A Kiss From A Rose

A Kearton Bay novel

(Book 2)

Sharon Booth

Copyright © 2015 Sharon Booth. Published by Fabrian Books.

All rights reserved. This book or any portion thereof may not be reproduced or used in any manner without the express written permission of the publisher, except for the use of brief quotations in a book review.

Typesetting and Design Fabrian Books – fabrianbooks.com.

Sharon Booth asserts the right to be identified as the author of this book. All the characters and events in this book are fictional. Any resemblance to individuals is purely unintentional.

For my mum—who made the gravy

xxx

To Mam
With all my love
always
Sharon
xx

About the Author

Sharon wrote her first book when she was ten. It was about a boarding school that specialised in ballet and, given that she'd never been to boarding school and hadn't a clue about ballet, it's probably a good thing that no copy of this masterpiece survives.

Her first published novel was *There Must Be An Angel*, which is the first in a series of four Kearton Bay stories, set in a fictional village on the North Yorkshire coast, inspired by the beautiful Robin Hood's Bay.

She lives in East Yorkshire, with her husband and their dog, and regularly yells for tea and biscuits while writing, to remind them that she exists.

She is one tenth of The Write Romantics, has a love/hate relationship with chocolate, is a devoted Whovian, and just a little obsessed with *Sherlock*, *The Musketeers* and *Poldark*. She freely admits that she would write more books if the BBC didn't insist on employing gorgeous men.

Find out more about Sharon Booth at:

sharonbooth.co.uk

Twitter: @Sharon_Booth1

To see the real-life village of Robin Hood's Bay, which was the setting for fictional Kearton Bay, and other things which inspired *There Must Be an Angel* and *A Kiss from a Rose*, visit:

https://www.pinterest.com/sharonbooth1/the-kearton-bay-novels/

CHAPTER ONE

I was flying through space, watching in amazement as stars hurtled around me. I was in the Tardis. I must have been, because I could distinctly hear the whooshing sound of its engines. What the stars were doing inside the Tardis was anyone's guess. I couldn't even remember how I'd got there, come to that.

'Is she all right, Doctor?'

Doctor! That was it. I was with The Doctor, in a blue box, hurtling through time and space.

'Oh, Rose, I'm so sorry.'

Rose? Oh, yes, that was me. Rose. I remembered now. Of course, The Doctor and Rose—made for each other.

'I'm The Doctor's one true love,' I murmured.

'Bloody hell. How hard did she hit her?'

I knew that voice. Fuchsia. Who the hell was Fuchsia? My daughter. Did Rose have a daughter?

'Mam, are you all right? I'll kill that sodding maniac when I get my hands on her.'

That was most definitely Fuchsia. The stars were fading away and the engine noise of the Tardis was dimming, to be replaced by a chattering of voices. I didn't want to leave the little blue box behind. It was so much nicer there, and I was with The Doctor.

'I love you, Doctor.' I sighed.

'Yes, well, I'm only doing my job.'

I realised that my face was freezing cold and blinked as a pair of eyes, as blue as the Tardis itself, swam into focus. 'What's that?' I demanded.

Flynn cupped the back of my head with his free hand and told me to keep still. 'It's just ice. I got it from the barman and wrapped it in my handkerchief. It will ease the swelling.'

I remembered now. I knew exactly who I was, and exactly where, too. Well, this was embarrassing.

'Your handkerchief? I hope it's clean,' I muttered, thinking *trust Flynn to have a hanky*. I mean, who else bothers with them nowadays?

'Don't be so ungrateful,' said Fuchsia. 'Will she be okay, Doctor?'

'Well, she'll probably have a bit of a shiner for a few days, but I doubt there'll be any lasting damage.'

Was that a hint of regret in his voice? What a cheek. I squinted up at Eliza and her new husband, Gabriel, who were peering down at me.

'You all right, Rose?' There was a suspicious gleam of amusement in Gabriel's eye. 'Whoever would have thought a bouquet could cause so much damage? How funny.'

'Yeah. Absolutely hilarious,' I said.

'Will you keep still?' said Flynn.

He pressed the ice even harder against my face, and I tried not to wriggle, all too aware that dozens of pairs of eyes were upon me and I'd made a proper show of myself. Again. I tried not to look at him. I'd never been this close to Flynn before. It was a surprisingly disturbing experience.

'It's my fault,' admitted Mrs Travers, Eliza's old friend who had come all the way from Margate to be at the wedding. 'My sister said Kylie was desperate to catch the bouquet. I should have taken her seriously.'

I pushed Flynn's hand away and stared at her. 'Desperate? She's insane. What the hell was Eliza doing throwing it at me, anyway? I'd rather have my bikini line plucked than get married.'

Eliza blushed. 'I thought it would help. I want you to be as happy as I am.'

'Well, congratulations. How can I not be happy, getting walloped by a desperate maniac and landing flat on my arse in front of a hundred people? Cheers, Eliza.'

Flynn looked thoroughly fed up. 'Do you want my help, or not? Because if you do, stop moaning and let me hold this ice to your face.'

'Sorry,' I muttered, thinking that, really, this was beyond endurance. I could feel myself trembling. I probably had concussion. I took the handkerchief from him and put it gently to my aching cheekbone. 'I'll hold it myself, thanks. I think I need some paracetamol,' I added, suddenly aware that my face was throbbing.

'Poor Rose. How is she, Gabriel?'

Oh, marvellous, that was all I needed. Sophie, Gabriel's sister, stood over me, peering down in sympathy. How she didn't topple over, given the size of her hat, was beyond me. It was like a sodding sombrero.

'Have you got any paracetamol, Sophie?' asked Flynn.

She rummaged in her bag and handed him a box of tablets. He pressed a couple into his palm and handed the box back to her. 'Right, I'll just get you a glass of water, and you can take these. Gabriel, can you move her somewhere more comfortable?'

'Isn't he kind?' Sophie said, as Flynn headed to the bar. She followed Gabriel and Eliza, as they helped me to stand and led me to a chair. 'Honestly, Rose, all that for a bouquet. It's just an old wives' tale, you know.' She laughed. 'Still, at least you caught it. That's all that matters, eh?'

'Oh, for God's sake!' I dumped the ice-packed handkerchief on the table and glared at them all. 'I was not, I repeat *not*, trying to catch the flaming bouquet. I'd actually turned to get away from it, which is when that maniac elbowed me in the eye. She's welcome to it. If you ask me, men are a pointless waste of space.'

'Your water.'

I looked up and saw Flynn standing before me, his face expressionless. I gave him an apologetic smile and took the glass from him, gratefully swallowing the paracetamol then returning the handkerchief to my face. 'Cheers, Flynn. You're very kind.'

'Was that my mother being polite? She must have

3

concussion.'

'Oh, nice of you to drop by,' I said, peering up at my youngest daughter, as she stood there, hands on hips, looking not-too-concerned about her poor mother at all.

Cerise rolled her eyes. 'That's more like it. Well, Mam, if you must go making a fool of yourself in your desperation to get hitched, what do you expect?'

Was no one listening to me? Why was everyone so eager to believe that I wanted a husband? I'd gone thirty-seven years without being married, and I didn't see any reason to ruin things now. My life had never been so good. I'd survived being used and dumped, and brought up two very bright—well, two very decent—okay, two daughters all alone. I was pretty good at taking care of myself. Men, in my experience, were best kept at a safe distance.

'How are you feeling now?' Flynn crouched down before me and carefully peeled away the handkerchief to check on my face.

'Fine,' I said, then hissed into his ear, 'Shouldn't you be outside? They'll be going in a minute.'

He looked baffled.

I tried to hide my irritation. 'The car? You need to sort the car out.'

He stood up, looking none-too-sure of what I was talking about, but turned and headed to the door anyway. I shook my head. Some best man he was. Honestly, he didn't have a clue.

'We'll have to go soon,' said Gabriel, taking Eliza's hand and squeezing it, before holding it to his lips and kissing it gently. She smiled at him and reached out to stroke his hair.

I felt sick. 'Give it a rest,' I said. 'At least wait till you're on your honeymoon. Some of us are feeling quite ill enough, without all that malarkey.'

Gabriel scooped Amy, Eliza's four-year-old daughter, into his arms. 'Now, you'll be a good girl for Uncle Joe, won't you?'

Amy nodded, looking adorable in her ivory flower girl

dress with its purple sash. I had to admit, the colour scheme did work, although I still thought Eliza should have gone for pink, something I'd tried to persuade her ever since we started planning the wedding six months ago.

'Where *is* Joe?' asked Eliza, looking around for her uncle, who'd given her away and had been beaming with pride and happiness all afternoon.

It wasn't that difficult to spot him. He was in a corner of the room surrounded by giggling women. Joe's sexuality didn't seem to stop them all throwing themselves at him. That was what fame did, I supposed.

He'd been a top chat show host for many years, before a heart attack, eighteen months earlier, had made him reassess his life and priorities. Now, he lived here in Kearton Bay, on the farm once owned by Eliza's grandmother, and wrote books and grew vegetables. The career change didn't seem to have lost him any fans, though.

'We'd better get off,' said Gabriel, looking at his watch. 'It's a long drive to Manchester. Where's Lexi? Honestly, I've hardly seen her today.'

Lexi, his own daughter, was sitting at a table with her cousins and grandparents. I sat nursing my aching face, as Eliza and Gabriel went to round up their relatives to say goodbye.

'Don't they make a lovely couple?' said Sophie, and I had to agree.

Eliza had never looked more beautiful in her long ivory dress, her chestnut hair swept up and adorned with tiny purple and white flowers. Even Gabriel, in his grey suit, with purple cravat and crisp white shirt, had scrubbed up well, and he hadn't stopped smiling all day. Come to think of it, he rarely did anything but smile these days. I blamed Eliza for that. Before she had arrived in the village, he was a miserable bugger, but at least we knew where we were with him. Now, he was far too free and easy with the laughter and jokes, in my opinion. Doctors were supposed to be quiet and serious, weren't they? Like Flynn.

Eventually, Gabriel managed to persuade his mother to stop crying, and Joe managed to prise Eliza away from Amy, and it was time for the bride and groom to go. Everyone made their way outside, braving the freezing February air to wave them off on their honeymoon. I stood in the car park, my teeth chattering with cold, glad I'd left the ice pack indoors. Who needed ice on an evening like this?

Gabriel put his arm round me. 'Thank you for looking after my wife, Rose,' he said. 'I know how much you've helped with this wedding, and I do appreciate it. Your turn next, eh?'

'Sod off,' I said, nudging him, and laughing when I noticed the twinkle in his turquoise eyes as he squeezed my shoulders with affection.

'Fancy you catching the bouquet, Mam. I wonder who my new stepfather will be.'

'Very funny, Cerise,' I muttered, taking her hand and wishing everyone would stop gawping at me. Everyone knew that the whole bridal bouquet tradition was complete rubbish, surely? It didn't mean anything. It was just an excuse to take the piss out of the poor wretch who caught it—simple as.

Rhiannon was at my side next, her brown eyes warm with amusement.

'Don't even think about it,' I warned her.

She raised an eyebrow. 'What *can* you mean?'

'You know what I mean, Rhiannon,' I said. 'Don't be making any of your weird, witchy comments about how the bouquet was always meant to be mine, and there's a mysterious stranger about to appear on my horizon at any moment to whisk me away from all this.'

She gazed at me steadily for a moment, making me a bit nervous. Rhiannon was the landlady of one of our local pubs, The Hare and Moon. It sat right on the seafront, and was one of the oldest places in Kearton Bay. Centuries ago, it had been the headquarters for smuggling in the area, and with its ancient beams and huge old inglenook fireplace, it had an unworldly feel to it, which was shared by Rhiannon herself. Stunningly beautiful, she was also a bit eccentric—all tumbling hair, Edwardian skirts, ankle boots and lace. She wasn't your average pub landlady. You'd be more likely to find her reading tarot cards than a glossy magazine, and she had a weird way of—well—knowing things. So, when Rhiannon gave you that look, you felt kind of spooked, to say the least.

'Just the opposite,' she said, laying her hand on my shoulder.

Now, what exactly did she mean by that? 'Well, good,' I said. ''cos a husband is the last thing I need, thank you very much.'

'Oh, I dunno,' Cerise mused. 'It would be nice to have someone with a bit of cash who wanted to buy my affection. I might get a new laptop out of it.'

Eliza kissed my cheek—the one without the rapidly-growing bruise. 'We're going,' she said, hugging me tightly. 'Thank you so much for everything, Rose. You were the best chief bridesmaid ever.'

That's probably true, to be fair. I'd spent hours trawling round every wedding dress shop in Yorkshire with her, given her a fantastic hen night, spent the whole morning calming her down and reassuring her that she looked marvellous, and that everything was under control, and stayed depressingly sober throughout the entire wedding. I doubted anyone could have done more.

I looked across to where the other bridesmaids were standing by Gabriel's car. Twenty-year-old Lexi was gorgeous, all long legs and flowing red hair, and Amy looked so cute with her basket of flowers and pretty dress, but they hadn't been by the bride's side for the last six months, studying bridal magazines, going to wedding fayres, sampling cake and arranging seating plans, while this wedding took shape. I certainly had. I'd earned every bit of praise going.

'Are you absolutely sure you don't want the bouquet?' she asked, her eyes suddenly serious.

I shook my head. 'How many more times? Of course I don't. Never did. Don't know what you were thinking.' I looked across the room towards Kylie, who was drowning her sorrows in a pint of bitter. 'And she's not having it. Not after this performance.'

'Then, could I ask a favour? May I have it back?' she murmured. 'Only, I'd quite like to make a detour to the churchyard.'

I smiled, understanding, and went to fetch the bouquet. I couldn't think of a better place for the wretched thing to end up than on Hannah's grave. Eliza's grandmother had adored Gabriel, and longed for the two of them to get together. She would have been so happy if she'd lived to see this day.

Eliza took the flowers from me with a grateful smile, and I watched as she and Gabriel climbed into the car, waving and laughing as they drove off.

Something was wrong, though. I frowned, turning away as I realised what it was. 'Where's that bloody best man?'

Rhiannon smiled. 'He's over by the door talking to Joe. Be gentle with him, Rose.'

I rolled my eyes and headed back to the entrance of The Kearton Arms, where Joe and Flynn were deep in conversation. 'Some best man you turned out to be.'

They both turned to look at me in astonishment.

'I'm sorry?' Flynn said, with some indignation.

'I should hope you are. What kind of best man lets the bride and groom go off on honeymoon without so much as a tin can attached to the car? Where was the "Just Married" sign, the strings of cans, the balloons? And what kind of stag night was a meal in a restaurant? Dear God, have you ever actually been to a wedding before?'

I was beginning to think that maybe he hadn't. I'd heard

from Eliza that the stag night was just about as tame as it could have been. Not a stripper in sight, for goodness sake. Eliza said that Gabriel had wanted it that way, but really, who cared what the groom wants? It was the best man's duty to make sure that the groom got absolutely plastered, was thoroughly humiliated, and preferably left tied stark naked to a lamppost. What was the point of a stag night otherwise?

As for the speech—well! There were no dark secrets exposed, no mockery, nothing for any of us to really get our teeth into at all. Totally dull, and full of kind and complimentary remarks about the couple. It had been a massive disappointment, although everyone had been very polite, and laughed and clapped, as dutiful guests should. I think I'd have made a better best man, to be honest.

'Gabriel wanted a quiet evening,' he said, casting a nervous look at Joe.

I couldn't see what difference that made. There were traditions that should have been carried out, whether Gabriel wanted them, or not. It struck me that Flynn had been entirely the wrong man for the job. It was on the tip of my tongue to say "Bugger Gabriel", but Flynn looked mortified, and I knew the effort it must have taken him to even turn up for the wedding, never mind the stag night—and he *had* packed his handkerchief with ice for me, after all.

'Yeah, well it doesn't matter now. It's done. I shouldn't think the happy couple even noticed, they're so loved up,' I said. 'To be fair, if I was on my way to Thailand, I wouldn't care about some tin cans on my car. Nice present, Joe,' I added. 'Quite appropriate, sending them to Phuket.'

Joe laughed. 'I don't think that's quite how you pronounce it, Rose. Are we going back inside? It's bloody freezing out here.'

'I know. Who gets married in February? Why they couldn't have waited for the summer, I don't know.' I pushed my way between them into the pub and looked back. 'Aren't you coming in?'

Flynn shook his head. 'I'm heading home, now they've gone,' he said.

'You can forget that,' I said, grabbing his arm before he could do a runner. 'You're the best man, and I'm chief bridesmaid, and now that the happy couple have gone, it's our job to make sure that the guests have a good time. There's loads of grub left in there, and the day is still young, so don't think you're clearing off and leaving me to deal with it all on my own.'

He looked appalled, but there was no way I was letting him off the hook. We walked into the function room, grateful for the central heating, after the bitter cold outside. Within minutes, the rest of the guests had joined us, and soon people were stuffing themselves with food, or lining up at the bar, or jigging around on the dance floor. Flynn wandered over to a corner of the room and stood, sipping a drink and watching everyone from a safe distance.

'How's your eye?' asked Joe, smiling across the room at Amy, who was dancing with Mrs Travers and putting on a quite spectacular show. They should never have let her watch *Strictly Come Dancing*.

'Throbbing,' I admitted. 'Caught me well and truly on the hop, didn't she?'

'I'm just glad it was you she aimed for and not me. I was convinced she'd throw it my way. I've been having nightmares for weeks.'

'Well, maybe you do need a nudge,' I said. 'We're never gonna get you fixed up at this rate.'

'You hypocrite.' He laughed. 'Why don't we both agree that it's a case of once bitten twice shy and leave men out of our lives for good?'

'Amen to that,' I said, although in my case it was twice bitten, thrice shy, as I'd been dumped and let down by the fathers of both my daughters. Talk about unlucky in love—

although, if I was being really honest, love hadn't come into it in either case.

'Do you think Amy will settle without Eliza?' I asked, watching the little girl and Mrs Travers, who were now doing a fantastic impression of Anton Du Beke and Ann Widdecombe, which wasn't surprising, given the old lady's dodgy knees and clicky hips. Or was it the other way around?

'She'll be fine,' he said. 'It's not like she hasn't stayed with me before, and she loves feeding the chickens and being around the donkeys. My only problem is going to be peeling her away from the farm and getting her to school.'

Sophie almost took my other eye out with her hat as she rushed over. 'Bless you, that's quite a bruise you've got forming. Mind you, I'm sure it was worth it,' she said, her hat wobbling dangerously as she spoke. If there'd been a strong wind, I'm sure she'd have taken off.

Archie, her ever-patient husband stood beside her, a pint in his hand and a weary expression on his face.

'Can't believe my own brother will be away for my birthday,' Sophie said, dropping a massive hint, if ever I heard one. 'I'll be fifty-three next week, although you'd never believe it, would you? I've always moisturised, that's the trick. Have you seen your Fuchsia?' she whispered, nodding with some difficulty towards the corner of the room. I looked across and saw my eldest daughter standing beside Sophie's twins, Oliver and Pandora, deep in conversation and with a weird expression on her face that quite unnerved me.

'She looks—happy.' I blinked, to double check what I was seeing. Fuchsia, my darling surly, sulky daughter was smiling, her eyes bright with interest. What miracle had brought that about?

'I think someone has a little crush on Oliver.' Sophie beamed with pride, and I groaned inwardly.

That was all I needed. Fuchsia being sulky was tough enough to cope with. Fuchsia in the throes of unrequited love would be unbearable. And it would be unrequited, let's face it. What would a high-flyer like Oliver Crook want with a village girl who worked in an office?

Oliver was at university. He had a bright future ahead of him, following in his father's footsteps as a solicitor. His life was already mapped out for him.

Fuchsia could barely be arsed to turn up to the office every day, and she was hardly solicitor's wife material.

I foresaw trouble ahead. Brilliant.

I reached for a bottle of wine that stood on the top table and poured myself a large glass. Now that the bride and groom had gone, I could relax and get thoroughly sozzled. I gulped the wine down and poured another, while Sophie chattered on about how popular Oliver was, and how all the girls threw themselves at him wherever he went. Blah, blah, blah.

'We all know how perfect Olly is, Mum,' said Tally, Sophie's youngest daughter, rolling her eyes at me in sympathy. 'Rose, have you got everything covered at the shop while Eliza's away?'

I took another slug of wine and nodded. 'Chrissie's doing really well. Her marshmallows are almost as good as Eliza's. Between us we'll manage.'

'I'd have happily helped you out, but I have to be back in York for Monday. I could come back on Friday night, though, if you need me for the Saturday?'

'Aw, thanks, Tally,' I said. 'I'm sure we'll be okay, but thank you for the thought.' She was a lovely girl. You'd never think she was only a year younger than Fuchsia.

Of course, I loved Fuchsia and would do anything for her, but she wasn't the sweetest person you could meet. She was moody, grumpy, far too serious, and never happy with anything. She'd hated school, hated college, and she hated her office job. She'd done some part-time work in Mallow Magic, our gourmet marshmallow shop, and Eliza had suggested taking her on permanently, but she'd hated that, too. Nothing and nobody could help Fuchsia. God knows what would become of her, but I couldn't see someone as popular and bright as Oliver putting up with her attitude for long. Just something else for me to worry about.

I put down my empty glass. To hell with it. 'Archie, do you want to dance?' I said, grabbing his arm and steering him onto the dance floor before he could answer.

'You okay, Rose?' he asked, as we jigged away to One Direction.

I shrugged. I wasn't really, but I wasn't sure why. Things were going so well for me, and I really couldn't complain. I didn't understand why I suddenly felt so unsettled and uneasy. Maybe I did have concussion, after all.

From the corner of my eye, I saw Flynn standing alone by the door, his face impassive as he sipped occasionally from his glass and tried to avoid eye contact with anyone. Flynn had come on quite a bit since Gabriel had started working with him—coming out of his shell enough to visit his friend now and then, and even going to the pub once—but he still had a long way to go before anyone could call him sociable. I wondered why he was so aloof. At first, I'd assumed he was shy, but I didn't think it was that anymore. He just didn't seem to want to mix with anyone, simple as that. Oh, well, it took all sorts, I supposed.

Archie and I had two dances together before Sophie came to claim him back.

I grabbed another glass of wine and slugged it down. It was a wedding, when all was said and done. I had done my duty and now it was my turn to forget everything and enjoy myself. The night was young and I was—well, thirty-seven and on a mission to get rat-arsed, frankly. Joe was paying, after all.

****

Flynn sipped his orange juice slowly. His eyes scanned the

room, looking for a flash of pink hair. There she was, on the dance floor. She was doing the Twist, with a laughing Derry Bone, Rhiannon's twenty-one year old son. Flynn watched, fascinated, as the two of them swayed dangerously, performing their drunken dance. Eventually, they fell together, helpless with laughter, and he marvelled at their ability to make absolute fools of themselves without feeling in the slightest bit self-conscious. It was a gift, and one he didn't possess.

Flynn wondered again if Rose had been right. Had he failed in his duties as best man? Gabriel had insisted that he didn't want a fuss, and Flynn couldn't imagine his friend and colleague wanting anything as embarrassing as a stripper at his stag night. Then again, maybe a meal in Helmston, followed by a few hours at a wine bar, hadn't been the sort of thing he'd expected? He'd checked with Archie, and he'd seemed agreeable with the plans. Was he just being kind?

Taking another sip of juice, Flynn tried to picture Gabriel's face as they'd said goodnight. Had he looked, in any way, unhappy? Or was he right in thinking that his friend had looked the picture of contentment as they parted ways?

'You're deep in thought, Dr Pennington-Rhys. Penny for them?'

Flynn started as Meggie appeared beside him. Meggie was his receptionist and his friend, and he trusted her absolutely. Maybe she'd know?

'Meggie, has Gabriel said anything to you about the stag night?'

She looked at him in surprise. 'Not much. Why?' Her eyes narrowed. 'Don't tell me someone got up to no good?'

'Oh, goodness, no. Nothing like that,' he reassured her.

She nodded, taking a bite out of a cheese sandwich and chewing happily.

'I was just wondering if he was happy with what I'd arranged. You know, the meal and the wine bar.'

'As far as I know, he was. My Ben enjoyed it, any road. Said it were a right good laugh. Why?'

'Did he? Really?'

'I just said so, didn't I? Why, what are you thinking?'

'Oh, just something Rose MacLean said.'

'Rose?' Meggie laughed. 'You don't want to take any notice of her. What's she been saying?'

'That perhaps I've let Gabriel down—failed in my duties as best man.'

'Oh, rubbish. That's just Rose. You know what she's like. You've done a damn good job, so stop worrying.'

'But I didn't get him a stripper, or take him to one of those lap dancing places that seem to be the norm on these occasions.'

Meggie, in the process of taking a bite of quiche, almost choked. 'I should hope not! If you'd taken my Ben there, I'd have flaming strangled you. Besides, can you imagine Dr Bailey in a place like that? He'd have died with his legs up.'

'Well, that's what I thought. You agree?'

'Of course! Bloody hell, Doctor, horses for courses. Some blokes might be up for all that palaver, but Dr Bailey isn't one of them, and neither are you. And neither,' she added firmly, 'is my Ben. No, you made the right choice.'

'And you don't think I let him down by not decorating the car?'

Meggie rolled her eyes. 'What use would that have been, trundling down the motorway to Manchester? Rose is pulling your leg. Take no notice of her.'

Flynn nodded, slightly mollified.

'You worry too much,' she told him, her eyes soft with sympathy. 'You always have. Why don't you stop dwelling on things and go and enjoy yourself? Have a dance, go on.'

'I think not.' He almost shuddered at the thought.

Meggie seemed to hesitate for a moment, then shrugged. She looked down at her plate, piled high with food. 'Sausage roll?'

'No, thank you. I was thinking I might sneak off home soon. Would it be wrong of me, do you think?'

He looked at her, full of confusion. What was the form for these occasions? Did best men have to stay to the end? He wasn't used to socialising, preferring his own company.

Meggie shook her head. 'You shouldn't worry about what's right or wrong. You've done your bit. It's up to you now. Mind you, I wish you'd stay a bit longer. Loosen up, enjoy yourself. You deserve a bit of fun.'

'Oh, I've had fun, Meggie,' he assured her. 'It's been a lovely day, and I think Gabriel and Eliza enjoyed it, which is the main thing.'

He paled as a flash of pink caught his eye, and suddenly Rose was there beside him, swaying and jabbing her finger at him. 'Are you all right? Perhaps you should sit down?' He couldn't help noticing that her cheekbone was badly bruised and her eyelid was turning purple.

'Oh, don't be daft! Who sits down at a wedding? Now, Dr Paddington Bear, or whatever your bloody name is, come and have a dance with me. Best man and chief bridesmaid always have a dance. Isn't that right, Meggie?'

'Oh, aye, if you say so,' said Meggie, biting into a ham sandwich. She nudged a horrified Flynn and nodded towards the dance floor. 'Go on! You'll enjoy yourself.'

'No, no, certainly not!' He was appalled at the thought.

Rose put her hands on her hips and glared at him. 'Not good enough for you, eh?'

'I didn't say that.'

'Prove it.' She linked her arm through his and began to pull him onto the dance floor.

He stood, utterly mortified, as she began to wave her arms around, bobbing up and down to some pounding music he'd never heard before. All around him, he could feel people staring. He was sure he could hear sniggering. He felt desperately hot and tugged at his shirt collar, beads of sweat appearing on his forehead. 'Really, I don't do this sort of thing —' he began, but she wasn't listening. He didn't want to leave her on her own in such a state but, really, this was horrific.

He paled as the music changed, and a ballad that even he recognised began to play. He hesitated, wondering if he could leave, but he caught her eye and saw the look in it, and was paralysed.

While he stood, frozen to the spot, she lunged towards him, wrapping her arms around him and swaying against him, forcing him to move in spite of himself. 'I love this song,' she slurred. 'It makes me all emotional. Does it make you emotional, Dr Paddington Bear?'

'Pennington-Rhys,' he muttered, looking around him for help.

No one seemed in any hurry to come to his rescue. Will Boden-Kean stood by the bar with Lexi, and Flynn tried to flash him a distress signal, but Will merely raised his glass like he thought Flynn was actually enjoying the experience.

Rose wrapped her arms around his neck and snuggled her head against his chest. She was incredibly unsteady on her feet. Flynn wasn't sure how she was still standing. He put a reluctant arm around her to help secure her, and she gave a loud sigh.

'I'm sorry I was mean to you, Paddington,' she murmured.

'That's quite all right,' he assured her. 'Perhaps we should sit down now?'

'You know, all this time I've lived in the village, and I don't think we spoke two words to each other till Eliza and Gabriel booked this wedding. Isn't that sad?'

'Is it? Well ... I suppose.'

He looked down at her, and his face softened. She wasn't a bad person, after all, just rather noisy. She was right, too. They had rarely spoken until he'd been asked to be best man, and she'd been chosen as chief bridesmaid, but over the last few months, they'd been thrown together quite a bit, with pre-wedding dinners, meetings and rehearsals. He'd been terrified of her at first, but she was quite sweet really, when one got to know her. Just scarily opinionated and rather loud.

She lifted her face to his, and her grey eyes were blurry with tears. Oh, God, she wasn't going to cry was she? Drunken women often cried, apparently.

She lifted a trembling hand and stroked his hair, pushing it away from his face and staring as best she could into his eyes. 'You're such a lovely man,' she told him.

He was baffled. 'Am I? You didn't seem to think so an hour ago.'

'Eh? Oh, that was just me mouthing off. Ignore me. I'm a gobby cow,' she told him, as if he needed telling.

He smiled half-heartedly and tried again. 'I do think you should sit down, Rose,' he began.

She put her hands on his face, cupping it and staring at him intently. 'You're a gorgeous bloke, Paddington,' she told him.

Heat spread over him. 'Yes, well,' he murmured, trying to prise her hands away from his face. 'I wouldn't say any more. You've had a nasty injury and a bit too much to drink.'

She wrapped her arms tightly around his waist. 'Don't make me sit down, Paddington,' she protested, her voice slurry. 'I haven't been held for so long, and you smell ever so nice. What are you wearing?'

'Clothes.'

'I mean your aftershave, silly. What is it? It's gorgeous. You're quite gorgeous. Has anyone ever told you that?'

'Yes.'

'Really? Who?'

'You, a few seconds ago.'

'Oh. Well, I was right, wasn't I?'

She lifted her face to him again, and they looked at each other for a moment. Flynn wished he could click his fingers and disappear. He'd never felt so embarrassed, and that was saying something. Then he noticed her eyes had dropped to his lips, and she was moving her face ever closer to his. His heart did a funny little jig, and then she was kissing him.

Warmth flooded through his cold body. All his synapses seemed to be firing at once; hot lava was coursing through his icy veins. Suddenly, he was kissing her back, and she held him tightly, as his hand cupped the back of her head, and he drank her in, like Meggie with a McDonald's chocolate milkshake.

'Oh, for God's sake, Mother, pack it in.'

Flynn's eyes flew open in shock, as Rose was torn away from him, and Fuchsia shot him an apologetic look.

Rose glared at her daughter. 'Do you mind? Me and Dr Paddington Bear here were having a meaningful conservation. How dare you interrupt?'

'Yeah, yeah, sure you were. I'm sorry, Doc,' said Fuchsia, beginning to lead her away. 'She always gets this stupid when she's pissed. Just ignore her.'

Rose looked as if she was about to protest, but then crumbled and allowed herself to be led away.

Flynn was trembling all over. What the hell just happened? He had to get out of there.

'Had enough?' Joe asked, helping a sleepy Amy into her coat near the door.

Beside them, Mrs Travers was pulling on her gloves, while somehow managing to keep an iron grip on her sister's granddaughter, Kylie, who was looking much the worse for wear.

Flynn felt dazed. 'More than enough. I'm going home.'

Joe grinned at him. 'Good looking woman, Rose MacLean. You could do worse.'

Do worse! Flynn left the pub without a backward glance.

It was just a kiss—a stupid, meaningless kiss. She'd have forgotten all about it by now. And maybe, by tomorrow, he'd have forgotten about it, too.

CHAPTER TWO

Monday morning. I hated Mondays. Having to drag myself out of bed and accept the fact that, for the next six days, I'd be chained to my place of work. Crap.

Not that I minded my place of work. It wasn't everyone who got to work with their best friends all day, and it wasn't as if I had far to go. I only had to trundle downstairs, and there I was. It was just the principle of the thing—the fact that I wasn't free to go wherever, whenever I wanted. Though, where I'd go, I couldn't imagine, come to think of it.

I suspected part of the problem was Fuchsia. She was always a nightmare to get out of bed, and I got pretty sick of having to drag the duvet from her and nag at her for ages to get herself ready to catch the bus into Helmston. That particular Monday morning, though, I didn't get the chance. I felt pretty rough still, and I had a rare lie-in, not getting up until eight thirty, which was awful of me considering the shop opened at nine, especially as, with Eliza being away, there was a lot to do, and I really shouldn't expect Chrissie to do it all.

By the time I'd dragged my ancient, weary bones out of bed and forced myself into the shower, Fuchsia had gone. I had no doubt she'd be late but at least she'd get there—eventually. Cerise had also got herself ready and gone off to school. I felt pretty bad about that. Cerise was a good kid, and I usually made her a packed lunch, and we had a bit of a gossip before she went out, but I would try to make it up to her when she got home.

Chrissie was all smiles when I entered the kitchen behind the shop. 'You made it, then? Wasn't sure you'd be up to working today,' she told me.

I frowned. 'I don't see why. What are you talking about?'

'I saw you on Saturday night, remember? You were pretty far gone, by the time the reception ended. Fuchsia had to practically carry you home.'

'Oh, don't you start. She spent the whole of yesterday telling me I made a complete fool of myself. As if! I had a few drinks to celebrate the fact that my best friend got married and all went well with the wedding. If you knew how much planning that day took, you'd not begrudge me a few drinks, I can tell you.'

'Oh, I don't begrudge you anything, Rose.' Chrissie laughed. 'I think Dr Pennington-Rhys may be steering well clear of you for a while, though.'

Dr Pennington-Rhys again. What on earth had I done? Fuchsia had been banging on about him, too. What was the big deal? So I told him off for not making more of an effort with the festivities, and I made him have a dance with me. So what? Would it kill him to let his hair down for once?

'You don't remember?' Chrissie was watching me, her blue eyes bright with amusement.

'What's to remember? I had a dance with him, didn't I? Big deal.'

'Hmm, you keep telling yourself that. I'm saying nothing.'

I had a sudden vague picture of my fingers pushing his raven hair away from his forehead, and a flash of panic in his indigo eyes. What had I done? I decided it was best to change the subject.

'Have any new orders come in?'

'Yep, quite a few. And we've had some lovely emails, complimenting us on the Valentine gift bags. I think we should start promoting the Easter baskets. What do you think?'

'Blimey, let's get February over with first. Still, it's nice to be appreciated. I'm going to make a coffee. Want one?'

'You need to ask?' She flashed me a grin and reached for her apron.

It was working out well, having Chrissie as part of the team. We'd taken her on a few months ago, when it became obvious that Eliza and I needed full time help. A few hours here and there from Fuchsia weren't enough, and she didn't want to work in a shop full time, so we'd advertised, and Chrissie had been our first applicant. I'd known her for a few years and, as she was Meggie's daughter, I knew she was trustworthy. She'd been made redundant from her job in a book shop in Helmston and had expected to be unemployed for months. Jobs in this area were few and far between, so it was a happy coincidence for all of us that we advertised within a week of her finishing work. She worked hard and was keen to learn. She'd picked up the marshmallow making really quickly, which had been a relief to us all, since I'd never been able to make them very well, and if Eliza was ever sick, or away—such as on honeymoon—the business would have ground to a halt. It meant I could serve in the shop, which I liked, take and package the orders, keep the website updated, do some marketing and help around the kitchen as necessary. We made a pretty good team.

The morning passed quickly. In spite of the fact that it was only February, there were a few tourists in the village, and a couple of them bought mallows as gifts to take home with them. I had a few internet orders to get ready for posting, and some locals also popped in for a treat and a chat.

There were lots of comments about the wedding and how lovely Eliza had looked, and how well it had all gone, but there were also some sly digs about my drunken antics. Honestly, you'd think no one had ever got tipsy at a wedding before. It seemed I'd attracted quite a lot of attention, and I wasn't in the least bit surprised when Sophie turned up just before lunchtime.

'You've recovered, then?'

'I wasn't that drunk, Sophe. Come on, you've seen me in a worse state. What about the hen night for a start?'

She couldn't deny that. Denise, who ran the local hairdressing salon Klassy Kutz, and I had had a drinking competition, and I'd won hands down. Mind you, I only knew that because I'd been told the next day. I couldn't remember a thing about it. Apparently, I'd had a fantastic night.

'Ah, yes, but on Eliza's hen night, there were no handsome doctors around. I wonder how Dr Pennington-Rhys is feeling today.'

'Him again. What is it with everyone? I had one flipping dance with him, and, suddenly, everyone's pairing us up. Are you all that desperate for gossip?'

'Pairing you up? You must be joking.' Sophie thought the very idea hilarious, obviously. 'I wouldn't dream of pairing you two up. The poor man looked positively horrified.'

'Did he?' I was a bit miffed about that. Who did he think he was, anyway?

'Oh, Rose, you were all over him. Made him dance, and then draped yourself round him and stroked his hair. You know how proper he is. How you had the nerve to kiss him, I'll never know.'

'Kiss him?' My stomach lurched as the memory of his lips on mine scorched through my brain.

Oh, Jesus, I had, too. What the hell had I been thinking? He'd looked scared stiff.

Oh, sod it. 'He shouldn't be such a wimp,' I snapped. 'Anyway, weddings are about getting drunk and dancing with people you shouldn't. I bet it's the first time a woman's bothered with him in years.'

Sophie looked sad. 'I know, such a shame. He's a lovely man—very good looking, too. Just so withdrawn. I'm sure there must be someone out there for him.'

'Well, don't look at me,' I said.

'I wasn't,' she assured me, far too quickly for my liking. 'The very idea. You'd be the worst possible woman in the world for him.'

'What do you mean by that?' I said, trying not to sound too indignant.

'Well, he's so quiet and reserved. And you're so … loud. I mean, you'd finish him off. He needs someone elegant, a real lady.'

'Charming,' I said. 'So, basically I'm too gobby and common for him.'

'Well ...' Sophie looked uncomfortable.

'For your information, Sophie, I'm not in the slightest bit interested in Dr Pennington-Rhys. He's far too miserable and boring, for my liking. If I were ever daft enough to get involved with a man again, I should hope he'd be a bit more outgoing and fun than that dull git.'

'Oh, really?'

'Too true. And bollocks to all this, anyway. Who can be bothered with men? I mean, never having control of the television remote again, not being able to slob on the sofa eating a bucket of ice cream to yourself, having to shave your legs every single day and not just for special occasions ...'

She raised an enquiring eyebrow and I cleared my throat, embarrassed.

'I mean, obviously, I shave my legs every day, but what I mean is, I do it because I want to, not because I *have* to. Anyway,' I continued, aware that I'd just revealed my deepest, darkest secrets to Sophie, of all bloody people, 'my life at the moment is as perfect as it can get. Long may it continue.'

Me and my big mouth.

It was just after twelve-thirty that the trouble started.

'Rose, is Cerise home for lunch today?' Chrissie was standing at the kitchen door, wiping her hands on her apron.

I shook my head. 'No. She stays packed lunch, why?'

'I don't want to alarm you, but I'm pretty sure I heard someone moving around upstairs.'

I stopped arranging the stock on the shelves and looked at her. 'Are you sure?'

'Well, pretty sure. Come into the kitchen and listen.'

I followed her inside, and we stood together in silence, our eyes wide.

'There!'

It was unmistakable—the sound of drawers being slid open and shut, and then footsteps padding above our heads. I felt sick.

'Should I call the police?' Chrissie asked.

I shook my head. 'I'm going upstairs to see who it is.'

'You're not serious?'

'I have to. I can't call the police for this. It could be a cat, for all we know.'

'Clever cat, opening drawers.'

'Well, maybe Cerise did come home, after all. I'll be careful.'

'I'm coming with you.' Chrissie took hold of a large saucepan. 'Best to be armed,' she whispered.

We headed into the shop and cautiously opened the door that led into my hallway.

'You sure about this?' she asked.

I nodded, although I was far from sure.

'Here, take this,' she said, handing me the pan.

I looked at her.

'I wouldn't have the guts,' she admitted. 'Besides, you're going first. You'll need it more than I will. I've got time to run downstairs.'

'Oh, thanks,' I muttered.

We crept as quietly as we could up the stairs, my heart hammering against the bars of my ribs in protest.

'They're in the kitchen,' whispered Chrissie.

I thought of all the knives I had in my drawer, and, suddenly, the saucepan didn't seem like much of a defence. I was just about to tell her to go back downstairs and ring the police, after all, when the door opened, and there on the landing was Fuchsia.

'For God's sake!' I nearly fell backwards, I jumped so hard, and the saucepan swung dangerously close to Chrissie's head.

'What the hell are you doing, Mam?'

'What the hell am *I* doing? What are *you* doing, you mean.

Why aren't you at work?'

Fuchsia looked distinctly shifty. 'Oh, well, er, I have to talk to you about that.'

Chrissie cleared her throat. 'Well, if all's well here, I'll get back to work. I'll take the saucepan, Rose.'

I handed it to her, my eyes never leaving Fuchsia's face. Slowly, we headed into the kitchen, and I sat at the table, still staring at my daughter.

'Go on, then.'

She stood by the sink, obviously nervous. 'Shall I put the kettle on?'

'Not for me. What are you doing home? What's happened?'

Though she hesitated, she pulled out the chair next to me and sat down, her eyes large and pleading. 'Don't get mad.'

'Jesus, Fuchsia, what have you done? Please tell me you haven't been sacked.'

She folded her arms, suddenly defiant. 'All right, I won't.'

I had a strong desire to shake her. 'Are you saying you've been sacked?'

'Make your mind up. Do you want to know, or not?'

'For God's sake, what have you done?'

'Oh, yeah, I might have known it would be my fault.'

'You've been sacked! People don't get sacked unless they've done something pretty bad.'

'Not bad. Well, not really.'

She twisted a lock of her dyed black hair around her finger and looked at me with large grey eyes that were apparently just like my own. It was the general consensus that she looked very much like me. I couldn't see it myself. 'Thing is, it wasn't that I did anything bad, or anything at all, really. I just—well, I just didn't go.'

'What do you mean, you didn't go? You've been going every day. I've been dragging you out of bed myself every single morning, to make damn sure you got there.' I narrowed my eyes at her. 'Are you telling me you've been going somewhere else?'

She nodded, guilt all over her face.

'Where? Where would you go? And how long has this been going on?'

'Three weeks.'

'Three weeks! For God's sake, Fuchsia, where have you been?'

She shrugged. 'Just hanging round.'

'Hanging round? Hanging round where? If you'd been in the village, I'd have known.'

'Been going to Whitby,' she admitted eventually. 'Just walking about, drinking coffee in a café. Nothing much.'

'Whitby? In February?' It had been bitterly cold recently. The thought of her walking around by the seafront in such freezing weather was beyond me. 'Are you having me on?'

'No, honest. That's all I've been doing. There was nowhere else to go. Like you said, if I'd been in the village, someone would have told you, and I daren't go into Helmston, in case someone from work saw me. At least in Whitby there are shops and cafés to go into to keep warm.'

'But why? I don't understand. Why would you rather wander round Whitby than go into work? It doesn't make sense.'

She shrugged.

'There must be more to this than you're telling me, Fuchsia. Why did you hate the job so much?'

'Just boring,' she said.

'Boring!' I was furious. 'Boring—like college was boring? For crying out loud, how many more times? Life isn't all fun and excitement. Sometimes, you just have to get on with it.'

'I didn't like the office,' she protested. 'It was a crap job, and they were crap people. I'll find something else.'

'Of course you will,' I said. 'Because jobs round here are so easy to come by, aren't they? For God's sake, Fuchsia, just when I think life is finally on the up, you go and spoil everything again.'

'Oh, well, thanks for your support,' she yelled. 'I should have known you wouldn't listen.'

'Listen to what? My spoilt brat of a daughter telling me she's bored with her cushy office job, so she didn't bother to go in for three weeks until her boss was pushed into sacking her.'

She glared at me.

'Well? Is there anything else you'd like to add to that?'

For a moment, she looked as if she were about to say something, but then she shook her head.

'Okay, so I guess we're done.'

'I'll get another job.'

'Yes, you will. You'll go into town this very afternoon, and register at the job centre, and start applying for every flaming job going. You understand? And I don't care how boring it is. We all have to do things in this life we don't like, Fuchsia. Welcome to the world of adulthood.'

She stood up and went to her room, slamming the door behind her. I put my head in my hands and tried not to give way to tears. It wasn't so much the financial situation, although her board money had come in useful, but the fact that I just didn't know what was going to happen to her. She seemed so angry and resentful all the time, and she simply didn't enjoy anything. She'd never made friends easily, or had a boyfriend, or any hobbies. She'd hated school and college, and now she was throwing away her job. Whatever she thought, I loved her dearly. She was a sulky brat, but she was my sulky brat, and I wanted her to be happy. I just didn't know what to do with her.

I headed back into work, the day totally spoilt. Chrissie was very tactful and said nothing, flashing me a sympathetic look but asking no questions. I tidied the shop, which really didn't need tidying, then sat down with the laptop and began to think about Easter baskets. Chrissie was right. We needed to think ahead.

It was almost two o'clock when the phone rang.

I answered it, expecting to talk to a prospective customer or, at worst, somebody wanting to flog me something like double glazing, or nag me into claiming back PPI charges. When the caller identified himself as a police officer, my blood ran cold. Immediately, I thought about Fuchsia. She was still upstairs, wasn't she? I hadn't heard her go out, but then, I hadn't heard her come in, either. What if I'd pushed her to the limit? What if she was really unhappy and I'd tipped her over the edge? What if she'd gone out in a temper and caused trouble? Or was it Cerise? Had something happened at school? Had she made it to school? Had there been an accident? It was amazing how many scenes of disaster a brain could fire at you within the space of a few seconds.

'Miss MacLean? Are you there?'

'What? I'm sorry, yes, yes, I'm here. What's happened?'

'I'm afraid I have some bad news about your mother. She's been the victim of a crime. She was mugged just outside her home, and she's sustained some injuries.'

'Oh, my God. Is she all right?'

'She will be. I'm at the hospital now. She's just given her statement, but she asked me to contact you and let you know. She's rather shaken up, as you can imagine.'

'Of course, yes. Do you want me to come up there now?'

'Well, obviously that's up to you, but I think she'd appreciate it. She's had a nasty shock.'

'I'll be there as soon as I can.'

Chrissie looked up, as I popped my head round the kitchen door. 'I'm really sorry. I'm going to have to go out.'

'What's wrong?'

'That was the police on the phone. My mother's been mugged. She's at the hospital. I'll have to go to her.'

'Of course. Oh, Rose, I'm so sorry. What a shock.'

She wasn't kidding. The thought of anyone having the guts to mug my mother was surprising enough—the fact that they'd succeeded was astounding. My mother wasn't one to go down without a fight. I guessed it must have been someone who didn't live on the estate.

'If you get really busy, yell for Fuchsia. She can come and help in the shop. It's the least she can do.'

'I will. Don't worry about the shop, just get yourself off. Give her my regards.'

I grabbed my coat from the hallway and checked my pockets for money. Buttoning up my coat, I headed out into the freezing February air and began the ascent to the top of Bay Street, wondering what else the day was going to throw at me.

****

Flynn handed the Lloyd George notes back to Meggie and rubbed his forehead wearily.

'How were they?' she asked.

He shrugged. 'The same as usual. Mrs Lancaster wanted to tell me all about her granddaughter's awful boyfriend, and Mr Marks spent twenty minutes complaining that the price of prescriptions has gone up again and he doesn't see why the workshy mob next door don't have to pay for them, when decent hardworking men like himself have to fork out.'

Meggie laughed. 'Bless you, it never changes. One day, you'll visit someone, and they'll be genuinely ill. It will scare the life out of you.'

'Are you coping all right on your own, Meggie? I can't believe what Lorna did—of all weeks.'

Meggie tutted. 'She was worse than useless, any road. Dr Bailey couldn't stand her. Miserable sod, she was. Never did a stroke of work. Mind you, she could have picked a better time, I'll give you that, what with him being on his honeymoon.'

'I don't understand why she'd think a job in a supermarket

was worth leaving here for. It's very puzzling.'

'Nothing puzzling about it. She's a proper lazy cow and probably thinks she'll get away with a lot more, working in a bigger place. I can't wait till she finds out she's wrong.'

'Well, perhaps.' Flynn scratched his head. 'We'll need to organise a replacement as soon as possible. I don't want you struggling with the workload, and I don't want Gabriel coming home to a backlog. Would you draft an advertisement for me? I think you're better placed than I am to know what's needed.'

Meggie nodded. 'Let's hope we get someone who hasn't got lazy-itis for a change, eh? I'll get cracking on it this afternoon.'

'Thank you. I'll email it to *The Gazette* tomorrow morning,' he said.

'Okey dokey. Now, why don't you head out and grab yourself something to eat before afternoon surgery?'

'Have I time? I should be here when the locum arrives.'

'Not due to arrive for another hour, and I'm here, aren't I? I can show him round. You get yourself off.'

'Yes, I think I will,' he said. 'I may pop into Farthingdale first and check on Mr Fry's leg.' He patted his pockets, checking that he had his wallet and car keys. 'See you soon, Meggie.'

'Dr Pennington-Rhys.'

He popped his head back round the door. 'What is it?'

'Be a love and bring me some crisps in from the shop while you're out. I've had me sandwiches and I'm still proper peckish.'

****

It was freezing at the bus stop. My teeth were chattering, and I stamped my feet hard on the ground to keep the circulation going. I glanced at my watch. Why hadn't I checked the timetable first? I could have had another twenty minutes in the warmth. Why the buses round here only ran every hour was beyond me.

I turned up my coat collar and peered down the street, hoping to see the bus appearing from the Farthingdale junction. No such luck. I turned my head and looked up the Whitby road, wondering how my mother was coping, wondering what I would find when I reached the hospital. I was so deep in thought that, when the car pulled up beside me, I took no notice at first.

'Rose?'

Oh, God. I felt my cheeks begin to burn as I looked into Flynn's eyes. What did he want?

'Can I offer you a lift?'

A lift? Why would he, of all people, offer me a lift? After what I'd been hearing all day about my embarrassing behaviour at the wedding, I'd have thought he'd be keeping well away from me. That was the type of bloke he was, I supposed. Too well-mannered for his own good. He just wouldn't be able to see me standing in the freezing cold at the bus stop if he could do something about it.

'It's okay. I'm not going your way.'

He raised an eyebrow. 'How do you know? You don't know where I'm going.'

'You're facing the wrong way,' I pointed out. 'And, right now, you're parked on the wrong side of the road at a bus stop. If the bus comes, you'll get a right mouthful off the driver, especially if it's that miserable git, Lance.'

'Oh. Well, I was heading into Farthingdale but I can make a detour. It's terribly cold, and the buses are not very reliable.'

'Like you'd know,' I muttered, then tutted impatiently at my bad attitude. He was offering a lift, for God's sake. Why was I being so ungrateful? 'Thing is, I'm going into Whitby,' I said, almost regretfully. 'I expect that's too far out of your way.'

He hesitated. 'Not at all,' he said. 'I can be there in ten minutes. Plenty of time.'

I shrugged. I wasn't stupid enough to turn down an offer of a lift, when I could be waiting ages for the bus to arrive and my mother needed me. Besides, it was cold enough to freeze the balls off a brass monkey.

I climbed into the car, closing the door and shutting my eyes in relief as the warmth seeped through me. 'Ooh, that's lovely,' I murmured, leaning back and sighing. 'Thank you so much.'

'You're welcome.'

He turned the car around, and we drove towards Whitby in silence for a while. I supposed I would have to broach the subject of the wedding at some point, since it seemed to have been a talking point with so many people.

'Er, I'm sorry for having a go at you at the wedding,' I muttered.

He said nothing, but I saw the tips of his ears go red.

'I hope you didn't take it to heart,' I continued. 'I mean, I just wanted them to have the perfect wedding, but to be fair I think it was. And you're probably right about Gabriel. He's not a tin can sort of person, is he? Never mind a stripper.'

'A stripper? Good God.' Flynn cleared his throat. 'I don't think he is, no.'

'Well, anyway, sorry if I was a bit of a mare.'

'That's quite all right.'

'And also, I seem to remember that I made you dance with me. Sorry about that, too.' I decided that it was better to pretend the kiss had never happened. I was sure he'd prefer it that way. His ears were now completely red. I watched them in fascination.

'It's fine,' he said. 'It doesn't matter. The wedding went very well, that's the main thing.'

'Yeah, it was great. Have you heard from them?'

'No, have you?'

'No. Mind you, I expect they've got other things to think about at the moment, don't you?'

Now his ears looked as if they were going to start smoking at any moment. I grinned to myself. He was so easy to embarrass. You'd never think he was a doctor. How the hell did he cope, when patients came in with more intimate complaints?

'How's your face?' he asked eventually.

'Bit sore, but not too bad, thanks. More embarrassing than anything. People seem certain that I got this bruise because I was so desperate to catch the bouquet. They won't believe I was trying to avoid it.'

'Ah, well, people tend to believe what amuses them the most,' he acknowledged.

We drove in silence again. I couldn't think of anything to say to him. His close proximity was giving me flashbacks of things I'd rather forget.

'Er, whereabouts in Whitby do you need to be?' he asked, as we saw the sign ahead for Whitby Abbey.

'The station. I have to get the bus to Oddborough Infirmary. I'm visiting my mother.'

'Oh, I'm sorry. Has she been ill for long?'

'She's not ill. That is, she's just been taken there. She was mugged earlier today. The police just called me.'

'Good grief.' He looked genuinely horrified. 'Is she badly hurt?'

'I honestly don't know. She's given a statement to the police, so I guess she's still making sense. Well, as much as my mother ever has done. I don't know what state the mugger's in, though.' I gave a half laugh and Flynn turned to me, wearing a bemused expression. 'Sorry. Just my little joke.'

He didn't answer but turned his gaze slowly back to the road, which was probably a very good thing. After all, one member of the family in hospital was enough for anyone. 'Your mother doesn't live in the village, does she?'

'No. She lives in Oddborough, on the Feldane Estate. You know it?'

'I know of it,' he admitted.

I'll bet you do, I thought. It was pretty well known, and for all the wrong reasons. I'd grown up there, and Fuchsia had been born there, but I was damn sure that we were never going back. My mother had never seemed bothered by it. She had lots of friends on the estate and had never shown any inclination to move. I wondered how she kept so cheerful, living in such a depressing and rather menacing location. I was pretty certain that the posh Dr Pennington-Rhys would never survive in such a place. His idea of an estate was probably Kearton Hall, or Chatsworth.

'I'm so sorry I can't take you all the way,' he said, as we pulled up at the bus station. 'I have surgery soon and the new locum's arriving, otherwise ...'

'Don't be daft. I wouldn't expect you to. Besides, you've done more than enough. It was really kind of you. Thanks ever so much.'

'You're welcome. I hope she's all right.'

'Yeah, me, too. Well, er, thanks for the lift. See you.'

He nodded, and I climbed out of the car, shutting the door behind me and fumbling in my pockets for change.

Despite my apparent humour, I was worried. What had that bastard done to my mother?

CHAPTER THREE

I found my mother quite easily. I heard her all the way down the corridor, telling someone all about her ordeal and how, if the bugger hadn't taken her by surprise, she'd have ripped his goolies off and worn them for earrings.

I popped my head round the cubicle curtain, expecting to see a policeman sitting there taking a statement. Instead, I found a terrified-looking young man who, it transpired, had come looking for an elderly relative and walked into my mother's cubicle by mistake—ten minutes ago.

'Oh, so, you've finally come, then,' she said, folding her arms and eyeing me disapprovingly. The man saw his chance and bolted, but my mother didn't even notice. 'Took your bloody time, didn't you?'

I gritted my teeth and pulled up a chair. 'You know buses don't run very regularly from Kearton Bay, Mam. I left as soon as I found out, but I'd probably still be standing at the bus stop now, if a friend hadn't given me a lift.'

'Well, that's what you get for moving to the back of beyond. You can't say I didn't warn you. At least on the estate, you get buses every ten minutes.'

I bit my lip, reminding myself that she'd just been through a very frightening experience and I couldn't get angry with her. Not yet. Maybe I could set a twenty-four hour limit? Or twelve?

She adjusted the blanket on her bed, eyeing me curiously. 'You been fighting?'

'Of course not!'

'Well, you've got a bruise on your face. Who bashed you?'

'A nutcase trying to catch a bridal bouquet.'

'Are you taking the mickey?'

'No, honestly. The bride threw the bouquet in my direction and someone wanted it more.'

'Huh. Waste of time that was. I've given up waiting for you to find Mr Right.' She tutted. 'Not brought me anything, then?'

I shook my head. 'I'm sorry. I never thought.'

'No, you wouldn't. Oh, well. I shouldn't think I'll be in here very long.'

'What have they said?' I studied her. I'd been expecting a black eye and swollen lip, at the very least, but she looked fine. I wondered how the mugger had fared.

'Oh, I'm right as rain. You can't keep me down for long,' she said.

Was I imagining it, or was there a slight quaver in her voice? I reached out and took hold of her hand, and she winced. Looking down, I saw that her wrist was swollen and bruised. 'Mam, what did he do?' I murmured, stroking her fingers gently.

'Bugger played dirty,' she said. 'Didn't even see him. Just got off the bus and was only two minutes from me front door. Next thing I know, it was like a rock had fallen on me head, and I was on the floor.'

'He hit you on the head?' Horrified, I stood up and peered over her. There was a dressing on the back of her head. She'd obviously been well and truly walloped.

'Aye, he did. But he didn't knock me out. Oh, no. He grabbed hold of me bag and tried to leg it, but I wouldn't let go. Just kept tugging at it and yelling me head off. He kicked me in the ribs, then, and I had to let go, dirty rotten swine, but then one of me neighbours started to run over, and the ratbag legged it.' She sighed. 'He got me bag, though, Rose.'

I wanted to find the bastard who had done that to my mother and kick him in the ribs, and somewhere a lot more delicate, too. How dare he do that to her? I tried to keep my voice calm. 'Well, you didn't have a lot in there, did you?'

'Me purse, half a pound of mince, an onion and me *Woman's Weekly*,' she said. 'I only had about three pounds fifty in the purse, so he wasted his time, really, didn't he?'

'What about your keys?' I asked.

'In me coat pocket,' she said triumphantly. 'I got them ready when I was on the bus. Didn't want to be standing on the doorstep, rooting around in me bag for them.'

I nodded. 'Well, that's something, then.'

'But I had that photo of you and your dad in me purse,' she said sadly. 'The one of you at your cousin Billy's christening. That time you screamed all the way through it, and me and your dad had to take you out of the church to shut you up, and your dad was pulling faces to make you laugh. I loved that photo. You were both laughing in the end, and I caught it just right. I've carried it with me for thirty-five years. Bugger's taken that away from me.'

'I'm sorry, Mam,' I said, squeezing her hand gently. 'But that's all he did get. It's just a picture. You've got the memories up here,' I added, tapping my temple.

She shrugged then winced again.

'Does your arm hurt?'

'Yeah. Think I twisted it, or something, when I pulled the bag from him. Waste of effort.'

'Don't you know who it was? Didn't you recognise him?'

My mother knew almost everybody on the estate. I thought it was a fair bet that she'd at least dimly know him, but she shook her head.

'He came up behind me, and the only time I saw him was when we were struggling over the bag, but I was too preoccupied with that to take much notice of his face. Besides, he had one of them hoodie things on and a scarf up to his nose.'

'Blimey,' I said. 'That should make him stand out.'

She gave me a withering look. 'Don't be daft. They all dress like that, except when they're in court. It's like a flaming uniform these days.'

'Would you like a drink?' I asked, desperate to do something for her, even if it was only finding a vending machine and bringing her a coffee or a cup of tea.

She seemed to think for a minute, then nodded. 'Aye, go on. Nice cuppa would do the trick.' As I stood up to go, she tapped my arm. 'Make sure it's milky, with two sugars.'

'I'll do my best,' I said, 'though I'm not sure how specific a vending machine can be.'

'Well, I'll not drink it if it's too strong,' she informed me.

I managed a smile and headed off to find a vending machine.

At the entrance to the ward, I found the reception desk, and asked if there was someone I could speak to about my mother. A jolly looking nurse told me that she'd been with her from the moment Mam had arrived at the hospital, and was more than happy to put my mind at rest.

'She'll be fine,' she told me. 'Badly sprained wrist, bruised shoulder and ribs, a nasty cut to the back of her head and some bruising to her hip, but she's been lucky in a way. No broken bones. We're keeping her in for twenty-four hours, to make sure there's no concussion, but she should be able to go home tomorrow.'

'Home?' I wasn't too sure about that. 'Are you sure she's up to it?'

'She can't stay here forever,' the nurse said firmly. 'And it's not like she's elderly. She's only in her early sixties, after all. She'll be fine. I think the policeman who spoke to her is getting in touch with victim support, and he gave her the number to ring if she wants to talk to anyone about what happened.'

'And that's that, is it?' I said.

'Well, that's up to you,' she said. 'If you're not happy about her being at home alone, perhaps you could stay with her for a while, or maybe she could stay with you?'

I'd had a bloody awful feeling she was going to say that.

****

I'd planned a quiet night in, but the thought of sitting in front of the television all night, with Fuchsia sulking and

Cerise caught between the two of us, didn't fill me with joy. I decided I was better off out of the way, and so, after making myself look beautiful—which was a very long and pointless exercise—I headed out to The Hare and Moon to see Rhiannon.

She beamed at my arrival and poured me a drink before I even had chance to ask for one. 'Double vodka and Coke,' she said, pushing the glass towards me, as I sank onto the barstool and dumped my bag on the counter.

'Cheers, Rhiannon. How did you guess it's been a double sort of day?'

'You look awful,' she admitted.

'Oh, well, thanks for that,' I said. 'I've just spent forty minutes tarting myself up. Took me ages to cover the bruise. Does it still show?'

'A little.' She smiled. 'Never mind. I'm sure it will be worth it in the end.'

'Don't start,' I warned her. I put the glass to my lips and knocked back half the drink in one mouthful.

'Oh, dear,' she said. 'That bad? Why don't you tell me all about it?'

'Fuchsia,' I said. 'She's been sacked. Hasn't been turning up for work, even though I've been getting her up every day and making sure she had bus fares and lunch money, and a decent breakfast. Turns out she didn't even go to the sodding office.'

'Really? So, where has she been going?'

'Whitby, can you believe? Hanging round the cafés and walking the streets. In this weather. I ask you, what's wrong with the girl?'

Rhiannon shook her head. 'She must have been very unhappy, if she'd rather walk the streets in this freezing weather, Rose. Not to mention the boredom. I wonder what's troubling her?'

'She's a lazy mare,' I said. 'Can't settle to anything. God knows what's going to happen to her. And as if that wasn't enough, some git only went and mugged my mother today.'

'Oh, heavens! Is she all right?'

I shrugged, knocking back the last of the vodka. 'She says she is, but I think she's a lot more scared than she lets on. Stubborn old fool. She's hurt her arm and ribs, and she's got a nasty cut on the back of her head. I don't know what to do about her. They're discharging her from the hospital tomorrow, and how do I know she'll be okay? She won't stay with me, and there's no way I'm going back to the estate, even for a few days.'

'Is it so awful?'

'Worse than you can imagine. Makes me feel sick every time I go. Why she moans about Kearton Bay when she's stuck in Oddborough is beyond me. Anyway, sod them. She and Fuchsia can sort themselves out. Pour me another drink, please, Rhiannon.'

She nodded. 'I think a single will be enough for now, though, don't you?'

'If you insist.'

I looked round to see if there was anyone I knew in the bar. It was pretty empty. Even the dining room, which was chaos in summer, had only a couple of people eating there. 'Where is everyone?' I asked.

'Derry's playing a gig at Moreton Cross,' she said, referring to her son who was a guitarist in a local band. 'Jack's in the kitchen, of course, and as for Michelle, well, she's no longer employed here.'

'Really?' That was good news, at any rate. Michelle had been a barmaid at The Hare and Moon and not known for her pleasant disposition. 'What happened? Did you sack her?'

'No. She got a better offer—working in a hotel in Scarborough. I hope she'll be happy there.'

No doubt she meant it. Rhiannon wasn't one to wish people harm—even the worst ones. Not like me. I hoped Michelle had a bloody awful time and regretted every moment of her career change, but then, I'm a horrible person. If there was such a thing as karma, there was no wonder bad things kept happening to me, really.

'Are you managing all right in the shop without Eliza?'

'Oh, yeah. I suppose that's partly why she chose February to get married. It's pretty quiet in the village, and Chrissie and I can manage on our own. I do miss her, though. Funny how close you can get to someone after only a couple of years.'

'Absolutely, and working together can bring you much closer. That's what I was hoping for with Will and Lexi, though there doesn't appear to be any progress with those two, does there?'

I shook my head. 'I reckon he's left it too late now. She sees him as a mate, and that's fatal. He should have jumped in the minute she broke up with Derry. He's brought it on himself.'

'Will's such a darling,' said Rhiannon, who should know, having had a short-lived affair with him the summer before last. 'I do wish Lexi would open her eyes and see that. They'd be perfect for each other.'

'Will's got enough on his plate with that mausoleum Kearton Hall,' I said. 'Bernie says they're really struggling to keep it going, and Sir Paul's so stubborn. He blocks them at every turn. Every time Will comes up with a money-making idea, his dad complains and starts yelling that it's his home, and he doesn't want to turn it into a business. He's living in cloud cuckoo land if he thinks he can keep it open without the help of the great unwashed. Poor Will.'

'Well, some of the house is open to the public for one weekend every month, and he's managed to get the gardens open to visitors—have you been round them, yet? Quite magnificent. And the teashop's doing well, and Sir Paul's finally agreed to a shop in the grounds, which will be fun.' Rhiannon smiled. 'He's such a poppet.'

I stared at her incredulously. 'Sir Paul? A poppet? Have you been drinking the profits, Rhiannon?'

'Oh, you don't know him the way I do,' she said. 'He's not nearly so grumpy when you get to know him.'

'How *do* you know him?' I asked. It was something I'd often wondered. Rhiannon was such an enigma. She obviously came from the upper echelons of society, yet here she was, running a pub in an insignificant village on the North Yorkshire coast. She didn't even own it. It was part of the Kearton Estate, along with The Kearton Arms and several other properties in the area.

She laughed. 'That's another story for another time. It hardly matters, does it? What went before is unimportant. It's what happens from now that counts.'

'Yeah, okay.' I sighed. 'Pour me another drink, pet, and I promise I won't ask any more questions.'

'Goodness, look who's here,' she said, handing me my vodka and Coke a moment later.

I looked round, and was surprised to see Meggie and Ben making their way towards me.

Meggie seldom came down to Old Town any more, mainly because she struggled with the walk. It was quite a climb from one part of Kearton Bay to the other, and Meggie wasn't the fittest of people. In spite of the fact that, like Eliza and me, she was a regular member of Sophie's Lightweights Slimming Club, she hadn't lost any significant weight in all the time I'd known her, and lately she'd been finding walking much more difficult. She tended to drink in The Kearton Arms, which wasn't far from her home.

'Meggie, Ben! How lovely to see you here. What can I get you?' called Rhiannon.

Meggie waved and sank down, in obvious relief, into one of the chairs by the window.

Ben strolled to the bar. 'Evening, Rose, Rhiannon. Pint of bitter and a glass of white wine please.'

'It's not often we see you in here these days, Ben,' said Rhiannon, busying herself at the pumps and fixing him with a dazzling smile. She was gorgeous inside and out, but Ben only had eyes for Meggie, and everyone knew it.

'She wanted to see you, Rose,' he said. 'Got something to tell you that might help.'

'Come over here, Rose,' called Meggie, waving a piece of paper in my direction.

Rhiannon raised an eyebrow. 'How intriguing. Go on over, and I'll bring your drinks to you.'

Ben and I walked over to the table and sat beside Meggie, who handed me the paper.

'Chrissie told us about the day you've had, Rose. What a palaver. How's your mother?'

'She'll live,' I said. 'Bit shook up, but she's a tough old bird.'

Meggie nodded. 'Bless her. Anyway, I can't do anything about that, but I was thinking I might be able to help Fuchsia.'

'Really?' I was doubtful. I wasn't sure a magic lamp and a willing genie could help Fuchsia, but I was getting desperate. I looked down at the piece of paper. 'You're looking for another receptionist? What happened to Lorna?'

'Cleared off to a supermarket, and good riddance. Dropped us right in it, though. We need someone and fast. Now, Dr Pennington-Rhys asked me to draft an advert, and I have, as you can see, but it hasn't gone in *The Gazette* yet, and I was thinking, well, if your Fuchsia went to see him tomorrow morning, after surgery, there may be no need for it to go in at all. What do you think?'

'I dunno, Meggie,' I said. 'I mean, it's good of you to think of her, and I do appreciate it, but is he likely to take her on, given that she's just been sacked for non-attendance?'

'Thing about Dr Pennington-Rhys,' she whispered, leaning towards me, 'is that he doesn't like dealing with people.'

'Really? You amaze me,' I murmured.

'What I mean is, if he can avoid all the interviewing rigmarole, he'll jump at the chance. If Fuchsia turns up and is smartly-dressed and polite, he'll be happy to give her a go, I'm sure of it. Plus, he's bound to ask my opinion, and, of course, I'll be all for it.'

'Will you?' I couldn't think why. 'She's not the sort of co-worker I'd choose, Meggie. Are you sure you want to put yourself through working with her? She can be a bit of a sulky mare, you know.'

She laughed. 'Oh, that's teenage girls for you. Chrissie went through just the same phase, didn't she, Ben?'

'Did she?' Ben frowned like he was trying to remember. 'Well, maybe. Anyway, Rose, I can't see another opportunity coming up like this one, can you?'

I hesitated. I couldn't, in all honesty, but I didn't want Fuchsia to let Meggie down. On the other hand, what choice did I have? If she didn't grab this chance, it could be months before she got another.

'Thanks, Meggie,' I said, smiling. 'I'll make sure she turns up tomorrow, if I have to drag her there myself. I appreciate it.'

'Oh, no thanks necessary.' She winked. 'A free bag of marshmallows will be ample enough reward.'

CHAPTER FOUR

Flynn looked bewildered, when Meggie told him she had an interview lined up for him with a prospective receptionist. 'How did you manage that? I haven't even advertised yet.'

'A daughter of a friend is looking for a job. She's just, er, come out of work, so the timing's perfect.'

'Does she have experience?'

'As a receptionist, no, but she's trained in office skills. She went to college for two years, so I'm sure she'll pick it up, no problem.'

He shrugged. 'All right, if you say so. I suppose it will save me trawling through applications and trying to come up with a shortlist. Thanks, Meggie.'

'Oh, it was no trouble,' she told him with a smile.

Flynn went into his consulting room, relieved that, at least, that problem was sorted. If Meggie thought the girl was up to the job, then no doubt she would be. She was pretty hard to please.

When he'd seen his last patient of the morning, he went into the office to see what time the candidate was arriving.

'She's in the waiting room now,' Meggie informed him. 'Just go easy on her, eh? She's a bit nervous.'

She wasn't the only one, thought Flynn. He hated formal things like this, and, really, it would make more sense for Meggie to interview her. After all, it was Meggie who would be working with her every day, and Meggie who would have to train her up.

'Would you like to sit in on this?' he asked suddenly. 'I'd rather like your input.'

Meggie actually looked relieved. 'Absolutely. You go and sit yourself down, and I'll bring her in.'

Flynn collected Meggie's chair and took it back to his room, placing it at the side of his desk, and sat down to wait. Nervous, he shuffled things around a bit, hoping he could conduct the interview in a professional manner. He opened the top drawer in his desk and looked inside at the photograph that lay there. Gently, he touched the face of the subject, but slammed the drawer shut as his door opened.

Meggie walked in, followed by a familiar-looking girl with black hair, kohl-rimmed eyes and a sullen expression.

He was about to greet her when, to his astonishment, Rose MacLean entered the room behind them. She was wearing a pink woollen coat and black boots, and had a pink woolly hat pushed over her rather unruly pink-streaked hair.

He blinked in confusion, as she sat in the chair opposite his desk and took off her gloves as if he'd been expecting her. 'Rose?'

'Thanks for this, Flynn. I mean, Dr Pennington-Rhys. I do appreciate your seeing Fuchsia. She's got all her qualifications. Tell him, Fuchsia.'

'For God's sake, Mam.' Fuchsia looked as if she wanted the ground to swallow her up, and Flynn couldn't blame her. What the hell was going on?

He looked enquiringly at Meggie, who had the grace to blush.

'Fuchsia's here for the job interview,' she said, somewhat embarrassed.

'I can see that. And what about, er, Rose?'

Rose leaned forward. 'Just making sure that everything's in order,' she said.

He stared at her. 'In order? What exactly are you suggesting?'

'Eh? Oh, I don't mean anything by that. Not what you're thinking, any road. I wasn't saying you'd behave improperly.' She started to laugh. 'You'd never behave improperly, I'm sure.'

He looked at Meggie. 'Can you please escort Mrs MacLean outside so I can conduct this interview in a professional manner?'

'I'd rather sit in on it, if you don't mind,' began Rose, but he cut in.

'Actually, I do mind. This is a job interview, and, generally, candidates don't bring their mothers to such things.'

'Told you,' Fuchsia muttered. 'Making a proper show of me, aren't you?'

'And whose fault's that?' snapped Rose. 'If I hadn't dragged you here, you probably wouldn't have turned up. Your word means nothing these days.'

They glared at each other, and Flynn shuffled some papers and tried to be professional. 'Right, well, I think I've heard enough. Thank you for coming, but I don't really think Fuchsia is what we're looking for—'

'Oh please, wait.' Rose turned to him, and he was surprised to see a look of desperation in her eyes.

He swallowed.

'Please,' she continued. 'Fuchsia's got lots of certificates from college in office work. She knows what she's doing. She's worked in an office since she left college, and she can do this job, I know she can.'

'Where did you work, Fuchsia?' he asked reluctantly. Dratted Rose MacLean and her big, sad eyes. Talk about emotional blackmail.

Fuchsia shrugged. 'I worked at Carstairs' Insurance in Helmston, but I got the sack yesterday.'

'Fuchsia!'

'Well, what do you want me to say, Mam? He's going to ask for references, isn't he? Told you this was a waste of time. I couldn't see me wearing that anyway, could you?' she added, looking distastefully at Meggie's uniform of navy blue skirt and white blouse with a blue diamond motif.

Rose shook her head and stood up, pulling on her gloves. 'We'll be going,' she said. 'Thanks for your time. Sorry, Meggie,' she added, scraping back her chair and taking hold of Fuchsia's arm.

Flynn closed his eyes for a moment. 'Do you have your CV with you?'

Rose stared at him, as Fuchsia nodded. 'Yeah, why?'

He held out his hand, and, obviously surprised, she handed it to him.

Rose flopped back down in her chair, as he sat, reading through it in silence.

Eventually he looked up. 'Well, you've got office experience, no doubt about it. I do wonder about the people skills, though. You'll be dealing with people every day, Fuchsia—people who are ill, frightened, stressed. Some of them may get quite angry. Do you think you can deal with that?'

'Yeah, 'course. I'm used to living with my mother. You should see her when she's got PMS.'

Rose's face turned as pink as her coat. She looked at Flynn, and he, again, caught the pleading in her eyes.

He sighed. 'What do you think, Meggie? It's you who'll be working with her and will have to train her up. Would you be happy to give her a try?'

Meggie beamed at him. 'Of course. She's a good girl at heart, aren't you, Fuchsia? I'm sure we'll get along just fine.'

He considered as they all held their breath. 'A month's trial,' he said at last. 'If you behave yourself and settle into the work, then the job will be yours permanently. I can't say fairer than that.'

'Oh, thank you.' Rose was on her feet, shaking his hand.

Fuchsia mumbled, 'Do I have to wear that uniform?'

'Yes,' he told her firmly, and she rolled her eyes but added, 'Okay. Cheers.'

Rose's eyes bored into his, her gratitude unnerving him. Where was the bolshy, confident woman he was all too familiar with? This version of her seemed smaller, somehow, and vulnerable. It was all a bit confusing.

'When should she start?' Meggie asked.

He coughed, gently releasing his hand from Rose's grasp. 'Er, I think tomorrow will be fine. Eight o'clock sharp, Fuchsia. Don't let me down.'

'I won't,' she said.

'No, she bloody won't, don't you worry,' said Rose, bundling her daughter towards the door and smiling back at him. 'Thanks, Doctor.'

'Rose,' he called, as she headed into the corridor.

She popped her head back round the door. 'Yeah?'

'How was your mother?'

She fixed him with a huge smile. 'She's coming home this afternoon. Just some cuts and bruises. Bit shook up, but she'll live. Thanks for asking.'

He nodded. 'Glad to hear it. Goodbye.'

Meggie waited until Rose and Fuchsia had left and turned to Flynn with a grin.

'What?' he asked, and blinked in surprise when she planted a kiss on his cheek.

'You,' she said. 'I dunno. What a waste.'

He had no idea what she meant by that. He would never understand women.

****

My mother was discharged that afternoon, and I called Fuchsia in, to help Chrissie out in the shop, as I headed to the hospital to be with her.

'Are you sure you don't want to come and stay with me for a while?' I asked, as we waited for the nurse to bring her discharge letter and painkillers.

I'd discussed the matter with the girls that night, and though both had groaned at the thought of their grandmother squashed into our tiny flat with us, they'd agreed that it was the least we could do. None of us liked the thought of her going back to her flat on the estate, and we were willing to put up with her cantankerous ways, if it meant she felt safe for a while.

My mother was having none of it, however. 'Why in God's name would I want to stay there?' she demanded. 'What's at Kearton Bay for the likes of me? I mean, it's all right for a holiday, if you like that sort of thing, but live there? I don't know how you stand it. That flaming hill, for a start. It's enough to wear your legs down to stumps, tramping up and down that bloody thing every day. And with the wind blowing in off the sea, it would dissolve me bones. No, thank you very much, but I'm happy in me own little home.'

She wouldn't let me pay for a taxi back to her flat, saying it would cost a fortune and why throw good money after bad? I ended up having to take her home on the bus, since I never learned to drive, something she kept reminding me of, as we endured the twenty minute bus ride back to the estate.

'Well, neither did you,' I pointed out.

'Why would I learn to drive?' she demanded. 'Where do I ever go? And I told you, the buses to the estate run every ten minutes. With you living out in the wilderness, you should have at least got yourself a car by now. No wonder I never see you.'

That wasn't the reason, I thought. Staring out of the window at the boarded-up shops and graffiti-strewn walls at the edge of the estate, I felt the familiar sinking feeling as the bus trawled through the dingy streets. I hated this place. I'd always hated it, and when I grew up, the only thing I wanted to do was escape it. That was why I rarely visited my mother. I couldn't bear to be there. It made me give up hope, sucked all the joy from me. Being on the Feldane estate was like suffering a kiss from a Dementor.

We got off at the bus stop near her flat, where it must have happened. I looked around, almost hoping to see the mugger. God help him if I got hold of him. There was no one there, though, except a mangy looking dog with no collar, who cocked its leg against the bus stop and then trotted off, having demonstrated that its opinion of the place matched my own.

I was surprised when I felt my mother's arm slip through mine. I felt her tremble, though she said nothing. I took hold of her keys, and we walked slowly to her flat, mindful of her aching ribs and hip.

The flat was on the first floor of the block. We weren't brave enough to take the lift, climbing the concrete steps slowly up to my mother's neat little home. Mam was very house proud, and the little rooms were immaculate, as always. She didn't have a lot of money, but what she did have had always gone on her home, which was her pride and joy. Her furnishings may have been more Argos than John Lewis, but it always looked lovely. It was just a shame it was in such a horrible location.

I sat her down in her comfy armchair, although she argued at first, and then went to put the kettle on. We sat, sipping tea and watching the television. I put the gas fire on for her, although she protested that she didn't generally have the fire on during the day due to the cost of fuel, but I insisted that she needed to keep warm and just hoped that she wouldn't turn it off after I left. We watched Alan Titchmarsh for a while, after which I rummaged in the fridge and found some vegetables and some sausages and prepared her a casserole, which would be ready for her at teatime. She told me off, informing me that she wasn't a baby and was perfectly capable of making her own tea, but there wasn't the usual force behind her argument, and I sensed that she was secretly relieved. She wasn't herself, and I knew it. The question was, what could I do about it?

'Mam, are you absolutely sure you want to stay here?' I asked, buttoning up my coat and pulling on my gloves as I prepared to leave.

'I've told you, I'm fine. This is my home. No bugger's going to drive me out of it, after all these years,' she said.

I looked at her in alarm. I was sure there were tears

glistening in her eyes. My mother, crying? It had never been known, not even at my dad's funeral, when I'd sobbed my heart out. She'd sat there, her face frozen, refusing to show the grief I knew she was feeling. This was scary.

I put my arms around her and felt her trembling, but she raised her face to mine defiantly.

'Go on with you, I'll be right as rain. Stop fussing. Get yourself back to the wilderness and get them girls of yours fed. I'm going to have me tea and watch *Emmerdale*, and then I'll probably get meself to bed. Stop worrying.'

I nodded. 'If you're sure? You know my number if you need me.'

'Aye, I do. Now, off you go. If you hurry, you'll catch the ten-to bus.'

I left her in the hallway, trying to push down the guilt I was feeling. What could I do? If she didn't want to come to Kearton Bay, there was nothing for it, because I sure as hell wasn't ever going to live on that estate again.

****

'So, these little pockets are what we call Lloyd George files and they're where we put all the paper notes for each patient.' Meggie waved her arm in the general direction of the back wall of the office, which was entirely covered in shelves of large pull-out drawers.

Flynn watched as Fuchsia tried to look interested. He wasn't convinced she was even listening, as Meggie explained how all letters and test results were scanned onto the computer these days, and the files contained information from years before, from the days before the practice had invested in an efficient computer system.

Fuchsia stifled a yawn, but, catching his eye, quickly stood to attention.

Flynn frowned. He hoped he hadn't made a huge mistake

taking her on. Meggie had enough to do, without chasing round after a bored, lazy girl. Maybe he should have placed that advertisement, after all, but Rose had seemed so desperate.

He turned away, heading towards his consulting room and trying not to think about Rose. Really, she seemed to be on his mind far too much lately. Ever since the wedding had been announced, he supposed. He'd had to rein her in several times during those months, when she tried to manipulate Eliza into choosing pink for her colour scheme, and when she'd suggested a hen weekend in Benidorm and a stag weekend in Amsterdam. She was nothing if not ambitious, but all her plans had been firmly rejected, and thank God for it. No wonder his quiet evening at a wine bar had met with her scorn. He had to admit, though, she'd made him laugh on occasions. She certainly amused Gabriel, and Eliza seemed to adore her. He could see that she had their best interests at heart and was probably a good friend to have onside, but, my God, she was opinionated and loud. He didn't know who the fathers of her daughters were—he understood they each had a different one—but he imagined they'd had to be pretty strong to live with a woman like Rose MacLean. He didn't know how they'd stood it. But then, they hadn't, had they? Both had left her and their children to it, which he thought was a disgrace. She'd had to bring her girls up alone, and he knew she'd struggled financially and been through some very tough times.

He sat down and shuffled some papers around before switching on his computer. As he opened the top drawer of his desk to retrieve his smartcard, his gaze fell upon the photo inside. Sapphire blue eyes smiled back at him, and he felt his heart contract as he gently stroked the glass, tracing the outline of her smile. Placing his fingers to his lips, he transferred the kiss to hers, and then, trembling, he put the photograph back in the drawer and slid it shut, wondering if the longing and the pain would ever go away, wondering if he really wanted it to, because then it would really be over and he didn't think he would be able to bear it.

CHAPTER FIVE

My mother sounded almost like her old self.

'I'm famous,' she announced, without so much as a hello, the minute I picked up the phone. I could have been Chrissie or Eliza, for all she knew, not that I supposed it mattered much. She was far too full of herself to care.

'What are you talking about?' I asked, waving goodbye to a group of customers who had just come in and spent a very satisfying amount of cash on a selection of our finest marshmallows.

It had been a good morning, with a flurry of internet orders, and a couple of queries about hiring our handcart for weddings. The handcart had been Eliza's idea, and was proving very popular. We stocked it with a wide variety of our goods, decorated it with the balloons and banners of the customer's choice, and it took pride of place at parties, receptions and other functions, bringing in a good income, as well as widening our customer base, as people who'd never heard of Mallow Magic until then asked for our business card and began recommending it to other possible clients.

'I'm in the paper. Didn't you see?' she demanded. 'I'm a hero. My photo's on the front page.'

'Which paper?' Not that it mattered, as I didn't buy any of them. Too full of doom and gloom. Who needed that?

'*The Oddborough Herald*, of course,' she snapped. 'What other paper do I get?'

'Well, how should I know?' I demanded. 'I haven't lived with you for years. You could take *The Financial Times*, and I wouldn't know, would I?'

'Don't be bloody soft. Any road, you'll have to get a copy and read it. It's a lovely photo. I look quite good for sixty, if I say so meself.'

'You're sixty-two,' I reminded her, 'and I don't think we get *The Oddborough Herald* here. You'll have to save me a copy.'

'Save you a copy? Charming. And when are you likely to see it, may I ask? Probably be another five years before you bother to visit again.'

'You could always come here,' I pointed out. 'You might like to visit your granddaughters and see what we've done to the shop.'

'Pulled it down, if you've any sense.' I swear I heard her shudder. 'All that daft pink. And, no offence, Rose, but that cake you gave me last time, with me cup of tea, should have been used as a doorstop. Baking's never been your thing, has it?'

I gritted my teeth. 'I told you, Mam, the café's gone. We turned it into a marshmallow shop, remember? Me and Eliza. I told you this ages ago.'

'I'm quite sure you didn't,' she said. 'I'm not losing me marbles, you know. Who the buggery bollocks is Eliza? And whoever buys marshmallows? They're awful.'

'Not ours. They're delicious. We're doing really well,' I began, but gave up. What was the point? If she was really interested, she'd have remembered when I told her all about it the first time. 'I have to go, Mam,' I said. 'We're really busy.'

'Busy? Hell, it really must have changed, then. You could have heard a spider spinning its web in that shop last time I visited. Well, I'll post you a copy, but you'll have to wait. I'm not forking out for a first class stamp, and second class will probably take weeks to reach that backwater. Quicker to walk there. I'll leave you to it, then. Bye.'

I put the phone down and headed into the kitchen. I needed a cup of tea to steady me after that. My mother always left me feeling drained, and not a little angry.

In the kitchen, Chrissie was about to start cutting up some raspberry ripple mallows. Huge, fluffy pillows sat on trays, waiting to be cubed. I knew for a fact that they would be delicious. Mallow Magic was a success, and I wished my mother could believe that, instead of always wanting to think the worst of me.

It was just over an hour later when the phone rang again.

'Hello?' I answered.

'Rose, is that you?" Mam asked, sounding very different to her earlier phone call. "I've had an awful thought. What if I've made myself a target? I'm on the front cover of a newspaper. Everyone round here knows me. What if I've made it all worse?'

I frowned. 'What do you mean? How can you have made it worse? A target for what?'

I heard her tut, and I gripped the phone, my eyes closing as I battled my impatience.

'Don't be so thick. Look, I've been mugged once already, and now that I've advertised the fact, other muggers are going to think I'm a soft touch. What if they all decide to give it a go? If one succeeded, they might think they all can. And what if the one who mugged me reads it and gets angry? They've made out that I was a hero and fought back, but what if that pisses him off? What if he comes back for his revenge?'

'Oh, Mam, I think you're getting in a state about nothing,' I said. 'Anyway, I doubt that people like him bother to read newspapers.'

'But my photo's on the front page, and when he goes into the shop to buy his fags, he'll see it. He'll recognise me,' she said in a trembling voice.

'Then, I should think he'll be terrified and will vow to keep well away from a terrier like you,' I said, trying to sound light-hearted.

'I'm glad you think this is funny,' she said. 'I appreciate your support, I must say. Sod you, then.'

'I'm not being funny,' I soothed. 'Just want you to calm down, that's all. Look, if you're really scared, why don't you stay here for a week, or so? Let the dust settle?'

'I'm not scared,' she snapped. 'And it would take a lot more than that little shit to scare me out of me home, so you can forget that.'

'Fine,' I said. 'Well, if you don't want me to help, stop whining on about it.'

The phone went dead, and I replaced the receiver, cursing myself for my bad temper. She was obviously afraid, and I should have been more patient, more understanding. I picked up the receiver again, but hesitated. She probably wouldn't answer, and, if she did, it would just mean another argument. She'd got herself into a state, and when she was like that, nothing I said or did had any effect. It was better to leave her to it. She knew where I was if she needed me.

****

'I can't believe it's been two weeks already,' Eliza said. 'The time just seemed to fly by. It's lovely to be home, though.'

''Course it is,' I said. 'Who needs the clear skies and turquoise seas of Thailand, when you've got Kearton Bay in February?'

'March,' she reminded me with a smile. 'It's March now. Can you believe it? Soon be spring.'

Sometimes, Eliza was so bloody cheerful, it made me sick. Mind you, I was glad to have her home. I'd missed her much more than I would ever have admitted. No one else seemed remotely interested in my moaning. Only Rhiannon made any attempt at sympathy, but even she'd looked a bit glazed the other night, when I started telling her about my darling daughter's first day at work, her loathing of her uniform, and her disgust at having to handle and label urine samples.

'That's nothing,' I'd told Fuchsia with undisguised glee. 'Wait till the stool, saliva, blood, and semen samples start coming in.'

She'd turned pale and informed me that she'd puke if she had to so much as look at them, never mind touch them, and that if Meggie thought she was going anywhere near them, she could piss off. I had a horrible feeling she meant it, too, which didn't fill me with optimism for her job security.

'So, how was the honeymoon?' I asked, determined to forget about Fuchsia for a while and concentrate on my friend, Pollyanna. 'You're far too brown for my liking. You were supposed to be shut up in the hotel room getting up to all sorts, not out sightseeing.'

She winked. 'Oh, don't worry. We didn't get much sleep.'

'Yuk,' I said. 'Didn't really want to know, thanks, Eliza.'

She laughed. 'Shouldn't have brought up the subject, then. Anyway,' she continued, looking fondly round the shop as if she'd actually missed it, 'what's been going on here? Everything okay while I was away?'

'Absolutely fine,' said Chrissie firmly, just as I was about to launch into my tale of woe about Fuchsia and my mother.

I supposed she was right. It could wait. 'We've come up with some designs for the Easter gifts,' I said, 'and we had great feedback from the Valentine bags.'

'Good. I'm thinking of experimenting with some chocolate orange mallows,' she said. 'I was thinking about it on the way home, actually. With Easter round the corner, it's a good time to launch a new product. Might have a go at some this afternoon.'

'Are you crackers? Go home, unpack, and get some sleep. No one expects you to start work today,' Chrissie said, heading back into the kitchen.

Eliza yawned. 'Perhaps she's right. I am a bit tired, now I come to think of it. Just wanted to check that everything was okay.'

'As you can see, we're all fine, and the shop's still standing. Go home and be with that husband of yours. We'll finish the week, and you can start bright and fresh on Monday morning.'

'Are you sure?'

'Absolutely.'

'Okay, but look. We want to invite our wedding committee

to dinner. We can show you the photographs we took, and I'll cook you a Thai curry.' She must have seen the doubtful look in my eyes because she laughed and hugged me. 'Okay, you don't have to look at the photos. But we do have gifts. Oh, I have missed you, Rose!'

I smiled. 'I should hope you have. Now clear off home and leave us to it.'

'Tomorrow night? Seven-thirty for eight? I promise we won't bore you to death.'

I nodded. 'I'll be there. I quite fancy a curry, as long as it's not too healthy. And I don't want rice. Give me chips instead, okay?'

****

Eliza and Gabriel lived in a sweet little cottage off King's Row, down a narrow passageway called Tippet's Yard. No one knew who Tippet was, or why they'd named a yard after him, but we all hoped he'd been someone notorious and exciting. King's Row was full of little alleys like that, and rumour had it that, once upon a time, back when Kearton Bay had been the smuggling stronghold of the Yorkshire coast, a bale of silk could pass from The Hare and Moon Inn on the seafront, all the way up to the top of the hill, without ever seeing the light of day, as there was reputed to be a network of secret passageways between the cottages that were used to thwart the revenue men. No one knew for sure if the passageways still existed, or, indeed, if they ever had, but we all fervently hoped so. Life could be so dreary, and it was nice to think it hadn't always been so dull. I quite fancied myself as a smuggler. I wouldn't have bothered with the silk, though. Give me the barrels of brandy any day.

Lexi opened the door and rolled her eyes at me, as I stood there, clutching a bottle of wine. It had been on offer for three-pounds- fifty in Sainsbury's, and I thought I ought to make the effort. People were supposed to bring wine to dinner parties, apparently. I'd never been to one till I met Eliza, so I wasn't too sure, but it seemed to be the norm when I watched *Come Dine with Me*.

'You needn't have bothered with that,' Lexi said, nodding at the bottle. 'Those two are sozzled already.'

'What? I don't believe it. This, I've got to see.' I pushed past her into the living room, but stilled when I heard Gabriel singing. Singing! 'What happened?' I demanded.

She shrugged. 'They've been having visitors all day, coming to see how the honeymoon went and to chat about the wedding, and they've been drinking wine all afternoon with them. They're well and truly sloshed. Quite embarrassing really.'

I heard Gabriel's voice soaring through the kitchen door, then Eliza giggling, and then it all went quiet.

Lexi screwed up her nose. 'They'll be slobbering over each other again. It keeps happening. I don't know if I can take much more.'

'Where's Amy?' I asked.

'Upstairs with Joe. He's reading her a story and tucking her into bed. Don't think Eliza even noticed. Bad mother.' She grinned.

I opened the kitchen door, covering my eyes at the sight of the two of them kissing and pawing each other in a truly obscene manner. Poor Lexi, having to live with that.

Tessa, Lexi's German Shepherd, stared up at them as if she couldn't believe what she was seeing. I knew how she felt.

As if finally noticing me, Eliza squealed at me in joy. 'Rose! Come in. Look, Gabriel, Rose is here.'

'So I see,' said Gabriel. 'Come in, Rose, come in. Is that wine you've got there?'

I nodded, and he and Eliza exchanged glances.

'Look, darling. Rose has brought wine. Shall we open the bottle?'

Eliza giggled and nodded, and I clutched the bottle to my chest and shook my head.

'Forget it,' I said. 'I think you've had more than enough.'

Eliza pulled a face. 'I can never have enough, Rose.'

'Are you talking about the wine or me?' Gabriel asked.

They both laughed, and I slammed the bottle down on the worktop. 'Fine, well, you two get on with your slobbering, but can I just point out that I've been invited round for dinner, and forgive me if I'm wrong, but I can't see or smell anything cooking, and I'm starving. So what happened to the Thai curry you promised me?'

They both stared at me in something approaching horror, and Eliza clapped her hand to her mouth. 'I knew there was something. Didn't I say there was something?' she asked Gabriel, who nodded, suddenly quite subdued.

'I told you the same thing not fifteen minutes ago,' a voice said behind me, and I looked round, relieved to see Joe standing there stone cold sober. He shook his head. 'I dunno. You both seem to have lost the plot. Reckon it's fish and chips for us tonight,' he added.

Eliza seemed appalled. 'Certainly not. I am perfectly able to cook for my guests.'

Lexi entered the kitchen, closely followed by Flynn. I half-smiled at him, embarrassed as I remembered the last time I'd seen him, at the interview. I couldn't believe I'd got so emotional and more or less steam-rollered him into giving Fuchsia a job. What had I been thinking?

He nodded at me before looking in obvious bewilderment at our friends. 'What's happened?'

'The lure of the grape,' said Lexi. 'They've been socialising all afternoon, and it looks like the Thai curry's off the menu.'

'Oh, dear,' Flynn said. 'Perhaps I'll get off home, then. Another time, maybe?' He turned, hardly bothering to disguise his relief.

'Not so fast, sunshine,' I said. I wasn't going to let him off that easily. 'Joe's suggested fish and chips, and I think that sounds even better. What do you say?'

Flynn stared at me like he wanted to throttle me, but he was far too polite to argue, much as I'd suspected.

Joe beamed at us. 'Right, Flynn, shall you and I head to the chippie and deal with the food? Lexi, you sort those two out with some strong black coffee, and Rose, you can warm the plates up and hunt through the cupboards or fridge for something for dessert. There's bound to be something in this house that we can eat. What does everyone want?'

After making a list of everyone's requirements, Joe and Flynn headed out to the fish shop, and Lexi started on the coffee, while I put the plates in the oven then searched the kitchen for food.

Eliza hadn't done any baking so there was no cake, but I did find a tub of ice cream in the freezer, and there were a few tins of fruit in the cupboard, so that would have to do. So much for the perfect hostess, I thought, watching as Lexi carefully led her father and stepmother into the room and got them settled, before bringing them strong black coffees. I'd seen Eliza tipsy before, but I never thought the day would come when Gabriel would be out of control like that. It just showed you. Love had really loosened him up.

Joe and Flynn returned within twenty minutes, and there was a rustling of paper and clattering of plates and chaos in the kitchen, as we all sorted out the various portions and served our hosts with their meals. Thoroughly shame-faced, they couldn't seem to apologise enough.

'To be honest,' I said, 'I think I prefer fish and chips to a Thai curry any day of the week, so don't worry about it.'

'Quite right,' Joe agreed, feeding a drooling Tessa a battered sausage. 'Any road, nice to see you two letting your hair down and enjoying yourselves. I take it you had a good a time in Thailand?'

That did it. They were off, and for the next fifteen minutes we were treated to a comprehensive narrative about their hotel, the beach, the local people, their fellow tourists, the views, the weather, the food and the flights. Thank God they stopped short of telling us about the consummation of the marriage. I didn't think any of us could have coped. We all sat nodding and stuffing our faces with chips, and pretending to be interested, but, really, was there anything more boring than other people's holiday stories? Well, maybe their holiday photos, but luckily for me, Lexi had already seen them twice and refused point blank to have to sit through them again.

'Another time, then,' said Gabriel, and we all assured him that, of course, another time we would love to see them.

I wondered if anybody else had their fingers crossed, or was it just me?

'How are things at the surgery, Flynn?' asked Gabriel, who was making a valiant attempt to sober up.

Flynn hesitated, just a fraction too long, in my opinion. 'Fine,' he said. 'We, er, lost Lorna, but don't worry, we replaced her.'

Gabriel frowned. 'What do you mean, you lost her? And replaced her with whom?'

Flynn glanced at me. 'Er, she decided a supermarket would be more to her taste. Luckily, Fuchsia was on hand to step into the breach.'

'Fuchsia? You don't mean it? What on earth were you thinking?'

'Oy, do you mind,' I said sharply.

He seemed to remember that I was her mother, and had the grace to look embarrassed. 'Sorry, Rose, but you know what I mean. Fuchsia just doesn't seem receptionist material.'

'Oh, and what is receptionist material? They pick up a phone and mark people off when they arrive. Big deal. It's hardly brain surgery, is it?'

'It's a lot more involved than that,' said Flynn. 'Ask Meggie what she does. I simply couldn't manage without her.'

'That I could well believe,' I said. 'Point is, Meggie thinks Fuchsia's up to the job, so if you value her so much, you should have faith in her opinion.'

That shut them both up. They looked at each other, and I saw Gabriel's mouth tighten. Though I knew he was dying to say something, manners must have prevented him. Sometimes, I was glad I didn't worry about such niceties. Fuchsia may have been a brat, but no one was going to insult her when she wasn't around to defend herself. Only I could do that.

I accepted Joe's offer of a glass of wine and noticed that Flynn was sticking to fruit juice again. It occurred to me that I'd never seen him drink anything stronger.

'Are you an alcoholic?' I asked him suddenly.

Flynn almost choked on his orange juice, and the room went quiet as everyone turned to look at me in astonishment.

'Blimey, Rose, just come right out and ask,' said Joe.

Flynn shook his head. 'No, I'm not! Why on earth would you say such a thing?'

'Just, you never drink alcohol. At least, not in company.' I shrugged. 'Thought maybe you were on the wagon.'

'Flynn does drink sometimes,' said Gabriel. 'He drank at my stag night, didn't you?'

'I have the odd tipple, but really I prefer to stay in control,' he admitted.

Why didn't that surprise me? I took another sip of wine and eyed him thoughtfully. 'I reckon you ought to take a leaf out of Gabriel's book. I mean, he was a miserable git till he met Eliza, and look at him now. You need to loosen up a bit, mate. You'll never find a girlfriend if you don't crack a smile now and then.'

His face turned quite white. I wondered if he had a dodgy haddock.

Gabriel waved a chip in the air and laughed. 'Maybe he doesn't want a girlfriend? Although I can recommend it,

Flynn, and really, you've been on your own for ages. Time to put the divorce behind you and move on, perhaps?'

Now it was my turn to almost choke. I coughed and spluttered as the wine went down the wrong way, and Lexi banged me, rather unhelpfully, on the back.

'You were married?' Eliza's eyes were wide. 'Ooh, Flynn, I never knew that. Do tell.'

'Maybe he doesn't want to tell,' Joe said gently. 'Eliza have you finished with that? I'll collect up the plates if everyone's done.'

'Yes, but hang on, Joe,' I said, having got my breath back. I stared at Flynn. 'Seriously? You were married? You? When? How? Who?'

Lexi wasn't the most tactful person in the world, but even she seemed to think I'd overstepped the mark. 'Leave it, Rose,' she murmured. 'Can't you see he doesn't want to discuss it?'

Flynn looked as if he'd rather be anywhere in the world but this room right now. His ears had turned scarlet against his pale face. He looked awful. I felt rather mean suddenly, and decided Lexi was right.

Unfortunately, Eliza was still very tipsy and hadn't picked up the signals. 'Who was she, Flynn? Does she live near here? How long were you married? What went wrong?'

Gabriel seemed to sober up instantly and looked shame-faced at his friend. 'I'm so sorry, Flynn. I quite forgot myself. Eliza, leave it. He doesn't like talking about it.'

'Why?' she demanded. 'Was she horrible? Did she cheat on you, Flynn? I know how that feels, oh, yes.' She stared moodily at the floor for a moment then her face brightened. 'But then I met Gabriel, and life was so much better with him than it ever was with Harry. So, you see, you may meet someone absolutely lovely and forget all about that horrible bitch of a wife.'

Flynn's eyes narrowed. 'She wasn't a bitch. She was—is— a lovely woman. I still think the world of her, and I'd thank you not to pass comments like that about someone you know nothing about.'

There was a silence for a moment, and he hung his head, obviously mortified. Eliza looked shocked. Joe started muttering something about digging out the ice cream and fruit, and Lexi jumped up, offering to dish it out. Even Tessa stood up and padded into the kitchen, obviously sensing the awkward atmosphere.

As I sat there, wondering how to ease the tension, my phone rang. Relieved, I grabbed it from my bag and answered it without looking to see who was calling. It was my mother, and for the first time I could remember, I was glad to hear from her.

'You all right, Mam?' I asked, trying to sound cheery to deflect the gloomy feeling in the room.

'Oh, Rose, it's awful.' She sounded dreadful, really tearful and shaky.

'Mam, are you okay?'

Everyone looked at me. They all knew about her mugging, and I could see the concern in their eyes. Or maybe they were just glad to have someone else to focus on.

'Rose, I—I'm scared. I think someone's bin in here. It feels all wrong, and I daren't go out, and I can't sleep. Oh, Rose, I don't know what to do.'

I swear I heard her sob. My heart skipped a beat. My mother was obviously terrified, and all alone in her flat on that awful estate. I had to do something. 'Mam, try to stay calm. I'm coming to get you, okay? Don't worry. Just watch a bit of telly, and I'll be there as soon as I can.'

'What's wrong?' Joe asked, as I put the phone away.

'My mother. She's really scared. Think the mugging has shook her up much more than I realised. I'm going to have to go to her. I'm sorry, I'll have to pass on the pudding.'

'Do you want a lift?' Eliza asked, looking helplessly around as she must have realised that it was out of the question for either her or Gabriel to take me. Joe and Lexi had also had a few glasses of wine.

There was a silence, till Flynn said quietly, 'It's okay. I'll take you.'

'Oh, Flynn, you darling,' said Eliza.

He shrugged and stood up. I think he was quite glad to be able to leave, to be honest. 'Are you ready?'

I nodded and collected my bag and coat, wishing that Joe had stuck to fruit juice tonight. He rarely drank these days due to his heart attack, but, of course, tonight had to be the one night he decided to indulge. I had a feeling that the drive to Feldane was going to feel endless.

CHAPTER SIX

'You didn't have to do this, you know.'

Flynn looked at me, his face impassive. 'I'm aware of that, but everyone else has been drinking, and it would cost a fortune in a taxi.'

'I'll pay you petrol money,' I said.

His face darkened. 'Don't be ridiculous. That's not what I meant.'

'I know that, but you already did me a favour.'

'Fuchsia will earn her wages. It's not exactly a favour.'

'I meant, taking me to the station that day.'

'Ah.'

We were silent as we reached the top of Bay Street, from where we walked along Whitby Road and down Station Lane to where Flynn's car was parked at Ivy House. I peered up at the big, honey-coloured stone house, tucked away down the quiet lane, wondering what it felt like to have so much room to yourself. I'd never really lived anywhere that hadn't felt slightly cramped. I thought about our two-bedroomed flat above the shop, and my heart sank. Where was my mother going to fit in? It was already claustrophobic, sharing with two teenage girls. I had to acknowledge, though, as Flynn held the passenger door of the car open, and I climbed in, that even Ivy House would feel too small with my mother in it. She'd never been easy to live with.

We drove through the darkness, saying nothing, and I wondered what Flynn was thinking. He must have been getting sick of my family. I mean, first I hassled him at the wedding, then he had to take me all the way to Whitby, then I'd harangued him into employing Fuchsia, and now, here he was, answering my mother's SOS. Considering he didn't really like me very much, he'd certainly been drawn into my life, God help him.

I wondered about his wife. She must have instigated the

divorce. He was obviously still very fond of her, and it didn't sound as if the break-up had been his idea. Was he still in love with her? No wonder he seemed so lonely.

Flynn must have been feeling as awkward as I was, because he stretched out his hand and pressed some buttons on the dashboard, and the car was filled with the most depressing racket I'd ever heard.

'Jesus! What kind of crap is that?'

Flynn glanced at me. 'Don't you like it?'

'Music to slit your wrists to.'

He looked quite put out at my opinion but pressed the button, then started fiddling with the radio. As the sound of Pink filled the car, I heaved a sigh of relief and closed my eyes.

'That's better.'

'Really? Who is it?'

I couldn't believe it. 'Who is it? It's Pink, of course. Don't you know anything?'

'You didn't recognise my music.'

'Well, nobody under seventy would have known that. Apart from you, of course.'

'I assure you, a great many people of our age would have known Wagner when they heard it. Trust you to recognise Pink.'

'Meaning what?'

'Well, you like anything pink. That much is obvious.'

'And there's something wrong with that?'

'Well, no. But don't you ever get an urge to do something radical? Like wear blue?'

'Cheeky git. Don't you ever get an urge to crack a smile, or would that ruin your street cred? Oops, sorry, you haven't got none, have you?'

'Any,' he muttered through gritted teeth.

'What?'

'It's any, not none.'

'Jesus, sorry, sir.' I folded my arms and glared into the

darkness, wishing I'd learned to drive after all. That way I would never have to put up with this stuck-up prig.

'Are you sulking?' he demanded.

'No, I'm not. I'm just thinking.' I squinted at him out of the corner of my eye, and I swear I saw his lips twitch. 'Did you nearly smile then?' I asked in amazement.

'No,' he said. 'Of course not. I was just thinking.'

We glanced at each other, and, to my astonishment, he gave me the biggest smile. It totally transformed his face, and I found myself smiling back.

'I'm sorry you keep getting dragged into my family stuff,' I said. 'I know we must be getting on your wick.'

He shook his head. 'Look, you've had some bad luck lately. I don't mind helping anyone if I can.'

I frowned. Did he mean I was some charity case, or something? I bit my lip, trying not to make some sarcastic comment. He looked much nicer when he smiled. I didn't want to see that twinkle in his eyes disappear just yet.

Flynn very kindly kept the radio tuned to the station, even though it seemed intent on playing songs he'd never heard of, as if to annoy him. I leaned back in my seat and hummed along to some of them, my eyes closed, fingers tapping on the car door. I occasionally opened one eye and peered at him to see how he was reacting to the torture, and found him staring grimly ahead, his knuckles white on the steering wheel. I grinned to myself and closed my eyes again, letting the movement of the car and the music lull me into a relaxed state. Too relaxed.

'Rose, wake up.'

'Eh?' I sat up in shock, suddenly aware that I was drooling and had probably been snoring, too. Brilliant. 'I wasn't asleep,' I informed him.

He was obviously aware that this was a blatant lie, but merely raised an eyebrow and asked which street we were heading for. I gave him my mother's address, and we crawled along, the car seeming as reluctant as I was to reach our destination. We pulled up outside her block of flats, and I yawned and rubbed my eyes, as Flynn climbed out of the car.

I unclipped my seatbelt and stared at him as he opened my door for me. 'You really are like something from the olden days,' I said, wondering how many other men these days would open the door for a lady. Not that I was much of a lady.

'The olden days?' He grinned at me again, and I pulled a face.

'All right, eighteen seventy-two. Is that specific enough for you?'

'Yes,' he acknowledged and shut the door, as I stood on the pavement, looking up in dismay at my mother's flat.

In the doorway, a group of young men skulked, and another crowd stood a little further down the road, pushing and shoving each other and cat-calling.

I shivered.

'What's wrong?'

'I fucking hate this place,' I said. 'It sucks the life out of me.'

'I shouldn't think anything could do that,' he said.

Now, what did he mean by that, exactly? 'Oh, well, here goes nothing.' I headed reluctantly down the path, watching worriedly as the gang moved out of the doorway and walked past us. Hoping they weren't getting any ideas about Flynn's car, I pressed the button on the intercom.

'Who is it?' My mother's voice sounded shaky.

I beamed at the speaker as if she could see me. 'Mam? It's only me, Rose," I said, trying to look and sound positive. "Can you let me in? I'm freezing my tits off here.'

I heard Flynn clear his throat and found I was blushing. I must remember to be more ladylike around him. He was far too proper to be subjected to such language.

The door clicked, and I pushed it open, ushering Flynn into the hallway as I looked back to see what the group of young men were doing. They'd drifted off to join the other gang. I could only hope they had something else to do rather than breaking into the car. I wondered if one of them was the little shit who'd mugged my mother. I didn't suppose I would ever know.

Flynn blinked and looked around the foyer, and I could see the horror in his eyes that he tried valiantly to hide. He needn't have bothered. I didn't blame him in the slightest. The dingy, green-painted walls had been sprayed with graffiti, and there were empty McDonald's bags and discarded bottles on the floor.

I led him towards the concrete stairs, and he nodded at the lift. 'Aren't you going to use that?'

'Trust me,' I told him. 'You wouldn't want to get inside that thing.'

He looked worried, but said nothing as he followed me up the stairs onto the landing, visibly shrinking against the wall when a couple came out of a flat, pushing a buggy with a sleeping toddler inside it. They wore tracksuit bottoms and hoodies. The man carried a bottle of cider, and both smoked cigarettes. They pressed the button of the lift, and both Flynn and I reeled as the doors slid open and the pungent odour of marijuana and stale urine assaulted our nostrils. Flynn's lip curled, but the couple stepped inside the lift as if they hadn't even noticed the smell.

As the doors closed on them, Flynn looked at me in horror. 'Where were they taking the child at this time of night?'

I shrugged. 'Maybe they don't live here and they're going home?'

'They shouldn't keep a baby out this late. Fancy bringing him here, anyway. Disgusting. What chance has he got? And did you see the way they were smoking over him?'

'Oh, Flynn.' I sighed. 'Welcome to Feldane.'

He shuddered, obviously appalled, and I could see the estate was having the same effect on him as it did on me.

I knocked on my mother's door and waited. A shuffling noise came from within, and a small voice said, 'Who is it?'

'Who do you think it is?' I said. 'I've just spoken to you on the intercom.'

'That was five minutes ago. You could be anyone.'

'For God's sake, Mam.' I took a deep breath. 'It's me, Rose. Let me in, will you?'

There was a rattle and the sound of a bolt being slid back, then the door opened slightly and my mother peered cautiously out, keeping the chain on as she ascertained that I was, in fact, her daughter.

'Who's that?' she asked, nodding at Flynn.

'He's, er, a friend. He gave me a lift here. You can trust him, he's a doctor.'

'Huh. Can't trust flaming doctors any more than you can politicians, in my experience, but if he's brought you here, fair dos.' She took the chain off and let us in, shutting the door quickly behind us and sliding the bolt back in place.

Flynn looked around, the expression on his face letting me know he was pleasantly surprised by what he found. My mother was nothing if not house proud, though.

'What's happened, Mam?' I asked, as she led us into her neat little kitchen and switched on the kettle.

'Nothing,' she said. 'What's your name?' she added, as Flynn stood awkwardly by the door.

'Er, Flynn,' he told her.

'Flynn? What kind of a God-awful name's that?' she demanded.

'My grandmother was a fan of Errol Flynn,' he admitted coyly.

'You poor bugger. Stop hovering over there and sit yourself down. Cup of tea?'

'Thank you.'

'Mam,' I said, feeling my impatience rising, 'what do you mean, nothing? You rang me in a right panic, not an hour ago.

Something must have happened.'

'That's you, reading too much into things,' she said.

I flopped down onto the chair next to Flynn's and stared at him. The expression in my eyes must have told him how pissed off I was, because he turned to my mother.

'You really worried Rose, Mrs MacLean,' he told her gently. 'You sounded quite panicked on the phone, and she thought —'

'How would you know how I sounded?' she demanded. 'Had me on speaker phone, did she?'

'Well, no, but —'

'So, you've only got her word for it, then, haven't you? You can't take that, I promise you. Always did exaggerate. Proper drama queen, aren't you?' she said, pouring boiling water into the cups before going to the fridge and getting the milk.

My mouth was a straight line by that point, and I struggled to keep my temper.

Flynn gave me a sympathetic look before looking back to my mother. Mug. 'Well, whatever was said, Mrs MacLean, the fact is that we're here now, so if you've been alarmed by something, we're here to help. Just tell us what the problem is, and we'll do what we can for you.'

My mother fixed him with a beady stare. 'Oh, it's *we* now, is it? Who are you, exactly?'

'I told you. He's a friend,' I said.

'Since when? I've never heard you mention him before. What's a posh bloke like him doing being friends with you? Doesn't ring true, at all. Doctor, are you, did you say?'

'That's right,' said poor Flynn. 'Dr Pennington-Rhys.'

My mother stared at him incredulously. 'Dr who?'

'No, Dr Pennington-Rhys. Just a regular human, I'm afraid. Not a Timelord.'

Flynn's feeble attempt at humour fell spectacularly flat. 'Listen, Dr Piddleton-Rice, or whatever your stupid name is, you can drop the act. I'm not senile, and I'm not stupid, okay?'

'I'm sorry?'

'Doctor of what? From the funny farm, are you? Think I need locking up?'

Flynn looked most indignant. It would have been quite amusing, if my mother wasn't worrying me so much.

'I can assure you, Mrs MacLean, I'm not a psychiatrist. I'm a GP, and I'm here as Rose's friend, nothing more. Would you prefer that I waited outside?'

'You're not going out there!' I said in horror. Flynn would be eaten alive. The streets would be crawling with vermin by that time of night. And perhaps rats, too. 'If you want to talk to me in private, Mam, we'll go into the living room, but you're not sending him outside, and I should think you should stop being so bloody ungrateful, given that a total stranger has come all this way for your sake, and is quite prepared to take you back to my place, if you want to go.'

She stared at me for a moment, then her expression sort of crumpled and she flopped onto the chair, rubbing her face with a shaking hand.

I rushed to her side and put my arm round her shoulders. 'What is it? What's wrong, Mam?'

'I keep hearing noises,' she admitted. 'I keep thinking there's someone in the flat. Oh, I know there isn't. Place is locked up, and I haven't been anywhere, so there's no way anyone could have got in, but I feel uneasy, you know. I get prickles up me back, and on the back of me neck, like there's someone there and I just can't see them. And there's a gang keeps hanging round outside. I don't recognise them, and I know most people round here. Well, I used to. Crackpot council keeps moving problem families in here, and sodding teenagers with nowhere else to live. Used to be nice here, but now .... And I swear I can smell that flaming marry jewana through the doors. Wonder I'm not seeing pink elephants. No wonder you think I'm going daft, I'm always drugged up.'

'Oh, Mam,' I said softly. 'It's no wonder you're hearing

77

noises. You've just been mugged. It's bound to be scary for you.'

'I'm not scared.' She sat up straight, glaring at me for even suggesting such a thing. 'I just don't want people nicking any more of me stuff, that's all. If anyone breaks in here, God help them, that's all I can say. No,' she added, shaking her head defiantly, 'I'm not scared, at all. Just don't like this feeling of being watched, that's all.'

'Of course not,' said Flynn. He looked at me and I saw the query in his eyes.

I could hardly turn my back on her, could I? But, God knows, it wasn't going to be easy.

'I'll help you pack, Mam,' I said, rubbing her back gently.

'Pack? What for? I'm going nowhere.'

'Oh, Mam.' I glared at her, beyond exasperated. She was such a stubborn woman. Why had she dragged me all the way there if she didn't want me to do anything? I looked helplessly at Flynn. It was no use arguing, she would never back down.

'Rose, could you do me a favour? Could you check on my car? That gang outside looked most interested in it. I can't see it from this window. Would you mind?'

I stared at him. All right, it was a nice car, but timing, mate, timing! Then I saw the silent appeal in his eyes, and I nodded and left the room, wondering what he was going to say to her. He was wasting his time, either way. Nothing would budge her when she made her mind up.

I wandered into the living room and peered through the net curtains down onto the street. Flynn's silver Peugeot was certainly attracting attention. A crowd of hooded young men had gathered round it, peering in at the windows and casting furtive glances around.

I pulled the net curtain aside and leaned out of the window. 'Oy, get away from that car, you little shits.'

Startled, they looked up, then laughed, and several of them stuck two fingers up at me, jeering and swaggering around.

'I'll come down there and throttle you,' I yelled. 'Piss off, or I'll call the police.'

They laughed again, nudging each other. Then one of them held up his hand to silence the others and reached into his pocket. Slowly and deliberately, he held something up, though I couldn't make out what it was. Still watching me, he leaned towards the car and ran his hand along the length of it.

I frowned. What the hell was he doing? It took me a few seconds to realise, and then I was out of the flat and running down the stairs, my mind full of fury.

'What the fuck?' The ratbag who was gleefully keying the side of Flynn's car didn't know what had hit him as I hurled myself into him, smacking him on the back and arms, and screaming abuse at him.

'Gerroff me, you mad 'ead!' he shouted, pushing me away.

No way was he getting away with it. I charged back at him, wrestling with him for the key and taking no notice of the other gang members, who'd circled us and were laughing at their friend's embarrassment.

Like he suddenly realised I was making a laughing stock of him, his face changed. 'Get off me, bitch.' He grabbed my wrists and held them tightly.

As I struggled to free myself, aware that I may have made a teensy error of judgement, I looked into his face and, seeing the contempt there, felt a flicker of fear—until my gaze landed on the mess he'd made of Flynn's car, and my anger resurged. 'Look what you've done, you scumbag!' I yelled into his face. 'Who the hell do you think you are? Waste of space. Too bone idle to do anything for yourself, so you spoil things for other people.'

He grinned at me, and I snapped, aiming a sharp kick at his shin. He yelled, and suddenly his hand shot out and connected with my face.

My head spun, and I would have fallen if some of the gang members hadn't caught me and pushed me back towards the thug, who gave me a look of pure venom. I rubbed my face and tried not to look scared, blinking as I tried to get my focus back. I felt a bit dizzy and wondered how exactly I was going to get out of such a mess.

I didn't have time to think about it for long, because he suddenly pushed me back into the crowd. Hands on my back shoved me back at him. Immediately, he pushed me back again, and so their game began, with me feeling like a bloody ping pong ball, being bounced backwards and forwards, while all around me I could hear jeering and laughing.

I began to feel sick, and my back was hurting, not to mention the pain in my face where his hand had connected with it. It was exhausting.

There was an increase in volume, and I heard some yelling, then I was falling, and I wondered if they would kick me when I hit the ground. Except, I never hit the ground. I was caught and pulled out of the crowd, and felt my mother's arms go round me as she steadied me, stroking my hair with trembling hands.

I took a few deep breaths, relieved that the earth had stopped spinning, then looked up, wondering what had happened.

Flynn was standing in the middle of the circle, talking to them. I mean, talking! He was pointing at his car and shrugging his shoulders, as if to ask, why?

'What's he doing, the moron?' I muttered.

My mother tutted. 'That moron just saved your bacon. Charged in there and shoved them out of the way, and caught you, just as it looked like you were going to hit the deck, so don't be so ungrateful.'

He had? Amazing. All the same, I had a feeling he was way out of his depth with this lot. I edged closer, patting my mother's hand as she tightened her grip on me.

'I'm okay,' I whispered, 'but I don't think he knows what he's dealing with.'

I heard Flynn demanding to know who'd been responsible for keying the car. There was a silence as the gang members stared at him.

'You wanna be careful what you say,' said the leader. 'We don't take kindly to knobheads like you coming round here and making accusations.'

'Is that right?' said Flynn. 'Well, I don't take kindly to idiots like you ruining my car, for no good reason. I ask you, what's the point of it? Is it just that you're bored? Or is it simply that you don't like to see other people with things you don't have?'

'Meaning what?' The gang moved inwards, the circle tightening on Flynn.

I swallowed. Oh, hell, this could be really bad. I looked round for my mother, but she'd disappeared. Probably barricaded herself in the flat and left us to it. Not that I could blame her.

'Think you're asking for a good smack, mate,' said a burly-looking lad with some very menacing tattoos.

'Come away, Flynn. Leave them to it,' I said.

He didn't answer, and I wasn't sure he heard me, but the leader had.

'Back for more, bubble-gum brain? Should've run when you had the chance.'

'Leave her alone,' Flynn said, his voice calm and steady. 'It's my car, my argument.'

'Flynn, please. Just leave it,' I said, but my voice seemed to inflame the situation.

The leader nodded, and tattoo-man grabbed me and clamped me to his side. 'Think you need teaching a lesson, darlin',' he said.

'Don't call me darling,' I snarled. 'And let go of me,' I added, struggling to get the thug's filthy hands off me.

'I told you to leave her alone,' Flynn said. 'Violence is never the answer.'

'Wanna bet?'

Tattoo-man laughed and grabbed hold of my hair, yanking my head back with a violent tug. I yelped, and then staggered as Flynn's fist flew out and hit my assailant squarely on the jaw.

He let go of me immediately, and I took the opportunity to thump him in the ribs. I turned to Flynn, who stood there, his jaw pulsing and his eyes dark with fury. I barely recognised him.

I reached out my hand and grabbed his. 'Run!'

It was too late, though. The gang piled towards us, and I felt myself being kicked and pushed, and then gripped tightly, as Flynn was jumped by three or four furious young men.

I heard myself screaming, and struggled, desperate to free myself so I could help him. Oh, God, he was going to die, and it was all my fault.

Tears streamed down my face, as fists flew and I lost sight of him in the crowd, which suddenly seemed to have got bigger. Much bigger. Like they'd got reinforcements.

We were both dead.

Then I realised the reinforcements seemed to be on our side. The thugs who had been attacking us were themselves being attacked. The person holding me was knocked to the ground, and someone caught hold of my arm and dragged me to the safety of my mother's hallway, where I found her standing, safe and sound, with several people I recognised as her neighbours.

'Went for help,' she said, putting her arm round me. 'I thought Doreen's lads might be in, and I knew they'd come to our rescue.'

'My lads won't see anyone set upon like this,' said Doreen proudly. 'They can fight each other all they want, but they're not getting away with hitting you and that nice young man. No chance. My lads will sort them out, don't you worry.'

'But Flynn.' I gasped. 'They have to get Flynn out of there.'

'Looks like he's doing okay to me,' my mother said,

nodding in satisfaction at the crowd.

I turned, and my jaw dropped as I watched Flynn wading in beside Doreen's boys, seeming not to notice or care that his car was being smacked into and scratched and kicked in the general confusion.

'My God,' I murmured.

'I like that fella,' said my mother. 'May not be a psychiatrist, but he tried the reverse psychology on me, bless him. Tried to tell me it would be for your benefit that I moved into your flat with you. That if I didn't, you'd be worried sick, and it would be bad for your health. Ha! Like I didn't see through that trick, but nice of him to care enough to try.'

'So, you're not coming, then?' I asked, aware that I was shivering and my face was aching. Another bruise. Great.

'What, after this performance? Too bloody right I'm coming. Had it with this place. The council can stick it up their arse. No way am I staying put, not now they've let the likes of this lot run riot round here.'

I felt weak with relief. Yes, we were going to be crowded, but there was no way I could leave her there. It was all right for Doreen, with her burly sons, but who did my mother have to protect her? I'd have tied her up and carried her home if I'd had to.

Flynn was suddenly at my side, and I looked up at him, noting with dismay the cut lip and torn shirt, the bloodied nose and the rapidly swelling cheekbone.

'Oh, God, Flynn. I'm so sorry,' I said. All he'd ever done was try to help me, and look what I'd got him into. I felt the tears splash down my cheeks and rubbed my eyes, mortified by my feebleness.

'Hey, hey, it's all right. It's not your fault,' he said, gently wiping my tears. 'You were very brave, trying to stop them from damaging my car. Incredibly stupid, but brave.'

I looked up at him, and then beyond him, to where Doreen's boys were running down the road, chasing the gang off the estate.

'Your poor car.' I gulped. 'I'm so —'

'Stop saying you're sorry.' He smiled. 'The main thing is, we're both all right. You are all right?' he added, checking my face and looking suddenly concerned. 'I think you're going to have another black eye.'

'You, too,' I said. 'That's two-one to me.'

We looked at each other and then we both started to laugh.

Doreen and my mother stared at us, totally perplexed.

'Well, I'm buggered,' said my mother. 'You two must have been hit harder than I thought, if you think that's funny. Come on, let's get upstairs and get packed. I'm out of here.'

'Aw, bless you, Maisie. I'll be sorry to see you go. Can't blame you, though. If I didn't have my lads, I'd be off, an' all,' Doreen admitted.

Flynn and I left them to say their goodbyes and headed back into the flat, where I found my mother's suitcase and began to pull some of her clothes out of the wardrobe.

'We'll get what we can now,' I said, 'and then I'll ask Doreen if one of the boys will drop the rest round in his van. God knows where we're going to put it all, though. It will have to go into storage.'

'There's always my garage?' Flynn offered. 'It's never used and there's plenty of room. I'm sure I can fit most of her things in there, and anything else can go in the spare bedrooms. I've got a few of those.'

'Really? Thank you. You've been really kind. I don't know what to say.'

'You two still mithering?' asked my mother, walking into the bedroom and standing with her hands on her hips. 'Nice of you to start packing, I'm sure, but if you don't mind, I'd rather handle my own smalls, thank you very much.'

Flynn's ears turned red, and I grinned and pushed him out of the room and into the kitchen. He had been a total star with my mother, and had proved to be a real hero, but I didn't think even he was brave enough to cope with some things. The thought of my mother in red lacy briefs may have been too much for even that lion heart to bear.

****

I sat in the back seat of the car with my mother on the way home. Since the adrenaline had worn off, I could feel the throbbing in my face, and my back hurt where I'd been repeatedly shoved. I felt weary to my bones, and the gloom had set in, as I faced up to the reality that my mother was going to be living with us.

I wondered how Fuchsia and Cerise would deal with it. It was all right saying it would be okay when it was all just an unlikely theory, but now it was real, would they stand it? The flat was small and crowded, as it was. With my mother charging her way through and dominating the room the way she did, it would seem even tinier.

My heart sank as I remembered what living with her was like. Constant criticism, nagging, telling me I was doing it wrong, no matter what "it" happened to be. Could I stand it, after so many years of freedom?

I would have to give up my bedroom, too. I couldn't ask her to sleep on the sofa, so guess where that left me? The bedroom was the only personal space I had, my only escape from the girls and the television. I would have no sanctuary left.

I glanced at my mother. She was looking out of the window, her shoulders hunched, her hands clasped tightly on her lap. I felt angry at myself for being so selfish, when she'd lost everything, including the only home she'd lived in since the day she got married to my dad. She was giving up so much, and there I was, moaning about a bedroom. I'd cope. I would have to.

Flynn played some soothing classical music all the way

home. I had no idea what it was, but it was nice, and much better than that miserable opera music he'd been playing earlier. I didn't feel in the mood for any upbeat pop music, anyway.

In the rear-view mirror, I could see that one of Flynn's eyes looked as if it was swelling rapidly. He must have been in pain, but he said nothing, just concentrated on the driving. His car looked as bad as he did, too. It would cost a fortune to repair, and that was down to me. I should have got a taxi to Mam's instead of roping him in. He'd said not to worry, and that was what insurance was for, but I still felt terrible. Wouldn't that mean his premiums would go up? Either way, he'd be paying for helping me out, and I'd already landed Fuchsia on him. Why did he have to be so amenable? Why couldn't he just tell me to get lost and make my own way to my mother's, or tell me that he wouldn't take Fuchsia on if she were the last woman left on the planet? No, always too nice. That was his curse, if you asked me. Look where it had got him.

I found myself wondering about his wife. Had she taken advantage of that niceness? Played him for a fool? Broken his heart? I looked into the mirror again. For a moment, his eyes met mine, and I found myself blushing. It was guilt, I thought. Guilt for the state of his face and for speculating about his wife. He'd defended her so quickly. Was that Flynn being the gentleman as usual, or did he still have feelings for her?

Mentally shrugging, I pulled myself together. What did it matter? For God's sake, I had more important things to think about. As the car pulled up outside The Kearton Arms, I took a deep breath. We were home, and I still had to break the news to my daughters.

'We have to walk from here, Mam,' I reminded her, as she looked at me blankly for a moment.

'Oh, oh, yes, 'course we do. Another downside to this place.' She pulled her coat tightly around her and unclipped her seatbelt. 'Right, well, best get it over with.'

She looked surprised when Flynn opened the car door for her and offered his arm, but accepted his help without a murmur, which showed how out-of-sorts she was. I scrambled out after her, and Flynn closed the door before rounding to the boot and taking out her suitcases.

He refused my offer of help, so I linked my arm through my mother's, and the three of us made our way down the scarily steep Bay Street towards home.

Kearton Bay was a former fishing village on the North Yorkshire coast, not too far from Whitby and the Yorkshire Moors. In a glorious location, the village itself was full of history and quaint buildings. The area at the top of the hill was known to locals as "Up Top", and was the newer part of the village that held lots of Victorian villas, and some fairly modern houses, too. Up there, the farms, the church, the riding school and the beautiful Elizabethan Kearton Hall could also be found.

Bay Street was the main route down to "Old Town", which huddled into the cliff side, and consisted of chocolate box cottages, tiny little shops, narrow passages and ancient pubs. Halfway down, Bay Street became a little bridge, which carried you over a fast-flowing stream. Known as Kearton Beck, it ran from the moors and threaded its way down to the sea, rushing out onto the sands from beside The Hare and Moon pub, one of the oldest buildings in the village.

I loved the village, heart and soul, but I had to admit that hill was the very devil. Walking down it was hard enough, but coming back up was doubly hard, especially when I'd had a few. Luckily, I lived down Water's Edge, which looked down over the beck, and so the climb wasn't as long for me, but even so I was aware of my mother's disapproval as we made our way down the wide concrete steps that had been put in place at the side of the cobbled road.

She clung tightly to the handrail the council had installed

many years ago, to help the elderly and infirm, and paralytic drunks, make their way up and down the hill. She tutted as we climbed the short flight of broad steps that led off the main street, and I heaved a sigh of relief as we entered the narrow little street that was Water's Edge, and the ground levelled off again to the thoroughfare between Bay Street and King's Row.

Mallow Magic, and my home, was situated about a third of the way down. I unlocked the front door, and Flynn stepped aside to let my mother and me into the hallway first, then he followed us up the narrow stairs, the edges of the suitcases bumping against the walls as we climbed up to the flat.

The living room was in darkness, apart from the light of the television. Fuchsia and Cerise were on the sofa, wearing pyjamas, eating ice cream, and watching *Nightmare on Elm Street*. Cerise screamed and nearly fell off the sofa in fright, as I walked up behind her and laid my hand on her shoulder.

'What have I told you about watching films like this?' I demanded. 'Fuchsia, you should know better.'

'I'm not a kid,' Cerise said sulkily. When she glanced behind her, her eyes widened. 'Grandma, what are you doing here?'

'Charming,' my mother said, flicking the light switch on.

I really wished she hadn't. The flat was a tip. I'd gone out in a bit of a hurry, and it didn't look as if the girls had done any tidying up since I left. Dirty plates and cups from their tea littered the coffee table, and Fuchsia's magazines lay on the floor. Her coat was draped over the back of her chair, and her shoes were scattered on the rug in front of the fire. Cerise's school bag was on the sofa beside her, her text books in a jumble on the floor, and her packed lunchbox lying open on top of the bag, revealing an empty crisp packet and an apple core.

My mother looked around, her eyes wide, and I could see she was wondering what the hell she'd got herself into. I could have killed the girls. They'd had all evening to tidy up and, instead, they'd slobbed around watching unsuitable films and left it all for me when I got home. That was bad enough, but for my mother and Flynn to witness such a mess was mortifying.

My face burned as defiance kicked in. 'Right, well thanks for all your help, Flynn,' I said, taking the suitcases from him and dropping them on the spare armchair. 'We can manage now. Get yourself home and see to that eye.'

'Dear God,' said my mother. 'I should think the least you can do is make the poor bugger a cup of tea, given all he's been through tonight, for your sake.'

My sake! That was rich.

Fuchsia had been doing an obvious job of avoiding eye contact with her employer since he walked in, but when she finally looked at his face, she burst out laughing. 'Jesus! What have you been up to? And you, Mam? You two been wrestling, or summat?'

I wanted to throttle her.

'Dr Peddleston-Rice has been very heroic,' said my mother, glaring at her granddaughter. 'There was some unpleasantness on the estate and your mother, being your mother, waded in without putting her brain into gear first. If it hadn't been for him, she'd have looked even worse than she does now, I can tell you.'

I was so stunned by this miscarriage of justice that I couldn't speak. Instead, I turned to Flynn, who seemed horrified by the state of the place, and began to push him to the door. 'Like I said, Flynn, cheers, and all that. Doreen's boys will be round some time tomorrow with Mam's stuff. They said they'll call you before they set off, make sure you're in. Appreciate your help, but, as you can see, we have a lot to sort out here, and I'm sure you're ready for home. Hope your car insurance gets sorted. 'Night.'

He mumbled something, but I could only hear a rushing in my ears, and I just wanted him to go. As he turned and headed for the stairs, I shut the door behind him, not even bothering to check that he shut the front door properly as he left the building.

Fuchsia and Cerise looked at each other, then at me. 'What's going on, Mam?' Cerise asked.

My mother put her hands on her hips and glared at them both. 'What's going on? Your mother's making a show of herself, as usual, and you two have behaved like slobs. Look at the state of this place! Absolute pig-sty. Well, neither of you need think you're sloping off to bed. No one's getting out of here until this room is spotless, and I'll be checking the kitchen, an' all, so don't think you can just dump everything in there. Rose, you've let them get away with murder. Well, it ends now, I can promise you that.'

'Mam, what the heck's happened?' whispered Cerise, as Fuchsia folded her arms and gave my mother a look that could have turned lesser mortals to stone.

I sighed. 'I'll tell you what's happened, love. My mother's here, and she's going nowhere. And so it begins ...'

CHAPTER SEVEN

Easter was always a busy time in Kearton Bay. The tourists flooded in, and the first really big money started to flow into the village. All the teashops, cafés and gift shops reopened, and the streets were crowded with holidaymakers and day-trippers, all admiring the pretty little place I was proud to call home.

Rhiannon always made a big thing of Easter, or Ostara, as she referred to it. It had a great deal of significance to her, being a Wiccan or a Pagan, or whatever she was, and she liked to make a fuss of all the kids in the village, making sure there was an Easter egg hunt and an Easter bonnet parade. She had her own private religious ceremony away from the crowds, and then, on the evening of Easter Monday, she had a party for all the adults in the village—a time to draw breath after the busy weekend, and a chance to catch up before the holiday season began in earnest.

I wasn't sure I was going to go, to be honest. I was knackered. Mallow Magic was hectic. We had a steady stream of customers during the day, and Chrissie had been making deliveries to the shops in Helmston and Whitby, which also stocked our products. The Easter baskets were flying off the shelves, as they made nice alternatives to Easter eggs, for the grownups; the new chocolate orange mallows were a sell-out, and we had several bookings for the candy cart.

I'd been going home every night completely exhausted. The one good thing about my mother being there was that the house was spotless when I arrived home. She had cleaned right through, and she made damn sure it stayed in pristine condition. We only had to stand up and she'd be plumping the cushions behind us. I knew I should be grateful, but sometimes it got on my wick. I mean, it was a bit much when I couldn't even put my cup of coffee down without someone screeching "coaster!" in my ear. Plus, there was the whole sofa thing. It was comfy enough to sit on, but sleeping on it every night was rough. I couldn't relax, and it didn't feel as if I was getting much rest. Also, all my clothes and stuff were in my old room, so I had to wait till I heard my mother up and about before I could get anything, and I was sick of creeping about the living room and kitchen so I didn't disturb her.

Cerise's school had broken up for the Easter holidays, and she'd been invited to stay with her friend and her parents in their holiday home in Cornwall. Lucky sod. I'd said no at first, sure it would cost too much, but the parents had phoned me and assured me that she would only need a little spending money, and that they didn't want anything towards her board. She was welcome company for their daughter, who got bored down there on her own. I felt like a proper charity case but I could hardly let Cerise down, could I? So I agreed and managed to scrape together fifty quid for her spending money. We were both pretty stunned when Fuchsia gave her twenty-five pounds out of her wages. She pushed it in Cerise's hand with a muttered, 'Have a good time, kid.' Cerise gaped at her and I'd had to sit down with the shock of it. Fuchsia was such a mystery to me.

Mallow Magic had stayed open through the Easter holidays, as we wanted to catch all the holidaymakers, and we'd done really well. Gabriel had Amy through the day, as the surgery was closed, but on the Monday he rang the shop and said his father had been taken ill, and could someone look after Amy so he could visit the hospital?

Eliza, naturally enough, wanted to go with him to Whitby to see how Raphael was. Chrissie was holding the fort at the shop, and I had the candy cart to prepare for a sixteenth birthday party that afternoon.

'What shall I do?' Eliza asked. 'Lexi's working, Sophie and Archie have gone to Scarborough for the day with the kids, and Chrissie said Meggie and Ben are visiting Ben's parents in Sandsend. Besides, Meggie's supposed to be having Amy tonight, while we're at the party, although I doubt we'll be going if Raffy's not well. Oh, God, I hope he's okay.'

'There's always Fuchsia?' I suggested hesitantly.

We looked at each other.

'Would she want to babysit?' Eliza sounded doubtful, and I couldn't blame her, but we were in a quandary and could only ask.

To my astonishment, Fuchsia agreed. What's more, she refused payment.

'Are you sure?' Eliza was stunned. She wasn't the only one. I felt like checking Fuchsia's temperature.

'Yeah, I'm sure. I hope Dr Bailey's okay. Will you—will you send the family my love?'

'Of course. Thank you so much, Fuchsia.'

The fog lifted, and it began to make sense. Raphael Bailey was Oliver's grandfather. Any chance to ingratiate herself with the family and Fuchsia was taking it. Poor little lass. She really had it bad.

Gabriel dropped Amy off at the shop, and Fuchsia took her upstairs, while Eliza grabbed her jacket and issued last minute instructions to Chrissie.

'Hope everything's okay,' I told them, seeing Gabriel's anxious face and crossing my fingers tightly for them. I liked Dr Bailey. He was a nice old bloke and had been lovely to Eliza. I'd hate to see anything happen to him.

Praying that all would be well upstairs, and telling Chrissie to listen out for trouble from the flat, I headed to the village hall, where the candy cart was waiting to be transformed. We kept it in an outbuilding at Whisperwood Farm, to save us dragging it up and down the hill, and Eliza had a trailer there, which she used if we needed to take it far. She'd dropped it off at the village hall, earlier that morning, as the birthday party was being held there. Sweet sixteen. How long ago that felt, now that I was a jaded thirty-seven year old. Had I ever been sweet, I wondered?

Ruby Simmons, whose party it was, was a very girly sort of girl. Her mother and aunt were already at the village hall, decorating the room with balloons and banners. It was all very pink—a girl after my own heart.

I worked all afternoon, trying not to worry about Raphael's health and how Fuchsia was coping with Amy. I hoped she wasn't watching any horror films with her. If Amy had nightmares that night, I'd flaming well kill Fuchsia.

By two o' clock, the cart was ready, and it looked stunning, if I said so myself. I'd attached some pretty, vintage bunting to the canopy, and to the edge of the cart, and wrapped bows of pale pink gauze to the posts. Baby pink vintage, enamel pots stood on the shelves, ready to be filled with various flavours of marshmallow, and, at the back of the cart, taking pride of place on the top shelf, was a three-tier vintage cake stand, which we were going to fill with mallow pops and mallow cupcakes. Dotted between the pots were little glass jars containing small branches of cherry blossom. I had placed more jars of cherry blossom on the tables, with the approval of Ruby's family. They were delighted with the cart. So far, so good.

I opened the tins of mallows and put them in place, just ten minutes before the guests were due to arrive. Leaving a stack of business cards in a dish on the lower shelf, I headed home to see how things were going there.

The shop was very busy when I stepped through the door. 'Any problems?' I asked.

Chrissie shook her head. 'Haven't heard a peep from up there. Rushed off my feet down here, though. Could use a hand?'

'Give me five minutes.'

I rushed upstairs and popped my head round the living room door. Fuchsia was sitting at the table with Amy and they were painting eggs. I couldn't believe it. Amy was concentrating very hard on her own little creation, and Fuchsia was encouraging and praising her, making suggestions on how to improve it, and asking her what she thought of her own egg, which Amy pronounced "rubbish", making Fuchsia laugh and nudge her in mock indignation. I wondered if she'd had a close encounter with an angel called Clarence and he'd shown her the error of her ways.

After sneaking back down to the shop, I put my apron on and got on with the job.

Eliza and Gabriel arrived home at five, looking most relieved.

'Is he all right?'

'He will be. It's a virus. They're keeping him in for now, but he'll be okay, thank God.' Gabriel shook his head. 'He's just taken ten years from me. I was scared stiff.'

'How's Amy been?' Eliza asked, a bit nervously.

I smiled. 'Absolutely fine. I checked on them, earlier on. They were painting faces on hard-boiled eggs.' I frowned as a sudden thought occurred to me. 'Crikey, I hope Fuchsia thought to boil them first.'

Eliza laughed. 'We'll soon find out. Can I go and get her?'

"Course. I'll come with you. Won't be a minute, Chrissie. Time to lock up, anyway.'

Fuchsia and Amy were sitting on the sofa, watching *Bedknobs and Broomsticks* on the television. On the coffee table in front of them lay a cardboard egg box, its lid open to reveal six colourful, decorated eggs inside.

'Look, Mummy, look, Gabriel, I've made you.'

Amy jumped up, eager to show her parents her marvellous creations. We examined them admiringly, as she pointed out eggs bearing the likeness of Eliza, Gabriel, Lexi, me, Fuchsia and Amy. It was easy to tell which one was me and which was Lexi, by the colour of our hair. The others were a little more difficult, but we nodded and praised her, delighted to see her so excited and proud. I felt quite weak with relief.

'Thank you so much, Fuchsia. She's obviously been well

looked after.' Eliza smiled at her, as Gabriel looked quite amazed by the turn of events.

'Yes, thank you. Are you sure you won't take payment?'

'No, no, it's fine. Just glad your dad's okay.'

The two of them seemed stunned into silence by the uncharacteristic display of altruism, the shock compounded by Amy informing them that she loved Fuchsia and could she play with her again soon?

'Well, er, I'm sure Fuchsia has a lot of things to do ...' began Eliza, but Fuchsia shrugged.

'I don't mind if you ever need a babysitter. She's a smart kid, aren't you, Ames?'

Amy beamed at her.

Eliza stared at her, then at Fuchsia. 'Well, er, thanks. I'll bear that in mind.'

Standing at the door, we waved them off as they left. Amy managed to prise her hand out of Gabriel's, and ran back to give Fuchsia a hug.

Fuchsia smiled—a proper, full-on smile. I almost keeled over.

Amy ran back to Gabriel, and they walked away, no doubt needing a lie down after the strange turn of events.

Fuchsia turned to me and caught me gaping at her. 'What's up with you?' she said. 'Standing there, all gormless.'

'I can't believe how well you did,' I admitted.

She shrugged. 'Amy's okay. We had fun. Better than watching telly all afternoon on my own.' She grinned at me, and for the first time in ages I felt optimistic. Had I finally had a breakthrough with my daughter?

I slipped my arm through hers and felt a warm glow, as, for once, she didn't shrug me away.

****

I didn't know if it was because she was still basking in the warm glow of admiration, or the promise of bumping into Oliver, that persuaded Fuchsia to attend Rhiannon's Easter party. Whatever the reason, I was surprised to find her looking quite presentable as I came out of the bathroom, newly-showered and wearing full makeup for the first time in months.

Actually, she looked more than presentable—she looked very pretty, and had made a real effort, wearing a berry-red skater dress, with a lace overlay and narrow belt. It was the first time I'd seen her legs in ages. She'd even put her hair up and was wearing raspberry lipstick, which really suited her dark colouring, and smoky kohl around her large, grey eyes.

Looking at her, I felt a clutch of fear. She obviously had it bad for Oliver, because there was no way she would have dressed like that usually. We'd made such progress today, I was afraid a knockback from him would put her right back in her usual sullen state. I just couldn't imagine him being interested in her, no matter how I tried. I didn't see any spark between them when they were together. I wasn't sure I'd even seen him look at her properly.

I tried to push all my worries away, just for one night. Life was always so complicated, but I wanted a night off from it all, to let my hair down and enjoy myself for once.

My mother had gone into Oddborough to meet Doreen. They were heading to the bingo hall, where there was, apparently, a big Easter jackpot on offer. She was sure she was going to win it. I hoped she did. Her pension didn't stretch far, and maybe, with a big wad of cash, she could find a flat of her own to rent in the area.

I allowed myself to dream for a few minutes, but then forced myself back to reality. My mother winning big on the bingo was as likely as Oliver Crook declaring his undying love for my daughter and whisking her away to live happily ever after.

The Hare and Moon was heaving when we arrived, and I

struggled through the crowd round the bar and ordered a lime and soda for myself, seeing as I was at work the following morning, and half a lager for Fuchsia. Looking around to see who'd turned up, I spotted Will and Lexi tucked away in a corner, deep in conversation. That looked promising. Had Will finally told Lexi how he truly felt about her? God knows, he'd been promising that he would for long enough. Way before she started working for him at Kearton Hall.

'They're talking shop,' Rhiannon said, spookily reading my mind as she handed me our drinks. 'And I mean that literally. They're discussing plans for expanding the shop on the estate, and maybe supplying other shops with produce from the estate farm. It all sounds rather splendid. Will's awfully clever, and now his father's backed off a little, he's getting the chance to put his ideas into practice at last.'

'Hmm, he may be clever, Rhiannon, but he's bloody dense when it comes to women. How long has he been mooning after Lexi, now? Why in God's name doesn't he just tell her how he feels?'

She shrugged. 'Who knows? I'm sure, when the time is right, he will tell her. Everything always unfolds exactly as it should. The universe doesn't make mistakes.'

I rolled my eyes. She was in one of her philosophical moods again. Rhiannon was an eternal optimist, and, to be honest, it quite got on my wick. Sometimes, I liked a good wallow, and she wasn't one to allow it. Everything was moonbeams and rainbows in her world. I doubted Will felt so confident, poor sod. As for Lexi, I mean how blind can you be? If she couldn't see that he fancied the pants off her then she didn't deserve him, because it was obvious to everyone else around. They were a good team. Pair of idiots.

Well, if they weren't going to get together tonight, there was no harm in joining them, was there? I nudged Fuchsia over to the table and plonked myself down beside Will, who looked rather startled, but greeted me as politely as always.

'You look lovely, Rose, and you, too, Fuchsia.' As he turned to my daughter, his eyes widened a little, and he sounded rather shocked as he added, 'You look absolutely stunning, doesn't she, Lexi?'

Lexi looked across at Fuchsia and nodded. 'Yeah, you do, actually. Oy!' she added, poking Will suddenly on the arm and fixing him with a stern look. 'You never said I looked stunning, or lovely. In fact, you never mentioned my outfit, at all.'

Will seemed stricken. His Adam's apple bobbed up and down, and his lips moved as he tried to formulate a response.

Lexi laughed. 'I'm only kidding. Jeez, I don't expect my boss to compliment me on my outfit. I'm not that needy.'

Will's expression drooped, and I was tempted to shake him. In fact, I was tempted to shake them both. Luckily for them, Sophie arrived at that moment and made a beeline for our table, while Archie went to the bar to get a round in.

'You all right, Sophe?' I asked, seeing that she wasn't her usual bubbly self.

'No I'm not actually,' she admitted, looking decidedly put out. 'Bloody kids. I don't know why we have them. Nothing but trouble.'

Lexi's lips twitched. 'But your kids are perfect, Sophie,' she reminded her. 'Surely, you must be mistaken?'

I smirked, but Sophie didn't seem amused. 'How many people would kill for the chance of a decent university education?' she demanded. 'The trouble with my lot is they don't know how well-off they are. Had everything handed to them on a plate, and do they appreciate it? Do they hell. I don't know why we bother.'

'What's happened?' I asked, my amusement that her perfect children weren't behaving so perfectly for once tempered by my understanding of her bewilderment. Kids were a nightmare, no doubt about it. They never did what you expected or wanted them to do. Then again, neither had I when

I'd been young, to be fair.

I heard Fuchsia murmur something and saw her rise from the chair. I looked around, and my heart sank as I saw that Sophie's children had entered the bar and were standing by the door to the dining room, deep in discussion. Tall, blond Oliver was waving his arms around and seemed to be arguing with his dark-haired twin, Pandora, while Tallulah, as ever, seemed to be trying to calm them both down.

Fuchsia headed straight for them, and I tried not to worry. Rhiannon was right, much as I hated to admit it. What would be would be, and if Oliver sent her packing, she would just have to deal with it. I couldn't protect her from life, as much as I wanted to.

I turned my attention back to Sophie, who'd started sniffing into a tissue.

'I just know she's going to do it, and I'll be having words with Georgia if she does, I'm telling you. I'm sorry, Lexi, I know she's your best friend, but, honestly, she shouldn't be encouraging such stupid thoughts.'

'Blimey, Sophe, are you still banging on about this?' Archie, Sophie's husband, handed her a glass of wine and pushed his way round the table to sit opposite her, clutching his pint tightly, as he did so. He looked desperately in need of it. Weary wasn't the word.

'I'm sorry, have I missed something?' I asked. 'What are you talking about?'

'Pandora,' said Sophie, looking at me with exasperation. 'I've just said so, haven't I? She's dropping hints that she's fed up with university and is thinking about changing her career.'

I blinked. 'Well, what's that got to do with Georgia?'

Sophie tutted. 'For God's sake, Rose. Haven't I just explained? She wants to work with horses, and who has a riding school round here but Georgia?'

'Well, that doesn't mean that she's intending to work with her,' I said. 'She could be thinking of somewhere farther afield, for all you know.'

Sophie's face crumpled, and Archie groaned. 'Oh, God, you had to say that. We've just had this out with Olly. I think they're trying to kill her off.'

'What have I said now?' I demanded.

Sophie sniffed into her tissue again. 'As if Pandora wasn't bad enough, now Oliver's talking about doing his training contract down south when he finishes his Legal Practice Course. I mean, why? He can do his training with his father in Helmston. That's always been the plan. I'm sure they're doing it to wind me up.'

'I'm quite sure they're not, love,' reassured Archie. 'They're twenty years old. They want to spread their wings. You can't blame them.'

'I wish Fuchsia had the chance to explore the world a bit,' I mused, sipping on my lime and soda. 'She's never been farther than Helmston. I'd have loved her to go to university. I wouldn't worry about the twins, Sophie. They'll always be all right. At least they've got the choice.'

'And what use is choice if you keep making the wrong ones?' she snapped. 'It was bad enough, anyway, with Oliver in Manchester and the girls in York, but if Pandora's planning on working God knows where with her damn horses, and Oliver decides to clear off to London or somewhere, what will be left? My family will be scattered. I may never see them again.'

'I think that's a bit dramatic, Sophie,' said a voice behind us, and I turned to see Gabriel and Eliza had arrived, with Joe in tow. Gabriel hugged his sister, before he and Joe brought chairs over to our table, although it was a pretty tight squeeze with eight of us sitting round it.

'You know Sophie,' Archie said to the new arrivals. 'Never one for underplaying a situation.'

'Why can't you all see how bad this is?' she wailed. 'Thank God for Tally, that's all I can say. She'll never let me down.'

'How are you getting on with your studies, Lexi?' Archie asked. 'Must be halfway through by now?'

'A couple of years left.' She sighed. 'I've only signed up for one course next time because of work. Still, I've got the summer school out of the way, and it will all be worth it in the end.'

'How are things going at Kearton Hall?' asked Archie, obviously determined to keep the conversation well away from his own children.

I vaguely heard Will telling him about his plans, but I was more interested in watching Fuchsia, to be honest. I could see her standing with the Crook kids, and she looked distinctly awkward. I would have said nervous. There was a light in her eyes that was unmistakable, but she was obviously unsure that her interest was reciprocated. Judging by Oliver's body language, I would have said not, but I could have been wrong. I prayed I was. Poor kid looked as if she was trying way too hard to fit in. My heart ached for her, but what could I do? She certainly wouldn't have thanked me for going over there and trying to play matchmaker.

'Penny for them?' Eliza nudged me, and I tried to smile.

'Our Fuchsia,' I whispered. 'Looks like she's got a crush on a certain someone.'

She glanced over to where the kids were standing, and smiled. 'Bless her. You don't look too happy about it?'

'Would you be happy if Amy grew up and fell for someone totally out of her league?'

Eliza frowned. 'What do you mean, out of her league?'

'My God, look who's here!'

We both turned at Gabriel's exclamation, and I felt a sudden rush of pleasure as I saw Flynn heading towards us. I supposed it was the shock at seeing him in a pub again, as it very rarely happened.

'What on earth brings you here?' Gabriel asked, as Flynn hovered near our table, nodding at us all and looking as if he was already having second thoughts.

Dressed in a black shirt and black jeans, he looked, quite frankly, pretty fabulous. I thought again what a waste it was, and that he should be out every night socialising and having fun. He would have been snapped up ages ago if he had, I was sure of it. Maybe that was what he was afraid of. Maybe he was still too hung up on his wife to risk it.

'Well, Rhiannon asked if I would come for once, and I thought I'd refused so many of her invitations, it would be rude not to accept this one,' he said. 'Er, would anyone like a drink?'

Everyone declined, stating that their glasses were still half-full. Well, mine wasn't. I'd swigged that lime and soda pretty quickly, but I didn't think Flynn owed me anything, not after what he'd gone through because of me.

'Rose?'

I looked up at him and found myself blushing. I wondered if he'd got his car fixed okay and how much it had cost him. At least his eye seemed all right. I hadn't even checked on him. What a nightmare I was, really. 'What?'

He grinned. 'Would you like a drink? Your glass appears to be empty.'

'Oh, no, it's okay, thanks. Let me get you one. It's the least I can do after everything …' The very least, I thought with some embarrassment.

'Don't be silly. I wouldn't hear of it. Are you sure you don't want one?'

'No, honest. I'll get my own.' I'd cost him enough, after all.

He hesitated as if about to say something, then went over to the bar. I looked at Eliza, who seemed puzzled.

'Fancy him coming out all on his own. Wonder what's brought him here?' She turned to Gabriel. 'Did you know he was coming?'

He shook his head. 'Never mentioned it on Thursday. Maybe it was a last-minute decision.'

'Strange. I wonder ...' Eliza's voice trailed off, and I turned to see what she was looking at.

Flynn stood at the bar, and, as I watched, Rhiannon leaned over the counter and touched his face. It was only for a moment, but the way she looked at him was most odd. I felt a weird clutching at my stomach as the thought occurred to me that maybe she was the reason he'd come here, after all, and not because of guilt. I couldn't blame him. Rhiannon was gorgeous, and, anyway, why shouldn't he get together with her? He was single, after all. They both were.

'Well, that looks interesting,' said Eliza. 'What do you think?'

I shrugged. 'Dunno. I suppose there has to be some reason he'd come out tonight. Not like he makes a habit of mixing with us peasants, is it? And, let's face it, Rhiannon's been pretty quiet on the bonking front lately. Don't think she's been with anyone for ages, so she's probably desperate.'

Eliza looked stunned by my comments, and I couldn't say I blamed her. I felt my face beginning to burn, and it didn't help matters when Flynn suddenly appeared at my side and handed me a glass.

'What's this?'

'Lime and soda,' he said, putting his glass of fruit juice on the table and glancing round as if searching for a spare chair.

'How did you know I was drinking lime and soda?'

He shook his head slightly, but didn't answer, and I took a large gulp of the drink, as it came to me that Rhiannon had probably told him. I expected he thought I was some kind of charity case, having seen my cramped little flat and the estate I had grown up on. Well, I didn't need his charity. I would buy him a drink next time. I didn't want to be any more in his debt than I already was.

'I called the hospital earlier,' Archie said to Gabriel. 'Your dad's doing fine. Good job. Sophie was apoplectic that she only found out this evening.'

'We tried calling you, Sophie, but your phone was off.'

'And whose fault was that?' she demanded. 'Turn your phone off, Sophie. Let's have a proper day out together with no distractions, Sophie.'

'Well, can you blame me?' said Archie. 'You're always on that damn thing lately. Sodding Twitter.'

'And how else do I keep up with the celebrity gossip?' she demanded. 'Anyway,' she told her brother, 'you should have called one of the kids. They never turn their phones off.'

'I don't know their numbers,' he admitted shame-faced. 'Still, all's well that ends well.'

'Who looked after Amy?' asked Sophie suddenly.

Eliza smiled. 'Fuchsia. And a brilliant job she did of it, too. Oh, yes,' she added, at Sophie's disbelieving face. 'Amy was quite taken with her. Wanted to stay with her tonight, but I told her Fuchsia was going to the party. She's with Meggie instead. She offered, but I daresay she'll regret it. She'll be hearing about nothing but that new Disney film all night. Amy's obsessed with it.'

'Has she seen it?'

'Joe and I took her for her birthday last week,' she said. 'I'm not sure who enjoyed it most, out of the two of them.'

'Neither am I,' admitted Joe with a grin. He leaned forward and cleared his throat. 'I have a bit of an announcement to make while you're all here.'

We all looked at him in surprise.

Eliza's eyes were like saucers. 'What announcement?' she demanded.

'Well, you know *Death by Default* comes out next month?' he said, referring to his new murder mystery novel set in the world of dog shows.

We all nodded.

'Well, I have to do a load of publicity for it, and I've been booked to go on *The Charlie Hope Show* to plug it a bit.'

Lexi nearly fell off her chair in excitement. Charlie Hope

was her favourite comedian. I reckoned he was a lot of peoples' favourite judging by his DVD sales figures and the way his tours sold out so quickly. Fancy Joe landing a guest spot on his show.

'Wow,' Eliza said. 'How fabulous!'

'Oh, please, please get me his autograph,' Lexi begged. 'Or, even better, a signed photograph.'

'I can do better than that,' he said, smiling. 'How do you fancy coming with me to watch the show being filmed?'

Lexi looked stunned. She turned to Will, who was beaming at her. 'Is that okay? Can I have the day off?'

'Of course you can.' He laughed. 'As if I'd come between you and Charlie Hope. What date will this be?' he added, taking out his diary.

'The eighteenth.'

'Just before my birthday.' Lexi beamed. 'What a fab present.'

'And I'll take you for tea, too,' Joe promised. 'We'll make a night of it. Stay over at a hotel. It is your twenty-first, after all.'

Lexi threw her arms round his neck and kissed him, then she rushed over to the bar, where she proceeded to inform everyone about her forthcoming treat.

'That's made her day,' Will said, the affection for her shining from him as stared toward where she was telling Derry and Robbie, her face bright with excitement.

My gaze slid over to the corner of the bar, where Fuchsia was standing next to Oliver. She was sipping her drink and looked forlorn. Pandora and Tally were giggling about something, and Oliver was texting on his phone. She looked so lost and alone, I just wanted to rush over and hug her. Beside me, I heard Flynn excuse himself and head back to the bar. Within seconds, he and Rhiannon were deep in conversation, and I turned away and finished my drink, suddenly depressed beyond words, in spite of the excited buzz around the table. It was all spoilt. I couldn't feel happy any more.

Lexi came back and sank into her chair, still looking stunned.

Will smiled at her. 'Have you calmed down now?'

She shook her head and looked round at us all, her eyes wide. 'I don't know. What a day. First a trip to London, and then a date.'

I saw the colour drain from Will's face, and my heart went out to him.

'A date?' asked Gabriel. 'Who's asked you out?'

She nodded her head towards the bar, where Robbie and Derry stood, chatting over a pint.

'Not Derry again?' Eliza said.

Lexi shook her head. 'Of course not. Robbie. Robbie just asked me out. Can you believe that?'

'And Derry doesn't mind?' Eliza asked, mindful of the fact that he and her stepdaughter had been "friends with benefits" for a while.

'Don't be daft. That's ancient history.' Lexi nudged Will. 'See? Someone thinks I look lovely, even if my own boss doesn't think so.' She laughed.

I didn't know how Will kept his face so neutral. I wanted to weep for him. I wanted to weep for Fuchsia. Hell, I just wanted to weep. I decided that, work or no work, my next drink would be vodka.

'Thank God for that,' Archie said, as Jack, Rhiannon's chef, began to bring out plates of food and lay them on the table closest to the bar. 'I'm starving. Sophie wouldn't feed me. Said I could fill up here instead.'

'Well, as if I'm in the mood to cook, with everything that's going on,' Sophie said.

I watched, feeling my anger rise as Oliver Crook headed straight over to the food and began to fill up a plate, leaving Fuchsia standing with his sisters as if she didn't matter a jot.

I drained my glass and headed to the bar, ordering a double from Rhiannon.

The vodka and Coke was gone in seconds, and I asked for another.

Rhiannon frowned. 'My goodness, that was quick. Are you sure you want another double, Rose?'

'Positive,' I said, all too aware of Flynn standing beside me. What were they suddenly so cosy about, anyway?

'Are you okay, Rose?' His voice was gentle.

I turned to him, feeling full of hurt and confusion, but I forgot my own emotions for a moment when I saw his face. He looked tired, dark shadows beneath his eyes as if he hadn't slept. What was wrong with him? 'Never mind me,' I said. 'What about you? Are you all right?'

He looked surprised at the question. 'Of course. I'm fine. Why do you ask?'

'Because you look bloody awful,' I told him.

His face fell. 'Oh.'

Rhiannon laughed, handing me my drink. 'I'm quite sure Rose didn't mean that the way it sounded,' she assured him.

I frowned. I wasn't too sure what I meant anymore. Things were becoming rather deliciously foggy, and I sipped my drink, anxious to hold onto that feeling. The good thing about vodka was that, before I knew it, I was all cocooned in a lovely warm blanket, and nothing seemed to matter that much—not having my mother living with us and stealing my bedroom, not a lovelorn daughter, nothing. When in that blanket, I was as good as anyone else, and nothing could really touch me. I didn't want that feeling to end, and, before I knew it, I was putting down my empty glass and asking Rhiannon for another double.

Flynn shook his head. 'I really think you should slow down, Rose.'

'Oh, you do?' I put my hands on my hips and glared at him. 'And I really think you should mind your own sodding business.'

He glanced at Rhiannon, and I felt suddenly overwhelmed with misery. I didn't need either of them judging me, or even worse, pitying me. I took a deep breath and tottered off to the toilets.

After splashing my face with cold water, I stared into the mirror and pulled a face. What was wrong with me? Bloody Oliver Crook, that's what, I decided. So Fuchsia wasn't in his league, socially. She wasn't middle class, and she didn't have a pony, and she wasn't bright enough to go to university and have some hotshot career, but did that make her less worthy? Did that mean she wasn't good enough for him? How dare he just ignore her the way he had? How dare he wander off and spend all evening chatting up Rhiannon?

Eh? I shook my head, trying to clear the fog. What was I talking about? I meant, how dare he wander off to fill his face with food, without so much as offering to bring her a flaming sausage roll? Christ, I was pissed. Two double vodkas, and I'd gone to pieces. I could have downed triple that amount, with no effect, back in the day. This was what working for a living and having kids did to you. Shameful.

Flynn was outside the toilets when I stepped into the passageway. I blinked as he took hold of my arm.

'Are you all right?'

'Yes. What exactly are you doing, hanging round the toilets?' I felt suddenly very defiant.

'I'm just ... I was .... Well ...' His voice trailed off, and I gulped as I looked into his weary face.

'Oh, Paddington.' I sighed, reaching out to stroke his hair. He looked so damn gorgeous. I leaned forward and brushed his lips with mine. When he tensed against me, I realised what I was doing and leapt away, horrified.

'Rose, you're drunk and I —'

'I'm going home,' I snapped. 'Sod the lot of you. I didn't want a bloody sausage roll, anyway.'

He frowned at me, eyes full of confusion.

I pulled open the door of The Hare and Moon and left him behind me, probably looking as bewildered as I felt.

CHAPTER EIGHT

'Hangover, is it?' my mother asked, brimming over with sympathy, as usual.

I blinked and tried to focus on her face, as she loomed over me, a monstrous vision to behold first thing in the morning. Or any time of day, really. 'I may have had a few,' I admitted, thinking I'd been quite restrained, actually.

When I'd got home, I'd limited myself to just four glasses of wine, and considering how miserable I'd been feeling last night, I could have downed quite a lot more. Anything to wipe out the memory of how disgracefully I'd behaved towards Flynn. I felt hot with shame when I remembered how rude I'd been. Oh, and, for God's sake, I'd kissed him again! Why? Why did I keep doing these things? I'd never dare look him in the face again.

My mother looked at me as if I'd committed some heinous crime, even though she had no idea that I actually had. I supposed she just automatically assumed the worst of me, although, to be fair, she was right on that occasion.

'I wouldn't say no to a cup of tea, if you're offering,' I murmured, wincing as a dagger was thrust through my brain and twisted very slowly.

'Well, I'm not,' she said. 'Best thing for you is a glass of water and a couple of paracetamol. You'd better hurry up about it, an' all. Don't see why your friends should have to open up the shop for you, just 'cos you can't be trusted round booze.'

I rubbed my aching head and yawned. 'What time is it?'

'Twenty-to nine.'

'What?' I sat up straight, throwing the duvet from me and ignoring the pounding in my skull as I struggled to my feet. 'Has Fuchsia gone to work?'

'Oh, aye.' My mother pursed her lips and folded her arms. 'Little madam, that one. Barely spoke two words to me.

Wouldn't have any breakfast, sipped half a cup of tea, and went. Never cracks a smile, does she? Dunno how you put up with her. Meanwhile, the other one's living it up in Cornwall like Lady Muck. I dunno. She should get herself a holiday job, never mind swanning round with her rich mates.' She sounded bitter. She hadn't won the jackpot, then.

'It's the Easter holidays,' I said. 'Weren't you ever fourteen?'

'I was working in Woolworth's at fourteen,' she said. 'You lot don't know you're born.'

'Was that before or after they sent you up the chimneys?' I muttered, heading to the bathroom and slamming the door behind me, an action I immediately regretted when the sound bounced around my poor, tortured brain.

Surveying myself in the mirror, I realised, with some shame, that I hadn't even cleaned my makeup off the night before. I looked like Alice Cooper, standing there with mascara and kohl smeared round my eyes, my hair its usual frizzy mess. I peered more closely and realised my pink streak was growing out. I would have to fix an appointment with Denise at Klassy Kutz. Was it me, or did my skin have a green tinge? Jesus. I wondered if Rhiannon ever looked so awful. Somehow, I doubted it. It was impossible to imagine her looking anything but stunning. It was my dodgy genes that had done it. You only had to look at my mother to see I'd never stood a chance.

I was twenty minutes late for work, but Chrissie and Eliza never commented. I had a feeling they'd been expecting it, which unnerved me a bit. Was I that predictable?

Eliza was full of the joys of spring, which was annoying, but Chrissie seemed a bit down. Not like her, really. Chrissie was the steady sort.

'Your mum cope all right with Amy last night?' I asked her, as we dipped mallow pops in white chocolate and hundreds and thousands.

'What? Oh, yes, fine.'

'So, what's up with you?' I asked, unused to seeing her so quiet.

She shrugged. 'Nothing. Just one of those days.'

'Right. Fair enough.'

It was only when she'd nipped to the loo that Eliza told me what was wrong.

'Think I slipped up,' she whispered. 'She was fine as I was telling her about last night, but you should have seen her face when I told her Robbie had asked Lexi out. Didn't realise she had a thing for him. Turns out they were childhood sweethearts. Went out through their school years, till Robbie left to go to college. She thought, one day, once he'd had a bit of freedom, he'd ask her out again, but instead he asked Lexi. I had no idea.'

'Neither did I,' I admitted. 'Sodding love. It's never straightforward, is it? You can keep it.'

She gave me a funny look and cleared her throat, pushing Smarties onto mallow pops. 'Did you notice the way Rhiannon and Flynn were last night? Seemed very close, didn't they? Do you think there's something going on there?'

'How the hell would I know?' I bit a marshmallow off its stick, chewing savagely.

'Well, she's been very quiet on that front lately, and at least he's not married. It would be lovely if they'd found someone at last. I'd like to see them both settled.'

'Why?' I demanded. 'Why must everyone be settled? Why do you always think people can only be happy in pairs? It's perfectly possible to be happy alone, you know. Look at me.'

She did look at me, and I squirmed, aware that I probably wasn't a great example, especially this morning, what with my green skin and shocking hair.

'I'm not saying it's not possible,' she said, 'and Rhiannon is probably perfectly happy as she is, but I do think it would add something to her life if she met someone special. She once told me she's never been in love. Isn't that dreadful?'

'Not really. I've never been in love, either. Does it matter?'

She stared at me in horror. 'Never been in love? Not even with Jimbo?'

Jimbo was Cerise's father, and the closest I'd got to married bliss, till he buggered off with a rich widow and left me stuck with the café that had been his dream and sod all to do with me or *my* dreams. Not that I'd had any dreams. Too busy with the kids and trying to pay the bills to have those.

'Nope. Jimbo was all right, but he never made my heart pound, or anything. Good job, as it turned out. Can you imagine the state I'd have been in when he cleared off?'

'Yes, I can,' she said, and I knew she could, since she'd been in that state herself when her husband started dipping his wick in his glamorous co-presenter. Eliza had loved Harry, but not in the way she loved Gabriel. Those two were completely smitten with each other. No wonder she thought everyone needed to feel the same way.

'Anyway,' I said, 'I thought Flynn was too besotted with his ex-wife to look at another woman, even Rhiannon.'

She looked at me in surprise. 'Is he? Is that what he's told you?'

'No, but look at the way he jumped to her defence, when you dared to criticise her.'

'Oh, well, that's Flynn, isn't it? He's far too much of a gentleman for his own good. She can't have been that nice, can she? I mean, she left him. It's pretty obvious it wasn't his choice, and what sort of woman would leave someone as lovely as Flynn? What more did she want?'

I stabbed a marshmallow with a lollipop stick. 'Maybe someone who knows how to loosen up and live a bit?' I suggested. 'Frankly, I can't imagine him keeping Rhiannon entertained for five minutes, so I wouldn't harbour many hopes of everlasting love there.'

'You never know.' She giggled. 'Maybe he's a fantastic lover. Maybe that's what she sees in him? Maybe he saves all his energy for the bedroom. What on earth are you doing to that marshmallow?'

'Turning it into a hedgehog,' I said. 'Thought I'd try something new for the kiddies. Just making little holes all over it, and I might put sugar strands in to make the prickles.'

She raised an eyebrow then took the marshmallow away from me. 'I don't think so,' she said.

Chrissie returned, and I took the opportunity to head back into the shop, away from all the ridiculous talk of love and sex. Honestly, didn't women ever think of anything else? Maybe I should have been born a man. I'd rather have ignored the whole subject and drank vodka.

Fate obviously had it in for me that day. Just as I was giving a customer his change, the phone rang. It was my mother, sounding completely different to the way she had that morning.

'Rose? You'll never guess what's just happened.'

'Okay,' I said.

I heard her tut. 'Well, aren't you going to guess?'

'What's the point? You've just told me I'll never get it, so why bother?'

'You're a complete pain in the arse, you know that?' she snapped. 'I don't know why I bother to tell you anything.'

'Because who else is going to listen?' I said, quite truthfully.

'I've a good mind not to tell you now,' she snapped. I was silent, and she quickly gave in, as I knew she would. '*The Oddborough Herald* just called me. Tracked me down through Doreen, bless her. You'll never guess who saw the story about the mugging and got in touch?'

'The mugger?' I suggested.

'Very funny. No, only Alec Thoroughgood. Can you believe it?'

'I might well believe it,' I said, 'if I'd any idea who the hell Alec Thoroughgood was.'

'Don't be daft, you know all about him. I must have told you about him?'

'Er, nope. Not a word. Should I know him?'

'Well, of course! He was the love of me life. I mean, apart from your dad, of course.'

'Of course,' I said, while thinking, *my mother had two loves? My mother?* I was still gob-smacked that she'd managed to attract my dad, and there she was telling me there'd been another one? 'Hang on,' I said, 'was this before, during, or after my dad?'

'Well, of all the cheek,' she said. 'What a thing to ask your mother! Before, of course. We were engaged for a short while, but your gran and grandad soon put a stop to that, and then his parents moved him away to Keswick, so I never saw him again.'

She made it sound as if they'd emigrated to Australia, not roughly eighty miles from Oddborough. They'd hardly fought for their love, had they?

'Anyway, his cousin still lives on the estate, and she saw the article and told him all about it. He rang the *Herald* and asked for my number, but obviously they won't give any contact details without my permission. He's living in Redcar now, less than an hour's drive away.'

'You're not going to get in touch with him?' I said.

'Why wouldn't I?' she demanded. 'Ooh, he was a looker, was Alec. If my mother and father hadn't been such miseries, I'd have been Mrs Thoroughgood now.'

'When was all this?' I asked, knowing that she'd met my father when she was just sixteen.

'The day I started at Woollies. He was working in the record department, and I was on the pic 'n' mix. Our eyes met across the liquorice torpedoes. I tell you, he was a bit of all right.'

'For God's sake, Mother! You were just kids. No wonder Gran and Grandad didn't approve of your engagement. And, anyway, he'll have changed a lot by now. He may be fat and bald and have false teeth.'

'That's typical of you,' she said. 'You shouldn't judge a book by its cover. You're so shallow, Rose.'

I was stunned into silence by such an outrageous slur. From my mother, too. Unbelievable.

'I've told the *Herald* they can give him our number,' she continued. 'I'm a bit nervous, though. I hope he isn't disappointed when he sees me, although I've always kept myself in shape and made an effort. Not like some.'

'Surely, it doesn't matter?' I said. 'Unless he's very shallow.'

She carried on, oblivious to my sarcasm, and began reminiscing about the time he'd taken her to the pictures to see *Alfie* and amused her all the way home with his Michael Caine impressions, telling her, "Blimey, girl, you ain't as ugly as I thought." He sounded all charm.

'So, what if he wants to meet up again?' I asked, when she finally paused to draw breath.

'Well, of course he'll want to meet up again,' she said. 'Why else would he want to get in touch? Honestly, Rose, you can be so dim. You have no idea about love. I shall meet him, obviously. It's about time this body was put to good use again, although I might need a little oiling to loosen me up.'

She cackled, and I nearly dropped the phone in horror. 'Mother!'

'Oh, lighten up.' She laughed. 'Honestly, it's time you got yourself a fella. You'll be forgetting what it's for, before long.'

I hung up. Really, there was only so much of that kind of talk any daughter could stomach.

****

'Are you here again?' Derry laughed, as I plonked my handbag on the bar counter and asked for a lime and soda. 'Might as well bring your sleeping bag and have done with it.'

'Don't you start,' I said. 'If you'd seen what I'd just seen, you'd be giving me a medal for not asking for a triple bloody vodka.'

He raised an eyebrow and turned to fix my drink, while I rubbed my eyes, trying to dismiss the images that were burned into my retinas—my mother in the briefest, laciest underwear I'd ever seen, far racier than anything I possessed. She was sixty-two, for God's sake! A mother. A grandmother. I mean, it couldn't be right, could it? What was she thinking?

Scrap that. I knew only too well what she was thinking, because she made a point of telling me—several times.

'It's been that long,' she'd wailed, as she paraded round the bedroom in her scanties, hunting for her stockings, as tights were apparently far too much of a passion killer. 'If I'd thought about it, I'd have had a Brazilian. Isn't that what you're supposed to do? In my day, we just let it all hang out, but nowadays, they like you to have a bit of a trim, at least, don't they?'

'Mother, please,' I begged. 'I really don't want to talk about this with you.'

'Why not? We're both adults, aren't we? Now, what do you think, Rose? Should I take some condoms with me, or would that put him off, do you think? He's bound to have some of his own, isn't he? But then, I've got flavoured ones, and his might be ordinary, and I do think I prefer the flavoured, as long as it's not chocolate. They taste horrible, not like chocolate, at all, don't you agree?'

She turned when I didn't answer, frowning when she found me sitting on the bed, my fingers tugging at my hair, rocking backwards and forwards as my face burned with embarrassment.

'What's wrong with you?' she demanded. 'You're a grown woman. Stop acting like a soft teenager.'

'But you're my mother,' I wailed. 'And how the hell do you know about flavoured condoms?'

'Your generation didn't invent sex,' she pointed out. 'Me and your dad had our fair share of fun, you know. What did you think? That we only did it once to conceive you?'

'Of course not, but, well, I don't need to know any details. And besides, won't it feel funny going with someone other than Dad?'

'It won't be the first time,' she said, rummaging in her top drawer and finally finding a pair of stockings, which she inspected for ladders.

'What do you mean? There's been someone else?'

'Not since your dad, no. But Alec and I—well, we were very much in love.'

'But you were only sixteen when you met Dad.'

'Aye? And?'

I shook my head. After the way she'd carried on, when I got pregnant with Fuchsia at seventeen, I'd assumed she'd been pure as the driven snow till she got married. What a bloody hypocrite. The only difference between us was that she and Alec weren't daft enough to take risks. They'd obviously been smarter about contraception than I had. I should have dragged Fuchsia's dad to see *Alfie* instead of *Forrest Gump*.

'Now, how do I look?'

She stood before me, and I had to admit she looked very presentable for a woman of her age, or any age, come to that.

'All right, I suppose,' I said, aware that I was beginning to sound like Fuchsia.

Her eyes narrowed for a moment before she shrugged. 'Okay. I do understand.'

'Understand what?'

'That you're jealous.'

'Jealous? Of Alec Thoroughgood! He sounds like a proper w—'

'Not about Alec,' my mother cut in. 'About me going on a date at my age, when you're sitting here, drying up as we speak.'

'Oh, lovely,' I said.

'It's your own fault. You need to grab life by the horns while you're still young enough to enjoy it. How long is it since Jumbo left?'

'Jimbo,' I said.

'Aye, that's the fella. Well, how long is it?'

'Dunno, three or four years.'

'Three or four years, and no action since?' She shook her head. 'What's wrong with you? You're not bad looking, when you make an effort. Hair needs a good brush, and you could do to get rid of that daft pink streak, and you're a bit saggy and lumpy, but nothing some good underwear couldn't fix. I'm sure someone would have you.'

'Well, thanks very much,' I said. 'I feel ready to take on the world after that glowing reference.'

'What about that doctor?' she asked. 'Him with the daft name? Isn't there anything happening on that front?'

'Of course not. I told you, we're just friends.'

'Are you sure? Only, I thought I saw a definite look in your eye when you saw the state of him after that fight.'

'It's called sympathy, Mother. You wouldn't know about it.'

'Oh, is that what they call it these days? In my day it was called lust.'

'Lust!' I snorted. 'For Flynn? You must be joking.'

'Dunno why,' she said. 'Even I can see he's a good looking fella. Still, if you think you're too good for him, that's your lookout.'

'Too good for him?' Was she taking the piss? If anything, it was the other way round. Good job I wasn't interested, because someone like Flynn would definitely think himself far too good for the likes of me. In my experience, opposites didn't attract, they repelled. Look at Fuchsia and Oliver.

'Well, if you're not interested in him, there must be someone else round here who floats your boat? Even this backwater's got to have some fellas in it. Don't leave it too late, that's all I'm saying. Now, I'm off to have fun, so don't wait up.'

'Where are you going and what time will you be back?' I asked.

She rolled her eyes. 'No idea and who cares? Don't be getting all protective of me now. Alec's a good man, and I'm not clock-watching for you, or anyone else, so don't be mithering me. I'll see you when I see you.'

She'd popped a pack of condoms in her bag and waved me goodbye, a smug grin on her face as she shut the bedroom door, leaving me sitting like the saddo I was, on what had once been my bed. How had it come to this?

The Hare and Moon was the obvious place to go, given that Fuchsia was in her bedroom, listening to music through her headphones, and Cerise was still away. It was either that or an evening watching telly on my own—again. I couldn't face that, so The Hare and Moon it was, and I was glad I'd made that choice when Eliza and Lexi arrived. Lexi was dressed to kill, and spotting Robbie sitting across the room looking nervously into his pint, I realised why. Tonight was first date night. There must have been something in the air.

'What are you doing here?' Eliza asked, and I explained about my mother, earning a sympathetic look as I did so. 'Poor you. Gabriel's catching up with paperwork, so I thought I'd come here and make sure Robbie turned up, then have a drink with Rhiannon. Cheer up, Rose. Things can't be that bad.'

'You wouldn't say that if you had my mother living with you, not to mention Fuchsia mooning around like a lost soul over that Oliver Crook.'

'Ooh, I meant to ask you about that,' she said. 'Hang on a minute. Why don't you find us a seat, while I get a drink, and then we'll have a chat.'

I found us a seat in the corner of the bar by the fireplace. The lovely roaring fire that had blazed away all winter had been replaced with Rhiannon's cauldron, which always stood in the inglenook during the warmer months, often filled with flowers and grasses.

Eliza made her way over and sat beside me, clutching a glass of what looked suspiciously like orange juice.

'What's with the drink?' I asked.

She flushed. 'I, er, I'm cutting out alcohol for now.'

'Really?' I said curiously. 'Any particular reason, Mrs Bailey?'

She flushed. 'Thing is, well, with Raffy being ill and everything, it got us thinking. Me and Gabriel, I mean. We thought, well, we decided it's time to try for a baby. His parents aren't getting any younger, and we want them around to see our child. No point in waiting really.'

'No, there isn't. You're not getting any younger, either,' I said. 'Isn't Gabriel forty now? Soon be past it.'

'Oh, well, that's charming,' she said. 'With friends like you, and all that.'

'Oh, wind your neck in.' I laughed. 'I was only joking! Congratulations. You two are fabulous parents.'

'So,' she said, fixing me with a very stern look. 'What was that you were saying about Fuchsia the other night? About Oliver being out of her league, I mean?'

I shrugged. 'Well, let's face it, Eliza, he is. Don't look at me like that. You must see it, surely? He's got his future all mapped out for him, and he's going to be a successful solicitor, just like Archie. What's going to become of Fuchsia? She's working as a doctor's receptionist, and she doesn't even enjoy that. She doesn't speak posh, and she'd never fit in with all his upper class friends. She's hardly going to set the world on fire, is she? What would someone like Oliver want with her?'

Eliza looked horrified. 'Rose MacLean, you snob!'

I spluttered on my vodka. 'Snob? Me? You must be joking.'

'I'm not joking. Why should anyone think Oliver's too good for Fuchsia? Just because he has a decent career mapped out, doesn't make him a better person. I'm stunned that you'd think that.'

'So, it hasn't even occurred to you?'

'Of course not.'

'Bet it occurred to Sophie,' I muttered.

She shook her head. 'I doubt it. Sophie's not bothered about stuff like that. No one thinks about social status and class these days. It's the twenty-first century, for goodness sake.'

'It's always the posh ones with money who say that,' I said. 'When you're skint, and you've been brought up on a rough estate like Feldane, you soon find out that the class system is alive and kicking.'

'I'm sure that's not true. And honestly, it wouldn't occur to Sophie to look down on Fuchsia just because she's not going to be a solicitor, or something. Oh, I know she makes a big show of Archie's success, and how clever her kids are, but that's because she loves them so much and she's proud of them. It's nothing to do with money or prestige. If they were working as road-sweepers, she'd be just as proud of them. She just wants them to be happy.'

'That's not what she said the other night,' I said. 'She was furious when she thought Pandora was going to throw her education away to work with horses.'

'That's because she can't understand where it's come from. It's so sudden. Pan was quite happy studying sociology, and all of a sudden, she's got it into her head to quit uni.'

'But she's always been horse-mad,' I pointed out. 'So what does it matter?'

'I don't think it would, if it was definitely what she wanted. Just that it seems to have come from nowhere, and that's why Sophie's worried. And, of course, with Oliver thinking about moving away in a year or two, to finish his training, she's already in a state. Wherever he trains, he may stay there permanently, and she can't bear the idea of him leaving the village for good. You can understand that, surely?'

Frankly, I'd have paid good money for someone to take my

family away from the village permanently. Oh, to be alone and live in my little flat in peace and quiet, with no one to traumatise or nag me. Bliss.

'I think Oliver thinks he's too good for Fuchsia, anyway,' I said. 'He doesn't seem in the slightest bit interested.'

Eliza sighed. 'I don't think that's the reason. I think the truth is, Oliver's only ever had eyes for one woman, and that's Georgia. Not that it's reciprocated, or probably ever will be.'

Well, that was understandable. Lexi's best friend was the owner of the White Rose Riding School on the outskirts of the village—a petite blonde with a pretty face and fabulous figure. I couldn't blame Oliver for fancying her, even if Georgia was a good six years older than him. Fuchsia had no chance, especially since Oliver was horse-mad, too, and Fuchsia wouldn't know one end of a horse from the other.

'Wish she'd set her sights on someone else,' I said. 'There must be someone round here who'd be able to cope with her. She's not that bad, is she?'

'Fuchsia?' Eliza looked startled. 'Of course not. She's very pretty. Just needs to smile a bit more, but then, she's in the throes of unrequited love. I expect she doesn't feel much like smiling at the moment.'

'I suppose not,' I said gloomily. I watched as Lexi and Robbie left The Hare and Moon, arm in arm. 'Where are they going?' I asked.

Rhiannon appeared at the table and sat down beside us. 'Robbie's booked a table at The Fox and Hounds in Helmston. Very expensive, but frightfully good food, although please don't tell Jack I said that. I must say, it's a shame. I do like Robbie, he's a charming boy, but really, poor Will.'

'I know,' said Eliza. 'Gabriel and I were hoping he'd have spoken up by now, but he seems quite unable to bring himself to ask her out.'

'Well, it's his own fault, then,' I said. 'He shouldn't be such a drip.'

'He's not a drip,' Rhiannon said with indignation. 'He's an absolute darling.'

'Well, you should know.' I said, 'Maybe you should rekindle your affair with him. Might give him the balls to man up and ask her out at last.'

She blinked as if startled, and Eliza cut in hastily. 'Is there anyone in your life at the moment, Rhiannon? Only, you seem to have had a bit of a glow about you lately.'

Rhiannon beamed, and I waited on her answer, wondering why my stomach was suddenly fluttering. 'Well,' she said, almost coyly, 'there is someone. It's early days, though, and I don't want to say anything about it just yet.'

'He's not, er, married?' Eliza looked worried, and I knew why. Rhiannon had a bit of a reputation for dabbling with married men. She never saw it as adultery, looking upon it as a kind of marriage counselling, but, needless to say, the women of the village didn't share her viewpoint, and she and Eliza had had a bit of a falling out over it when Eliza first moved to the village. Not surprising really, given what Eliza had been going through at the time.

Rhiannon shook her head, her dark, glossy curls bouncing, and her brown eyes shining. 'No. Well and truly single. Well, divorced, but that was a long time ago. He's rather lovely, actually, and surprisingly adventurous in the bedroom.'

My eyes narrowed in suspicion. She was talking about Flynn. She had to be. I thought of the way they'd been so deep in conversation the other night at the bar, the way she'd reached out and touched his face, the weird look in her eye as she leaned towards him over the counter. No doubt about it. Flynn had succumbed. Well, I hoped they'd be very happy.

'How lovely,' said Eliza. 'I hope it works out for you, Rhiannon.'

'Yeah,' I said. 'Though, I reckon you'll be climbing the walls with boredom within two months, and you'll be seeing Will as Mr Excitement all of a sudden.'

'Goodness, you're in a lovely mood tonight, Rose.' Rhiannon laughed. 'What's put you in such a frame of mind?'

'My mother talking chocolate condoms and pubic hair,' I said.

That shut them up. Served them right for being so bloody cheerful.

CHAPTER NINE

Flynn stared out of the rain-spattered window of the surgery, over the car park. Concrete ground met charcoal sky on a dismal horizon. It matched his mood perfectly.

'Have you ever seen a more depressing sight than that?' he said, turning to Gabriel.

Gabriel's eyes flickered over toward the desk, where Meggie was licking jam from her fingers, having demolished a jam doughnut. 'I can think of something,' he murmured.

Flynn frowned. Meggie was always about to start a diet, but never seemed to get round to it. He knew Gabriel shared his concerns about her health, but neither of them knew what they could do about it. She was an adult and had to make her own choices. They all did.

'You're a bit down today, Dr Pennington-Rhys,' Meggie said, smiling brightly up at him. 'What's wrong with you? Is it the weather? Bit of a downer, after all the nice days we've been having. Still, you can't expect miracles. It's still only April, and you've got to put up with a bit of rain. Makes you enjoy the sun even more.'

'Very philosophical, Meggie,' said Gabriel. He glanced at Fuchsia, who was flicking through her phone. 'Keeping you busy, are we?'

Fuchsia didn't even look ashamed. 'Finished my work,' she said. 'Nothing else to do.'

'You could wash the cups for Meggie,' he pointed out. 'I haven't seen you do them once.'

Fuchsia put down her phone and collected the cups without a murmur. Flynn and Gabriel looked at each other in surprise.

Meggie leaned forward as Fuchsia left the room and whispered, 'Summat wrong with her, I'm telling you. Haven't had any lip from her all week, and she hasn't cracked a smile. Not a one.'

'Does she ever?' asked Gabriel, surprised.

'Well, she usually laughs at them daft photos people put on Facebook, but she hasn't even looked at it for days. Today's the first time she's picked up her phone this week. And another thing, she's not eaten a scrap of food. Doesn't want to know. I ask you, is that healthy?'

Gabriel coughed. 'Well, er, I'm sure she's eating at home, Meggie. Not everyone's so fond of jam doughnuts and crisps, you know.'

'She doesn't even eat her sandwiches at lunchtime. I've seen them in the bin. I hope she hasn't got that anorexia.' She shuddered. 'Doesn't bear thinking about.'

'I'm sure she's fine,' Gabriel reassured her. 'Just a bit lovesick, from what I've heard. It will pass.'

Flynn turned back to the window, frowning as he looked out at the almost-empty car park. It had been a long, dreary day and he was tired.

'Why don't you get yourself home, Flynn?' Gabriel said, his eyes full of sympathy. He must have remembered.

Flynn shook his head. 'I've got that medical arriving any time now,' he pointed out. 'In fact, he's a bit late.'

'I'll do it. There are no visits tonight. Why don't you go now and leave it to me? Have a bath, listen to some music, relax a bit.'

'Am I missing something?' Meggie frowned. 'What's happened?'

'Nothing's happened,' said Gabriel. 'Just think Flynn, here, could do with a break.'

She didn't look convinced, but Flynn shook his head. 'It's nothing, honestly. I always get a bit down at this time of year. A lot of bad things happened. Eight years ago today, my divorce became final.'

'And it still upsets you?'

He shrugged. 'A lot of things around it still upset me. Not so much the divorce but what led to it. There are ... unhappy memories.'

'Aye, well, we all have those,' said Meggie, reaching in her bag. Bringing out a baby wipe, she removed the last of the stickiness from her fingers.

'I'm sure we do,' he murmured. 'Are you sure you don't mind doing the medical for me, Gabriel?'

'Of course not. Get yourself home.' Gabriel patted him on the shoulder. 'Better day tomorrow, maybe?'

Flynn nodded, but he could only see things getting worse. He hated this time of year. Usually around this date, the sun was shining, and everyone was looking forward to the summer and feeling optimistic. He didn't know which was worse—the blue skies and pretending he felt as cheery as everyone else, or the grey skies and admitting to himself that he never would.

He left the modern brick surgery and walked next door to his home. The honey-coloured stone had darkened with rain, making the house look cold and unwelcoming. He let himself in and dropped his bag in the hallway, feeling himself suffocating in the silence as he stood looking around. Maybe he should get a dog. At least that way there'd be someone to greet him when he got home.

Wandering into the kitchen, he headed to the fridge. It was twenty-to six and he was hungry. He glanced at the shelves, neatly stacked with an assortment of fresh pasta, sauces, meats, cheeses and yoghurts. He couldn't be bothered to cook, that was the trouble. Maybe he'd have a shower first, then make some cheese on toast.

First thing's first. A cup of tea before he did anything else. After filling up the kettle under the tap, he flicked the switch and stared out of the window at the garden. He liked to have a wander round there when he got home from work, if it was still light, but the rain made it out of the question tonight. When his attention strayed, inevitably, to the riot of colour at the end of the lawn, he turned away abruptly, reaching for a mug and a spoon and taking a teabag from the canister.

After his cup of tea, and a shower, he sat at the breakfast

bar, eating cheese on toast. The silence crushed him, though, and he switched the radio on, half listening to someone babbling on about roadworks in Whitby while he washed his plate and cup. Once he'd finished, he sat drumming his fingers on the worktop and wondering what to do with the evening. He may as well have done that medical, after all. There was nothing for him at home.

When the phone rang, he was almost relieved. Whoever it was, even if it was someone trying to sell him something, at least it was a voice—unless it was one of those annoying recorded messages, of course. That would put the tin hat on a perfect day.

'Dr Pennington-Rhys?'

Flynn frowned. He didn't recognise the voice at all. 'Speaking.'

'Dr Flynn Pennington-Rhys?'

'Yes. Who is this?'

'Sorry to bother you at home. My name's Elsie Robbins. I live next door to Dr Taylor. I understand he's a close friend of yours?'

Flynn's hand tightened on the receiver. Maurice Taylor. What was wrong with him? Why was someone calling about him? 'That's right. Why, what's happened?'

'Oh, nothing serious. At least, I don't think so. Like I say, I'm his neighbour, and I keep an eye on him, pop round now and then to check he's all right and take him a bit of stew for his dinner, or a crossword book—that kind of thing. I don't want to alarm you, but I know you're all he's got now, and I was wondering if you'd consider popping down to see him one day? Only, well, he's not himself, and, to be honest, I think he's getting worse.'

'What do you mean, not himself? What's wrong with him?'

'Well, you know, he's never really been right since poor Matilda died, and, of course, that's understandable. I mean, they were married a long time, and it was a shock, even given that she was ill and it was expected, but even so you can never prepare for that kind of thing, can you?'

'No,' murmured Flynn, 'you can't.'

'I know it's been five years, and he should be moving on, but I think he's going downhill. He's proper down in the dumps. Off his food and, well, maybe you should come and see for yourself. Let's just say he's not his usual dapper self. Not by a long chalk.'

Flynn closed his eyes in shame. Maurice Taylor had been his dear friend and mentor when he'd arrived in Helmston eight years ago, broken and alone. Maurice had taken him in, encouraged and supported him, and never asked questions or pried into his personal life. He remembered Matilda and her zest for life, her habit of including him in their lives, inviting him for dinner most nights, buying him a ticket when they went to the theatre or a concert. The shock of her illness, so soon after Maurice had given up work. They'd planned a long and happy retirement together, but it had been cut so short. Not long after Maurice left the practice, Flynn had taken a partnership with Gabriel's father at Ivy House Surgery. He'd meant to keep in touch with the couple, but then Dr Bailey had decided to retire, leaving him to run the practice alone, and he'd heard about Matilda's illness and found himself paralysed with fear. He couldn't deal with seeing her suffer, and though he'd tried hard to deal with Maurice's grief, he'd convinced himself that his old friend was coping and didn't need him. Now he knew he'd lied to himself and had been a coward. Maurice and Matilda had helped him through the worst time in his life, and he'd abandoned them to deal with their fate alone. How could he have been so gutless?

'Dr Pennington-Rhys? Are you still there?'

He forced himself to concentrate. 'Yes, yes, I'm here. How did you get my number?'

'Well, he keeps it by the phone, of course. You're all he talks about—you and Matilda. Hasn't got anyone else, has he?

They never had kiddies, of course. Such a shame.'

'Yes, a real shame.'

'So, will you come and see him, then? Only, I don't know what to do about him, and it's not like I've got any right to try, is it? I mean, I'm only a neighbour, when all's said and done. I hardly know him.'

Only a neighbour, but one who had shown more kindness and compassion to his friend than he had himself.

'I'll be there as soon as I can,' he promised.

'What? You mean tonight?'

'Yes, tonight. I'll get ready now.'

'Oh, that is kind of you. That's a weight off my mind. What a diamond you are.'

As Flynn reached for his car keys, he thought savagely that a diamond was the last thing he was. He'd been utterly selfish. He had a lot of making up to do.

****

Tucked away down Station Lane, Farthingdale Village Hall was a fifteen minute walk away from my home, but in the heavy rain it seemed to take ages to reach. Inside was a dreary scene, too. Wet footprints left trails on the wooden floor, and people stood dripping water and moaning about the weather, wondering why they'd bothered to come out on such a night when they could have been at home watching *Coronation Street*.

It seemed that at least half of the Lightweights members had made that choice, anyway. Only about eighteen people had turned up to be weighed, and the hall echoed with their moaning and exclamations of shock that they'd managed to gain weight.

'Surely, someone's lost some weight tonight?' asked Sophie, staring at Meggie's writing in horror. 'They can't all have gained?'

'Clarissa, Eliza and Joan all stayed the same,' said Meggie with a shrug, 'but everyone else put on. Mind you, some only put on half a pound, so it doesn't really count, does it?'

'What on earth have you all been doing?' demanded Sophie.

We all looked at each other, guilt in our eyes. I tried to think if I'd been particularly bad that week, but couldn't recall eating anything out of the ordinary. Usually, I stayed the same. I never expected to actually lose weight but I'd gained three pounds recently. Then I remembered all the vodka and wine I'd knocked back and blushed. Better not mention that.

There was a silence, before someone mumbled something about it being her birthday, and others started confessing about leftover Easter eggs, and fish and chips.

'Never mind, Sophe,' said Hattie, a cheery woman who worked at the fishmonger's down King's Row. 'We'll be back on track next week, eh?'

Sophie threw down her notebook and glared at us all. 'And that's the right attitude, is it? Well, you may as well take these marshmallows back, Eliza, because no one's Slimmer of the Week this week, and quite obviously they no longer serve as any motivation, so don't bother making them anymore. I want to see some serious weight loss next week, or you might as well forget it. I've got better things to do than stand here trying to get through to a bunch of women who obviously don't give a monkey's about losing weight. I'm not here for the fun of it, you know. This is my job. Obviously, I'm completely useless at that, as well.'

She rushed out of the hall and into the adjoining kitchen, slamming the door behind her, while we all stared at each other in shock.

Meggie looked appalled. 'You won't stop making the marshmallows will you? If there's no prize for Slimmer of the Week, what's the point?'

Clarissa tutted. 'To lose weight. Is Sophie going to take a

class tonight, or not? Only this has cost me four pounds fifty, and it's not my fault you lot have no will power.'

Eliza got to her feet. 'I'll go,' she said, and I followed her to the kitchen, where we found Sophie sobbing over the sink.

'Oh, God, Sophe, what's happened?' I'd never seen Sophie like that before. She was always so upbeat, so relentlessly cheerful, that it was quite unnerving.

Eliza put her arms round her sister-in-law, and Sophie cried onto her shoulder, mumbling something about being a useless mother, and everything going wrong.

'Useless mother?' I demanded. 'You? Blimey, what am I, then? Don't talk daft. You're a cracking mum, and everyone knows it. What's made you so upset? Tell your Auntie Rose all about it.'

She sniffed into a tissue and dabbed her eyes, seeming embarrassed as she looked at us. 'I'm sorry. What must you think of me?'

'That you're upset, and we'd like to help,' said Eliza. 'Come on, Sophie. I'll put the kettle on, and we'll have a chat, eh?'

In the end, we all had a cup of tea. The meeting turned into a little party, as we pulled our chairs closer together, sipped tea, scoffed marshmallows, and discussed our errant families.

Sophie had been informed by Oliver that he was definitely heading south when he finished his degree the following year, and was moving to Bristol to complete his Legal Practice Course and training contract. Archie's brother, Gordon, had a practice there, and had apparently informed Oliver that he would be more than welcome to live with him and his wife while he finished his training. Pandora, meanwhile, had decided to complete her second year at University and then leave. She'd spoken to Georgia, and Georgia was quite willing to take her on as a groom and general help, while she studied part time at college to be a riding instructor.

'It's such a waste,' Sophie wailed. 'Pandora wanted to study sociology for years, so I don't understand where it's come from all of a sudden. And Olly. My little Olly heading to Bristol!'

I thought about Fuchsia. Did she know of his plans? She'd been very quiet lately and hadn't been giving me as much grief. I had thought she was settling down, but was she upset about him leaving? Was she harbouring hopes of going with him? The thought of her moving away was awful. She would be so vulnerable, so alone in Bristol, wherever the heck Bristol was. I could sympathise with Sophie, although Oliver seemed quite confident and capable enough of managing in any city, if you asked me. As for Pandora, well, who cared? She'd always been horse-mad, so what did it matter?

'At least she's doing what she wants to do,' I said. 'I don't see why you're so upset about it.'

'Me neither,' said Meggie. 'And at least she'll be close by, which is what you want isn't it?'

Sophie sipped her tea and nodded. 'Well, yes, but there's something not right about it all. She's not herself, I'll tell you that much. She's sort of edgy, shifty. And there's something between us, some barrier. There never used to be. We were very close. Now she seems to be keeping me at arm's length. I can't help worrying about her.'

'Well, that's what parenthood seems to be about—worry,' said Joan, whose son was in the army and had served in Afghanistan and Iraq.

None of us could argue that we had it any worse than her. The thought of our children being so far away and in such danger was horrific. Sophie had to concede that, compared with what Joan had been through, Oliver going to Bristol was pretty tame.

'And I'm sure he'll be back as often as he is now,' said Eliza. 'He comes home most holidays from Manchester, and I'm sure he'll do the same from Bristol. Besides, he may not even like it. It may sound very exciting, but the reality may prove to be very different. Living with an aunt and uncle isn't exactly thrilling, is it? He may be heading back and begging Archie to take him on, after all.'

'You think?' Sophie sniffed.

'Almost guaranteed,' I said. 'Bristol may be a big city, but Kearton Bay will always be home.'

'He's just trying to fly the nest,' Meggie soothed. 'They all try, but nine times out of ten, they end up back with their families. You're a lovely mum, Sophe. You've done nothing wrong. It's just kids testing their wings.'

'Really?'

'Of course.' We all laughed at her hopeful expression.

She sat up a bit straighter and looked at us all in shame. 'I'm ever so sorry for sounding off like that,' she said. 'I can't think what I was playing at. And Eliza, you must carry on with the marshmallows, of course. I'm sure next week there'll be a slimmer of the week.'

We all promised immediately to try harder, before heading out into the wind and rain. I wondered if anyone would be home when I got there. Cerise was doing homework at her friend's, but I wasn't sure about Fuchsia, who seemed to have become a hermit lately. My mother had gone on another date with Alec, the first one apparently being so successful that he'd asked her out again immediately. I hadn't asked if the condoms had been needed. Better not to know.

The flat felt empty when I walked in. I popped my head round Fuchsia's bedroom door to see if she wanted a coffee or something, but she was fast asleep. She seemed to be sleeping an awful lot lately. Having to do some actual work for once was obviously knackering her out.

I flopped down on the sofa, pointed the remote at the TV, and flicked through the channels. There was nothing of any interest on. Oh, crap, if I couldn't find something to occupy my thoughts, they'd turn to my mother and her date, and that was the last thing I wanted to think about.

I had a quick shower and changed into my pyjamas, then dragged the spare duvet and pillows out from under my bed. I carried them into the living room and plonked them on the sofa. Might as well get comfy. I snuggled under the duvet and scanned the television channels again, finally settling on an old film that I'd seen about eight times already. Bloody telly was a rip-off. All that money for what? Same old tosh, night after night.

I heaved myself off the sofa, heading into the kitchen for something to eat. There was nothing in the cupboards, but I thought I had some quiche in the fridge, and I was suddenly starving. I opened the fridge door and pulled out the quiche, cutting myself a large slice before returning it to the fridge. My eyes fell upon the bottle of wine that lay on the top shelf. I could have just one glass of that, surely? It would help me relax. Maybe help me sleep.

I pulled it off the shelf and poured myself a glass, then rummaged in the cupboards. There was almost a full packet of chocolate digestives in there. They'd go nicely with the quiche. I carried it all into the living room, sinking back onto the sofa and pulling the duvet over me, trying to ignore my sudden feelings of guilt. I was bored, fed up, and depressed beyond words that my mother had more of a social life than I did. I deserved some empty calories. Sod the diet.

****

As Maurice Taylor opened the front door, Flynn tried hard to mask his shock. His friend had always been so smart, so dapper. He couldn't believe it was the same man standing there, in a shabby green cardigan, his hair un-brushed, and his face drawn and suddenly old.

'My word, Flynn! How good to see you,' said Maurice, breaking into a smile and holding out his hand.

Flynn shook it, but swallowed when he was dragged into an embrace and held as if he was the most precious thing in the world.

'Come in, come in.' Maurice closed the door behind them and ushered him inside, leading him from the hallway into the adjoining room.

Flynn glanced round at the lounge that had always been so beautifully neat and tidy—Matilda's favourite room, as she'd often told him. She would be horrified at the state of it now. Dirty plates and cups lay on the floor, newspapers covered the sofa, and the furniture was thick with dust. Flynn felt sick to his stomach. Why hadn't he checked on his friend before now? Obviously, he hadn't been coping as well as he'd imagined, and Flynn felt ashamed as he realised that he hadn't questioned it much, trying hard not to think about it. He'd been so selfish. He had to put things right somehow.

'Would you like a cup of tea, or perhaps something stronger? I think I have some brandy left over from Christmas. Or was it the Christmas before? Anyway, I think there's some in the house, somewhere.' Maurice looked around vaguely and shrugged. 'Do you drink brandy? I can't remember.'

'A cup of tea would be fine,' said Flynn. 'Why don't I make it?'

'Oh, well, there's no need, you know. Still, if you like. ..' Maurice sank into an armchair and stared at the television set. 'I'm not sure what this programme is. If there's something you'd like to watch, you can turn it over, you know.'

'Really, I'm fine. I'll make that drink,' said Flynn, shocked by Maurice's rather bewildered expression. He headed into the kitchen and stared in horror at the overflowing bin, the piles of dirty plates and the open tins of beans and soup on the worktop. Peering inside them, he saw mould growing in one, and his stomach turned. Rummaging in the drawers, he found a roll of bin liners and tore one off, opening it up and collecting up all the rubbish that was scattered on the floor.

Maurice was silent in the other room, while Flynn worked for nearly an hour, clearing the worktops, discarding food, checking the fridge and clearing it of out-of-date products, scrubbing it clean, doing the dishes before mopping the floor then taking the bin bags outside to the wheelie bin.

When he entered the living room, carrying two cups of tea, Maurice was still sitting in the armchair, staring at the television.

He smiled as Flynn handed him the cup. 'Ah, thank you. Found everything all right, then?'

There was no hint of embarrassment, and no sign of any awareness that almost an hour had passed since Flynn had offered to make the drink. Flynn closed his eyes. This wasn't good. This wasn't good at all. Matilda would be so disappointed in him for neglecting her poor husband.

'So, how have you been, Maurice?' What a stupid question, but what else could he say?

Maurice shrugged and peered around him, not seeming to see anything. 'Oh, right as rain, Flynn. What about you? How's things with Raphael? Bet he's making sure you know who's boss, eh?' He chuckled.

Although the emotion threatened to overwhelm him, Flynn tried to keep his voice steady as he answered, 'Raphael retired, Maurice. Remember? I told you at the time, although ...' Although, he'd probably had other things on his mind, like his poor wife dying, for instance.

'Retired? Well, I never thought I'd see the day,' Maurice said.

Flynn tried to smile. 'He hung on as long as he could. He was seventy before he finally surrendered. Wendy had persuaded him to go part-time when I joined him, but it was another year before he finally gave in completely. He seems happy enough now, though, with his allotment to tend.'

'Ah, yes. Always loved his garden, didn't he? You had that in common, at least. And, of course, Wendy will keep him on his toes. Good woman, that. Lucky man.'

They were silent as they sipped their tea, and Flynn tried again. 'So, what have you been doing with yourself lately?'

Maurice looked blank. 'Eh? Well, I—I watch a bit of television. Read a bit. I'm getting quite good at crossword puzzles, you know. My neighbour buys puzzle books for me. Very kind. So you work alone now?'

'I did for three years, but now Gabriel works with me. You know, Raphael's son?'

'Ah, yes. Keeping it in the family, eh? I've been thinking about going back to it, you know. Maybe doing some locum work, just to keep my hand in. What do you think?'

Flynn thought it was an impossible dream, but how could he say so? Maurice had retired six years ago when he'd turned sixty-five, and had been looking forward to many happy years with his wife. He'd been alert and competent, and nothing like the broken man who sat before him now. He studied his friend's face, noticing his gaunt appearance and the stubble on his chin. Maurice used to shave every day. He didn't approve of stubble.

'Have you eaten, Maurice?' he asked gently.

Maurice looked startled. 'What, today? Well, er, I think I had some soup at lunchtime. I'm not sure, exactly. Is it almost time for dinner already?'

'It's almost nine o' clock,' said Flynn. 'I'll fix you something to eat.'

'No, no, don't worry about that. I'm not hungry.'

'You have to eat something,' Flynn said. 'Let me make you something. It doesn't have to be anything heavy.'

He headed back into the kitchen, checking the cupboards and realising that, apart from an ancient box of stock cubes that had probably been there since Matilda was around, and a few packets of jelly and half a bottle of soy sauce, there was nothing in there. He would have to do a shop. He would head to the supermarket tomorrow. In the meantime, it would have to be a takeaway.

'Would you like Chinese, Indian, or pizza?' he asked, sitting back on the sofa, after pushing the newspapers out of the way and taking out his mobile phone.

Maurice looked at him blankly. 'Sorry?'

'To eat? Would you like Chinese? You always enjoyed a chow mein as I recall?'

Maurice shook his head. 'Is it nearly time for dinner already? Not for me, Flynn. I'm really not hungry.'

Flynn's hand trembled as he looked down at his phone. For a moment, the screen swam before his blurry eyes, but he said, quite calmly, 'Well, I'm starving. I think a chow mein for both of us, don't you?'

It took him only moments to Google the nearest takeaway and place an order for the food. He didn't feel hungry, either. In fact, he felt quite nauseous, and a chow mein was the last thing he felt like eating, but it had always been Maurice's dish of choice whenever they visited a Chinese restaurant, and it wouldn't lay too heavy on him.

Maurice didn't look as if he'd eaten a big meal for a while. He wondered if Mrs Robbins had actually seen him eat any of that stew, or if she just left it with him and hoped for the best. Somehow, Flynn had to coax him into eating again, and more to the point, he had to try to bring his friend back to life. Part of him had died with his wife, and Flynn had been too selfish to realise it. It was time to make amends. Tonight was just the start.

CHAPTER TEN

'Can you believe they've picked Susan Skelton to be the May Queen?' Sophie sounded disgusted. 'She looks like she's been smacked in the face with a frying pan. Not that you can blame her. Blood will out. Hello, Hattie. Lovely day for it. Can't wait to see your Susan in her costume.'

Hattie smiled and waved, as she headed towards the bonfire in the middle of the paddock.

Sophie tutted. 'Thinks she's royalty now. Who chose her? Was it Rhiannon? Because we have far prettier girls in the village than Susan. Pan and Tally for a start—no one can deny they're beauties. Then there's your Fuchsia, Rose, she's a looker, too. But Susan? What a terrible representative for Kearton Bay she'll make.' She looked around furtively. 'I wonder if we can nobble the camera?' She nodded toward the lone reporter from *The Farthingdale Echo*, who had turned up to snap the Beltane festival.

'Sophie, honestly.' Archie shook his head. 'That's hardly the spirit of the thing, is it? Anyway, Pandora and Tallulah are away at university, so they couldn't have made it, even if they'd been picked.'

'They could have got the day off. Anyway, Fuchsia's here, isn't she? Don't you agree, Rose? I think it was a fix.'

'I'm not sure there was anything to fix, Sophe,' I said. 'Don't remember there being a ballot. And, to be honest, I think Fuchsia would rather die than dress up as the May Queen. Can't really see her in that costume, can you?'

'Well, perhaps not,' Sophie conceded. 'And I suppose,' she added with a sigh, 'that Pandora would only agree if they let her keep her jodhpurs on. But Tally, oh, she'd be perfect. Do you remember the other year when our Lexi was chosen? Wasn't she stunning? All that gorgeous red hair.'

I looked around, seeing Lexi leaning against the paddock fence, chatting amiably to Georgia and Robbie. She held

Amy's hand in hers, and the poor kid was looking extremely bored. There was no sign of Will. Maybe it was all too much for him, seeing her with her new boyfriend. Poor sap.

Rhiannon was standing by the gate, her eyes dancing with excitement. She loved Beltane, and set great store by its deeper spiritual meaning. She'd picked a spotty teenager called Darren to be the Green Man, something else of which Sophie didn't approve, given that he wasn't half as handsome as her beloved Oliver.

'Still,' she admitted grudgingly, 'at least he'll be wearing that creepy mask, so we won't see his face in the papers.'

'That's the spirit, Sophe. Aren't Eliza and Gabriel coming?' Archie asked, glancing at his watch. 'They're cutting it fine. This thing's about to start.'

I tutted. 'They'll be at it.'

Sophie and Archie stared at me. 'Pardon?'

'Sorry. Just that, well, Gabriel's on call, and I don't mean for his GP duties. Hasn't Eliza told you?' I started to laugh. 'She bought one of those ovulation kits, and now whenever her hormone levels are right, she summons him to her, and they ... well, I'm sure you can guess.'

'Good grief,' said Sophie. 'Whatever happened to letting nature take its course?'

'I dunno.' Archie winked. 'But I can think of worse things to be summoned for.'

Sophie giggled. 'He'll be exhausted. I can't think why they're being so technical about it all. Half the fun of getting pregnant is the trying.'

'Only half the fun?' queried her husband, and she nudged him.

'I think it's because of their age,' I said. 'With Eliza being thirty-five in July, and Gabriel being forty, they've decided there's no time to waste. They've been at it like rabbits since they decided to go for it.'

'I thought Gabriel was walking funny last time I saw him.'

Archie laughed. 'Oh, speak of the devil, here they come. Pardon the pun.'

Eliza and Gabriel came rushing into the paddock, their faces flushed. 'Have we missed anything? We were a bit busy.'

Gabriel frowned. 'What's funny?' he demanded, as we all started to laugh. 'Oh, Christ, you've told them, haven't you?'

Eliza blushed. 'Only Rose.'

Archie pulled a sympathetic face. 'Poor Gabriel. Has she been cracking the whip, then, mate? Wonder you managed to get up the hill after all that exertion.'

'Oh, shut up,' said Gabriel. 'It will all be worth it in the end.'

'If you say so,' said Archie. 'Personally, I can't think of anything worse than starting again with bloody kids.'

'Me neither.' I shuddered.

'Well, aren't you all cheery?' said Eliza. 'Thanks very much for your support.'

'It's Gabriel who'll be needing the support.' Archie laughed. 'A flaming truss before long, if you keep making your demands, you wanton hussy, you.'

I laughed, seeing Gabriel's obvious embarrassment, then my laughter died and I muttered, 'Oh shit.'

My mother waved gaily at me as she tottered across the paddock in her high heels, dragging along a short man with a comb-over and a camel coat, uncannily like that worn by Del Boy Trotter. 'Yoo hoo! By, it's a bit nippy the day, isn't it? We all want our heads read, stood out here for some weird ceremony. Rose, this is Alec. Alec, this is my daughter, Rose.'

Alec took hold of my hand and kept hold of it, while he told me that he'd been longing to meet me for ages, and how beautiful I was, and so like my mother. If he wanted to get into my good books, he was going the wrong way about it. 'And are these your friends?' he asked me, as if I were about six. I looked round in embarrassment, to see Sophie, Archie, Eliza and Gabriel all standing there, trying not to look as if they were listening.

'Er, yeah.' I introduced them to him with some reluctance, explaining that Alec was my mother's good friend.

'Good friend?' she trilled. 'He's a bit more than that, I hope.'

'So do I, my sweet,' he smarmed, 'especially after last night.'

I thought how easy it would be to push him onto the bonfire. He wasn't that tall, and I bet most of his weight was in the heavy coat and gold sovereign rings on his fingers. All that oil on his hair, he was bound to burn easily, too. I tried to pull myself together. I was getting extremely violent in my old age.

'Your mother's told me all about you,' he said, flashing me a terrifying smile, which revealed rather long, yellow teeth. 'You and that little sweet shop of yours. Well done. I run a car showroom myself.'

How did I know he'd say that? 'My ex ran one of those,' I informed him.

'Really? Was it successful?'

'If it was, it was no thanks to him. He was a complete tosser,' I said.

He frowned. 'Oh, dear. No love lost there, then.'

'You could say that. He moved to Spain with some rich widow. Always did have an eye out for any money-making opportunity.'

'Really? Well, I hope you realise we're not all like that.' He gave a feeble laugh, and I shrugged.

'Obviously. You wouldn't be with my mother if you were. She hasn't got two pennies to rub together.'

My mother gave a girlish giggle. 'Oh, Rose, what a thing to say. Ignore her, Alec. She's always teasing.'

I tutted. Knowing my mother, she'd probably told him that she owned the flat and was just letting me and the girls stay there out of the kindness of her heart. I wouldn't put anything past her. She was a slave to her libido.

Those of us who had been to these things before knew what

it meant when the sound of drumbeats began, and we all turned. Alec finally dropped my hand and stared in disbelief, as Susan, wearing a long white dress and a crown of flowers, was carried into the paddock on a mock throne by four men.

'By heck,' he murmured.

'Who's that funny-looking sod?' my mother asked.

'See?' said Sophie triumphantly.

Archie shook his head at her, and we watched as Susan climbed unsteadily down from the throne before it was carried back to the gate by the men.

'She's had a few clouts with the ugly stick,' Alec murmured to my mother, who nodded in agreement.

Then the drumbeats grew a bit louder, and from out of the trees, Darren stepped forward, dressed all in green, with a huge mask of leaves and deer antlers covering his face.

'He looks a bit sinister,' said Alec.

'He looks better than he usually does,' Sophie assured him.

'Will you behave?' said Archie.

The drumbeats started a steady rhythm, and I heard Alec gasp as the Green Man pointed at the May Queen in a very dramatic fashion. She stared at him in terror, and he waited, before he dropped his hand and looked round.

Everyone glanced at each other, rather bemused. Rhiannon stepped forward and whispered something in Susan's ear. Then she nodded at the Green Man, who stood there, rather awkwardly shuffling from one foot to the other, and he pointed again. That time, Susan turned and began to run, somewhat clumsily, round the bonfire.

'What on earth's going on?' asked Alec.

'Told you it was a weird place,' said my mother. 'We never got stuff like this in Oddborough.'

We watched, holding our breath, as Susan clumped her way through the bystanders, and tripped and fell headfirst into the mud.

'Thank God she missed the fire,' said Gabriel.

'I know. She'd have put it out,' said my mother, lighting a cigarette and drawing on it heavily. 'What a flaming shambles. Is it always like this?'

'Certainly not!' said Sophie. 'You should have seen it when Lexi was our May Queen. She was very elegant. It's all that Rhiannon's fault, picking that dozy girl.'

The Green Man had easily caught up with her, and was standing there, looking very uncertain, while Hattie rushed to pick his May Queen up. There didn't seem much point in chasing her any farther, so the drummers stopped drumming, and there was a silence, till Rhiannon murmured in Darren's ear, and he reluctantly stepped forward and gave Susan a kiss on the cheek. She immediately wiped her face and turned her back on him, rushing back to Hattie.

'How old is that lass?' demanded my mother.

'About sixteen, seventeen.'

'Jesus. One sandwich short of a picnic, is she?'

'No! She's just very shy,' said Eliza indignantly.

Alec started to laugh. 'Well, I've never seen the like. What a fiasco. Mind you, that woman over there looks interesting. What's she come as?'

Sophie snorted. 'That's Rhiannon. She's come as herself. She always dresses like an extra from *Downton Abbey*.'

'Well, I see what they mean about these rural villages,' he said, taking out a cigar and lighting it with a very flashy gold lighter. 'Everyone's a bit barmy, aren't they?'

We all stared at him in stony silence, but he didn't seem to notice.

Rhiannon was making her speech, thanking everyone for coming, and asking us to give thanks to the god and goddess for their blessings.

'Bugger that,' said my mother. 'What is this? Salem's Lot?'

'They didn't bless that loopy girl with the white dress,' Alec pointed out, practically choking me with smoke from his cigar. 'Tried to kill her off, more like.'

'Can you blame them?' asked my mother. 'How insulting, picking her for the May Queen. I bet they thought we were taking the piss out of them.'

'I did say Fuchsia would have made a better May Queen,' Sophie whispered, mindful of the silence that was being observed by most other people at the gathering.

My mother flicked her ash on the ground. 'I wouldn't go that far.' She looked around. 'Where's that Dr Peddleton-Ross? Is he not coming?'

'Flynn doesn't really do social events,' murmured Gabriel, looking at Alec with some distaste. I couldn't blame him. Alec was puffing on a cigar and watching Rhiannon with a very unsavoury gleam in his eye.

'He was at the Easter party, though,' said Eliza. 'I thought maybe he was making progress. Anyway, hasn't he got a bit of a thing for Rhiannon?'

My mother stared at her. 'Rhiannon? Him? No way.'

'Meaning what?' I said. 'Are you saying Rhiannon's too good for Flynn?'

She looked at me with a baffled expression. 'No. I'm saying I thought ... oh, never mind.'

Gabriel looked puzzled. 'Flynn and Rhiannon? What on earth makes you think that?'

'She was very touchy-feely with him at the pub. Didn't you notice?' asked Sophie. At Gabriel's and Archie's blank expressions, she tutted in exasperation. 'Why do men never notice these things? He was standing at the bar, and she stroked his face in a very intimate way. All very strange, even for her. I tell you, he's probably yet another notch on her bedpost. Wonder that damn bed's still standing.'

Gabriel shook his head. 'I doubt it very much. Flynn's been going through some stuff—I'm not sure what. He's been really down lately. Rhiannon's probably being sympathetic. You know what she's like.'

'Don't we just,' said Sophie and sighed. 'Poor Flynn. I wish he could find someone. He's such a nice man, and he deserves some happiness.'

My mother took another drag on her cigarette and hooked her arm through Alec's. 'Aye, well, you never know. Maybe there's someone just round the corner for him. I reckon he'll be in the pink before you know it.'

I felt my heart pounding as she winked at me. Please God, let no one else have noticed that, nor picked up on her pathetic attempt at humour. Why was she so insistent that Flynn and I were meant for each other? It was never going to happen.

We all headed back to The Hare and Moon for the food that Rhiannon always laid on after the Beltane festival. My mother and Alec slunk into a corner, where they sat, feeding each other bits of food and slopping over each other.

'How disgusting is that?' I said, as Alec picked up a sausage on a stick and proceeded to tease my mother with it, putting it to her lips and then withdrawing it several times. 'I feel sick.'

'It's a bit much at their age,' admitted Eliza.

'It's nothing to do with age,' I said. 'Look at them. I'm surprised my mother doesn't slide off the chair, sitting next to that oil slick. I mean, what does she see in him?'

'There's no accounting for taste,' said Eliza. She hoisted Amy up onto her knee and handed her a sandwich. 'Where are your kids, anyway?'

'Cerise is on the beach with her mates, and Fuchsia is, well, who knows? Probably sitting in her room, listening to miserable songs with suicidal lyrics. That's all she ever seems to do these days.'

'Oh, dear. Still no progress with Oliver?'

'You know what, Eliza? I'm not sure he even knows about it. I mean, have you ever seen them even talk? I think maybe it's just a crazy crush that she's developed. An obsession even. I don't know. I can't quite fathom it all out.'

'It must be worrying for you.'

'Yeah, and you want to go through it all twice? You must

be mad. Bad enough that you've got this one growing up so fast,' I said, smiling at Amy, who beamed back at me. 'Fancy wanting a baby. I can't think of anything worse.'

'But it will be perfect,' she said dreamily. 'It will be Gabriel's baby. I can't think of anything better.'

Yuk. All this lovey-dovey stuff was beyond me. For a brief moment, Flynn's face flashed into my mind, and I pushed it away, not wanting to admit to myself that, without him, the packed little bar of The Hare and Moon felt surprisingly empty.

****

I was knackered. I felt quite nauseous and still had a pounding headache from last night. The last thing I felt like doing that morning was going into work, to be surrounded by all those sugary sweets.

I emerged from the shower, looking and feeling like death warmed up.

My mother opened her bedroom door and stood, leaning against the frame, looking at me with undisguised contempt. 'Well, don't you look lovely?'

'Good morning to you, too,' I muttered, rubbing my head and wondering where I'd put the paracetamol.

'Have you seen the time? Cerise got her own breakfast, you know. Don't you think you're getting a bit old for all this malarkey?' she demanded. 'I mean, how many did you have last night? I had no idea you were such a big drinker.'

'Big drinker?' I shook my head, but wished I hadn't when the room swung dangerously for a moment before settling back into position. 'I had a couple of drinks, that's all. Stop making such a big deal out of it.'

'Sure you did. No wonder your kids are so out of control, with a mother who's a borderline alcoholic.'

'Borderline alcoholic!' The nerve of the woman. I'd had

two vodka and Cokes, and my nausea was more down to the plateful of sausage rolls I'd scoffed, while I listened to Eliza droning on about babies and tried not to look at my mother and Alec, practically hoovering each up over the vol au vents. 'I've only got a headache because you and lover boy practically choked me to death in here last night, with your cigarettes! I've told you not to smoke in the flat. When I got home, it was like bloody foggy old London town in here, and I've got to sleep in this flaming room, remember.'

My mother shrugged. 'You're in denial. Well, when you're ready to talk about it, let me know. I'm going back to bed. I had a late night,' she said with a smug grin.

Feeling even sicker, I pulled a face as she closed the bedroom door behind her. Now, where the hell were the painkillers?

Casting a despairing glance around the kitchen, I noted that Cerise had left her cereal bowl and mug on the draining board of the sink, instead of putting them in the dishwasher, and her dirty PE shorts and shirt were thrown on the floor in front of the washing machine.

'Lazy little mare,' I muttered, trying to ignore the guilt I was feeling that she'd got herself ready and off to school without even seeing me. I picked up the clothes and dropped them into the laundry basket. Well, at least Fuchsia must have put her breakfast dishes away, which was unusual for her. Maybe she was finally growing up.

I found the paracetamol and poured myself a glass of water, considering the matter. As the cold liquid poured down my throat, I decided that the possibility of Fuchsia's new-found maturity seemed unlikely. On a sudden impulse, I pulled open the door of the dishwasher and peered inside. No dishes. Would Fuchsia really have gone off to work without even a cup of tea inside her? Come to think of it, she wouldn't have been as considerate as Cerise. She would have banged and clattered, and made damn sure my sleep was well and truly disturbed. I looked at the clock. Twenty-past eight. Fuchsia should have started work at eight.

'Oh, God.' I groaned. 'The little git's done it again.'

I threw open Fuchsia's bedroom door, and, sure enough, there she was, fast asleep in bed.

'Fuchsia, for God's sake,' I yelled, dragging the duvet off her and shaking her frantically. 'Get out of bed now. You're late for work again.'

'Gerroff me,' muttered Fuchsia, reaching for the duvet and shrugging my hands away from her shoulders.

'It's twenty-past eight. You're late, and you'll get the sack.'

'For God's sake, Mam, I won't. I rang in sick at quarter-to eight.'

'What do you mean? There's nothing wrong with you.'

'I've got period pains. I feel rubbish. I can't work today, feeling like this.'

'You lazy little git.' I felt perilously close to tears. 'You'll end up getting fired. There's nothing wrong with you. They'll get rid.'

'Oh, give your head a bang,' snapped Fuchsia. 'They can't sack me for being ill.'

'You're not sodding ill. You're bone bloody idle.' I sank onto the bed, suddenly exhausted. 'Why do you do this to me?'

'Do what? I'm pre-menstrual. What can I say? I can't help my bloody hormones, can I?'

'You know what? I'm sick of worrying about you. If you want to throw your life away, go right ahead, but I'm telling you now, sort yourself out, or you can go and sponge off someone else, 'cos I've had it with you.'

Stomping out of her room, I slammed the door, tears of frustration blurring my sight. I walked past the chaos in the kitchen and went to collect my apron for work. Fuchsia could tidy the house if she wasn't going into work. I had enough to do.

Trudging downstairs, I entered the shop, and, head held

high, I shut the door to my domestic hell behind me.

CHAPTER ELEVEN

'Lexi says their hotel's lovely,' said Eliza, plonking herself down on the sofa and peering at her mobile phone. 'They had a fabulous tea with finger sandwiches, and different types of buns, and gorgeous scones with clotted cream and delicious jam, but the prices are horrendous, and it's a bloody rip-off in London, and she can't believe they dare charge so much.'

Gabriel grinned. 'Sounds like Lexi. Always practical. Glad she's enjoying it, though.'

'Oh, she is. They've had champagne, too.' She frowned. 'She says Joe's really nervous about tonight. He's been rushing to the loo non-stop for the last couple of hours.'

'Aw, what a lovely picture,' I said, wrinkling my nose in disgust.

'Why's he nervous?' said Gabriel. 'He's appeared on television for years. What's so different now?'

'Wasn't someone else's show,' she said, putting her phone back in her bag. 'He told me he doesn't want to muck it up for Charlie. He says it's much tougher being the guest, in his opinion, than it is being the host.'

'And how's he going to muck it up?' I asked. 'He knows what he's doing. Charlie will look after him.'

'It's the idea of having to sell his novel,' she explained. 'It was different with his autobiography. They basically asked him about his life story, and it was simple enough to talk about that, but he feels awkward trying to explain the premise of *Death by Default*. He's worried people will think it sounds daft.'

'It *is* daft,' I said. 'A murder mystery set in the dog show world. How can it not be? What does he think they're expecting? *Wolf Hall*?'

'Lexi will be so excited,' said Gabriel. 'She's loved Charlie Hope for years. I don't think our birthday present is going to beat this, Eliza.'

'I dunno so much. A bloody car! What a twenty-first she's having,' I said. I remembered my twenty-first birthday. I spent the day on the market stall, trying desperately to sell cut-price Christmas cards and budget tree decorations in the freezing cold, then went home to find out that Fuchsia had been sent home from nursery with a bug, and spent the evening cleaning up vomit, while my parents went out to the pictures and left me to it. What a fun day that had been.

'Are you sure you don't want to stay here and watch it with us?' asked Eliza, as Gabriel reached for his jacket.

He shook his head. 'No, I'll leave you ladies to it. I'm going to see Flynn. I'll take a few beers with me and try to cheer him up. He's been rather low recently. Besides, I wouldn't want to get in the way of you two. I'm sure you'd rather have a girls' night in. I'll see you later.'

He kissed Eliza and left the house, taking care to shut the door quietly so Amy didn't wake up.

'I'm so looking forward to this show,' said Eliza, reaching for the remote and settling herself down. 'I quite envy Lexi. I watched some of her Charlie Hope DVDs recently, and he's very good.' She paused, but only for a moment. 'He interviewed Melody Bird a couple of weeks ago.'

'He did? Blimey, wish I'd known. You never said.'

'No.'

'Does it still rankle?'

'Not about her and Harry. No way. She's welcome to him. What gets me is that their son gets to see his father every day, whereas Amy—well, it's a couple of weeks in the summer holidays and a few days after Christmas, if she's lucky. I know they're busy but really ...'

She picked at the buttons on the remote quite savagely. 'I suppose I feel angry on her behalf. Melody was sitting there, banging on about her successful career, and I just thought, you've got everything you wanted. What about Harry's little girl? Why is she being pushed out?'

'At least Amy's got Gabriel,' I pointed out. 'I know he's not her real dad, but, really, he couldn't be better if he was, could he? And he loves her to bits, anyone can see that.'

She smiled. 'Oh, yes. He treats her just as if she were his own. I do know how lucky I am, Rose. I suppose it just hurts that Harry doesn't seem to appreciate her. She deserves better. Oh, well, sod him. I'm not going to let him spoil this evening. Don't let your coffee get cold,' she added, nodding at the mug on the coffee table.

I'd forgotten it was there. I reached for it and took a sip. It was still warm, luckily. 'So, what's wrong with Flynn?' I asked, trying to sound casual.

'I don't know. Gabriel mentioned the other day that he's a bit down, but he didn't say why. That's if he even knows. It's hard to find anything out about Flynn, really. He keeps himself to himself so much. Maybe Rhiannon would know?'

I gulped down the rest of my coffee and put the mug back on the coffee table, wondering if she'd heard any more about their possible relationship. I was about to ask, when she squealed and pointed the remote at the television. 'It's on! Oh, I hope Joe copes all right.'

In the event, he coped brilliantly. Joe had always been entertaining, but even Eliza said she'd never seen him enjoy himself as much as he seemed to with Charlie. From our point of view, it was hilarious, though the actual interview was a shambles, as both men were helpless with laughter.

'Oh, my God, that was brilliant,' Eliza said, wiping her eyes. 'I hope Lexi texts me after the show to give me the gossip. Would you like another coffee? Or would you like some wine?'

'Crack open the wine,' I said. 'Aren't you watching the rest of it?'

'I'm not that fussed,' she admitted. 'I don't like that awful actress, and I'm sick of seeing that band. They're on every bloody programme lately. I'll get the bottle. Would you like some cake? We'll have to starve for the rest of the week, obviously, or Sophie will have another meltdown.'

I grinned and nodded, and she went into the kitchen, returning within minutes with a bottle, two glasses and two slices of cake. We sat watching the rest of the show, criticising the Hollywood starlet who took herself far too seriously, and didn't understand a word Charlie was saying, and wondering what on earth all the girls in the audience were screaming for when a boy band, whose members seemed to have an average age of twelve, appeared. The bottle of wine was empty before we knew it, which was a bit worrying, as Eliza had restricted herself to one glass, due to her mission to conceive.

'Crikey, you got through that quickly,' she said. 'Are you okay?'

I wasn't okay, really. I felt unsettled and a bit depressed, but I couldn't for the life of me think why.

Eliza's phone beeped, saving me the bother of answering. It was Lexi, informing us that Charlie was ever so friendly, and he and Joe were still laughing, seemingly oblivious to the other guests, and that they really seemed to have hit it off. In fact, there was a definite chemistry. She added that one of the band members had tried it on with her, and she'd patted him on the head and told him to come back when he'd finished puberty.

'Oh, she does make me laugh,' said Eliza fondly. She looked at me hopefully. 'What do you think? Joe and Charlie, eh? That would be wonderful, wouldn't it?'

I nodded and waved my empty glass in the air. 'Too right. Joe's far too gorgeous to be left all alone. Is there any more wine?'

She frowned. 'Rose, don't you think you've had enough?

'You're not my sodding mother, Eliza. If I want a lecture I can go home.'

She narrowed her eyes and pursed her lips. For a moment, she was the spitting image of Hannah, her late grandmother. 'I may not be your mother, but I am your friend, and I'm only looking out for you. Is something wrong? It's not like you to drink so much.'

'You mean, apart from the fact that my mother has taken over my flat, her creepy walking oil-slick of a boyfriend keeps dropping round and slopping over her, the flat stinks like an ashtray, even though I've told her not to smoke indoors, my back aches from sleeping on that dratted sofa every night, and Fuchsia's moods are up and down like Rhiannon's knickers. Nope, all fine.'

'Oh, Rose.' She sighed, putting her arm around me. 'I'm sorry. I've been so preoccupied with my own life, I never gave much thought to how difficult things must be for you. I'll get you that bottle,' she added, making me feel incredibly guilty. I mean, yeah, all those things were driving me crazy, but deep down I knew there was another reason for my sudden depression, but it was one I could never confide in her about.

Halfway down the second bottle, I was feeling a whole lot cheerier. Eliza was extremely excited about Joe and Charlie's "chemistry" and had texted Lexi for an update. She was now in an agony of impatience as there was no response.

'She'll be too busy with her new showbiz pals.' I giggled. 'Maybe the Boy Wonder suddenly seemed attractive, after all?'

'No, she wouldn't do that to Robbie,' said Eliza confidently.

'They're hardly love's young dream,' I pointed out. 'They've only been going out for five minutes and the passion's already worn off. That's if it was ever there.'

'I don't think Lexi will ever settle down. She's got no faith in relationships, and who can blame her? Her parents' marriage was so bitter, and she was at a vulnerable age. She'll never trust in love enough to get truly involved with someone. Robbie's just someone to hang out with.'

'And shag,' I said. 'Lucky bugger. God, it feels like years

since I got any action. What am I talking about? It *is* years! Nothing at all since Jimbo left, and not much when he was around, to be honest.'

'That's what's really wrong with you. You need a man. I wonder how long it takes the wedding bouquet to work its magic?' she mused. 'It's been nearly two and a half months now. There should be someone on the horizon.'

'You do talk shit,' I said. 'Like there's anything to that old wives' tale. And if there was, I'd send him packing, have no fear on that score.'

'So, you got a black eye for nothing?' She grinned. 'Harsh.'

'I wouldn't say it was for nothing,' I said, aware that I was smirking, and seemingly unable to stop myself. 'I got lots of medical attention from Flynn, after all.'

Her eyes widened, and I realised I may have made a blunder. 'Rose, you're blushing!'

'I am not!' I protested. 'It's the alcohol.'

'Don't you dare!' she said, 'I'm not daft. You're blushing. Oh, my God, it's all making sense now.'

'What's making sense? Not you, that's for sure.' I folded my arms, wishing I'd stuck to coffee and kept my big mouth shut.

'Oh, Rose, do you like Flynn? Really?' Eliza's eyes were shining.

'I have no idea what you're talking about,' I said, sipping my wine, while Eliza sat there, her face screwed up in concentration, as she obviously tried to make sense of the whole imaginary romance.

'Now I think about it,' she said, 'he did rush to your side when that stupid girl elbowed you in the face.'

'So what? He's a doctor,' I pointed out.

'So is Gabriel. He could have left it to him. The old Flynn would have. He never pushed his way forward for anything. But the minute you got hit, he was at your side, and he rushed off to get ice for you and used his own handkerchief. For which, I might add, you weren't the tiniest bit grateful.'

'Oh, well, I'm very sorry, but I was in pain,' I pointed out. 'Anyway, you're talking rubbish. He did what he'd do for anyone. Nothing more. He certainly didn't dance with me because he wanted to. He only got up because I forced him.'

Eliza stared at me. 'He danced with you? When did this happen? Where was I?'

'After you'd left,' I said, wondering what I was doing telling her all this. My mouth seemed to have developed a life of its own.

She clapped her hands in excitement. 'Oh, Rose, why didn't you tell me?'

'Tell you what?' I said, perplexed.

'That you have feelings for Flynn, of course!'

'I don't have any feelings for Flynn,' I said. 'Honestly, aren't you listening? You're making this up as you go along.'

She definitely wasn't listening. She was chewing her thumb nail, and I just imagined her trying to recollect every meeting Flynn and I had ever had.

'Look how he came to your rescue at your mother's. He got a black eye for his trouble, and all for you. Can you not see what you're doing to him? You're turning him into a hero.'

'What the hell are you talking about?'

She clapped her hands again. I think she was turning into a seal. 'Of course! He turned up at the pub for the Easter party. When does Flynn ever go to things like that? Yet, there he was, uninvited. He came to see you, Rose.'

'Bollocks,' I said. 'He spent the entire night talking to Rhiannon.'

'But it was you he bought a drink for,' she pointed out.

'I told him I didn't want one,' I protested.

'We all did, but funnily enough, it was only you that he bought one for. Oh, Rose, I think somehow you've awakened him.'

I nearly spat my wine out. 'Awakened him?' I snorted. 'Who is he? Sleeping Beauty? That kiss probably sent him into a coma, more like.'

'Hang on, rewind,' said Eliza, while I stared at her in horror and vowed to myself never to touch alcohol again. 'What kiss?'

'While we were dancing. You have to understand, I was pissed,' I muttered, my face burning. 'It meant nothing. And besides, what did he do afterwards? Shot out of the pub like a bullet from a gun. Couldn't escape fast enough, so don't tell me it mattered to him. Honestly, you're starting to get on my wick. There's nothing between Flynn and me and there never will be, so shut up, will you.'

'Oh, but Rose—'

'I said, *shut up*, Eliza!'

I was horrified to find there were tears running down my cheeks, and my throat felt full, as if I was going to choke. What was wrong with me?

Eliza's expression changed to one of concern, and she held out her arms to me, but I shook my head and ran upstairs to the bathroom. I locked the door and sat on the bath mat, staring at the wall and wondering how I'd managed to make such an idiot of myself. Why had I told her all that? I should never have drank all that wine. It did funny things to me. And now Eliza would be convinced that I fancied Flynn. Did I fancy Flynn?

I buried my face in one of Eliza's thick, fluffy towels. What did it matter, really? Even if I had cared about Flynn Pennington-Rhys, which I didn't, what use would that be? People like Fuchsia and me, we had to be realistic.

I thought of my poor lovelorn daughter, mooning around after the snooty Oliver Crook. I imagined him at Manchester University, regaling everyone with amusing stories about the lovesick girl he'd left behind, while he flirted outrageously with someone called Felicity Fossington-Jones, who was destined to be a barrister and earn shed-loads of money, just like her father. I was so busy weaving the story of Oliver's imaginary girlfriend that it took me a while to realise that someone was tapping on the bathroom door.

Reluctantly, I opened it, sitting down again as Eliza shuffled in. She sank down onto the floor beside me, saying nothing, but put her arms around me and let me cry.

'It's 'cos I've had too much to drink.' I sobbed.

'I know,' she said.

'I should have stuck to coffee, shouldn't I?'

'Perhaps.'

'It's poor Fuchsia. She loves Oliver, and someone like him would never look at someone like her, would he?'

'Wouldn't he?'

'She's not clever enough, not middle class enough. He'd get bored with her. I'd—she'd embarrass him.'

'I see,' she said, stroking my hair.

'It's a little bit sad, isn't it?' I said.

She kissed the top of my head and sighed. 'I wish you knew how lovely you are, Rose.'

Sometimes, I remembered exactly why she was my best friend.

CHAPTER TWELVE

Helmston was a beautiful place, and Flynn wondered why he didn't visit more often. Its main claim to fame—and the thing that had visitors swooping there in huge numbers—was its castle. Over nine hundred years old, it stood overlooking the bustling market town, its popularity never dimming. Owned and cared for by ECHOES, the Enterprise for Conservation of Historic Old English Sites, it dominated the neighbourhood, and there were dozens of local businesses that bore the word "Castle" in their titles. There was no doubt that it had brought wealth to the place, and Flynn knew that Will had hopes of achieving a similar success one day, with Kearton Hall. He doubted that it would happen in Sir Paul's lifetime, though, which was a shame. Kearton Bay could have done with some year-round tourism. As it was, the place was half-empty through the winter.

The market square was chaotic today. Most days it was used as a car park for visitors and locals doing their shopping, but on Wednesdays and Saturdays it was market day, and the town descended into madness as people fought for parking spaces in its narrow back streets—all because they were too lazy to walk for ten minutes from where the council had put a secondary car park in to cope with the overflow. People wanted to be as near to the market as possible, and it was all too much trouble, apparently, to actually use their legs to get to it.

Flynn had nipped into the town centre to get some fresh fruit and vegetables for Maurice. His friend was looking a bit better, now that he had regular company and was eating properly. Flynn managed to visit every night after work, even if it was only for an hour or so, to make him a meal, wash the dishes and tidy up. Some nights, if he wasn't too tired, he would sit with him, watching television for a couple of hours, and they would chat and reminisce. Maurice seemed to like that. He loved talking about Matilda. His eyes would light up, and he would tell Flynn some anecdote from their marriage, something amusing that his wife had said or done, and he would laugh and shake his head, saying fondly what a character she'd been. It seemed to be doing him the world of good, having someone to talk to, someone to share his memories with.

Flynn had decided to give the house a thorough cleaning that afternoon, but first he wanted to get some supplies in from the market. Parking in the council car park, he walked into the centre of town and braved the heaving crowds, all jostling for bargains round the dozens of stalls.

He found a second-hand book stall and stopped for a moment, never able to resist the lure of an old book. Browsing through the piles of old hardbacks with yellowing pages, creased paperbacks, and the occasional pristine copy of a novel that had obviously never even been read before, he was completely absorbed in his mission to find something worth taking home and adding to the far-too-large pile of books he already owned. It was some moments, then, before he realised that the general buzz of conversation around him had become more focused, more urgent. He saw people rushing past him and heard someone ask if they were all right. If who was all right?

He turned round, still holding a book in his hand, and the first thing he noticed was the flash of pink hair. What had happened to Rose?

He dropped the book and rushed forward, calling, 'I'm a doctor, let me through.' Had he really said that? Good grief. Still, it actually worked, as the crowd parted for him, and he felt quite weak with relief as he saw that Rose was standing and looked perfectly all right.

It was her mother who was on the ground.

He knelt beside her. 'Mrs MacLean, are you all right? What happened?'

'Oh, Errol, pet, I've had a nasty turn.'

'Flynn,' he said automatically.

'Eh?'

'Flynn. Not Errol.'

'Oh, aye, that's the one.'

She didn't look hurt. Her breathing and pulse were fine, her skin seemed perfectly normal with no sweating, and she wasn't pale.

'What exactly happened, Mrs MacLean?'

She shook her head. 'I dunno, pet. Just came over all funny, didn't I, Rose?'

He looked up at Rose, who stood with her arms folded, looking as if she'd like to throttle her mother. 'Yeah, you did. Very funny. Just after she spotted you, Flynn, actually. It was very sudden.'

'Did you have any pain?'

'No. Just went a bit dizzy, and then the next thing I knew, bang. On the ground. I'm lucky I haven't fractured me skull.'

'Hardly likely, since you fell on your arse,' said Rose, who didn't sound in the slightest bit sympathetic.

Flynn helped her mother to her feet. 'How do you feel now?'

'Well, truth to tell, I still feel a bit woozy,' she informed him. 'What I could do with is a sit down and a nice cup of tea. Are there any cafés round here?'

He heard Rose gasp and wondered what was going on between them. The crowd drifted away, seeing that there was no blood and no drama worth hanging around for.

Flynn shrugged. 'There are lots of cafés round here, Mrs MacLean.'

'Yeah. Like the one we were in not ten minutes ago, for example?' Rose grabbed her mother's arm and hooked her own firmly through it. 'Come on, Mother. I'm sure you'll be fine. Time to get the bus, I think.'

'The bus? Ooh, Rose, I don't think I'm up to that long bus

ride, pet. I feel proper shaky.' She looked appealingly at Flynn. 'I shouldn't risk it, should I, Doctor?'

Rose looked away, but he saw the distinct flush of pink on her cheeks. 'I could give you a lift,' he said hesitantly. 'The trouble is, I'm not going home yet. I'm just getting some fruit and vegetables for a friend, and dropping them back at his house. Then I was going to clean up for him. I may be there some time.'

Mrs MacLean's face brightened. 'That's no problem. We'll come with you. We're not doing anything else. Rose has got the day off, and we decided to spend it together, didn't we?'

'Yes, you did.' Rose looked at Flynn, her eyes full of apologies. 'I'm sorry. We'll be fine on the bus.'

'Don't be daft,' her mother said. 'He just said, didn't he? We can go back to his friend's and get a nice cup of tea there, then he can take us home. He doesn't mind, do you, Flynn?'

Flynn's ears were scorching. 'Er, no. Of course not.'

'Mam, we don't even know his friend. You can't just invite yourself round.'

'Well, I like that! As if I would. It was Flynn's idea, not mine. Don't you be so ungrateful, miss. At least he cares about me health, even if me own daughter doesn't give a monkey's.'

Rose looked furious and ashamed all at once.

Flynn shook his head. 'Honestly, I'm sure it will be fine. Will you be all right for a couple of minutes, while I just get the shopping? The car's parked in the Garrison Street car park if you want to be walking up there? I'll catch you up and take you to Maurice's.'

'Oh, Flynn, you really don't have to ...' Rose's voice trailed off and she sighed. 'Thanks,' she finished, obviously having decided that she was fighting a losing battle.

They turned and began to walk away, and Flynn headed off to the fruit stall, wondering what on earth Maurice was going to make of the arrival of two total strangers on his doorstep.

****

Honestly, I could have killed my mother. I'd barely registered that Flynn was standing just in front of us, head in a book, before my mother did her pathetic swooning thing and plopped down on the ground. I could have died of embarrassment. Talk about a dying swan. How anyone who saw that believed it was genuine, I have no idea, but within seconds there was a crowd round us, and people were acting all concerned, and my mother was lying there, one hand across her forehead, like a heroine from a silent movie.

Flynn, being Flynn, was the perfect gentleman. Surely, even he wasn't naive enough to believe her cock and bull story? Still, he couldn't defeat my mother, whether he believed it, or not. She decided what she wanted, the minute he mentioned his friend, and that was it, the die was cast.

Within ten minutes, we stood in the Garrison Street Car Park beside Flynn's car, waiting for him to catch us up, my mother having made a miraculous recovery and fairly galloped down the street the minute his back was turned.

'What the hell do you think you're playing at?' I said, as we stood beside his silver Peugeot, now thankfully restored to its former glory—though, at what cost, I shuddered to think.

'I have no idea what you mean,' she said, folding her arms and glaring at me. 'And even if I did, I should think you could be a bit more grateful. I got you what you wanted, didn't I?'

'What I wanted? What are you talking about?'

She laughed. 'Don't be playing the innocent with me, miss. I know what you think of him, it's plain as day. You fancy the pants off him. I saw it the first night I met him, when you brought him to the flat—couldn't take your eyes off him. Don't try to deny it. I'm your mother, remember? There's no hiding place from my eyes.'

'You're frigging barmy,' I informed her. 'I do not fancy Flynn. He's a mate, nothing more. And of course I couldn't take my eyes off him. I was checking he was still alive! You do remember what happened that night? He could have been killed.'

'Aye, and all for your sake,' she pointed out. 'You two are made for each other. All you need is a nudge.'

'A nudge? Oh, for God's sake, Mam. I'm thirty-seven. He's forty. We hardly need people to set us up. You've got this all wrong. We're different people. There's nothing between us. It would never work.'

'Stranger things have happened,' she said. 'Are you telling me, hand on heart, that you don't fancy Flynn Piddleston-Rice?'

I swallowed. 'I swear.' Though, how I felt about Flynn Pennington-Rhys was a slightly more confusing matter.

'Hmm, we'll see,' she murmured and leaned feebly against the car as the man himself approached. 'I made it, lovey, though it was a long walk. Ooh, I'm really ready for a sit down and a cuppa.'

I could have strangled her. Flynn opened the car door and helped her into the back seat, before putting the shopping in the boot. I hesitated, wondering whether to sit beside my mother.

'You sit in the front seat, Rose,' she called, like she'd sensed my indecision. 'I don't want to be all penned in at the back, not the way I'm feeling. I need air.'

Blushing, I climbed into the front seat. Flynn slammed the boot shut and got in beside me.

He smiled weakly. 'Right, well, here goes, then.'

We left the car park and began to drive down Garrison Road.

'So, who is this friend of yours?' asked my mother. 'It was a man, you said? School friend?'

Flynn shook his head, while I stared stonily ahead of me, dreading to think what she might ask next. 'No. Maurice was my employer, when I worked at the Castle Street Practice eight years ago. I only worked with him for two years, but he was more than my boss. He was a very good friend. He and his wife used to look after me as if I were their own son. When he decided to take early retirement, I moved to Ivy House to work with Gabriel's father, but I stayed in touch with them. Then, about five years ago, Matilda died and I ... I lost touch with Maurice for a while. But I've been visiting again lately. He's a good man. I owe him a lot.'

'Aw, that's nice. What about your own mam and dad, Flynn? Do they live round here?'

'No. My mother lives in Portugal. Has done for years. My father—well, who knows? He travels a lot. Always did. They were both rather, shall we say, bohemian. I was left at my grandmother's in Surrey mostly—apart from when I was away at school, obviously.'

'Oh, obviously,' said my mother.

I could just imagine her eyes boring into the back of my head, urging me to speak, but I was too busy digesting the fact that Flynn had been more or less abandoned by his parents and shoved in a boarding school. They might have had money, but it seemed that hadn't made them any better parents. In fact, it all seemed a bit cruel to me. But then, people with money didn't seem to see boarding school that way. It seemed to be an accepted part of life. I supposed it took all sorts.

'So, does this Maurice live far away?'

'We're here now,' he informed her, sweeping the car into a neat little cul-de-sac, and pulling up outside a large semi-detached house, with a paved drive, and a front lawn that badly needed cutting. He must have seen me looking, because his face flushed a little, and he said, almost apologetically, 'I haven't got round to mowing the lawn yet. Probably next weekend.'

I wondered why it was up to him to mow the lawn, and why he was shopping, cleaning and cooking for the man. Did Flynn rush to help everyone? Was I just another on his list of charitable causes?

He collected the shopping from the boot, and we followed him up the path to the front door. He had a key, so he obviously visited regularly. He pushed open the door, and we all went inside, me and my mother standing in a large hallway, while Flynn nudged open the door on the left and popped his head into the room beyond.

'Maurice? Hope you don't mind, but I've brought some visitors. Is that okay?'

'Visitors? Why, yes, of course, Flynn. Any friend of yours is a friend of mine. Bring them in.'

Flynn glanced back at us, worry in his expression. I tried to give him a reassuring smile, but my mother had barged past me and was already in the room. I rolled my eyes and followed her in, while Flynn headed through another door, which I guessed led to the kitchen.

'Maurice, is it?' My mother stood over a man, probably in his seventies, who was sitting in an armchair, looking up at her with a slightly bemused expression. Clean-shaven, he wore a pair of dark trousers and a brightly-coloured jumper. His white hair was neatly combed, and he had a big smile on his face, which was pretty bloody decent of him, considering he'd just been hijacked by a gobby woman. 'I'm Maisie, Maisie MacLean. This is my daughter, Rose. You've probably heard all about her.'

Maurice looked baffled, and I suddenly felt like it was me who was having the funny turn. Honestly, she was a nightmare. Why in God's name would he have heard of me?

'I'm sorry, I don't think I have, no,' he confirmed, and I felt strangely disappointed, which was ridiculous. 'I'm very pleased to meet you, Maisie, and you too, Rose.'

Flynn entered the room, having put the fruit and vegetables away. He seemed to be checking his friend over, and I saw the look of relief in his eyes. I wondered what he'd been expecting.

'You're looking very well, Maurice,' he said, smiling. Had he been ill, then? I supposed that explained Flynn's mission to take care of him. Hell, and here we were forcing our company upon him. How embarrassing.

'I'm feeling well, Flynn,' Maurice replied. 'I've been out this morning. Went to the newsagent's and got myself a morning paper. Lovely day out there. Was thinking I might cut the grass later on. Front garden's a disgrace. Matilda would be ashamed of me.'

Flynn looked delighted at his friend's words, and watching his face, I realised how much he cared. What an amazing man he was, I thought, always bothering about other people.

He turned to look at me, as if my thoughts had attracted his attention, and I realised I was smiling at him. I tried to temper my enthusiasm, and he looked a bit puzzled and turned back to his friend.

'So, to what do I owe this pleasure?' Maurice was asking. 'You've never brought friends here before. Is this your lady friend?' he added, nodding in my direction.

My skin burned until my face was probably as pink as my hair. Flynn gulped, and my mother let out a hearty laugh.

'Well, she's his friend, though how much of a lady she is, is debatable, Maurice. We all live in the same village, and my granddaughter works for Flynn. Have you ever been to Kearton Bay, Maurice?'

'Oh, not for some years now. I expect it's changed quite a bit since I was last there.'

'I doubt it. Never changes, that place. Still dull as ditch water.'

'I was rather fond of the place,' he mused. 'Used to visit it when I was courting. And Whitby, of course.'

'Oh, aye. Whitby's another matter. Got amusements there, at least, and that *Dracula Experience.* My God. Have you ever been round that, Maurice?'

He shook his head. 'No, I can't say I have. What is it?'

'Name of God! It's enough to put the wind up your sails. I nearly shit meself, honestly. You'll have to go one day, unless you've got a dodgy ticker. Have you got a dodgy ticker, Maurice?'

I held my breath, praying that his heart was just fine. If he'd been ill because of heart problems, I'd kill my mother with my own bare hands.

Maurice considered for a moment. 'Not dodgy, Maisie, no. Bit battered and bruised, but not dodgy.'

'Aye, well, we've all been there. Lost your wife, didn't you? I know how you feel, pet. I lost me husband. Tragic day. Tragic.'

'Really?' Maurice leaned forward, his eyes all sympathy. 'When was that?'

'Ooh, nigh on twelve years ago now. And there's not a day goes by when I don't pine for him,' she added, apparently forgetting all about her recent nights of passion with Alec Thoroughgood, and her assertion that she'd never been shagged like that by anybody before in her whole life.

Flynn cleared his throat. 'I'll make that cup of tea I promised you, Mrs MacLean. Would anyone else like one?'

'I'd love one,' Maurice said, and I nodded as it didn't look like I was going anywhere soon.

'Do you need any help?' I asked, but he shook his head.

'I'm fine. You stay here and have a chat.'

I tried to ignore the feeling of disappointment and concentrate on my mother, who was telling Maurice all about the funeral she'd given my father, and how he was the love of her life, and how lucky she was to have met him so young and have so many blissful years with him. I thought about the Michael Caine impressionist and wondered if she'd forgotten all about him, or was she just a consummate liar?

Maurice seemed totally spellbound by her, as she gabbled on, practically telling him her life story, while I sat cringing as she effed and cursed her way through the ups and downs of her life. God, she swore a lot. I wondered why I hadn't noticed before. It was excruciating to listen to her.

Flynn brought us the cups of tea, and we all sat there, making conversation like the civilised people we were. I say *making conversation*, but really I meant listening to my mother yakking on, while Maurice chipped in occasionally, and Flynn and I sat in uncomfortable silence. At least, it was uncomfortable for me, but when I sneaked a glance at Flynn, he looked positively delighted. His eyes were shining as he watched Maurice with undisguised joy. What a funny bloke he was.

Eventually, Maurice seemed to remember that we were in the room, too, and turned to me, his eyes crinkled in a smile. 'So, how about you, Rose? What do you do for a living?'

'Works in a shop,' my mother informed him, taking a sip of her tea and smacking her lips together appreciatively. 'Smashing cuppa that, Flynn,' she said with a wink. 'You'll make someone a lovely husband one day.'

'What kind of shop?' asked Maurice.

'A sweet shop,' said my mother.

I glared at her. 'Actually, it's a gourmet marshmallow shop, and I don't just work in it. I'm a partner in it, as a matter of fact, and very successful it is, too, for your information.'

My mother took another sip of tea. 'She used to run a café, but she went bust. Not surprising really. It was crap. You should have seen the way the place was decorated. Enough to bring on a bilious attack with all that pink. Still …' She looked at me grudgingly. '… she's doing well now. I'll give her that.'

'Jeez, thanks,' I muttered.

'Well, lucky for her, she met a friend with money, who went into partnership with her and bailed her out. Hopefully, things won't go tits up this time,' she added, as if not wanting to make me feel too good about myself.

'Rose runs Mallow Magic with Gabriel's wife, Eliza,' Flynn chipped in. 'It's one of the most successful businesses in the village. Not many stay open through the winter months, but they manage it. Not surprising, really. Their marshmallows are absolutely delicious.'

I wasn't aware that he'd ever tasted one, and even if he had, I didn't make them. That was all down to Eliza and Chrissie. However, I realised he was trying to help, and I was grateful, even if it did mean that, yet again, he was seeing me as someone who needed rescuing.

My mother winked at Maurice. 'Always sees the best in her, doesn't he? I dunno. Not many true friends like Flynn, eh?'

Maurice shook his head. 'Very true, Maisie, very true. Always was a good, kind man. Don't know where I'd be without him.'

'Oh, I can imagine. I'm very fond of him. Did I tell you about the time he came to me rescue? I was surrounded by thugs and vandals, and our Rose butted in, but of course she made it all worse. God knows what would have happened if he hadn't been there. He saved us. Proper hero. Got a punch in the face and a vandalised car for his trouble, an' all. By, I'd be proud to have a son like that, Maurice.'

'Absolutely. Matilda and I never had children, Maisie. But if we had, I'd have loved to have a son like Flynn. Or indeed a daughter, like the lovely Rose, here.'

Flynn and I were both scarlet by this time and were both shrinking into the sofa like it could make us disappear. I wondered if he was feeling about twelve, too. Really, was there anything more embarrassing than grownups discussing their kids? They'd be asking us how we were getting on at school next. One thing was for sure, the next time my mother wanted a mother-and-daughter day in town, she could bloody well whistle for it.

****

I'd had an awful day. The shop had been hectic, and we'd

been rushed off our feet. The last thing we'd needed was a phone call to say Cerise had been in trouble at school for fighting.

My mother was nowhere to be found and didn't answer her phone, so I had no choice but to leave Eliza and Chrissie to cope. Livid, I'd waited ages for the bus into Helmston, then had to go into the school to grovel to an irate headmaster, as well as a furious parent, whose child had boasted a split lip and grazed cheek, thanks to Cerise's handiwork. Cerise also had battle scars, but the headmaster assured me they were done in self-defence.

'The art teacher saw it all. Cerise just flew at her. It was totally out of the blue. I must say I'm very disappointed in her. So unlike her.'

Cerise refused to apologise. 'Taking the piss out of me,' she muttered. 'Deserved everything she got.'

'You can't just hit someone,' I raged. 'If she was taking the piss out of you, take the piss back. Don't thump her, for God's sake. You'll end up being expelled, at this rate. What was she saying, anyway?'

'Nothing.'

'Nothing? So, you hit her for nothing? Way to go, Cerise. It's all I bloody need, isn't it?' I noted the bruise on her cheek and the scratches on her neck, totally bewildered by her attitude. It was so unlike Cerise. What on earth was going on?

My mother, when she arrived home, inspected my daughter's face and tutted. 'Taking after your mother, then?'

'Meaning what? When did I ever get into a fight at school?'

'You've got a short memory. You were fighting just a few weeks ago. Turned up at the hospital with a black eye, remember?'

'That was at the wedding. Some nutter wanting to catch the bouquet. I told you.'

'That's your story. And then you were scrapping again with that gang, and you roped poor Finn into it.'

'I was defending his car. And it's Flynn. Not Finn.'

She shrugged. 'Whatever. All I can say is, the apple doesn't fall far from the tree. You can't blame her when you're setting her such a bad example.'

'And where did I learn it from, then?' I demanded.

She didn't miss a beat. 'Bad genes, from your father's side,' she told me, sweeping past me into the bedroom and shutting the door with a bang.

When Fuchsia came home at twenty-past six, I'd already worked myself up into a state and was in no mood for her sullen behaviour. When she informed me that she didn't want the tea I'd cooked for her because "liver is rank", I snapped. I tipped the whole lot in the bin and told her she could starve to death, for all I cared, and it was all thanks to her moody behaviour that Cerise was turning into a delinquent.

'My behaviour? Have you seen how you carry on when you've had a few? And, anyway, what's Cerise done? Got a B for her homework instead of an A-plus?'

'She's been in a fight.' I could hardly believe I was saying those words, and Fuchsia turned to her sister, looking stunned.

'You've been fighting? You? Who with?'

'What does that matter? The point is I had to go to school and grovel to the headmaster and she's well and truly blotted her copybook. She's turning into you, and that's all I flaming need, isn't it?'

'Oh, well, thanks. So Cerise starts scrapping, and it's all my fault? Jog on.'

My mother stabbed a piece of liver with a fork. 'I think the simple truth is you're a dysfunctional family. You see them all the time on Feldane. It's because you've got no man in your lives. You need a bloke to keep order, and that's a fact.'

'Don't you dare,' I murmured, feeling the familiar churning of guilt and sadness and anger whenever someone pointed out that, as I was a single mother, my children had been somehow deprived.

She shook her head, waving her fork in the air. 'It's true. You can try to be modern and independent, all you like, but the truth is, kids need two parents. You can't say we didn't warn you. Me and your dad told you to stick with Bazza, but you weren't interested. Where would you have been, if it wasn't for us? And then to go and make the same mistake twice. I mean, that's just stupidity.'

Cerise and Fuchsia glared at her. 'Thanks, Gran,' said Cerise. 'So, we were mistakes?'

She chewed on the liver and considered. 'Well, maybe not so much you. But the men she picked to father you, definitely. I mean, where are they now? Where have they been all your lives?' She gave a big sigh and glanced around the flat. 'Your mam's done her best on her own, I suppose, but really, she should have been at home, bringing you up properly, while your father went out to work and looked after the finances. That's how it works best, you know. Your mam never wanted to stay in and take care of you. Even when she had Fuchsia, she couldn't wait to get back to work on that flaming market stall, leaving me to look after the baby. Not that I minded. It was for the best. God knows what she'd have done if she'd been left all alone with the poor little mite.'

I slammed my fork down on my plate and put my head in my hands. 'Thanks, Mam.'

'I'm not saying it was all your fault. You picked a bad 'un. But then, you didn't really think it through, did you? You should have been more careful. Me and your dad just couldn't understand why you went back to work so quickly. Your place was with your baby. It wasn't decent.'

'I went back to work because I needed to start saving money, so that Fuchsia and I could get our own place.'

'There was no need. We had room in the flat.'

'It was a two-bedroomed flat.'

'And the council would have re-housed you, eventually.'

'Yes. On Feldane! I wanted out of there. I wanted Fuchsia

brought up somewhere better, somewhere she'd have a chance of a decent upbringing.'

My mother laughed. 'Well, that worked out well, didn't it? One can barely hold down a job, and the other nearly got expelled for fighting. Well done.'

'Grandma, you can be a proper bitch,' said Fuchsia. She pushed her chair back and stood up.

Cerise looked up at her. 'Are you going out?'

'No. Just to my room to watch telly.'

'I'll come with you.'

We all stared at her. Since when had Cerise ever wanted to spend time with Fuchsia?

Fuchsia shrugged after a moment. 'Okay. If you like.'

They headed into the bedroom, and my mother and I turned to each other.

'Well,' said my mother, leaning back in her chair and giving me a smug grin. 'There you go.'

'What?'

'Left all this to us again.' She waved at the dirty dishes on the table. 'And what's worse, they've ganged up. They're a team now. God help us all.'

I tried not to show any emotion as I stood and scraped the remains of everyone's meals onto one plate, but my mind was whirling. Cerise had never shown any interest in her big sister before. What had she been fighting about? And why did she want to spend an evening in Fuchsia's company suddenly? Was she going the same way? Was I going to end up with two moody, sullen girls under my roof, as well as my smug, gobby mother?

I carried the plates into the kitchen, feeling that if something didn't happen soon, I'd pack my bags and clear off, leaving all three of them to it.

CHAPTER THIRTEEN

Meggie was eating a fig roll when Flynn walked into the office that morning, a thoughtful expression on her face. Flynn wondered if she was even aware that she was eating, or if it was an automatic response to arriving at work.

'Morning, Meggie,' he said, putting down his bag and looking round cautiously. 'Any sign of Fuchsia?'

Meggie gave him a wary look. 'She's just gone to the loo. You want a cuppa?'

'It's okay, I'll make it. Do you want one?'

'Aye, go on, then. You've twisted my arm.' She smiled, but there wasn't the same sparkle in her eyes that usually greeted him.

'What is it? What's wrong?'

'Did I say there was anything wrong?'

'You didn't have to. I know you well enough by now. What's happened?'

Meggie put down her fig roll. 'I'm worried about that little lass. There's something wrong, I'm telling you. She's not given me any lip for ages, and I had a go at her this morning for not locking the prescriptions away last night, and she didn't kick off at all. Just muttered she was sorry and went to the loo. That's not Fuchsia, is it? And I don't care what Dr Bailey says, she's not eating properly. The weight's dropping off her. Why hasn't anyone else noticed?'

Flynn frowned. 'Maybe it's as Gabriel says. She's got a bit of a crush on Sophie's son, hasn't she? You remember what that's like, surely? Unrequited love.' He sighed. 'I wouldn't worry too much, Meggie. It's a teenage thing.'

'But she's twenty,' Meggie pointed out. 'Fine, though, I'll shut up. You're the doctor, after all.'

She resumed eating her fig roll and began tapping on her computer keyboard, her lips pursed. He'd obviously insulted her. Oh, well, a cup of tea would put her in a better mood.

He headed out to the kitchen at the back of the building, passing the toilets as he went. As he neared the kitchen door, his steps slowed, and, cautiously, he turned round and went back to the toilets. Feeling rather embarrassed, he pressed his ear to the door and listened. He was sure he'd heard it. There it was again, and it was unmistakable. Someone was crying. At this time of the morning, there were no patients around, and the cleaners had long gone. It could only be Fuchsia.

He looked towards the kitchen. Should he just pretend he'd heard nothing? But then it came again, a heart-rending sob. He couldn't ignore that. How could anyone?

Gently, he tapped on the toilet door and pushed it open, praying that she was decent and that there was no one else in there with her. How the hell could he justify himself? His ears burning, he stepped inside the room and saw her standing by the washbasin, dabbing furiously at her eyes with a paper towel.

'Fuchsia?'

'I'm not late. I got here at five-to. Ask Meggie.'

'I'm not bothered about that. You were crying. What's wrong?'

She shook her head and straightened up. 'Nothing. I'm fine. Right as rain. Sorry, I'll get back to work.'

He stared into her grey eyes, so like Rose's, but wet with tears, and his heart ached. 'You're not fine. Is there anything I can do to help?'

She looked terrified. 'No. Honest, I'm okay. Just being daft.'

'Fuchsia, I may be your employer, but I'm always here, if you need to talk, you know? Anything at all, any time. I hate to see you so unhappy. Is it the job? Are you really miserable here? I know your mother kind of rail-roaded you into it, but she was just trying to help. You know that, don't you?'

She said nothing, staring at him like a wounded animal.

He felt totally helpless. 'Would you like a cup of tea? I'm

just about to make one.' What a banal remark, but he couldn't think of anything else to say, and at least it was something.

She gave him a weak smile. 'Meggie always says there's nothing you can't solve with a cup of tea. If only, eh?' Her voice caught, and he found himself putting his arm round her as she gave way to a fresh round of sobbing.

'Fuchsia, please, what is it? Please let me try to help.'

'You can't help. No one can. It's just one of those bloody cruel twists of fate.'

A sudden thought occurred to him, and he swallowed. 'Fuchsia, you're not—you're not pregnant, are you? Because if you are, well, it's not the end of the world. There are worse things to find on your doorstep than a baby.' He gave a feeble laugh. 'I'm sure there are plenty of people who would help you—not least your mother.'

She shook her head. 'I'm not pregnant. Far from it.'

He looked puzzled, and she gave a bitter laugh. 'It's all right. I'll be okay. And you needn't worry about me getting pregnant. That's never going to happen.'

Bless her. So Oliver had given her the brush-off. Well, it happened to everyone. She would have to get over it. She seemed to have taken it very hard, though, and now that he thought about it, Meggie was right. She had lost weight. He could feel her bones beneath his arm, and her face looked sunken. And she didn't answer back these days, either. She'd lost her spark. He thought about Maurice, and how thin and quiet he'd been that first night when he'd visited. Why hadn't he seen what was happening? Fuchsia was depressed. Rose had said something about her always sleeping—another symptom. Some doctor he was.

'If you need any help, you only have to ask. Would you like to make an appointment to discuss things? Maybe you'd consider counselling? I could refer you—'

'I don't need that.' Fuchsia moved away from him. 'Honest. Thanks, but I'll be okay. Best get back to work. Thank you.

Sorry.'

She shot out of the room and left him standing there feeling like a total failure. But what could he do if she wouldn't confide in him? Then it came to him. He could talk to Rose, see if she could get her to open up a little about how she was feeling. It wouldn't be breaking any confidentiality rules. Fuchsia hadn't come to him as a patient. He was just asking as a friend. And he wasn't telling her anything other people hadn't picked up on. He couldn't if he'd wanted to, as he had no idea what was going on.

Yes, he would speak to Rose. She would surely be able to get through to her daughter.

****

It was a lovely afternoon. Rhiannon and I sat at one of the tables outside The Hare and Moon, gazing out over the sea, feeling the sun on our backs, listening to the hum of conversation from the sands below and the occasional cry of a seagull swooping overhead. Farther up the sands, Eddie and Tally were hoisting young children onto the backs of Eddie's donkeys. He had about eight donkeys and kept them at Whisperwood Farm, Joe's home. Usually, Eddie worked alone, but Tally was home for the holidays, and he could always rely on her to give him a hand if he needed it. Tally was animal mad and spent most of her time at the stables, helping Georgia out.

'Do you know, it seems only five minutes ago that was Lexi working with Eddie.' Rhiannon sighed, having obviously been watching, too. 'Time goes so fast. So much has happened in the last couple of years.'

'You're not kidding,' I said. 'This time two years ago, I was struggling to keep Pinky's afloat, Lexi and Gabriel were living with Sophie, Gabriel was making rabbit hutches for a living, and Fuchsia was miserable, sulky and trying to avoid work.

Oh, scrap that one. No change at all.'

She laughed and sat up straighter, taking a sip of orange juice and eyeing me thoughtfully. 'She has made progress, Rose. She's got a steady job now, for one thing.'

'Yeah, if she manages to hang onto it.' I said. 'Let's not talk about Fuchsia. It's Sunday, and I'm trying to forget all about my family for today. I just want a bit of peace, and to enjoy the sunshine.'

'It is rather lovely out here. One forgets. I spend so much time inside, pulling pints and working in the kitchen, I seem to miss out on the beautiful surroundings. It's nice to sit out here occasionally and soak up the sun.'

'Yes, and the fresh air and peace.'

'I expect it's rather crowded in your flat at the moment.'

'You have no idea. My mother fills the place all by herself, and now she's got Alec oil-slick Thoroughgood round all the time—ugh. He's there now, actually. That's why I came out. I couldn't stand it. What the hell she sees in him is a mystery to me.'

'They do say love is blind.' She smiled, turning back toward the donkeys again. 'Though, I must say, it seems to be in the air at the moment. Derry's got a new girlfriend, a charming girl from Moreton Cross. Rather sweet. And there's Eliza and Gabriel trying for a baby, of course. And did you know Charlie Hope has been in touch with Joe? They're going to meet up. Eliza says Joe is rather taken with Charlie. I'm so pleased for him. It's all rather lovely.'

I eyed her curiously. 'And what about you? Who's this mystery lover, then? The one you've been seeing but insist isn't married?'

She turned back to me and took another sip of her orange juice, seeming to consider how much to tell me. I waited, my stomach suddenly fluttering as I wondered who she was going to name, and wondering, also, why it mattered so much.

'The thing is,' she said, rather regretfully, 'I think things are winding down there. It was wonderful to start with, but, well, I think I'm rather too much for him.'

'Too much for him?'

'Yes. You know what I mean, Rose. It was all jolly exciting for him at first, and he was up for anything, but now, well, I think I've exhausted him. Still, I think I've put the spark back for him, and I'm sure he'll find someone more suitable soon.'

I studied my glass for a moment, gazing at my lime and soda and wondering whether I dared ask. But I knew I would have to. I had to know.

'Was it—was it Flynn?'

She stared at me in surprise then gave a tinkling laugh. 'Good heavens, no! What on earth made you think that?'

I felt myself redden and reluctantly had to tell her what I'd noticed at the Easter party.

She shook her head in amazement. 'How odd that you'd think that. No, poor darling Flynn was rather low that night. He had … things on his mind. I was just being supportive. Fancy you noticing that. Now, why would that be, I wonder?' She smiled at me, and I sipped my drink hastily. 'I suspect you're quite drawn to Flynn.'

'Of course I'm not! That is, I do like him, as a mate. He's a nice bloke. That's all.'

'He's terribly sweet, and any woman would be lucky to have him,' she agreed.

'So, why aren't you with him, then?' I was genuinely curious. I had a feeling that if she set her cap at him, she could easily have him. What bloke could resist Rhiannon?

She shook her head. 'I'm not the right woman for Flynn. He needs someone who needs him. I don't need any man.'

'Me neither,' I said. 'That's what I keep telling everyone, but they're always trying to match-make for me. Chucking that stupid bouquet at me. What were they thinking?'

She gave a funny little smile. 'I can't imagine. Maybe they see something you don't?'

'Meaning what?' I demanded.

She seemed to hesitate, then her face lit up and she waved at someone behind me. 'Flynn, darling! How lovely to see you!'

My blood ran cold, and I felt sick. Was she winding me up? But there was a scraping of a chair, and suddenly he was sitting beside me, and Rhiannon's face was positively glowing, her eyes were dancing with delight. For someone who didn't fancy him, she sure looked pleased to see him.

I realised I was scowling and tried to switch on a smile. 'What brings you out?' I asked, attempting to sound lighthearted.

He looked at my glass, curiosity in his eyes. 'Would you like another? What are you drinking?'

'Lime and soda,' I admitted, 'but I was going to have a vodka and Coke next.'

Bloody hell, that sounded awful—like I could only afford the cheap stuff, but now he was buying I'd go for the more expensive option. Trouble was, I suddenly felt the need for alcohol. I wondered why Flynn had that effect on me.

'Oh, okay. What about you, Rhiannon? What can I get you?'

She shook her head. 'Sadly, it's time for me to get back to work. I've enjoyed my little sojourn into the sunshine, but now I have to chain myself to the bar again, or the boys will be getting awfully cross with me. I'll leave you to it.'

She beamed at me, and the two of them headed indoors, leaving me sitting there clutching my glass with white knuckles, while I wondered what it was that had brought him out all by himself. If it wasn't Rhiannon, I couldn't imagine what would drag the hermit away from his cave.

He seemed to be gone ages, and when he finally returned and handed me my glass, I felt distinctly nervous and more than a little impatient with myself. I took a large gulp of my drink and tried not to show my embarrassment, when he asked, 'Thirsty?'

I blushed and nodded. 'Er, yeah. Quite warm today, isn't it?' Good grief, was I actually discussing the weather? Shameful.

Noticing his own drink of beer, I stared from the glass to him.

He raised an eyebrow. 'What is it?'

'You're drinking beer. Since when?'

'Well, I, er, do drink occasionally. Sometimes, we need a helping hand, something to give us that extra bit of courage.'

'Why do you need courage?'

'I just meant in general. I wasn't being specific.'

'I don't think a doctor should be advocating alcohol as a confidence booster,' I said.

He was all serious immediately. 'Oh, I'm not, not at all. Just an observation, not a recommendation.'

I nodded and turned to watch the donkeys plodding up and down the sands, mainly because the sun was in my eyes and I had to squint to look at Flynn, which I suspected wasn't an attractive picture.

'Rose, I need to talk to you,' he said quietly.

I was so shocked, I forgot all about the squinting and turned back to him. What would he need to talk to me about? For some unaccountable reason, I felt my heartbeat quicken and tried to steady my breathing, as he put down his glass and seemed to be considering his next words.

'Can you shift?' I asked.

He glanced up, startled. 'Pardon?'

'I mean, can you move round the table so that I can see you? The sun's blinding me.'

'Oh, oh, I see.' He smiled and stood up, moving to the chair opposite me. 'Is that better?'

'Much.' I sat back in my chair, trying to look nonchalant, and said, 'So, what do you want to talk to me about?'

'Fuchsia.'

'Oh.' I felt the disappointment seep through my bones, and was sure I visibly slumped, as he watched me, a rather nervous expression on his face. He hadn't shaved, and the stubble was an undeniably sexy look. I gulped, and he leaned forward, obviously misunderstanding my expression.

'Please don't worry, she hasn't done anything wrong. I'm just rather concerned about her.'

'In what way?' I didn't understand what he was getting at. If she hadn't done anything wrong, what was his problem?

'The thing is, well, I rather think she may be suffering from depression.'

'Depression!' I laughed. 'What's she got to be depressed about? It's me who's got the depression.'

He considered me for a moment, a trace of frustration in his eyes. 'I mean it, Rose. I caught her crying at work on Friday. She was very distressed.'

'Crying?' I sat up, suddenly worried. 'What for?'

'She wouldn't tell me. I didn't want to break her confidence, and I wouldn't normally, but I do have a friend who suffers from depression, and I notice some of the same symptoms in Fuchsia. She's very quiet lately, and obviously tearful. We've had no cheek from her for a long time, which is quite unlike her.'

I couldn't argue with that. I tried to recall the last time she'd argued with me, and realised it was a good while ago, too. She just didn't speak much at all. In fact, I hardly saw her.

'You said that she was sleeping a lot?'

'Did I? Well, yeah, but she's a teenager. Well, near enough. That's what they do.'

'But sleeping a lot is a symptom of depression. Are you aware that she's not eating her lunch?'

No, I wasn't bloody aware. I packed her up every day. What was he talking about?

'Meggie has been checking. She finds it in the waste bin most afternoons. She's lost a lot of weight. I put my arm around her when she was crying, and I could feel her bones. Haven't you noticed?'

I shifted uncomfortably. No I hadn't, and I was suddenly feeling really awful about it. I should have done, shouldn't I? How embarrassing was that? 'I don't know what she'd be depressed about,' I said, 'apart from Oliver Crook, but surely he doesn't matter that much? I don't think they've ever been involved. I can't imagine he's had that much effect on her.'

'Have you asked her?'

I felt cornered. Who was he, anyway? What was he insinuating? That I didn't look after my own child properly? 'No, I haven't asked her. People don't always want to talk about stuff like that, especially if the bloke they fancy doesn't want to know.'

'I expect she's feeling the pressure at home, too,' he said thoughtfully.

My guard slammed up, but he seemed too busy staring into his beer, probably gathering his bullets for the next attack, to notice. 'Meaning what?'

'Well, I was just thinking how crowded it must be in your little flat, and your mother is rather, er, forceful. And she has to share a room with Cerise, doesn't she? So I expect she doesn't get much privacy, which must be quite stressful.'

Anger started gathering inside me, curling itself up into a cannonball in my stomach, ready to explode at him any moment.

'At least she's got a room,' I said through gritted teeth. 'Some of us are sleeping on a sofa. Some of us don't have any privacy at all.'

He looked up, seemingly shocked at the tone of my voice, and as his expression changed, he held up his hands. 'Oh, I know. I do see that, honestly. I feel for you. It must be so hard. When I came back that night and saw how small your living room is, and all that luggage of your mother's, and two young daughters with all the stuff they collect ... well, it must be really difficult for you all.'

Yeah, we were real charity cases. So he felt for us, did he? Well, I hardly needed his pity.

'Not everyone's lucky enough to live in a massive house all by themselves,' I said, trying to keep my voice steady, but hearing it rise in spite of my best efforts. 'I'm very sorry if our living arrangements fail to live up to your standards, but we do what we can. It's called being a family. You wouldn't know, living up there in your flaming ivory tower.'

'Rose, I'm not attacking you. I know how hard it's been, and you've done an amazing job—'

'Sounds like it. I can't provide Fuchsia with her own bedroom. I can't provide one for myself either, but why? Because I'm providing shelter for my mother, the way people do for their families. And if I didn't notice that Fuchsia had lost weight, maybe that's because I'm too busy working to keep the roof over our heads, the way I've done since she was born, because it's always been my job, and I've done it the best way I can.'

'I know that,' he said gently. 'I wasn't criticising. I'm just trying to help.'

'I don't need your help,' I said, my voice catching, and I swallowed, appalled to find tears in my eyes. This was mortifying. 'I get that you love playing the knight in shining armour—me, my mother, Maurice—but, if it's okay with you, I can look after Fuchsia myself.'

'I'm sorry,' he said, raking his hands through his hair and seeming totally bewildered. 'I seem to have made a bit of a mess of this. I didn't mean to offend you—'

'Well, you have,' I said. 'And if you don't mind, I'd like you to leave me alone. I came here to get away from everything and just relax for a couple of hours, and I'd appreciate it if you let me get on with it.'

He stared at me for a long moment and seemed about to say something, but he shook his head. 'As you wish,' he muttered and stood up, pushing past me as he left.

I didn't look round, but sat staring out over the sea, hot tears pricking my eyes, and cursing my temper and pride.

Why did he always see me as someone so useless, so lowly, that I needed his help, though? And why did I care, anyway? What did it matter how he saw me? He was just Fuchsia's employer, when all was said and done.

I watched the sunlight glinting on the water and felt the tears on my cheek. Rubbing them away furiously, I contemplated my daughter. What was going on with her? And, more importantly, how did I make it all better?

CHAPTER FOURTEEN

Gabriel was furious. 'She's really taking us for fools, Flynn. I know her trial's up, and she's a proper member of staff now, but even so. I think we should be thinking seriously about finding a replacement for her.'

Meggie began to protest, but Flynn beat her to it.

'We can't do that. She may be feeling really ill, for all we know.' Flynn doubted it, but he had to try. His heart had sunk when he'd arrived for work that Friday morning, to find Fuchsia hadn't turned up, and when Gabriel informed him that, according to Eliza, Rose had assumed she was at work, he felt even worse. He was running out of options with her. Gabriel would only take so much, and Fuchsia was really pushing all the buttons. What on earth was he going to do?

He and Meggie looked at each other. He hadn't confided in her about his conversation with Fuchsia in the toilets, but she wasn't stupid. She must have seen the state of the girl, when Fuchsia arrived back in the office, her eyes red with crying and her skin all blotchy.

Fuchsia had been behaving well for the last week, arriving on time, getting on with her work, no back-chat or moodiness. She rarely spoke, at all, in fact. He wondered if Rose had managed to get through to her? He wondered if she'd even tried, given her apparent impression that he was using Fuchsia to have a go at her parenting skills.

'If she was really ill, she'd be in bed,' Gabriel said. 'Rose said she went out at half-past seven, and she never said a word about feeling unwell, or not going to work, so let's face it, she's pulled a fast one. We're going to have to give her a written warning, at the very least.'

Flynn sighed. 'I suppose so. Let's hear her side of the story first, though. She may be back on Monday.'

In the event, she turned up at half-past nine, rushing in, her face flushed and her eyes bright.

'I'm ever so sorry I'm late. I overslept.'

Meggie shot her a warning glance, but she didn't appear to notice, just babbled on about her late night and how the alarm didn't go off. Flynn, who'd only gone into the office to ask Meggie if a fax had arrived from the hospital, could have throttled her. Why couldn't she just tell the truth? She was making it all ten times worse, especially as Gabriel had just come through to collect a sample bottle and was witness to her display of blatant dishonesty.

He stood, arms folded, as Fuchsia gabbled on, and Meggie covered her eyes, while Flynn gaped at Fuchsia in dismay, willing her to just stop lying and come clean.

Eventually, Fuchsia seemed to sense the atmosphere and her voice trailed off. She shrugged uncertainly. 'Oh, well, I'm here now. You can dock my wages, if you like.'

Gabriel cleared his throat. 'Fuchsia, does it ever occur to you that my wife works with your mother? And they talk? And my wife talks to me?'

Fuchsia paled. 'Have you been checking up on me?'

'I shouldn't have to, but yes, actually, I did. Not deliberately. I had to call Eliza for something else, and I happened to mention that you weren't at work and asked if you were okay. Imagine my surprise to discover that, as far as your mother knew, you were here. So, yes, we will be docking your wages, and you'll also be getting a formal warning. Do you understand?'

Fuchsia seemed to hesitate, but she nodded. 'Yeah, okay. Fair enough. Sorry.'

There was a silence, and Flynn wondered if the other two were as stunned as he was by her sudden change of mood. She looked flushed and happy, and as if nothing they said or did could really upset her. Had Rose talked to her, after all? Had she managed to get through to her? Or had something else happened?

Whatever the cause, he felt huge relief that Fuchsia seemed

to be happier. Even if she was skating on thin ice at work, at least she might start eating again and smiling now and then. That was worth more than a punctual receptionist, at least in his book.

It was half-past twelve when he went out on his first visit, having had a busy morning and grabbing a sandwich in his room the minute his consultations were over. He had a stack of paperwork to catch up on before afternoon surgery, and five visits to fit in beforehand, so he decided to head out to the Chantry farm over in Farthingdale, which was the furthest away from the surgery, and make his way inwards.

Mr Chantry had had an operation on his foot, and Flynn spent ten minutes examining him, chatting to him, and writing him out a prescription, receiving a dozen fresh eggs for his trouble, before climbing into his car and heading towards his next visit.

As he drove down Cherry Tree Lane, he slowed to pass a group of horses and riders out on a hack from the White Rose Riding School. Georgia was at the head of the group, and she smiled and waved at him, as he crawled past them, wary of frightening the horses. He nodded back and admired the beautiful horses and ponies, their coats gleaming, hooves clattering on the road. He'd ridden when he was a boy. With his grandmother's passion for the animals, he'd had little choice. He'd not been in the saddle for years, though, and he wondered vaguely if maybe he should take up riding again. At least it would get him out of the house, and it was good for fitness, too.

He drove slowly along, thinking about it, and his contemplation almost made him miss the sight of two people standing by the riding school gate, hand in hand, gazing into each other's eyes.

He wasn't sure what made him notice, really. Maybe it was the recognition of the uniform. Out of the corner of his eye, he must have seen the white blouse with the blue diamond pattern, and his brain must have flashed a message that this was a familiar thing to him, because he turned his head and gasped in shock as he registered that Fuchsia was standing there, looking so happy, so loving, so ... different.

She leaned forward, and the other person moved towards her, and their lips met in a kiss.

Flynn jerked his gaze away and stared back at the road, speeding up a little as he drove past, hoping against hope that she hadn't spotted him. How to deal with it, though? He'd been so wrong. They all had. Because Oliver Crook wasn't the object of Fuchsia's affections, at all. The person whose hands she'd been holding, and whose lips she'd been kissing, and whose eyes she'd been gazing into with such obvious love, was Oliver's twin, Pandora.

He really hadn't seen that coming, and he doubted very much that Rose had, either.

****

The afternoon flew by. The surgery was very busy, and Flynn dealt with fifteen patients, dictated two referral letters, and filled in some forms, before deciding enough was enough and it was time for home. He looked out of the window, smiling at the blue skies and realising that summer was well and truly on its way. He hated leaving work in the dark.

He thought about Maurice. Maybe they should go out for the day, one weekend. It would do them both good to spend the whole day away from home, enjoying themselves. Maybe they could visit Helmston Castle, or one of the many abbeys in the area. Maurice had always enjoyed that. Or had it been Matilda? He wasn't too sure. He would have to think about that one.

Meggie was switching off her computer as he walked into the office. 'All done?' she asked him. 'Dr Bailey's just in with that last medical. He said I can get off. He'll lock up.'

Flynn looked across at Fuchsia, who was logging some prescriptions into the chemist's folder. They always wrote the name, date of birth, and number of items prescribed, for every patient who had a prescription that was collected by the chemist's driver, who had to sign for them. It resolved any arguments about whether the prescription had been picked up, or not, and by whom. It was a bit of a chore, but didn't usually take that long. Fuchsia seemed to be writing very slowly.

Meggie glanced over at her in surprise. 'You nearly done, love? You can finish up in 'morning if you like, only I want to get off. Me belly's giving me proper jip,' she confessed, rubbing her stomach and pulling a face.

'It's okay. I'd rather get it done now.' Fuchsia looked up at Flynn, her expression defiant.

He sighed. She'd seen him, then. 'You get off Meggie. I just have some last minute things to see to.'

'Well, if you're sure. I dunno, not very often I'm the first to leave, is it? Oh, well, I'll get off home and start on the Gaviscon. See you Sunday?'

'Sunday?' He looked at her blankly.

'Sophie's anniversary garden party? You are going? You can't back out now. Sir Paul said no, so that was a proper blow to her. And besides, don't you want to meet Charlie Hope? Joe's bringing him to meet everyone. Eliza says they're right loved up, and I, for one, want me photo taken with them both. So, you see, you have to go. You can't miss it.'

'Yes, yes, I promised I'd be there, I just forgot for a moment. See you on Sunday, Meggie.'

Meggie picked up her bag and left, and Flynn sat down, his gaze flicking over to Gabriel's door, but it was still firmly shut.

Fuchsia's hand shook as she wrote in the folder. She put down her pen and stared at him. 'Go on, then.'

'Go on, then, what?'

'I know you saw us. Don't play dumb. I saw your car driving by really slowly. Copping an eyeful, were you?'

Flynn was outraged. 'Certainly not! I'd slowed down because Georgia had a string of riders and horses out for a hack, and I happen to know the Highway Code, as well as having a bit of common sense. Honestly, Fuchsia, you do say some things.'

She blushed. 'Sorry. Are you gonna tell my mam?'

'I hardly think it's my place to do that. So, you were never interested in Oliver Crook? It was always Pandora?'

Fuchsia gaped at him. 'Oliver Crook? Who the fuck told you I liked him?'

'Well ...' He shrugged. 'Not sure. It was common knowledge. Obviously a misunderstanding.'

'You're not kidding. Oliver's a proper tosser. He fell out with Pan because she's quitting uni and starting work with Georgia. Imagine what he'd say if he found out about us?'

'So, he doesn't know? Does anyone?'

Fuchsia shook her head. 'Not really. Tally, obviously, and Cerise—thanks to someone at school who found out and started taking the piss. Cerise walloped her and got in bother, but then she asked me if it was true. She'd got in trouble, so I couldn't lie to her, could I? She promised not to say anything.'

'Have you been together long?'

'On and off for a year.'

'A year? So, why is it a secret?'

She stared at him. 'Well, why do you think? It's not easy to admit that you're different, especially in a place like this.'

'I shouldn't think anyone would care in the slightest. It's the twenty-first century. People don't bother about such things these days.'

She gave a bitter laugh. 'That's all you know. You have no idea how bad it was at my last job. Some knobhead saw us in Helmston one lunchtime, and it was soon all over the office. You should have heard them. You'd have thought I had leprosy, the way they looked at me, and the comments they made .... God. I couldn't face it. Stopped going in in the end, and finished up getting the sack.'

'I see. Well, that's their wrongdoing, not yours. Why haven't you even told your mother? She's not going to be like those people, I'm sure.'

Fuchsia shrugged. 'I dunno. I suppose, partly, I don't want to see the look of disappointment in her face. And then there's the main thing. Sophie.'

'Ah.' Flynn considered. It might well be quite a shock for Sophie, but even so, he couldn't see her turning against her own daughter. 'I think you'll be surprised. Once she accepts it, I think she'll be fine.'

'Pan won't hear of telling her.' Her lip trembled and her eyes filled with tears. 'You just don't get it.'

'What don't I get?' Flynn's voice was gentle. It was obviously all still very raw for her.

'Do you know how many times Pan's broken it off? Kept trying to kid herself that she's straight? Dumping me for stupid lads at university? It's taken all this time for her to accept she's gay and admit that she wants to be with me. When she told me this morning, I was so happy. She rang me at seven, said she wanted to see me. She was at the stables. Took me ages to walk there, but I had to go, didn't I? Had to see what she wanted. Sorry I was late for work, but I couldn't not see her. That's when she told me she'd finally accepted it and wanted us to be together properly. I was over the moon. But when I went back at lunchtime to see her, she was still adamant that she wouldn't tell her mum and dad. Said they wouldn't approve. Approve of what? Her being gay? Or me?'

'You? Why on earth wouldn't they approve of you?'

'Well, look at me.'

Flynn only saw a pretty, courageous young girl, who'd been dealing all alone with a very emotional time in her life, coping with uncertainty and heartbreak, and even bullying, without confiding in anyone. She was more than worthy of Pandora. 'I am looking, and I don't see why on earth you think they wouldn't approve of you. You're a lovely girl, Fuchsia. You just have to believe in yourself.'

'Yeah, right. I'm hardly social worker or solicitor material, am I?'

'Neither was Sophie. You do know she met Archie because she was his secretary?'

Fuchsia's eyes widened. 'Was she?'

'Not even that, actually. She was a typist at the law firm where he worked. He fell for her just the same.'

Fuchsia considered. 'Well, yeah, but her dad's a doctor.'

'What on earth does that have to do with it?'

'Posh, aren't they? And look at me. I wouldn't even know which fork to use if we went anywhere classy, never mind anything about wine, or any of that stuff.'

Flynn laughed. 'Oh, Fuchsia, as if any of that matters! If you and Pandora love each other, that's all that counts. Sophie and Archie would be fine with it. You're seriously underestimating them. They're good people, and all they want is for their daughter to be happy. I'm sure your mother will be just the same. I think, if anything, she'll be relieved to know that you've met someone you care about and that you've cheered up a bit.'

'You can't tell her.'

'Of course not, but you should.'

'You know my mother. She'll be round to tell Sophie before I've closed my mouth. No way. Pandora would kill me, and she'd finish with me, for sure. I have to let her do this in her own time, do you understand? I can't frighten her off again.'

'All right, calm down,' Flynn said, aware that her voice was full of panic and she was staring at him with saucer-like eyes.

Gabriel's door opened, and he walked out of the room, accompanied by the taxi driver who had come for his medical. 'Everything okay here?'

The taxi driver looked at them curiously through the open door, before shaking Gabriel's hand and heading down the corridor and out of the building.

Gabriel looked at them both, his eyes full of suspicion. 'What now?'

'Nothing, nothing. We were just chatting.'

'Sounded a bit loud for a chat. What's going on? What have you done now, Fuchsia?'

Flynn shook his head. 'It was my fault. I thought she'd made an error in the logging, but I'd made a mistake. She was quite right. Are you done here, Fuchsia? You can get off now, if you like, and I'll put everything away.'

'Are you sure?' Her voice seemed small, her expression sheepish.

He smiled. 'Quite sure. Call it an apology, eh?'

She gave him a grateful look and collected her bag, giving a brief nod towards Gabriel and heading out of the office.

'Are you quite sure everything's okay?' Gabriel sounded doubtful.

Flynn didn't answer. He gathered up the folders and busied himself locking everything away for the weekend. He'd no idea what to tell Gabriel. He thought things were quite a long way from being okay.

CHAPTER FIFTEEN

The sun shone for Sophie's garden party that Sunday, which was a good job, as we'd never have fitted into her house. She'd invited what appeared to be the entire population of Kearton Bay and was in her element, showing people round her home, which was her pride and joy, and informing anyone who'd listen that Joe Hollingsworth would be in attendance, and he was bringing a very special guest.

'Is he really bringing Charlie?' I whispered to Eliza, and she nodded, her eyes shining. 'Yes. Isn't it exciting? They've really hit it off. Joe's never off that phone lately. It's so lovely to see him so happy.'

'So, he could be moving back to London, then?'

Her smile dropped. 'Oh, no, he wouldn't do that. Would he? I don't think so. I mean, he loves it up here, and London's so far away …'

'I dunno, Eliza,' I said, sipping my orange juice. 'Love makes fools of us all.'

She gave me a sympathetic hug, and I shrugged. I'd admitted to her what an idiot I'd been around Flynn the previous week, and she'd assured me that Flynn would understand. I didn't think so. I reckoned he must think I was a complete head-case, and he wouldn't be far wrong. I'd been adamant that I wasn't going to attend the garden party, but Eliza and Gabriel seemed certain that Flynn wouldn't go. Given his loathing of social events, I guessed they were right, and when my mother announced she wouldn't be attending, as she was going up to Redcar to meet Alec's friends, I decided that it suddenly sounded a lot more attractive. Better than moping around the flat all day, anyway.

Cerise decided to go with me, but Fuchsia said she was going out. When I asked her who with, she'd said, 'Just friends.'

I nearly keeled over. Fuchsia had friends? Wonders would

never cease. Still, it made me feel a bit easier about leaving her, and I decided to forget all about my worries, stuff my face with food that would definitely not be recommended by Lightweights, and have a bloody good time.

Archie was barely visible when we neared the barbecue, so many people were milling around, helping themselves to steaks, prawns, burgers, sausages and chicken breasts, as soon as they were ready.

Meggie was desperately trying to avoid Sophie, who was on a mission and had decided that she wanted one of her members to be the Lightweights Slimmer of the Year. Meggie, by far the largest of us, was her prime candidate.

Meggie, who had been attending the club for years without losing so much as a stone, thought differently. 'I can't just have rabbit food,' she wailed. 'Even the quiche is full of fat.'

'Now, Meggie darling,' said Sophie, 'think how you'll feel when you win that title. There's a five hundred pounds prize, you know, and we'll get to go to the event in London. Very swanky hotel, and there's usually a celebrity presenting the award. Imagine that!'

'Do you think I give a monkey's?' Meggie demanded.

'Well, even if you don't, you should think about your health. You're not getting any younger. It's time you followed the Lightweights plan seriously. No arguments.'

Meggie caught Ben's eye, and the panic in hers seemed to communicate itself to him. 'She can have some steak, can't she?' he asked.

'Can I?' Meggie seemed bewildered. Lack of food was obviously making her feel quite faint and disorientated.

'Meggie, this is best quality meat, none of your cheap rubbish,' Sophie said. 'You can have a steak. They're nice and lean, not fatty, like some. You could have just one with some salad. Just don't go eating too much. Stop when you're full, for a change.'

Meggie took her plate gratefully, and we headed away

from Sophie as fast as we could, taking refuge on the garden bench, while Ben wandered indoors to get a beer.

'Are you going to stick to the diet, then?'

Meggie sighed. 'Doubt I'll have much choice. Sophie's determined I'm going to be Slimmer of the Year. Imagine, no more marshmallows.'

'Jesus, Meggie.' I gasped. 'We'll go out of business.'

She nudged me, and I laughed, looking up in delight as Eliza and Lexi approached, with Joe and Charlie Hope. In real life, Charlie was shorter than he appeared on television and not quite as plump. He had a round, cheery face and thinning hair, and looked older than his thirty-seven years, until he laughed, at which point the years just seemed to fall away from him. He and Joe were laughing then at some joke. They obviously found each other hilarious. The hours must just fly by with those two.

'Rose, Meggie, this is Charlie,' said Eliza.

Charlie stopped laughing and held out his hand for me to shake. 'Pleased to meet you, love. Heard a lot about you. Eliza's business partner, right?'

'And best friend,' I informed him.

'And Meggie is also our friend,' said Eliza, 'and she works for Gabriel and his partner, Flynn.'

'Are they bossy?' asked Charlie with some sympathy. 'Doctors always strike me as bossy. Do they order you around and throw strops, like that horrible one on the telly?'

Meggie laughed. 'Definitely not. They'd get a clip round the earhole if they tried. I'm very lucky, they're both lovely.'

I felt a sudden sadness. She was quite right, they were both lovely. And I'd been so horrible to poor Flynn. He'd never speak to me again. If only he didn't see me as some charity case.

'So, what do you think to Yorkshire, Charlie?' Lexi asked.

'Not what I expected,' he admitted. 'Thought you'd all be wearing flat caps, and that you'd make me eat bread and dripping.'

Lexi laughed. 'Typical southern prejudice. All you lot are poncy know-it-alls who believe all that stereotypical rubbish,' she said, oblivious to the irony of her comment.

'You forget, Lexi,' I said, 'even you lot are poncy southerners to me.'

Eliza laughed. 'You only come from Oddborough! It's barely thirty miles away.'

'That's thirty miles *north* of here,' I pointed out. 'You all sound foreign to me.'

'Are you a Geordie?' Charlie looked thrilled. 'Do you know Ant and Dec?'

'No, I'm not a bloody Geordie,' I said. 'And don't mention those two in front of Joe. They've beaten him to the *TV Quick* awards every sodding year.'

Charlie grinned. 'Aw, they're lovely boys. Can never understand a single word they're saying to me, but they're cute. Anyway, thanks for the tipoff, Rose. And now I've seen for myself that you can get electricity past Watford, and I won't have to wear clogs, I may come up here a bit more often.'

'Really?' Eliza looked delighted.

'Well, I've got a reason to now, haven't I?' he said, nudging Joe, who blushed and looked distinctly embarrassed. 'I thought I could persuade him to come back to the bright lights of London, but he ain't having it. They'd bite his hand off, if he wanted to go back to work, but he's not interested, are you, Joe?'

'No,' said Joe. 'I've done all I wanted to do. It wasn't fun anymore. There's only so long you can go on at that pace before it burns you out. I'm happy at home now, with my writing.'

'Don't you get lonely?'

Joe laughed. 'Lonely? Most of my family and friends are up here, not to mention Jeeves and Wooster.'

'Micro pigs, I ask you.' Charlie shook his head. 'Ain't you ever gonna get another dog? Thought you would have replaced Bertie by now.' Bertie was Joe's little dog, who had died some years ago. He'd been almost as famous as Joe, although, surprisingly, the micro pigs had got more fan mail than either he or Joe had.

'I think I will soon,' said Joe. 'I'd like to get a dog again, and I want some pigs, too, and maybe a couple of sheep. But I have to get this book out there first. It will demand my full attention, so it's better to wait for now. Who knows, one day you may want a quieter life yourself, when the joys of showbiz start to fade.'

'Yeah, well, when that time comes, I'll be well out of it,' said Charlie. 'You'll never see me in the jungle with them two who shall not be named, or ballroom bloody dancing.'

'Jesus, I should hope not.' Joe shuddered.

Lexi plonked herself down on the bench next to me and took a sip of her drink.

'Is Robbie not with you?' asked Meggie.

Lexi shook her head. 'Nah, gone fishing with some of his mates.'

'You don't seem too upset about it,' I remarked.

'Why should I be? We're not joined at the hip.'

'Who's Robbie?' demanded Charlie.

'Lexi's boyfriend,' said Eliza.

Lexi spluttered into her glass. 'Hardly! We go out sometimes and—well, you know. It's a laugh, that's all.'

'Bet he's flattered,' said Charlie.

'Not true love, then?' Joe grinned.

Lexi shook her head. 'Who needs true love? You're better off keeping it casual, and that's a fact. Love leads to heartbreak and bitterness.'

'How old's this girl again?' said Charlie. 'Blimey. Who broke your heart?'

I looked at Eliza. 'I think we've all had our hearts broken

at some point,' she said. 'I know I have.'

'But look at you now,' said Joe.

'And look at you.' She grinned.

'What about you, Charlie?' I said. 'Have you ever had your heart broken?'

'Only twice,' said Charlie. 'I wrote to Chesney Hawkes asking him if I could be his one and only, and the bastard never wrote back.'

'Good God, how old were you?' asked Joe.

'Fourteen or fifteen,' Charlie said.

'Blimey,' I said. 'What was the other time?'

'Back in primary school.' He smirked. 'I wanted to play Mary in the Nativity play, and for some reason, the teacher had a problem with that. It took two visits to the headmaster's study and a letter from my doctor before I got my own way.'

We laughed, and I pictured a miniature Charlie sitting angelically on stage, dressed in a blue robe clutching a doll to his chest.

'Don't laugh,' said Charlie in mock outrage. 'My Mary was the talk of the school.'

'I'll bet,' said Joe, mopping his eyes yet again. 'Come on, we'd better go and mingle. Sophie will be up in arms if we don't introduce ourselves to every single one of her guests.'

They wandered off, still laughing, and Eliza hugged herself in delight. 'They're made for each other, aren't they? I'm so happy. I must go and find Gabriel and Amy,' she added, before rushing off.

Lexi finished her drink and stood up. 'Think I'll go and see how Will's doing,' she said.

'Will's here?'

'Yeah, thought he'd escape the hall for a couple of hours. Sir Paul's in a rage about something, or other, so he decided he was better off getting out of the way.'

'Poor thing,' I said. 'He's such a lovely bloke. Will, I mean, not Sir Paul. He's a twat.'

She laughed. 'Yeah, that's one way of putting it. See you later, guys.'

Meggie looked dolefully at her plate. 'I never even noticed I'd eaten that. I'd kill for some garlic bread. How am I going to get through this awful diet, Rose?'

I sighed. 'Never mind, Meggie. Things could be worse. You could be me.' I chewed rather despondently on a prawn, but my eyes widened in horror when I spotted Flynn near the barbecue, deep in conversation with Archie and Ben.

Oh, hell, that was all I needed.

Meggie followed my gaze and looked at me curiously. 'You okay, Rose?' she asked, although I should have thought it was bloody obvious that I wasn't.

What was he doing here? He'd spent years rarely leaving his house, and he was getting far too good at this socialising business, if you asked me. I wasn't safe anywhere. I needed a drink. A proper drink. Stuff this orange juice lark.

'I won't be long, Meggie,' I said. 'Just going to get a drink. Be back soon.'

****

For some mystifying reason, Cerise was furious with me.

'You're pissed,' she raged. 'How could you do that? I'm so embarrassed. We're going home, right this minute.'

'Do you blame me?' I spluttered. 'Christ, Cerise, give me one day off. Do you have any idea what I'm going through?'

'What you're going through? Like what?'

'Are you kidding me?' I asked, outraged. 'My mother's got my bed, and I'm dossing on the sofa, and have you seen that oily monstrosity she's dating? I mean, come on. And then there's Fuchsia …'

'What about Fuchsia?' Her eyes narrowed. 'What's wrong with Fuchsia?'

'What's bloody right with Fuchsia?' I said.

'I hope you're joking,' she said.

'What do you mean?'

'What do *you* mean?'

'Eh? What do you think I mean? She's a moody little madam, and God knows how long she'll hold down that job and—'

'Oh, for God's sake, is that all?' she snapped.

'Is that all? Well!' I tried to glare at her, but after four glasses of vodka, it was proving a bit difficult. 'Have you any idea how worried I am, and how crap my life is right now?'

'I don't care.' Cerise grabbed my arm and pulled me towards the gate. 'We'll discuss this later. We're going home.'

'I don't want to go home,' I said, shrugging my arm free of her grasp and swaying dangerously in the process. 'I hate it there. It's a prison.'

Cerise glared at me. 'Now's not the time, or place. Why don't you ever put your brain into gear before you open your mouth?'

'Excuse me, lady. Don't talk to your mother like that. Why would I want to go home? If it's not you fighting, it's your grandma having a go at me, or Fuchsia slamming doors and being the obnoxious little madam she always is. It's all right for you lot. My life sucks.'

'You don't know anything, Mam,' Cerise said, suddenly tearful. 'Fuchsia's not the bad one you think she is. Why don't you see what's right in front of your nose?'

'Meaning what? What are you talking about? Oh, God, she's not on drugs, is she?'

'There you go again, assuming the worst. You know, you're always banging on about the way Grandma puts you down, but you do it all the time to Fuchsia. Why don't you keep your head out of the vodka bottle and take a good look around? I'm off.'

She turned and stomped through the gate, leaving me standing there with my mouth wide open. What in God's name had just happened? Why was I the bad one? I'd only had four drinks. There were a whole lot of people there who'd drank a lot more than that. It was all desperately unfair.

Hesitating, I looked around Sophie's garden. What should I do now?

I made my way, rather woozily, towards the house. Standing on the step leading into the kitchen, I swayed slightly and looked inside hazily. The doctors were there. Well, wasn't that just typical? Thank you, God, I thought. Why don't you just let the roof collapse on me and finish the job?

Well, there was no way I was leaving just because of those two. I needed to sit down. Come to think of it, I needed to sit down pretty fast. I suddenly realised I wasn't feeling too bright at all.

****

Flynn and Gabriel sat quietly at the kitchen table, discussing a patient, though Flynn secretly watched the clock, wondering how soon he could leave without appearing rude. He thought, with some relief, the time was almost upon him. Looking longingly at the door, he saw a pink-haired, glassy-eyed woman, swaying dangerously on the step, and his heart decided to perform the paso doble.

The shock must have shown in his face, because Gabriel looked around as though to see what he was staring at. 'Oh, God,' he said wearily.

Flynn leapt up and grabbed Rose's elbow, as she almost toppled backwards onto the patio. 'Not again, Rose,' he said, leading her to the table and pushing her onto a chair.

'She's drunk,' said Gabriel. 'Marvellous.'

'I'm not bloody drunk.' Rose stabbed him in the chest with her finger and turned to Flynn. 'Why are you here?'

'Charming,' said Gabriel.

'You never used to go anywhere. Now, everywhere I look, everywhere I go, there you are.'

'Well, I'm very sorry if my presence offends you,' said

Flynn, sitting down beside her. 'And I'm very sorry that I upset you last week. I really didn't intend to.'

'I know. I know.' Rose nodded furiously, and to his dismay, she burst into tears.

Gabriel and Flynn stared at each other, and Flynn wondered which of them was the most terrified. Gabriel looked around, obviously hoping Eliza would materialize from somewhere, while Rose sobbed noisily, snot pouring out of her nose and mingling with her tears.

Flynn couldn't bear it. Tentatively, he put his arm around her. Rose wailed and threw herself against him, weeping into his shirt, tears seeping into the material. His heart went out to her, and he was quite offended on her behalf when Gabriel started to laugh.

'That's right. Make fun of me.' Rose sniffled. 'Some friend you are!'

'Rose, I'm sorry.' Gabriel seemed guilt-stricken. 'I wasn't laughing at you, I promise. We're both useless at this stuff. Do you want me to find Eliza?'

'No, I don't. Sick of people having to bail me out. I can manage myself,' she said, her voice muffled against Flynn.

He patted her shoulder. 'I don't know what's wrong, Rose, but if there's anything I can do ...'

Rose wiped her nose on his shirt collar and sat up straight, rubbing her eyes and sniffing loudly.

'There you go again,' she muttered, as Flynn pulled out his handkerchief and wiped his shirt collar as best he could. 'I don't need your help. I can manage my own life perfectly well, thank you very much.'

'Of course you can, but I just thought you may need someone to talk to,' Flynn began, but Rose turned to him, her eyes flashing with anger.

'What would you know about anything?' she demanded. 'Sitting up there in your posh house, reading books and listening to your depressing music like Inspector sodding

Morse. Some of us have families, you know. Some of us have to deal with stroppy teenagers, and bitchy mothers, and creepy old men. Some of us don't get a minute's peace. What do you know about kids or family, anyway? Jesus, what a life.'

She stared into the distance for a minute, before she folded her arms on the table and dropped her head onto them in despair. The two men watched her warily for a moment, but jumped when she emitted a loud snore.

Flynn felt himself pale.

Gabriel tried to smile. 'Don't worry, she'll be fine.' He glanced around. 'We'd better take her home, I suppose. We can hardly leave her here in this state. Are you all right?'

Flynn nodded slowly, and Gabriel patted him on the shoulder. 'Don't take any notice of what she said, Flynn. She's drunk. She'll have forgotten all about it tomorrow.'

'Perhaps. What do we do?'

'Maybe I should find Eliza, see if she can give me a hand to take her home.'

'I mean about her unhappiness? What do we do about that?'

'What do you mean? What can we do? I suppose I can ask Eliza if she knows what's up with her.'

'It's so awful, seeing her like this.'

Gabriel leaned back in his chair and surveyed him through narrowed eyes. 'You seem to be taking this very personally. Any particular reason?'

'I offended her the other day.'

'It's easily done.' Gabriel sighed. 'She's not her usual self lately. I suppose she's under a lot of pressure.'

'Quite.' Flynn studied the sleeping woman beside him and fought the urge to stroke her hair. In spite of her attack on him, he'd seen the pain beneath the anger and wanted to take it away. 'I'm going to take her home now.'

'What? By yourself? Are you sure?' Gabriel sounded doubtful. 'I'm sure Eliza would help.'

Flynn nodded. 'I'm sure. I'm ready to leave, anyway. Will

you tell Sophie and Archie I had to go, and thank them for me?'

Gabriel grinned. 'Good an excuse as any to leave, I suppose. Well, if you're sure you can cope with her?'

'I'm sure.'

Flynn shook Rose carefully, and, as she stirred, he put his arms around her and began to pull her to her feet.

'What are you doing? Gerroff me!' she muttered, sounding uncannily like Fuchsia.

'I'm taking you home,' Flynn told her.

Rose opened one eye and stared at him for a moment. Then she gave a slurry laugh and threw her arms round his neck. 'Ooh, Paddington, are you really?'

Gabriel gaped at them. 'Paddington?'

'Long story,' said Flynn. 'Come on, Rose. We're going, okay?'

'Ooh, yes, it's okay with me, if it's okay with you,' Rose agreed.

Flynn steadied her and began to lead her out of the kitchen, all too aware of Gabriel's amusement. No doubt he hadn't heard the last of this.

It took at least twice as long to get Rose home as it would normally have done. At first, Flynn wished he'd brought his car to The Old Vicarage. At least then he'd have been able to drive her as far as Bay Street, but all things considered, maybe the fresh air and exercise were the best things for her. The cool evening air appeared to be having a sobering effect on her, and, as they passed crowds of tourists heading out to the pubs, she seemed to make a determined effort to at least appear more in control. Although he still had his arm around her, she wasn't so heavy against him, standing properly and not swaying nearly as much.

Bay Street itself appeared a bit more challenging, and he tightened his grip on her as she wobbled precariously on the steep road, guiding her hastily over to the steps and placing her right hand on the handrail as they made their way down towards Water's Edge.

As they reached the little stone bridge, Flynn gently turned her to face the steps up to the alleyway, but she stopped short.

'What is it? We're nearly home now, Rose. Look, Water's Edge.'

She shook her head, saying nothing. He stepped in front of her, and when he saw the tears in her eyes and the tremble of her lip, he felt his heart contract.

'What's wrong?' he asked her gently, pushing her fringe from her eyes with suddenly shaky fingers.

'Can we just stand here a moment?' she pleaded. 'I'm not ready to go back in there just yet. Please?'

'Of course. Look, let's get a coffee, shall we?'

The Copper Kettle Café was at the beginning of Water's Edge, and stayed open till eight o'clock in the summer months. Outside was a little patio, with tables and chairs, that overlooked the beck and was usually full of customers. Tonight, though, it was empty. Most people had either headed home for their evening meal, or were on their way to the pub.

Flynn guided Rose into a seat before he went inside to get two coffees. When he returned, she was sitting, head in hands, staring down at the table.

She peered up as he put a cup in front of her. 'I'm sorry,' she said.

He raised an eyebrow. 'For what?'

'Everything. I dunno, Flynn. How did someone like you get all tangled up with someone as useless as me, eh?'

He sank into the chair opposite hers. 'What on earth are you talking about?'

She shook her head but winced. 'It's been one thing after another since the wedding. All you've done for me and my family. I don't know what I'd have done without you.'

He stared into his coffee cup, feeling his ears burn. 'Honestly, it's nothing.' He jumped when her hand grasped his, and he looked up to see her gazing at him intently with those amazing grey eyes.

'But it is,' she told him fiercely. 'It's so good of you. You're always kind and good. Why are you so kind and good to me, Flynn?'

'Well, er—' He didn't know how to finish the sentence, where to begin. How to tell someone as lively and popular as Rose that he was drawn to her like a moth to a flame? That she flooded his world with colour, and that when he was near her, he felt himself coming back to life. He'd never really thought about it before. He'd only known that he liked being around her. She pushed him into doing things he'd avoided for so long; she nudged him into wakefulness after years of sleep. When she wasn't there, life felt dull, meaningless.

As he watched her tucking her extraordinary hair behind her ears and taking a sip of her coffee, he felt his stomach lurch, and he realised that she was so important to him, he couldn't imagine not being around her. When had that happened? How?

She smiled at him. 'I guess you're just a good man, kind to everyone. Not many like you in the world these days, sadly. I'm so sorry I snapped at you. I know you were only worried about Fuchsia. You're not the only one. I just don't know what to do about her.'

'Fuchsia is a good kid at heart. She's just trying to find her own way, and she will. She'll come good, Rose. Give her time.'

'Do you really think that?' Her eyes seemed troubled as she watched him over her coffee cup, and he thought how pretty she was, even with her makeup smudged where she'd been rubbing her tears away.

'Of course. How old is she? Twenty? What were you like at twenty?' He realised that he really wanted to know. He wanted to know all about her, what her life had been like, what made her tick.

She put down her cup, tilting her head to one side. 'Twenty?'

As Flynn watched her vivid pink streak peel over to the wrong side of her parting, he had to fight the urge to reach over and smooth it down. He daren't touch her. He was suddenly aware of an inexplicable longing he had, to take her in his arms and kiss all her worries away. What had she done to him?

'Hmm,' she continued. 'I was running a market stall. Fuchsia was at nursery. We were living with my mum and dad, on the estate in that bloody flat. It was a nightmare, even worse than it is now. I mean, we were just as cramped there, but at least now I'm cramped in better surroundings. God knows how I survived Feldane.'

'How did you get out of there?'

'Jimbo. He was a bit of a shit in the end, but at least, through him, I came here. And I got Cerise, of course.'

'Did you—did you love him?'

Rose took a sip of coffee and stared out over the water for a moment. When he saw her shiver, he realised that the evening was turning cooler and took off his jacket. As he wrapped it around her shoulders, she stared at him. 'What is it?' he asked.

'You.' She shook her head and the streak settled back in its rightful position. 'I dunno. I've never met anyone like you before. Jimbo wasn't, I can tell you that much. Nor was Bazza. He was Fuchsia's father. Useless tosser.'

Flynn bit his lip, trying not to smile. 'Tell me about them.'

'Why? Why would you be interested in them?'

'I'd just like to know ... about Fuchsia. Maybe there's a clue in there somewhere.'

'You think? You mean genetic, or 'cos she was brought up by shit men? 'cos she wasn't really. It was mostly me on my own. Oh, unless that's what you're getting at?'

'Of course not! You've been amazing, taking care of two

girls all by yourself and providing for them the way you have.'

'Not really.'

'Well, tell me. Please.'

She seemed to consider for a moment before nodding. 'Okay. You asked. Bazza was a total knobhead. I was at school with him, and I didn't like him very much even then. But we got together on my seventeenth birthday.'

'Why? I mean, if you didn't like him very much?'

'I was feeling down. I'd had a row with my mam, as usual. She was busy telling me what a waste of space I was. I'd just lost my job, and she blamed me, though it wasn't really my fault. There was a proper creepy bloke there, kept putting his hands all over me, and I couldn't stand it. I complained loads of times. Turned out he was the boss's nephew, and in the end, they let me go, said I didn't fit in with the others and it was best that I leave. I was on a three month trial, so nothing I could do. 'Course, my mam wouldn't listen to me, so all I got for my seventeenth birthday was a lecture about what a useless lump I was and how I was going nowhere.'

Flynn tightened his grip on the cup but said nothing, waiting for her to continue.

'Anyway, I went out with my mates and got pissed, and Bazza was just there. He kept telling me how gorgeous I was, and how I was too good for the estate, and all the rest of the crap that I just lapped up.'

She pulled a face. 'We had exactly two dates—a night at the pictures, and a night babysitting for his sister's kids. Both nights ended with a crap shag in an alley. I'd never done it before, and it was awful. And I paid the price. A few weeks later, I found out I was pregnant. By then, I'd already decided that Bazza was a total prick and wanted out, but of course my mother said I had to stick with him. I refused point blank to marry him, thank God. He hung around for a little while, but then, when I was about six months gone, I found out he was shagging Clare Harper from the next block. My mam and dad were furious, but I was delighted. No way could I have lived with him.'

She sighed. 'Thing is, that left me at the mercy of my parents. I'd got a job on a market stall, helping out a mate, just before I found out Fuchsia was on the way, but I stuck at it and it was all right, really. Bit crap in bad weather, but there you go. Anyway, when she was born, I went back to it, and Mam looked after the baby. Trouble was, she started taking over. You know, telling her off and undermining me all the time. It was like she was hers. When I complained, they said I was being ungrateful, and was far too young to know what was best for her. I got my own stall eventually and started saving up for me own place. Then, when Fuchsia was five, I met Jimbo. It was on a night out for me mate's birthday. He was a car salesman and doing all right for himself. We got on really well. I can't say he was like Bazza, 'cos he wasn't.'

She twisted her hair round her fingers and sat in silence for a moment. Flynn wondered if she was missing him, and the thought unexpectedly hurt. He pushed his cup away, still half full. The coffee had gone cold, anyway.

'Jimbo and me, we had a laugh, and he was okay with Fuchsia, which meant a lot. We pooled our resources—I'd got a bit put by for me own place, and he had savings—and bought a house together. My parents didn't like it. They'd lost control of Fuchsia, you see, and they said it wouldn't last. They thought he was too middle class for me. Said he'd get bored, and I'd never fit in. Turns out, they were right. His parents loathed me. Said I was a common gold-digger. I mean, like they were loaded, or something. All right, they had a nice house and a car each, but they were hardly the Beckhams.'

She scowled, and Flynn hid a smile, although he felt indignant on her behalf. Who did those people think they were, treating her like that? Poor Rose.

'Anyway,' she continued with a shrug, 'Jimbo got promoted, and then I got pregnant with Cerise. He wanted me to give up work. Said it was embarrassing having a girlfriend who worked on a market stall. So I did. I wanted it to work, you see? Besides, truth to tell, I was knackered. So I gave up the stall, and it was the biggest mistake of my life, 'cos then, it was just me and the kids at home all day, while he was out meeting people and living life. I saw less and less of him. We started arguing. He was making lots of money, but it wasn't making us happy. Then he told me he wanted a change of direction, something new. He'd seen this little café in Kearton Bay and wanted to make a go of it, turn our lives around. Was I up for it?' She sighed. 'Well, I wasn't sure about running a café, but he said that would be his job, and I did love the area. I wanted out of Oddborough and away from our parents, so I agreed. We sold the house and bought the café ,and then, just as we were about to move in, he cleared off with a librarian.'

'A librarian?' Flynn blinked, wondering if he'd misheard.

'Yeah. She'd come into loads of money and was moving to Spain. I reckon that was the attraction there. Anyway, he told me he'd fallen in love with her and wanted to be with her. Said he was sorry, but she'd made him realise that he'd never really loved me, and that we had nothing in common, and his parents had been right that we were too different to make it work.'

'Oh, my God, Rose. I'm so sorry.'

'Nah, it's okay. He was right, wasn't he? And I never really loved him, either, so I can't call him for it, can I? And, anyway, at least he had a conscience. Jimbo signed the café over to me before they went to Spain, so I could be independent at last. No need for a bloke anymore, see? It was all for the best. I'm just glad my dad wasn't alive to see it happen. I was already a massive disappointment to him.'

'I'm sure that's not true,' he said softly.

Her eyes filled with tears, which she hastily blinked away. 'Oh, yeah, it is. Me mam told me so on the morning of his funeral. "He was so disappointed in you, Rose." Just what you want to hear in a crematorium, I must say. I've never got over it, really. Too late to make it right, though. Oh, well, to hell with it.'

He shook his head slightly, aware that she was far more hurt than she was letting on. No wonder she put on such a tough act. How could her mother be so tactless and cruel? And as for those useless men in her life … no wonder she didn't trust relationships.

He'd been so lucky to find Lindsey. She'd been so lovely, so kind. She would never have betrayed him like that. He felt desperately sad for Rose, never to have known that feeling of being totally loved and cared for, and desperately sad for himself that he'd lost it.

She looked at him, her eyes puzzled. 'Are you okay? Have I bored you into a coma?'

He smiled. 'No, no. Sorry. I was just thinking what a rotten time you've had.'

'Oh …' She shrugged. 'People have it worse than me. I'm all right. Things will work out. Sorry about earlier. I'm a nightmare, aren't I?'

'Not at all. Would you like another coffee?'

She shook her head. 'No. I'd better be going back in. No point putting it off. No doubt I'll get another lecture from them all. Oh, well.' She stood up, handing him back his jacket. 'Thanks, Flynn. You're a star. Honestly.'

He followed her to her front door and slowly put his jacket back on, as she turned to say goodbye. 'You're sure you're okay?'

She nodded. 'I will be. Thank you so much.'

'Please, stop thanking me. It's nothing. I'm always happy to help.'

'I know you are. I've never met anyone like you.' She looked up at him, no trace of a smile on her lips.

He gazed into her eyes, wondering what she was thinking, wondering if she knew how much he longed to take her in his arms and kiss her.

Before he knew what was happening, her lips brushed against his. He didn't have time to collect his thoughts, as she gabbled, 'Sorry. 'Night, Flynn.'

Then she was gone, and he was standing alone on the pavement, and the world had tilted yet again. He stared at the door and tried to collect his thoughts, but all he could feel was those soft lips on his, and all he could do was pull his jacket closer to him, breathing in the scent of her perfume that still lingered on it. It was the third time she'd kissed him. Without even realising it, Rose was pulling him down a dangerous path. Flynn had a feeling there was no turning back.

CHAPTER SIXTEEN

'A hundred and ninety-nine steps! Bugger that.' My mother looked up in horror, as we stood at the foot of the steps that led to Whitby Abbey. 'I'm not that fussed about looking round an old ruin, anyway, are you, Maurice?' She nudged him, and he shook his head.

'You've seen one abbey, you've seen them all,' he agreed.

Flynn and I gaped at them. 'It was your bloody idea,' I said. 'You can't come to Whitby without seeing the abbey. Those were your very words.'

'Aye, well, that was before I'd had me fish and chips. I'm too full to be climbing stairs now. You two are being very selfish. You ought to think about Maurice's old bones. He's in his seventies now, you know. He can't be climbing all that way up there at his age.'

'Oh, I think I can—' began Maurice, but my mother was having none of it.

'Fine,' said Flynn, letting go of the handrail. 'We'll go back along Church Street and head to West Cliff, if you like.'

'Now you're talking,' said my mother. 'I think we should go round *The Dracula Experience*. What do you say, Maurice?'

'Well, I don't know. If you think we'd all enjoy it?'

'Oh, it's a right laugh. Mind, you're not easily scared, are you? Only it's a bit spooky in there, pet.'

'I'm sure I'll cope.' He laughed. 'What do you reckon, Flynn?'

Flynn looked thoroughly undecided about it, but I knew there was no point arguing. My mother had made her mind up, and when she made her mind up about something, there was no swaying her. That's how we'd ended up in Whitby in the first place.

I'd had no idea that she'd visited Maurice again, until she came home one evening and announced that we were all going on a daytrip.

'Who's all?' I'd asked suspiciously, dreading the thought of Alec "Del Boy" Thoroughgood accompanying me anywhere.

'Me, you, Maurice, and Finn,' she said.

I'd nearly choked on my bacon sandwich. 'Are you kidding? Who says?'

'Me and Maurice decided today. I went to see him. Wondered how he was getting on, and I was in Helmston, anyway, so I thought, why not? Turns out, he's feeling a lot more like his old self, and is fairly desperate to get out of the house, so we thought, well, let's do it! Whitby's as good a place as any to start, and it will do us all the power of good to get away from this place for a day.'

'Flynn might not want to go,' I said, and after my recent behaviour, I wouldn't have blamed him in the slightest. From then on, I'd be sticking to soft drinks. A bit of alcohol, and I seemed pathetically unable to keep my lips to myself when he was around. I couldn't risk humiliating myself any further.

'Already agreed,' she informed me with a smug look. 'Maurice rang him and said we needed a lift into Whitby, and as he was going to have to take us there, he might as well stay the day with us while he was at it.'

'Charming,' I said. 'Talk about being railroaded into something. Anyway, you don't need me.'

'Of course we need you. Think I'm going to be the only rose between two thorns?' she said with a sinister cackle. 'Anyway, I should think you'd like to spend a bit of time with him. Don't look at me like that. I'm telling you, he's solid gold, that lad.'

I had no idea if Flynn was aware that I was going with them, or not, but if he was shocked, he hid it very well and was politeness itself to both me and my mother as we got into the car. Maurice had elected to sit in the back seat next to Mam, so I was forced to sit beside Flynn the whole way to

Whitby, which was pretty nerve-wracking.

We'd had a good day, though, despite all my expectations. It was a lovely sunny afternoon, and we'd paddled in the sea, played bingo, and stuffed our faces with fish and chips. *The Dracula Experience* was our final destination before we headed home.

I'd been round there once before, but even knowing what to expect didn't help. I couldn't cope with scary stuff like that. My imagination was too vivid, and hearing that sinister voice droning on about the creepy Count, and stumbling around in the darkness, having all sorts of scenes appearing in front of me, plus being confronted by a terrifying apparition in a hooded cloak, was all too much for me. I wanted to shut my eyes, but the steps and twisty passageways made it impossible.

Flynn and Maurice seemed to find it all highly amusing, especially when Dracula himself appeared in front of us, and I screamed blue murder. Flynn seemed to see the panic in my eyes, though, and his laughter stopped. I felt his fingers entwine with mine, and shivered as he squeezed my hand, suddenly unsure what scared me the most—a bloodthirsty vampire, or a gorgeous doctor with gentle blue eyes and a reassuring smile.

We stumbled into the street, blinking in the sunlight. Flynn seemed to realise that he was still holding my hand and dropped it, turning away from me in obvious embarrassment.

'Christ, that was horrendous,' said my mother. 'What did I tell you, Maurice? Hope your pants are still clean.'

I could have killed her. She was the most embarrassing woman ever.

Maurice, however, seemed to find her hilarious. He laughed and clapped his hands together. 'What larks! Now, before we have to go home, who fancies an ice cream?'

'Ooh, lovely,' said my mother. 'A ninety-nine with a big fat flake. What do you say, Flynn?'

'I'll get them,' I said, desperate to get away from her for a moment. 'Four ninety-nines coming right up.' I fairly ran across the road to the ice cream stall and gabbled out my order. While I waited, I turned to see what they were doing.

The sunlight reflected off the shop windows, making them difficult to see, but I could just about make out that my mother had lit a cigarette and was puffing away, deep in conversation with an animated-looking Maurice. I hated to admit it, but she really did seem to be doing him the power of good.

Flynn had moved away from them, and I could barely see him for the dazzling sunlight. He was a hazy figure standing by the kerb, his hands in his pockets. I lifted my hand to shield my eyes and saw he was watching me, his eyes sparkling, his lips curved into a gentle smile.

My mother was quite right about him. For one brief, shining moment, I saw gold.

****

My mother was quite insistent. 'Just drop me off at the bus station, and I'll be fine.'

'Are you sure?' Flynn looked a bit worried. 'I can drive you to Alec's house, if you like. It's no trouble.'

'Bless you, pet. Don't be soft. I quite like the bus ride, any road. You get yourselves home and don't worry about me. I'll probably stay over, Rose. Thanks for the lift, pet, it was a lovely day.'

We left her in Whitby, dropped Maurice off in Helmston, and headed back to Kearton Bay, suddenly awkward once we were alone in the car. My phone beeped, and I took it out of my pocket, almost choking as I read the text message from my mother.

'There's a chocolate condom in your bag. You're welcome. Don't let the bugger get away.'

'Would you like to come in for a coffee?' Flynn asked, as we approached the turn-off for Ivy House, and it seemed churlish to say no. I mean, where was the harm? We'd had a nice day together, and what was the point of rushing home, anyway? Cerise and Fuchsia would hardly be desperate for my return, and my mother was out enjoying herself with the walking oil slick. What was wrong with a cup of coffee with Flynn?

He seemed pleased when I agreed, so I didn't think he'd only said it to be kind. Maybe he was lonely. Living in that big house on his own couldn't be much fun, especially if he was still pining for his wife. Besides, I really wanted to see what the inside of Ivy House looked like.

I wasn't disappointed. Flynn unlocked the front door and showed me into a living room that was beautifully decorated, and far more contemporary than I'd expected. Actually, it looked as if he'd walked into a furniture shop, seen a display he liked, and uprooted the whole thing to his house. It could have been a picture in a catalogue, it was so perfect.

While Flynn made the coffee, I sat nervously on his leather sofa, looking hopefully around for a speck of dust, or a fingerprint on the furniture. He must've spent his whole life cleaning. It was immaculate. Then again, I supposed my flat would look a hell of a lot tidier if I lived there alone. All the same, I would still have had photographs on the wall, personal ornaments, things that meant something to me. Nothing in the room gave anything away about Flynn, not even a photo. It was a show house, not a home. I felt suddenly quite sad for him.

He walked into the living room, carrying two cups of coffee. Proper cups, not mugs with rude slogans on them, like the ones I had at home. I bet none of his crockery had a single chip in it. He was so organised, so controlled.

He sat on the armchair and sipped at his drink. 'Would you like anything to eat?'

'God, no,' I said. 'I'm still stuffed from those fabulous fish and chips.'

'They were really good, weren't they?' he agreed. 'Actually, it was a lovely day. I really enjoyed it. Thank you, Rose.'

'Why thank me?' I said. 'You were the one who drove us all there. I reckon you didn't have much of a choice about it, either. Sorry about my mother.'

'Stop apologising for everything,' he said. 'It's been the nicest day I've had in—well, I can't even remember.'

'You should get out more,' I told him. 'I don't know why you hide yourself away in here all the time. You're good company, you should mix with people.'

'Am I?' He seemed doubtful. 'I wasn't. Not for a long time. I suppose time heals everything ... eventually.'

'I suppose it does,' I agreed, wondering what he was talking about.

We finished our drinks without further conversation, and I stood up, announcing that I'd better be getting home.

Flynn stood, too, and took my cup from me, placing it on the coffee table. 'Really? Are you sure? You don't have to go. Not if you don't want to.'

I looked at him, surprised. 'Thought you'd be glad to see the back of me.' I laughed. 'Haven't you been stuck with me long enough?'

He didn't laugh. 'No. I don't think I have.'

My eyes widened when I saw the look in his, and then ... well, I'm not sure who moved first. It was like, one minute we were both standing there, staring at each other in a fairly shell-shocked way, and the next we were just together somehow. I didn't know how. All I knew was that his arms went round me, and we were kissing, and he was sort of holding me like he'd never let me go, and then he was murmuring in my ear and stroking my hair, and I was past all reasoning by then. I couldn't help myself, and anyone who'd seen the look on his face wouldn't have blamed me in the slightest.

Even so, I wasn't expecting him to respond so dramatically.

I mean, why would I? I should never have kissed him like that, but, for God's sake, I'm only human, and he was irresistible, standing there being all gorgeous in a very unfair way. What was a girl to do?

His hair was all messed up from the sea breeze, and his shirt sleeves were rolled up, and I did have a bit of a thing for a man's forearm. Well, both of them actually, not just one. That would be weird. And we'd had a nice day, and we'd laughed a lot, and he'd been so nice to me.

Oh, all right, I admit it, I'd been panting after him all day, but when we'd finally ditched the oldies and were standing in his living room, just staring at each other, it was a case of ... well, what now? Did I thank him for the nice day, bid him goodnight and leave? Or did I take the chance while I'd got it, because, let's face it, there might never have been another. Not to mention he was looking at me in a very peculiar way, and I was sure I was getting the right signals from him. There was pure static in the air between us. I bet my pink streak was standing on end. I could feel the room positively crackling, and, sod it, I needed earthing.

I grabbed his hand and pulled him into the hallway, and he led me upstairs and into his bedroom. I vaguely remember thinking how tidy it was up there, too. I mean, how do people manage that? My bedroom—when I was fortunate enough to have one—looked like a municipal tip, but where else would I put things? And I have lots of things. Well, too much for a two-bedroomed flat, anyway. Mind you, with the size of this house, I supposed Flynn could have put all his junk into a spare bedroom and kept the rest of the house immaculate. Christ, what did it matter? I was wrapped in his arms again, and he was kissing me with such passion that I wouldn't have given a shit if he lived in a dilapidated caravan on a roundabout on the M1. I had to get his clothes off and fast.

He was surprisingly easy to undress. In fact, I didn't think he even noticed what I was doing. If I didn't know better, I'd have said he was as sex-starved as I was, but surely not? Not when he looked the way he did.

I shoved him onto the bed fast, before he had chance to think about what he was doing, and pulled my clothes off as quickly as I could, hoping to God he didn't look up and see my wobbly body in all its lack of glory. It would be just my luck to come fully to the boil, just as the sight of me reduced him to a low simmer. Or worse, turned the heat off all together, which, given my saggy stomach and stretchmarks, was a distinct possibility.

Not giving him a chance to sit up and examine what it was he was getting himself into, so to speak, I quickly pounced and kissed him again. If I could keep him occupied upstairs, hopefully his eyes wouldn't have the chance to wander down below.

Shit! Had I shaved my legs? This was what came of being single for so long and letting yourself go. If I'd had a partner, I would never have had to ask myself that question. Then I remembered that I'd shaved them that morning, just in case. My God, I was shameless. Thankfully.

I wondered if he was enjoying himself as much as I was. Luckily, it was quite easy to tell with men. My hand reached down, just to double check. Oh, yes, most definitely.

It was quite exciting to think I'd turned him on that much. Bloody hell, hadn't I just! It practically leapt into my hand, and as I gave it a loving caress to thank it for being so flattering, it juddered in my palm. For a moment, I forgot all about my stretchmarks and turned my attention to Flynn's body instead.

Oh, my, it was good. I mean, every inch of it. How had I ended up in bed with someone who looked like him?

Flynn's hand touched my left boob, and I gasped in shock. What if he felt how saggy they were? Two babies had made sure they weren't exactly pert and perky—God, that sounded like something Joe would name his micro pigs. These days, they sort of sagged a bit, to put it mildly. When I took my bra off, they practically bounced off my knees—though that may have been a slight exaggeration. What if he found them disgusting? What if he wondered why they weren't all firm and pointing outwards like normal women's? Because mine definitely pointed south, like they were drawing the eye to my fat stomach on purpose. Flynn might ... oh, well, maybe he wasn't bothered.

He gently kissed one of them before taking it carefully into his mouth. Hell, I hoped it wouldn't choke him. They weren't exactly small. Not that I was of Jordanesque proportions, but, well, I wasn't Keira Knightley, either. Still, Flynn seemed to be enjoying himself, so maybe I should've stopped worrying?

I had to admit, it was terribly pleasurable to be wrapped around him, feeling his head against me, his lips on my breast, his arms holding me with such exquisite tenderness. I forgot all about my worries and just enjoyed the moment, aware that we were building up to something that there was simply no stopping.

Oh, crap! For a split second, I thought about protection and panicked, then felt a most unfamiliar sensation—gratitude to my mother. The chocolate condom. I could see Flynn was almost at the point of no return, and I didn't think I could hold out much longer.

Telling him not to worry and that I wouldn't be a second, I rolled off the bed and crawled around to my bag, hoping that he wouldn't peer over and see me in such an unflattering position. My fat arse stuck in the air, while my boobs practically swept the carpet would hardly be a turn-on, but I daren't stand up in case he recoiled in horror. Reaching my bag, I felt inside, pulling out the little packet with relief.

Back on the case in a second, I tore open the foil with trembling fingers. I did think briefly what a waste of a chocolate flavour condom it would be if I didn't actually taste it, but I dismissed the thought immediately. I mean, I barely knew the man. What sort of woman would he think I was?

Flynn lay there like some gorgeous god, as I carefully rolled the condom onto him. His eyes were full of pure lust. It was fabulous. I reached over and kissed him again, and his hands stroked my hair as he kissed me deeper and deeper. I climbed aboard, so to speak, and he didn't object or demand that he go on top, or anything like that. To be honest, I'd have done pretty much anything he suggested by that point, but as it turned out, we were both more than happy with the way things were going. Boy, were we ever.

I watched him with growing delight, seeing the expression on his face change, the intensity in his eyes, the tension in his muscles. The quiet man, who always seemed so detached, so remote, was suddenly all-too-human. And I loved him for it.

'Do you know how lovely you are?' I murmured, not even meaning to say it out loud. I don't know if he heard. I hoped not. I was suddenly aware that there were tears rolling down my cheeks and had no idea why.

I'd forgotten how emotional sex could be. Though, actually, I didn't remember it ever being that emotional. I mean, physically, sex with Jimbo had been good. He'd certainly introduced me to the big O, which was more than Bazza ever did, or the couple of blokes I had brief relationships with after him, but emotionally ... I didn't think it had ever connected, somehow. Not like with Flynn. This was something entirely new.

For a start, the timing was perfect. We even came together. I hadn't even known that was possible. I can't tell you how many orgasms I faked with Jimbo, waiting for him to hurry up and get it over with. He'd once read a magazine that told him women could have multi-orgasms and decided that was the way to go, so he refused to come until I'd had at least three. Problem was, after the first, I kind of lost interest, so then it was fake and fake again so that Jimbo could finally let go, accompanied by the sound of my Oscar-winning gasping and groaning, and a lot of eye-rolling and facial contortions that

I'd learned from watching *When Harry Met Sally*. No need for that on this occasion. Flynn was bang on time, and I certainly didn't have to fake anything. If anything, I was probably a bit too enthusiastic, but I was past caring, and luckily, he didn't have any neighbours to worry about.

Afterwards, he wrapped his arms around me and kissed my forehead, and we lay together, and as I watched his chest rising and falling, I felt a really weird feeling that felt surprisingly like contentment. We didn't speak, but just lay there, as darkness fell outside and my eyelids grew heavy, and I sighed against him. Gradually, his breathing became deeper, and I thought maybe he'd fallen asleep, and was filled with happiness at the thought of falling asleep beside him. As I began to drift away myself, I turned onto my side and wrapped my arm around him. The last thing I remembered was murmuring, 'I love you, Flynn,' into his ear. I'm not sure why.

Like I've always said, sodding hormones have a lot to answer for.

****

I opened my eyes the next morning wondering where I was. The duvet was thick and luxurious, not at all like the Asda Smart Price duvet I'd been huddled under for the last few months. I turned my head to see his beside me on the pillow. He was sleeping so peacefully, he looked like an angel—an angel with dark, messy hair and stubble on his chin. He looked terribly sexy.

What was I thinking that for? This was no time to remember how his hands had explored my body with such tender expertise, nor how his eyes had burned into mine with such passionate intensity, nor how ... *for God's sake, pack it in, Rose*, I thought. This was what you got for reading Mills and Boon.

My face burned, as I recalled the shameless abandon I'd

displayed. He must have thought I was a complete slut. I'd practically dragged him upstairs and pounced on him, the poor bloke. I didn't think I'd even given him a chance to protest. We hadn't even been drinking, so I couldn't blame the vodka, for once. I'd obviously inherited my mother's libido, after all.

I studied his face carefully. He wasn't snoring, and there was no sign of any drool. Trust Flynn to look so perfect, so utterly beautiful. I dismally recalled that I hadn't taken my makeup off before we fell into bed, so I probably looked like a panda. And I bet I'd drooled. And snored. Brilliant.

I lifted the duvet and looked down at myself. Yep. Not a stitch on. My eyes moved, almost of their own accord, over toward Flynn. He didn't have a stitch on, either. I let myself admire him for a moment. He really was perfect, no doubt about it. His chest with that soft, dark hair curling against his damp skin. That flat stomach, and ... *Jesus*! Jimbo had used to wake up with an erection all the time. It quite shocked me at first, but then, he'd always fallen asleep reading *Big Bums Magazine*, so I kind of thought it was all down to that. Took me ages to discover that men often woke up like that, for no real reason at all, and it struck me as terribly inconvenient. Imagine if women were the same—waking up every morning with nipples like chapel hat pegs? They could take someone's eye out. It must have been very cold for them—men, I mean—waking up with the duvet lifted up and the chilly morning air blowing round their vitals.

I stared at Flynn's swollen member and tried not to giggle. Swollen member? Sounded like a Tory MP. Then I blinked. I was sure it had just moved all of its own accord. I looked more closely. It definitely twitched. I wondered, if I waved at it, would it wave back?

Christ, I'd really lost the plot. I stifled a groan. How could I have been so irresponsible? Well, not irresponsible, exactly, because, actually, I'd been quite *responsible*, when I came to think about it. More than he had, and him a doctor. Mind you,

I couldn't take the credit for it, really. The cheek of my mother, dropping one of her chocolate condoms into my bag. All the same, I was grateful she had. What would I have done, if she hadn't? Would I have been sensible enough to walk away? Nah, no chance. The way I'd been feeling last night, there was no way I could have stopped myself. Funnily enough, I didn't think Flynn could have, either. I'd never seen him like that before—so out of control, so passionate. Well, at least now I'd satisfied my lust, I could put all those thoughts of him away and get back to normal. Maybe, in another four years, I'd have found someone else to indulge my wanton desires with.

I found myself lifting the duvet and examining him again. "It" was still standing to attention, like a royal bodyguard, ready to jump in at any moment, so to speak. I felt a distinctly dangerous tingling beginning all over again, and had to fight the urge to reach out and stroke it. Sod it, it wasn't a pet spaniel! Oh, no. No chance. I had to get out of there, or I may just lose all reason.

God knows how Flynn didn't wake up, with how loud my heart hammered against my chest as I slid out of bed and gathered up my clothes. I didn't even go to the bathroom, despite being desperate for the loo, but tiptoed onto the landing and put my clothes on as fast as I could. Finally, thanking God that Flynn had left the key in the front door, I crept out of the house.

The flat was in darkness when I sneaked into the living room. My mother would be at Alec's house. Fuchsia and Cerise wouldn't surface for at least another hour, not on a Sunday. I went to the loo, where I stared at myself in the mirror. It was as I'd feared. I looked an absolute fright. Thank God Flynn hadn't woken up and seen the state of me. I wondered if he was awake yet. What was he thinking? Was he horrified at what he'd done? What we'd done, I reminded myself. It was certainly not all him, not by any means. I imagined his shock as the truth sank in, that he'd actually had sex with someone like me.

I rubbed half-heartedly at the smudged mascara round my eyes and briefly contemplated getting a shower, but the noise of the boiler clicking into action and the running water might wake the others, and I wasn't ready to face them just yet. With any luck, they'd have no idea that I'd not come home last night. There was no way any of them could ever find out. My life wouldn't be worth living.

I slipped back into the living room and curled up on the sofa, hugging a cushion to me, but, much as I longed to forget, my treacherous mind kept replaying the events of last night. I thought of the way Flynn had held me, the expression in his eyes. That look! Hard not to get turned on when a bloke's looking at you with all that wonder and desire.

What had happened to him? How had we got ourselves into such a state? I'd only meant to give him a kiss, and I really didn't know why I'd done that. We'd just had such a lovely day and got on so well, and, well, he was gorgeous. I didn't expect anything else to happen. Why would I? If Flynn wanted sex, I had no doubt he could have taken his pick from any number of beautiful, intelligent women. Maybe he'd fancied a bit of rough?

I shook my head, angry with myself. He wasn't like that. I'd seen the way he looked at me, I'd felt the tenderness in his touch. It was me he'd wanted, I was sure of it. I just couldn't figure out why.

And I'd wanted him.

I hugged the cushion tighter, as I admitted that, actually, I'd wanted him for a long time. There was something about him. He was like no one I'd ever known before. He occupied my thoughts far too much, and I was in severe danger of losing all sense around him. I'd been a fool, but I'd had one hell of an itch, and I'd hoped that, if I let myself scratch it, that would be that.

I buried my burning face in the cushion and stifled a groan, as I realised that, really, all I'd done was spread the itch till it had become full-blown pruritus. I didn't just fancy Flynn. I loved him, and probably had done from the moment he'd flown to my rescue outside my mother's house, fighting off that bloody gang and not even caring about, or blaming me in the slightest for the state of his car. Well, a fat lot of use that was. People like me didn't end up with people like Flynn. Oh, he'd be polite and kind. He'd never tell me outright that it had been a mistake, but nevertheless I'd get the message loud and clear. It would never happen again.

I didn't even try to stop the tears. With any luck, they would wash away the mascara.

Always a silver lining.

CHAPTER SEVENTEEN

My mother hadn't been home all night again, which was quite disgusting. She'd sent me a brief text, assuring me that she was all right and would be back the next morning, and she was having a fabulous time at some swanky restaurant in Oddborough. I didn't know there *were* any swanky restaurants in Oddborough, and if there were, I shouldn't imagine they'd have been too thrilled to have my mother and Alec Thoroughgood as guests.

I trudged into the shop, pulled on my apron, and got down to the most important job of the day—making a cup of tea. Flicking the kettle on, I stared round the kitchen, trying to summon some enthusiasm for the day ahead. Chrissie and Eliza would be here any minute. I had to look like my usual self. Except, what was my usual self these days? I didn't know. My moods were so erratic, and I had to admit that, right then, I didn't know what I was feeling, or what I wanted.

Flynn had called me the morning I left him in bed, sounding very regretful. He said it was because he'd been asleep when I left, and he'd wanted to wake up with me, but I wasn't so sure. I had a horrible feeling he was wondering what the hell he'd been thinking. I'd tried to keep my voice light, my tone casual, to not give him any impression that I was taking it all seriously. He would probably be horrified by some clingy woman who assumed we were suddenly in some sort of relationship.

Obviously, I wasn't that woman. I had no expectations. It was just a one night stand, and one that should probably never have happened.

He'd texted me a couple of times since, asking how I was, but there was no mention of meeting up again, so I tried to put the whole experience behind me and forget about it. Blame it on Whitby. It had always had a magical effect on me, and it seemingly did the same for Flynn. Best to chalk it up to experience and move on, like the adults we were.

I switched on a smile, as Eliza let herself into the shop and headed straight for the kitchen, followed within minutes by Chrissie. They seemed surprised, and pleased, to find me all ready for work and holding out mugs of tea for them as they walked in.

'That's what I call service.' Eliza grinned, taking the mug from my hand and sipping at the tea. 'I'd better make the most of this week. School breaks up next Thursday, and Amy will be at home. It's going to be a bit manic.'

'Who's looking after her while you're working?' asked Chrissie.

'Harry's having her for a couple of weeks in August. Other than that, it will be Joe mostly, although Lexi will help when she can, and Tally's offered, too. I'm very lucky.'

'You'll need all that help when you've got two of them to find childcare for,' I pointed out.

'We ought to think about maternity cover, too,' said Chrissie thoughtfully.

Eliza laughed. 'I'm not even pregnant yet!'

'Yes, but we will have to think about it. Depending on the time of year, we could be rushed off our feet. We may need to take someone else on.'

'Oh, I think we'll manage,' I said. 'You make the mallows, and I'll flog 'em. It will be fine.'

'Careful. I'll begin to think I'm not needed.' Eliza yawned. 'Sorry. Bit knackered.'

'Let me guess,' I said. 'On second thoughts, I won't bother.'

'It is hard work, getting pregnant,' she admitted. 'I don't remember it being this exhausting when I was trying for Amy.'

'Maybe you're trying a bit too hard,' suggested Chrissie. 'You should just relax and let things flow. So to speak.'

They giggled, and I tried to push the thought of Flynn and me out of my mind. I felt a distinct longing for him for a moment. That was the trouble with celibacy. You could go for years without any hanky-panky, no bother at all, but then, when you finally indulged, it woke up all sorts of urges. I could feel my own previously comatose urges stirring at that very moment, which was a bit inconvenient, to say the least.

I gulped down the last of my tea and straightened up. 'Right, work.'

They both looked a bit shocked by my sudden enthusiasm and my surprising punctuality, as I turned over the sign on the shop door bang on nine o'clock. I needed to take my mind off things, though—quickly.

After a busy morning serving customers and dealing with internet orders, I'd almost succeeded in putting my misery behind me. Just my luck that, at about ten-past eleven, my mother waltzed through the door, looking as if she'd been dragged through a hedge backwards.

'What do you want?' I demanded, somewhat ungraciously.

'Well, that's a nice welcome,' she said, although she didn't seem too put out, as she was still smiling in a very unnerving manner. 'Something wonderful's happened, and I wanted you to be the first to know.'

'You've found a flat?' I asked, trying to keep the hope from my voice.

'No. Well, not exactly. Haven't you noticed?'

'Noticed what?'

Eliza came through into the shop, and her face lit up immediately. 'Oh, my God! When did that happen?'

'When did what happen?' I was baffled.

My mother waggled her fingers at me, rolling her eyes at Eliza, who'd already rounded the counter and was examining my mother's hand while squealing in delight.

'Ooh, it's, er, stunning. Congratulations.'

'Jesus!' I stared in dismay at the ugly rock on my mother's left hand, but quickly realised how bad that sounded. 'I mean, er, congratulations. When did this happen, then?'

'Last night at the restaurant,' she said. 'He dropped it into me champagne. Nearly swallowed the damn thing, but, luckily, he grabbed the glass just in time. Ooh, it was dead romantic. We got a couple of fiddlers playing at our table, and the butler brought me a red rose.'

'The butler?' Eliza bit her lip, and I nudged her. 'Well, that all sounds very lovely. So, when's the wedding?'

'I dunno yet. Alec said it should be soon. There's no point in waiting at our time of life, is there? Alec said we've been separated long enough, and now we'll never be separated again.'

'So, it will be this year?'

'Oh, yes. Alec said he's thinking somewhere along the lines of August or September.'

'Alec said quite a lot, didn't he?' I muttered. What was the rush, anyway? Was he scared she'd come to her senses if he gave her enough time?

'Gosh,' Eliza said 'That doesn't give you an awful lot of time to plan a wedding.'

'Oh, Alec will take care of that. He's getting on the internet this morning, to try to sort it all out.'

'Really?' I was a bit taken aback. 'Are you telling me you're not having any input at all? In your own wedding?'

'Well, I'm choosing my own outfit,' she said. 'Alec has good taste. I trust him.'

I thought about his oil slick hair, camel coat, and sovereign rings, and shuddered. I dreaded to think what kind of a wedding he was planning. Thank God she was choosing her own outfit. Left to Alec, I reckoned he'd choose a dress that would make the ones from *Big Fat Gypsy Weddings* look understated.

'Well, I'm sure it will be lovely, whatever you decide,' said Eliza, heading back into the kitchen.

'Thanks,' called my mother, then turned to me with a curious look on her face.

'What?'

'You'll never guess what I've just seen. Talk about a dark horse.'

'Surprise me,' I said, heading back round the counter.

'I might just do that. I got off the bus at the stop past the Farthingdale crossroads, and guess who was parked up opposite, texting away on his phone?'

'David Tennant?' I suggested hopefully. 'Matthew Rhys? The Musketeers?'

'Your hormones are popping,' she said, with uncomfortable accuracy. 'No. Flynn.'

'The only thing surprising about that is you remembered his name,' I said, trying to ignore the fluttering in my stomach at the mention of him.

'You're wrong there,' she said. 'First off, he should have been in surgery, shouldn't he? So I popped across the road, just to say good morning, like, and as we're exchanging pleasantries, I just happened to look past him, and you'll never guess what was on the passenger seat?.'

'Kylie Minogue?'

'Will you behave yourself? A massive bunch of red roses, that's what. Really gorgeous. Must have cost a fortune. Now, who do you think they were for, eh? And who's so important that he's skipping surgery to give flowers to them?'

She folded her arms and scrutinised my face for signs of emotion. I tried to look unimpressed, but my heart was thudding. For a brief moment, I considered that, just maybe, they were for me. But then, that didn't make sense, because why would he skip surgery for me? He could see me anytime. He could have seen me during the last few days, when I'd waited, half-hoping that he'd call round. He hadn't, though, had he? And he wouldn't need his car to bring me flowers, either. I felt bitterly disappointed in him.

'Anyway,' said my mother, 'whoever they're for, I hope she's worth it.' She sighed. 'Looks like I was barking up the wrong tree about you and him, after all. Ah, well, I'm going up for some kip, pet. I'm buggered.'

She left the shop, leaving me feeling utterly wretched and oddly betrayed, which was ridiculous. I wandered into the kitchen, deep in thought.

Eliza looked up and her face dropped. 'Go on, what's she said now?'

'Eliza, has Gabriel said anything about Flynn taking today off?'

She nodded. 'Yeah, he did say something. Not the full day, just a few hours, midday.'

'Do you know why?'

'Something about him having a train to meet at Whitby. I think a relative or friend was visiting.'

A relative or friend who merited a huge bunch of red roses? I didn't think so. And you know what, the least he could have done was have the decency to tell me there was someone else in the picture. Okay, so we weren't in a relationship, but a bloke couldn't just sleep with someone and not refer to it again, could he? Okay, so maybe he could. Maybe that was what I'd decided to do, but I expected better of Flynn. He must have been involved with this other person when we went to bed, and that made it my business.

Anger built up inside me as I considered the matter. I couldn't shake the feeling that he'd badly let me down, and I didn't like it. I was sick to death of being used and dumped by selfish men. I deserved to know the truth.

'Eliza, I know this is awful, and I wouldn't normally ask, and you know I wouldn't, but please, please can you run me to Whitby? It's important. Please?'

She and Chrissie looked at each other.

'Well, er, I don't know,' said Eliza. 'Can you manage here, Chrissie?'

'Sure, if I have to,' said Chrissie. 'You okay, Rose?'

'I'm not sure,' I admitted. 'There's just something I have to do.'

Eliza watched me for a moment, then she nodded and pulled off her apron. 'Okay, Rose. Let's go.'

****

'So, where exactly are we going?' Eliza asked as we headed along the Whitby Road in her beloved Fiesta. 'Am I right in thinking the station?'

'That obvious?'

'Well, yes. What's going on, Rose? You look really upset.'

I realised I was hugging myself, as if for comfort. My stomach was on spin cycle, and I had an awful feeling that I was going to need the loo before long. Why was I so nervous? Why did it all matter so much? This was what happened when you let yourself develop feelings for people. I'd known it all along and still allowed it to happen. My own fault.

'Rose?' She glanced at me briefly, clearly concerned. 'If you're making me take you to the station, the least you can do is tell me what's going on,' she said, in a blatant attempt at emotional blackmail.

I hung my head, mortified with shame. 'I slept with Flynn.'

The car wobbled rather worryingly, as she shrieked, 'What?' and stared at me in astonishment.

'The road, Eliza,' I reminded her, and she quickly turned back to face forwards and shook her head.

'When did this happen?'

'A few days ago, after we'd taken Maurice and my mother to Whitby.'

'But how? I mean, Flynn!'

'What do you mean by that?' I said.

'Well, I just can't imagine him making a move on anyone, that's all. I didn't realise you two had .... I mean, I knew you liked him and ..., Oh, what am I saying! I'm so thrilled for you, Rose. You really deserve this, you both do.'

'Huh.'

'What's wrong? What's happened?'

Briefly, trying to keep my voice steady, I told her about him making no effort to see me since, and about the two brief texts, which were the only contact I'd had with him since that first awkward phone call.

'Gabriel did say he was behaving a bit oddly lately. He's been rather down. Quiet. I think he's got something on his mind.'

'Yeah, the fact that he lowered himself to sleep with me.'

'Don't be silly. I'm sure that's not the case, at all.'

'Oh? Well, explain this, then.' Quickly, I told her about the roses, and she looked a bit awkward.

'Oh.'

I felt bitterly disappointed that she didn't immediately come back at me with a very plausible explanation for them, but she seemed pretty stumped, too.

'I suppose they could be for his mother? Maybe she's visiting?'

'He doesn't see his mother. She lives in Portugal. And I got the impression that if she did bother to visit him, he wouldn't be buying her red roses.'

'Oh. Well, has he got a sister?'

'Nope. Only child. He was mostly raised by his grandmother, and she shuffled off the mortal coil years ago.'

'Gosh, he's filled you in on quite a bit, hasn't he?'

'Not the important stuff, obviously. Like who he's seeing behind my back.' I shook my head, suddenly furious with myself. 'Listen to me, acting like some jealous harpy. Turn the car round, Eliza. It's none of my business, anyway. Just because we had sex, doesn't mean I own him.'

'But it's Flynn!'

'And?'

'Well, he's just not like that. He wouldn't cheat on anyone, I'm sure of it, so there must be a reason for all this. Don't you want to know? Put your mind at rest? Then you can start to work out how you really feel about him, and maybe ask him what it is he wants, too.'

Why did she sound so sensible? She made it seem really easy.

Reluctantly, I agreed to carry on, and we drove steadily towards the town centre, parking up in the car park and walking cautiously through the arched entrance into the station, towards the platform. I was shaking by that time, my eyes darting left and right, desperate to avoid being seen by Flynn.

'We don't even know which train he's meeting,' Eliza said.

'I shouldn't think there's that many to choose from,' I pointed out. 'It's hardly Piccadilly, is it?'

We clutched each other in sudden shock. 'There he is!'

He was sitting on a bench reading a newspaper. The roses were by his side—a huge bunch of beautiful, full-headed, deep red blooms. They were absolutely gorgeous. I hated them. I watched him as he scoured the pages, his dark head bent in apparent concentration. I wondered if he was really reading. He kept glancing up and looking down the track then at his watch. He seemed nervous. No wonder. He had a very dark secret he was keeping, after all. Me.

I was so busy glaring at him, I didn't even notice the train approaching until Eliza squeezed my arm, and I realised that people were standing up, picking up bags and checking tickets. Flynn stood, too, folding up his paper and shoving it in the nearest bin, before picking up the roses and staring down the line at the approaching train.

As it ground to a halt, there was a general mêlée on the platform, as doors opened and people surged forward. There was a huge buzz of conversation, and the odd air of panic that you found at a train station, as passengers hurried towards the train, desperate to ensure a good seat. I couldn't imagine why they were panicking. The train was hardly going to be full.

Flynn was craning his neck as if to see over the crowd, and

I saw him raise one arm tentatively.

Desperate to see who he was waving to, I hopped up and down, and as the train began to fill up and the platform gradually cleared, we were able to see at last.

Eliza gripped my arm, and we watched as a tall woman with dark hair approached Flynn, waving to him and smiling. She wore a navy blue jacket and pencil skirt, with matching high heels, and she looked impossibly elegant.

I looked down at my jeans, trainers, and pink T-shirt and felt ridiculous.

Eliza was watching open-mouthed, and I glanced up to see Flynn kiss the woman on the cheek then hand her the roses. She buried her head in them for a moment, seeming to breathe in the scent, then she raised her face to his and kissed him lightly on the lips. He wrapped his arms round her, taking care not to squash the flowers, and they stood for a long moment, seemingly clinging to each other. There was no mistaking the sense of intimacy.

Feeling as if we were invading their privacy, I turned away, sickened. 'Come on.'

'Are you sure?' Eliza obviously felt the need to check, but I could see in her face that she felt the same way I did. We had no place here. There was something so private about the two of them, it made us both feel shamed and small, somehow.

We walked back outside into the station car park. Across the harbour, I could see Whitby Abbey in the distance, watching over the town that had changed so much in the centuries that it had stood, like some sentinel, on the cliff top. Was it really only a few days ago that Flynn and I had strolled beside these busy roads, sunlit waters, bobbing boats? It seemed like another lifetime.

I rubbed my forehead, suddenly tired.

Eliza slipped her arm through mine and squeezed it tightly. 'There'll be a reason,' she promised.

I tried to smile but couldn't force my mouth to obey. Sure,

there was a reason—the reason I'd suspected all along. Someone like Flynn would never be interested in someone like me. I couldn't say I hadn't known. I'd asked for it from the start.

****

It took all my strength not to succumb to a very large vodka and Coke that night. I'd been too restless to stay indoors. Fuchsia was—amazingly—out meeting friends again. I had no idea who those friends were, but there'd been a massive change in her lately, and I couldn't say I wasn't hugely relieved. Whoever they were, they seemed to be doing the trick. She still had her moments of moodiness, don't get me wrong, and there were odd times when I caught her looking at me curiously, as if she was considering something, but she always hastily looked away, and I didn't push her. She was generally acting pretty normal. She'd regained a little weight, too, and Meggie had reported that she was eating her lunch and getting on with her work much better.

Cerise was staying over at her friend's house for a couple of nights, and my mother was round at Alec Thoroughgood's house and wouldn't be back till the following evening, as they were going to a wedding fayre. I didn't fancy being stuck in the flat all by myself that night. I knew only too well that I'd be brooding about those red roses, about the way Flynn had held that woman to him so tenderly. I felt my fists curl in anger every time I thought about it, and wondered when I'd turned into a jealous, over-emotional lunatic. What happened to not needing a man? What happened to independence and never getting involved? How had someone as reserved as Flynn managed to break down all my defences? And how had he turned into such a liar? Maybe he'd always been that way and just had a brilliant facade, or maybe it was me. Maybe there was something in me that turned decent, honest men into cheating pigs.

It was no use calling Eliza. I knew what she'd be up to that night, and I doubted she'd interrupt her evening to spend any time with her neurotic friend. Even if she would, I wasn't going to be the one responsible for putting her baby-making on hold, even for one evening. God forbid that I'd be held accountable for her next unwanted period. I had more than enough on my plate, thank you very much.

So, that evening found me in The Hare and Moon, slumped over the bar, sipping—rather nobly, I thought—on my lime and soda, while contemplating the huge disappointment that was my life.

Rhiannon leaned on the counter opposite me, her head propped in her hands as she studied me. 'What now?' she asked, as I slurped down the last of my drink and demanded another.

'Same again, I suppose,' I said grudgingly. 'At least it's a cheap night out when you avoid vodka.'

'I meant, what's happened now? Fuchsia?'

I shook my head. 'For once, Fuchsia seems to be doing fine.'

'Splendid. Well, that's something, isn't it? Your mother, then?'

'Nope. My mother's at her slime-ball boyfriend's house, going over wedding plans, as we speak. Everything in her world is rosy.' I considered the pun and snorted, rather unattractively. 'Everything's coming up roses,' I said, unable to keep the bitterness from my voice.

She glanced round before murmuring something to Derry, who nodded. 'Come on, Rose,' she said. 'Let's go upstairs and talk in private. I rather fancy a couple of hours away from the bar.'

'Are you sure?'

'Absolutely. Derry and Jack can manage the food, and Kerry's all right in here for a short while,' she said, referring to her new barmaid, who had settled in quite well, and was a good deal friendlier than the delightful Michelle.

I followed Rhiannon upstairs to her kitchen, where she tactfully put the kettle on and made us both coffee, rather than getting out a bottle of wine, which was what she usually did.

'Now,' she said, sitting down at the table and fixing me with a knowing look, 'what's gone on between you and Flynn?'

I peered at her suspiciously. 'Who told you?'

'No one. At least, that's not strictly true. You and Flynn told me, every time I saw you together. Chemistry. It's unmistakable and rather lovely. So, what's happened?'

Funnily enough, it was easier to admit to Rhiannon what I'd done than it had been to tell Eliza. Even the shameful spying episode seemed slightly less embarrassing, as I told her about it. She wasn't one to judge or condemn, and I felt better for pouring it all out while she listened quietly, sipping coffee occasionally, and nodding now and then as she watched me with sympathetic brown eyes.

'Goodness, you have been busy. And what a state to get yourself into,' she said, when I finished and gulped down some coffee in relief.

'It's a right pile of shit,' I agreed. 'I should have steered clear. There's no peace of mind when men are involved.'

'I rather think that depends on the man,' she said.

'Well, put it this way, I don't seem to have met one yet who wasn't a total arsehole,' I said, with some feeling.

'I am absolutely certain that Flynn is no such thing.' She smiled. 'It could be that you're putting a totally false interpretation onto things. It could even be that you're seeing what you want to see.'

'What I want to see? What do you mean by that?'

'Sometimes, we get what we expect,' she said. 'Rose, tell me exactly what it is that's upsetting you so much.'

'Well, isn't it obvious?' What was wrong with her? Did she need a flaming diagram?

'Humour me,' she said.

I was silent for a moment. What exactly was upsetting me? 'I slept with him,' I said. 'I really wish I hadn't.'

'Do you? Honestly?'

'Yes, I do. Because when you give yourself to someone like that, it opens you up to being hurt,' I said.

'So, it wasn't just sex, then? It meant something?'

I glared at her. Bloody witch. 'Yeah, okay. I don't just jump into bed with anyone, you know. No offence.'

She laughed. 'None taken. So, you have feelings for Flynn, you admit that?'

I ran my hand through my hair and wondered how much I dared confess. Sod it. In for a penny, in for a pound. 'I told him I loved him,' I muttered, waiting for the shriek of laughter, but she seemed delighted and gave a contented sigh.

'How lovely. And what did he say to that?'

'He didn't. I think he was asleep, to be honest.'

'It seems to me that Flynn isn't one to *jump into bed with anyone*, either. I think, if he went to bed with you, it meant something to him, too. *You* meant something to him.'

'Then, why give red roses to this other woman?' I demanded.

'Have you ever been to Flynn's house?' she asked.

I nodded. 'That's the scene of the crime. Where we did the dark deed.'

'Was it daylight?'

'Well, kind of. Just sort of starting to get dark. What the hell does that matter?'

'I just wondered if you'd seen his garden?'

I didn't think that was a euphemism. I stared at her in exasperation. 'Well, really, Rhiannon, who gives a toss about the bloody garden? I didn't go into the back of his house, at all,' I said, remembering. 'We went through the front door, into the living room, and then upstairs to the front bedroom. I left in the morning, straight out of the front door. Why?'

She finished her coffee and shrugged. 'He's awfully keen on his garden. He has a beautiful rose garden at the end of the lawn. Grows some stunning roses.'

Who did she think I was? Alan sodding Titchmarsh? Who gave a shit? Then I realised what she'd said. 'Are you saying he grew those roses? The roses for the woman?'

'Well, it's a possibility, isn't it?'

'Okay, so if he didn't buy them, am I supposed to feel grateful that he's too tight to go to a florist?'

She smiled. 'You're rather missing the point, Rose.'

'Well, what is the point?' I snapped, exasperated. 'He grew some roses and cut them for her. Loads of them. And you should have seen how he gave them to her. It was so ... so intimate. I can't explain it. Eliza felt it, too. Like we were intruding on something really private.'

'Perhaps you were. It doesn't necessarily mean that it was a bad thing. I rather think it depends on the variety of rose.'

'Big, fat, red ones,' I said. 'The kind you'd give someone on Valentine's Day, if you really, really fancied the pants off them.'

'There are lots of different varieties,' she insisted. 'A rose by any other name ...'

'I have absolutely no idea what you're talking about,' I said.

She squeezed my hand. 'It's not up to me, Rose. I just think you should give him the benefit of the doubt and be patient. Give him a chance. If you ask him, I'm sure he will tell you. Things are seldom what they seem to be to the casual observer.'

'But you didn't see the way they looked at each other.'

'No. But I can imagine.'

'You can? How? What is it you're not telling me?'

'I just think you should wait and see. That's all. And try not to worry too much. Now, how about another coffee?'

I just knew she wasn't going to tell me anything else. It rankled a bit, knowing that she knew stuff about Flynn that I didn't, and I was quite miffed that she wasn't going to tell me, but then, the thing with Rhiannon was that I knew I could tell her anything and it would go no further. I couldn't have it both ways, I guessed. She was a good friend to have onside.

Giving her a weak smile, I agreed that another coffee would be lovely. It wasn't as if I had anything better to do that night.

CHAPTER EIGHTEEN

Flynn rang me the very next day. I ignored it the first four times. The fifth time, I considered ignoring it again, but realising I would only be putting off the inevitable and I may as well get it over with, I answered.

'Hello.' He sounded relieved. His warm, gentle voice sent ripples of delight through me, and I gripped the phone, furious with myself for feeling that way, furious with him for putting me through all this. 'I've been calling you for ages. Didn't you hear the phone?'

'No,' I lied. 'Bad signal round here.' That was true. It was pretty dodgy in parts of the village, and I often had to go outside the shop to make calls. He'd only caught me then, because I was on my way to see Ted and Dawn at the ice cream shop at the top of Bay Street, taking them a big tub of marshmallow fluff for them to use in their ice cream.

'I'm sorry I didn't call you before. I've been a bit preoccupied, and I wanted to be able to give you my full attention. Can I come round?'

'No,' I said. 'It's Saturday, remember? I'm working.'

'Oh, of course. Well, what about tonight? Would you like to come for dinner?'

I felt sick with longing. How easy would it be to pretend that I hadn't seen him with that woman? To kid myself that none of it mattered, that being with him was enough? But I couldn't do it. Not again.

'I don't think I can tonight.'

He sounded concerned, hurt even. What a nerve. 'Is everything all right, Rose? I know it must seem as if I've neglected you, and I suppose I have, but it wasn't intentional. It was just very bad timing. I can explain it all, and I will, if you give me the chance.'

I'd almost reached the ice cream shop. I hesitated. 'Look, I'll be round in about fifteen minutes, if that's okay? I won't stay long. Unless you're ... busy?'

'No, that would be lovely,' he said immediately. 'I'll put the kettle on,' he added with a laugh.

I didn't answer, feeling too depressed to bother. I put my phone back in my pocket and dropped the marshmallow fluff off at the ice cream shop.

'Cheers, Rose,' said Dawn. 'Reckon we'll be getting through quite a bit of this during the summer. Very popular flavour it's turning out to be.'

'Great. Thanks.' I turned and trudged out of the shop and headed towards Station Lane. As I neared The Old Vicarage, I speeded up a bit. The last thing I wanted was for Sophie to spot me and rush out to enquire where I was going. I passed the surgery, the purpose-built brick building that had been put up just six years ago. Before then, the surgery had, apparently, been held in the house that Flynn lived in. The garden must have been huge at that time, but the new building had taken quite a lot of it up. I wondered what his garden looked like. I wondered about the roses that Rhiannon had said grew at the bottom of it. I wondered what Rhiannon knew.

Flynn greeted me at the door, smiling shyly at me, as I stood on the doorstep, my stomach churning. I felt it do a funny little backflip as I stared at him, thinking how gorgeous he looked, and wondering why it had taken me so long to notice.

The stubble on his chin was highly attractive, and he wore a denim blue shirt, open at the neck, and a pair of faded jeans. His hair was a bit messy, and he seemed to realise it, running his hand through it rather self-consciously. He needn't have worried on my account. It was having a very disturbing effect on me. How easy it would have been to grab his hand and drag him upstairs for a repeat performance. My treacherous body was practically screaming at me to go for it, my hormones popping, as I stood there, gaping at him like a moron.

'Come in,' he said, standing aside and ushering me in.

I stepped into the hallway, and he closed the door behind me. My eyes flickered toward the stairs, and I swallowed. I had to be strong. I couldn't let myself be fooled again.

I followed him through the doorway at the end of the hall and found myself in the kitchen. It was spotlessly clean, not a thing out of place, and ultra-modern. I thought of my own tiny, chaotic kitchen, and almost laughed at the contrast. If that didn't provide the perfect metaphor for Flynn and myself, I didn't know what would.

'Tea or coffee?' he asked.

I shook my head. 'Neither. I'm not staying.'

'Not staying?'

Hearing the disappointment in his voice, I turned away, my gaze drawn to the window. Beyond it, the expanse of lawn stretched outward and, at the end, a distinctive fusion of bright colours. A rose garden, full of orange, pink, white, and—most definitely—large, fat red blooms.

My resolve hardened as I turned back to him, my fists clenched tightly, as if to remind myself of my purpose.

'I don't understand?' Flynn's expression seemed anxious, his blue eyes showing his confusion.

It would have been so easy to reach out and stroke his cheek, soothe away his frown lines, make everything all right—but right for whom? Not me, that was for sure, and my feelings mattered just as much as his, didn't they? No one was going to make a fool of me, ever again.

'What's happened?' he asked. 'I know I haven't called you, and I apologise unreservedly for that. I can explain, I promise.'

'Go on, then.' Please, Flynn, I thought, make it a great explanation. Give me a reason to stay.

What appeared to be shock darkened his eyes. 'Well, I will. But it's not that simple. Not something I can just blurt out over a cup of coffee.'

'Thought not.' My voice was hard. I felt sick with disappointment.

'Rose, you have to believe me. I'm sorry, if you feel I've neglected you. I've not been myself for the last few days. Things are always difficult .... I'm not good to be around. But you and I, well, the other night ... I thought we—I thought things were ... going well?'

'Yeah, me, too,' I said, turning away so I didn't have to look in his eyes any longer. 'Just shows you, eh?'

'Rose!' He grabbed my arm, pulling me back to him, but I wrenched myself free and glared at him.

'Get off me. You've been rumbled, mate. Deal with it.'

He stared at me in bewilderment. 'Rumbled? I don't know what you're talking about.'

'Forget it.'

'Oh, no, you don't.' He reached out and grasped me by the shoulders, staring right at me. 'At least explain what's happened. The other night—did it mean nothing?'

'Oh, pur-lease.' I rolled my eyes. 'Get a grip. We had sex. We're consenting adults. Big deal.'

'We had sex? And that's it, is it? That's how you see it?'

'Yep.' I folded my arms, mainly to hide the fact that I was trembling. I tried hard to stay steady, focused, but I was in grave danger of crying.

He seemed to consider me for a moment, before he shook his head, releasing me as he did so. 'I don't believe you. I know what happened. I know how we felt. Something's changed. What is it? Don't you think you owe me that, at least?'

'I don't think I owe you anything,' I snapped. 'Not after what you've done.'

'What I've done? What have I done? Will you just stop being a brat and tell me what your problem is?'

'Well, that's rich!' My fury nearly over-spilled. 'Don't you dare lecture me. It's you who has the problem.'

'Oh, and what problem's that?'

'The same problem that most men have in my experience—you can't keep it in your fucking trousers.'

'I beg your pardon?'

I gripped the expensive granite worktop and leaned towards him, fighting back tears. 'I saw you at Whitby Station, giving red roses to that woman.'

He reeled back, obviously shocked. 'You saw me? How? What the hell were you doing at Whitby Station?'

'Does it matter? It's hardly the point, is it? The point is—'

'Yes? The point is what?'

'The point is, you've obviously got some other woman. There's no way that was an innocent meeting. I saw the way you hugged. I saw you kiss her. I saw the roses—red roses. Red roses are for love, aren't they?'

He was silent for a moment, then he shrugged. 'Yes, they are. Red roses are for love.'

'So, who was she?'

He cleared his throat. 'That was Lindsey. My ex-wife.'

I could hardly breathe. 'So, I was right? You are still hung up on your wife. My God. And does she know that while you're panting around after her, you're also screwing around with a bit of rough?'

'What?'

'Surprised you didn't make me take a test first. Make sure I was clean. I hope you wear protection with her, too. I mean, I wouldn't want to infect her, or anything.' I pouted, aware that I sounded like a stupid, neurotic woman with a brain the size of a peanut.

'Right, that's it.'

He grabbed my arm and dragged me out of the house, before I had the chance to fight back. Ignoring my protests and my struggles, he marched me over to the car and unlocked the door, before practically throwing me into the passenger seat.

'Stay there,' he barked, slamming the door shut, and, heading back to the house, he locked up. That done, he climbed into the driver's seat and started the car.

'What are you doing?' I demanded, but he said nothing.

We drove in silence for what felt like forever. I thought, at first, that he was going to Maurice's house, as we headed towards Helmston, but we passed the turnoff for his street and continued down the main road.

'Where are we going?'

'You'll see,' he muttered, his hands clenched tightly on the steering wheel.

We went through Helmston and out into the countryside beyond.

I began to get a horrible feeling of dread. 'Flynn, I mean it. Where are we going?'

'I told you, you'll see. Just shut up.'

It was on the tip of my tongue to have a go at him for talking to me that way, but I couldn't speak. I'd never seen him like that. He looked grey, and suddenly old. I had an awful feeling I'd made a big mistake.

We headed into a little village called Bramblewick. It wasn't somewhere I'd ever been before, so I'd no idea what to expect, as Flynn slowed the car and indicated left down a little lane.

We drove along for a few minutes before he pulled over and turned off the engine. 'Get out.'

I turned to him in surprise. 'What do you mean, get out? Where are we?'

He climbed out of the car and went to stand by the bonnet, resting against it as if in need of support. I stared at him through the windscreen for a moment. It was the first time he hadn't come round to open the door for me.

Nervously, I undid my seat belt and climbed out, going to stand beside him.

We were opposite a church—a small, rustic, Saxon church. Flynn took hold of my arm, and pulled me through the gate, up the gravel path towards the building. Blimey, I thought, don't tell me the ex-Mrs Pennington-Rhys is a vicar?

As we got near the door, Flynn turned left, and we rounded the side of the church, our feet crunching on the gravel. He was silent as he pulled me along, crossing the churchyard, striding purposefully through the graves until we came to a little white headstone.

There, he stopped, and I looked down, my stomach contracting as I saw the red roses that adorned the little grave.

'What—what is it?'

'You mean, who is it? This is my daughter's grave. My little girl.'

I felt the ground begin to spin beneath my feet.

His face held an impassive expression, but his hand clenched the headstone tightly as he looked down at the neat little grave that contained the remains of his child.

'I don' t.... I didn't .... I mean, when?'

'Her name is—was—is, Emily. She was four months old. It was Sudden Infant Death Syndrome—cot death—just one of those things. Nothing anyone could have done, apparently.'

'Oh, my God, Flynn. I'm so sorry.'

'Lindsey and I, we meet up every year on her birthday and bring red roses to her grave. They're special ones. They're called *Loving Remembrance*. I grow them in my garden.'

I felt sick. So, that's what Rhiannon had meant. Why hadn't I listened? Why did I have to go charging in like an idiot?

My body burned with shame.

Flynn stroked the headstone, his face lined with sadness. 'There's nothing between Lindsey and me anymore. Hasn't been for ages. Not in the way you think, anyway. We never really got over it. We tried so hard not to blame each other, tried to put it behind us, move on. We couldn't. Lindsey—she reached the point where she wanted to try again. Another baby. I couldn't contemplate it. It seemed cruel, disloyal. As if any child could replace my beautiful Emily. Eventually, we realised we couldn't make each other happy anymore. We were too much of a reminder to each other, of what had happened. Lindsey asked me for a divorce, and I agreed. Simple as that.'

'Do you still love her?'

'Yes, probably, but not in a romantic way. She's a lovely woman and we were happy until ... well, until Emily.'

'Oh, Flynn.' I shook my head, my vision blurred with tears.

'Lindsey's married again. They have a son. He's four. So, you see, you had no reason to accuse me. There's no affair. No romance.'

'I see that. I'm sorry. I didn't know.'

'No, you didn't. You just assumed.' He turned to me, and his eyes were dark with pain. 'I'm many things, Rose. Call me a coward and I'll hold my hands up—'

'You're not a coward,' I said immediately. 'You're a brave man. You—'

'I'm a coward. I couldn't face up to my own grief, never mind my wife's. Nevertheless, I'm not a liar, nor am I a cheat. Obviously, you don't know me at all.'

'It's not that,' I said, desperate to make him understand. 'It's just that I've been lied to in the past. I've been fooled by men before, and I just didn't want to go through it all again.'

'I would never have done that to you,' he said quietly. 'I thought you understood that. You followed me to the train station, you spied on me. You jumped to all sorts of conclusions and accused me without any evidence at all. All you had to do was ask me. If you'd asked, I would have told you.'

Wasn't that what Rhiannon had said? Why hadn't I just done that, instead of acting all paranoid? I hung my head.

He bent down and touched the roses gently, while I looked through tears at the inscription on the headstone. "Emily Grace Pennington-Rhys, Sleeping Peacefully In the Arms of the Angels." I strangled a sob. Poor Flynn. How had he coped with this? How could any parent cope with it? How would I have coped with the loss of Fuchsia or Cerise? It didn't bear thinking about.

I reached out and stroked his hair, but he sprang up as if I'd slapped him and cleared his throat.

'Come on. Let's go.'

'We don't have to. If you want to stay ...'

'No. Let's go.'

He turned and began to walk back up the path. I followed, casting one last glance over my shoulder at the little grave, wondering how he could bear to leave her there, wondering how he'd walked away from her when it happened.

We got back into the car and he drove us home in silence. I wanted to say something, but what could I say? Nothing sounded right anymore. Everything seemed trite and pointless, after the bombshell he'd just dropped on me. He didn't go back to Ivy House, but turned right at the junction opposite The Kearton Arms and stopped outside the pub, the engine still running.

I sat for a moment, before I realised he wasn't going to say anything and unclipped my seat belt. 'Flynn, I—'

'Just go, Rose. Please.' He turned his head, staring straight ahead of him.

Swallowing hard, I climbed out of the car, slamming the door, and almost stumbled to the top of Bay Street. Behind me, I heard the squeal of tyres, as he turned the car and headed to Ivy House. I didn't look back.

****

Flynn closed the front door and, leaning against it, closed his eyes as if to shut out the memory of the last couple of hours. He didn't know how he'd managed to hold it together. He'd prayed Rose wouldn't stay, wanting answers. He knew he could never have dealt with it. It had taken all his strength to take her to the grave, to show her where Emily lay, to drive her back home without the carefully-constructed facade crumbling.

After locking the door, he walked slowly, heavily, to the living room. The sideboard was like all the other furniture in his house—new, fresh, without any memories attached to it. Inside was another matter. He pulled open the door and stood for a moment, taking a deep breath before bending down and looking inside. There it was. The box. Untouched all those years. He'd resisted looking inside it all that time, but, somehow, he knew that he couldn't resist it any longer. He had to open it up, just this once, then never again.

He carried it over to the sofa and sank down onto the leather upholstery. Gingerly, he took off the lid, and took a sharp breath as the scent hit him. Was it even real? Talcum powder, baby shampoo, the gentle wash powder that Lindsey had always used on the baby clothes ... surely, after all that time, it wouldn't still be tangible? Yet, he could smell them—those beautiful scents that used to linger on Emily. He remembered the sensation of holding her tightly to him, feeling her dark hair, soft against his skin, breathing her in. He remembered it all, so vividly.

Staring down into the box, he gently pulled back the tissue paper, gasping at the shock of seeing her little knitted bootees. He remembered Lindsey's mother had knitted them. His own mother wouldn't dream of knitting. She'd never shown much interest in him, so she wasn't going to be overcome with love for her granddaughter. Lindsey's mother, though, was very maternal, and had knitted matinée coats, complete with little satin ribbons, and tiny little hats, which they hadn't been able to imagine would fit any real baby. They hadn't realised how small babies actually were, but she'd been right. They'd fitted perfectly. Lindsey had laughed and announced that they were far too old-fashioned. No one dressed their babies in hand-knitted clothes anymore. The shops had been full of trendy little dresses and dungarees, leggings and T-shirts. Their baby would look ridiculous in knitted matinée jackets and bootees.

Flynn had pointed out that it obviously meant a lot to her mother, though, so they'd dressed her in the clothes she'd made, and even Lindsey had admitted that Emily looked adorable in them—although, to be fair, Emily would have looked adorable in anything.

As he carefully placed the bootees on the arm of the sofa, he smiled sadly at the small teddy bear that had been hidden beneath them. She'd loved that teddy. She'd slept with it in her cot every night. It had also lain beside her when she left them, when they hadn't been there for her. He hoped it had been a comfort to her on her last night.

He stroked the soft fur gently. It had done its duty, never left her side. He'd wanted to bury it with her, but Lindsey couldn't bear to part with it. She'd placed Emily's toy rabbit inside the coffin instead, and Flynn had wanted to protest, sure that Emily would want the bear, but he couldn't cope with any more of Lindsey's grief, so he'd gone along with her wishes. Ironically, when they separated, she'd given it to him. Time for a fresh start, she'd said gently, as if she knew that he wasn't ready to let go, the way she had. Not that she'd ever forget her baby girl, but she was willing to start living life without her again. She knew that he wasn't. She'd understood that. It was why they'd agreed to part, after all.

Feeling the familiar stab of pain, Flynn forced himself to open the little box beside the teddy. It contained a lock of her hair, curled up in cotton wool at the bottom of the box, almost as dark as his own. He longed to touch it, but he was afraid it would disintegrate beneath his fingers. He couldn't disturb it, not after all those years.

He put the lid back on and, instead, picked up the rattle, nestled in the tissue paper beside it. She'd giggled so much when she played with it and had loved bashing it against the floor. He'd often wondered how it managed to stay intact.

There was her silver bracelet, too—a christening gift from Lindsey's grandmother. Neither he, nor Lindsey, had thought much about getting her christened, but it meant a lot to Lindsey's family, so they'd gone along with it. When the worst had happened, they'd been grateful that they had, clinging to the hope that it actually meant something. That she'd gone to a better place. That she was being loved and cared for.

He came to the bottom of the box, and his fingers closed around the pile of photographs that had been hidden away for almost a decade. He hadn't looked at them once. He had one photograph of her in his desk at work, and sometimes, when he couldn't help himself, he would take it out and look at it, staring into her laughing blue eyes and hoping, praying, that she would know that he was still thinking about her, still loving her. It was safer at work. He could never be sure that Meggie or Gabriel wouldn't walk into the room, and there was always a patient to deal with, or a phone call to make. No time to dwell. No time to give way to the emotion that threatened to choke him every time he looked at her dear face. Whereas at home, alone in the empty house, he had no one to distract him. If he had the photographs out there, he might not be able to stop himself crying, breaking down, letting go of the grief. Once he started, he may never stop. So, he kept them locked away, kept her locked away, the memory of her buried as deep within him as her little body lay buried beneath the ground.

It was all too much. He could feel the pain bubbling up inside him. He couldn't do it. Hastily, he jammed everything back inside the box and replaced the lid, quickly putting it back inside the sideboard and shutting the door. He would visit Maurice—that was what he'd do. No doubt, he would welcome the company, and maybe they could go for a walk somewhere. It would do Maurice good to get out of the house, get some fresh air. It was bad for him, being cooped up inside with only his memories for company.

Flynn turned his back on the living room and made for the front door, his car keys jangling in his hand like the sound of a baby's rattle.

CHAPTER NINETEEN

July dragged on. The verges were bright with daisies, buttercups and dandelions, wild poppies and harebells. Up on the moors, the heather was a carpet of purple flowers, and visitors flocked into the area, keen to explore the beauty of the moorland and its quaint villages. Kearton Bay was heaving with tourists, and the shop was doing a roaring trade, which was a very good thing, as I needed my mind occupying.

Eliza had expressed her concern that I was quiet and not my usual self, and urged me to talk to Flynn. I told her we'd decided to put our one night stand down to experience and part as friends. It wasn't true, but what else could I say? His secret wasn't mine to tell, and even if I'd confided in her, I could hardly expect her not to tell Gabriel. She told him everything, and he worked with Flynn. It wouldn't be fair on either of them. I was pretty certain that neither knew about Emily, and it wasn't up to me to enlighten them. I'd caused enough damage already.

At least things at home were looking up. My mother had confirmed that she was moving into Alec's three-bedroomed semi in Redcar after the wedding, so at least I'd get my bedroom back, and Fuchsia was positively beaming these days, although I still got the feeling that something was bugging her, and she was very cagey about where she was going and who those friends of hers were.

Cerise was spending a lot of time staying at her friend's house, too. They lived in Farthingdale, and had a lot more room than we had, and a garden where the girls could sit out in the sun and relax. She was growing up fast. She went out one day, fresh-faced, and with her hair in a ponytail, and came home with full makeup on and her hair straightened to within an inch of its life.

She also asked me if she could have highlights, but I refused. My mother said I was being mean, but I said, at fourteen, she was too young to start messing with hair dye and bleach. My mother said I had a short memory, and didn't I recall the electric blue streaks I'd sported at the age of thirteen? I said I recalled them only too well, and the photos were still dragged out to humiliate me, and I would be no sort of mother at all if I didn't protect Cerise from the same hideous fate. Cerise said I was an old misery, and Heidi's mother had agreed to Heidi having highlights. I said Heidi could do what the hell she liked, and I didn't care how many photos there were to embarrass her when she grew up, but there was no way I was letting Cerise dye her hair and that was that. After calling me a hypocrite, she'd huffed and puffed about it all day, but when I gave her twenty quid to go to Boots in Whitby and get some makeup of her own, she brightened up considerably and told me I was ace, so that was all right.

It seemed that I was the only unhappy person in our household, which made a change. My mother was in her element, spending a fortune on bridal magazines and scanning the pages for something suitable to wear. She decided that I would make the perfect maid of honour, which horrified me, especially as she insisted that she choose my outfit. God help me.

Alec had booked St Hilda's church for the second Friday in August, and negotiated a deal with Clifford for a cut-price reception at The Kearton Arms. Some bakery in Oddborough was taking care of the cake, and a florist in Redcar was doing the flowers. Alec didn't want to wear a wedding ring, but had bought my mother one. She had no idea what it was like, because he'd chosen it and kept it away from her, which I thought was a bit off. In fact, I thought the whole thing was off. He struck me as a total control freak. No wonder he'd never married before.

I couldn't believe my mother was actually going through with it. Surely the sex wasn't that good? The thought of it made me feel sick. She really should have lost her libido by now.

I wished to God I could lose mine, but it had been brutally awakened and was raring to go. I kept remembering Flynn's hands on me, the sight of him that morning naked under the duvet, and I would go hot and tingly and have to take my mind off it all very quickly. I found Alec was useful in that respect. I just thought of his disgusting leer when he'd clocked Rhiannon across the paddock, and that was usually enough to make me cool down very quickly.

My mother kept showing me pictures of hideous bridesmaid dresses in magazines and saying, 'What do you think of that one?'

I turned down every one of them, horrified at the thought of anything made of satin, anything that would cling too tightly to my, ahem, curvy body, and anything peach. She was getting a bit fed up with me, to be honest.

'You're a complete nightmare,' she said. 'It's not my fault you're a bit lumpy, and if you got rid of that daft pink streak, you wouldn't clash with the peach.'

'Peach is so nineteen-eighties,' I said defiantly. 'And I won't part with my streak. It's my last bit of independence. Jimbo forbid me to get it, so I did it, anyway. It means a lot to me.'

'Alec has chosen the colour scheme, though,' she said. 'I can't do anything about it now. He's ordered the flowers, and the cake's peaches and cream. Can't you just dye it, temporarily?'

'No,' I said, folding my arms. 'It stays.'

She was quite put out by the whole thing, so I suppose it was inevitable that when Cerise walked through the door that evening, with a whole waterfall of blonde streaks in her hair, she would find it highly amusing.

'What the buggery bollocks have you done?' I screeched, looking at my baby girl in horror.

'You gave me that twenty quid, so I bought a home streaking kit. Heidi did it for me. Looks good, doesn't it?'

'It looks awful. You'll have to dye over it.'

'I won't,' she said furiously. 'I like it. It stays.'

'Aw, leave her alone,' said my mother. 'She shouldn't have to part with it. It's her last bit of independence.' She gave me a smug grin, and I glared at her, furious that she'd thrown my own words back at me.

Bloody hell, did I have no control over anything in my life anymore?

My mother's phone began to ring, and while she answered it, Cerise and I exchanged further pleasantries, and I decided that I would really have to start doing the lottery, because it was the only way I was ever going to be able to afford to buy a house on a desert island and never have to see anyone in my family ever again.

'You'll never guess!' my mother said.

Cerise and I stopped arguing for a moment and looked at her, as she hopped up and down like Tigger on speed and waved her phone at us in excitement.

'Blimey, what now?' I hardly dared think.

'That was Alec. *Ti Amo Magazine* has just been in touch with him. They want to run an article about us. You know, all about our lost love, and how we rediscovered each other all these years later.'

'How did they know about it?' I asked, puzzled.

'They saw our engagement notice in *The Oddborough Herald*,' she said. 'They made some enquiries, and bingo! Isn't it exciting?'

I frowned. 'Why would *Ti Amo Magazine* be scouring the engagement notices in a local paper? And how did they know you'd been separated so long? And, anyway, surely they're not that hard up for stories?'

'You really are a killjoy,' said my mother, plonking herself down on the sofa and dropping her phone in her bag. 'I don't know where you get it from. I've always been very open to new experiences.'

'Haven't you just,' I muttered.

'Well, I think it's great, Gran,' said Cerise, giving me a poisonous look. 'I reckon Mam's just jealous.'

'Aye, that'll be it,' she agreed, her face brightening. 'It's gonna be lovely. They're going to meet us in York, and take us for tea at Betty's Tea Rooms. Can you imagine? And we're gonna have our photos taken and be interviewed like celebrities. Ooh, I'm that made up.'

She sat babbling on about her forthcoming interview as if she was preparing to go on *The Charlie Hope Show*, not chat a bit to some reporter from a trashy magazine. Cerise encouraged her just to spite me, of course. Great. It seemed that just as Fuchsia was approaching something like normal behaviour, Cerise was morphing into Miley bloody Cyrus. What the hell had I done to deserve all this?

Then I remembered Flynn's expression, the hurt in his eyes, the pain in his face as he'd told me about his daughter, standing over her grave and gripping the headstone with hands that were clenched so tightly the knuckles were white. And I knew I deserved everything I got.

****

Eliza wasn't happy. I'd been busy in the shop, while she and Chrissie worked in the kitchen, but I'd gone through during a lull and put the kettle on, sitting on the sofa, which we'd put at the end of the room, to give us a place to rest whenever we had the chance, while I waited for it to boil. I felt really awful. I reckoned I must have been coming down with a bug, or something. Even the sight of the marshmallows made me feel queasy. Maybe I shouldn't have been anywhere near the kitchen. But then, I hadn't had any real symptoms. Just nausea.

'Do you want a cup of tea?' I asked.

Chrissie nodded, not looking up from the big fluffy pillow

she was cutting up into squares. Usually, I adored the salted caramel mallows, but today I had to look away hastily.

Eliza was banging pans and muttering to herself. I looked at Chrissie, who rolled her eyes and shrugged.

'What's up with you?' I asked.

Eliza seemed delighted to be given the chance to explode. 'Bloody Harry! He can't have Amy because he and Melody are *having problems* and he needs to sort it out. She's taken Rufus and cleared off to the South of France for the summer, to think things over, and he's decided to follow her over there to try and patch things up.'

I winced. The South of France was where the two of them had cleared off after their affair was exposed, and it must have been pretty galling that Harry was going to all that effort to repair their marriage, when he'd done little to aid his first to Eliza. Not to mention the fact that Amy had been left out in the cold, yet again.

'He could have taken her with them. It will be Christmas before she sees him again, and I wonder if he'll come up with some excuse even then. What kind of a father is he?'

'A crap one, but, really, Amy's probably better off with you. She doesn't need to be around them if they're rowing, does she? Poor little Rufus. He's got the rough end of the stick, if you ask me. Amy's got you and Gabriel. Look who he's got to deal with.'

She stopped scowling and grinned. 'I suppose you're right. Gosh, Rose, are you all right? You look like you have a giant hangover.'

I took a deep breath. 'Yeah, I feel like I've got a hangover, too. I feel shocking.'

'Oh, no.' Her expression immediately changed, and she was all concern. 'Sit down, and I'll make the tea. Is it something you've eaten?'

'I hope not.' Chrissie looked worried. 'If she's got food poisoning, or any kind of bug, she needs to get out of here. We don't want environmental health on our case. Get yourself home, Rose, till we know what it is.'

'Don't be daft,' I began, but Eliza was nodding.

'She's right. Go home and rest up. If you're no better tomorrow, I'll ask Gabriel to take a look at you. We can't afford to take risks.'

'But I don't want to go home,' I complained. The thought of a whole day with my mother was too much to bear.

'It's for the best,' she said. 'We'll manage. Please, Rose, be sensible.'

Grumbling, I took off my apron and headed back upstairs to the flat, where I found my mother sprawled on the sofa, eating a box of chocolates. She nearly had a heart attack when she saw me standing there.

'What are you doing back?' She tried to hide the chocolates under her magazine, but it was way too late for that.

'Kept those quiet, didn't you?'

'They were a present from Alec. I'd forgotten all about them till this morning. Just had one, or two. Have one, if you like?'

My stomach churned at the thought. 'No, thanks. I'll pass.'

Her eyes narrowed, and she looked at me suspiciously. 'What's up with you? Hangover?'

'In case you hadn't noticed, I haven't had a drink in weeks.'

'Well, you look very dodgy.'

'Thanks. I feel dodgy. That's why I'm here. Eliza and Chrissie sent me home, in case I've got a stomach bug. Health and safety, and all that stuff.'

She nodded, picking up her magazine with a laugh. 'Oh, aye, got to be proper careful these days. You don't want to be poisoning the whole village. Ah, well, at least we know you're not pregnant. No chance of that, any road.'

I dropped down on the armchair, staring at the wall in front of me. Pregnant? Well, no, I couldn't be, could I? I mean, we'd been careful and responsible. What date was it, anyway?

I reached for my phone and clicked on the calendar. After a quick calculation, I shook my head. That couldn't be right. I checked again, and my entire body went cold.

I was ten days late.

Even so, I couldn't be pregnant. I'd put the condom on Flynn myself, and I'd done it properly, I was sure. It couldn't be that. It must just be a coincidence.

My mother was engrossed in the magazine, her hand dipping into the box of chocolates every now and then. I stood up and shakily made my way into the bedroom.

'Where are you going?' she demanded.

'Just going to get the duvet,' I said. 'Feeling a bit cold.'

'Cold? Are you mad? You must be ill,' she said, but returned to her reading, her motherly instinct apparently satisfied.

I shut the bedroom door behind me and looked feverishly around. Where did she keep them? I quietly slid open the drawers one by one, screwing up my nose as I hunted through the piles of underwear and stockings. It was like a tart's boudoir in there these days. I wouldn't have been at all surprised to find a garter and a pair of crotch-less knickers.

They weren't there. I looked around, wondering where else they would be. Then I saw her handbag, and, trying not to feel guilty, I opened it up and looked inside. Rummaging around, my hand closed around a familiar little package, and I pulled it out. A strawberry-flavour condom. Not a chocolate one, as she'd given me, but then she didn't like the chocolate ones. She'd told me so herself. No doubt they'd been bought at the same time.

I took a deep breath, and as I examined the expiry date on the packet, I dropped the bag on the floor and put my head in my hands.

The door flew open, and my mother stood there. 'What the hell are you doing, rooting round in here? If you're looking for money, you're out of luck. I'm skint.' She must have read my body language, finally, because her expression changed, her voice softening. 'What is it, pet? What's wrong?'

'Oh, Mam,' I said, my voice catching with emotion. 'I think I've done it again.'

****

It wasn't often that I had cause to be truly grateful to my mother, but that day, she really pulled out all the stops. As I explained about the expiry date on the condoms, she sank onto the bed beside me and put her arm around me, her face white with shock.

'Christ, who knew? I mean, I know food has dates on it, but condoms? Fancy that. Didn't think I'd have to check them. Jesus, I could have caught anything from Alec. Not that I would have done, obviously, but you know what I mean. And they're definitely out of date?'

'Put it this way,' I said wearily, 'you probably bought them when dad was still alive, right?'

She blushed. 'It was just a bit of fun. I thought they'd be all right. They'd never been opened so .... Aw, pet, I'm sorry.' Her face brightened suddenly. 'So, you and Finn? When did that happen, eh?'

'Flynn,' I said automatically. 'And it happened that night after we'd all been to Whitby.'

'Ooh, I knew it! I knew you two were made for each other. Aw, he'll make a lovely dad. You've picked a good 'un there at last, love.'

It was too much. My face crumpled and I gave way to tears.

My mother pulled me to her and let me cry, stroking my hair away from my face and wiping my tears with a tissue from her bag. I vaguely hoped it was clean, but I didn't want to spoil the moment. She hadn't been this kind to me since ... well, ever.

'What's wrong, pet? Is it your hormones, do you think?'

I shook my head and sat up straight. 'Me and Flynn, we're through. It was just a one-off. We're not together, and we never will be.'

'But why?' She looked puzzled. 'You're so right for each other. Me and Maurice were talking about it when you were queuing up for our fish and chips. We both said you made a lovely couple, and we hoped you'd realise it yourselves.' She pulled a face. 'Was he rubbish in bed?'

I half laughed and rubbed my face. 'Far from it. He was bloody amazing.'

'Well, there you go. That's half the battle, in my experience. They can be complete losers in life, but if they can take you to bed and make you forget all about it, who cares?'

'Oh, Mam.' I sniffed. 'It's all such a mess.'

'What is? What went wrong?'

I thought about it. Would I be breaking a confidence if I told her all about Emily? Could I trust her?

'If I tell you something, you have to swear that you won't repeat it to anyone. It's not my secret to tell, really, and I haven't told anyone else, but you have to promise, Mam.'

She looked quite indignant. 'As if I would! If you don't want me to, I won't. What it is?'

I hesitated, then, slowly, I told her all about the roses, and my jumping to conclusions, and trailing him to Whitby, and seeing him with his ex-wife. I told her about our argument, and then, shame-faced, I told her about our trip to Bramblewick, and seeing the grave of little Emily.

I waited for her to have a go at me for blundering in and upsetting him, but she was silent. When I looked up, I was astonished to see that she had tears in her eyes.

'Poor bugger,' she murmured. 'Four months old. Bad enough for me, but that ... aw, bless them.'

'Bad enough for you?' I was confused. 'What do you mean?'

She wiped her eyes. 'Five, I lost, Rose. Two before you, and three after. All at different stages of pregnancy. They could never give me a reason why. The first two were early miscarriages. I barely knew I was pregnant, and I was young. They said to just keep trying, so we did, and we got you. You were a month early, but you were healthy and strong. Always was a little fighter. Afterwards, well, it wasn't so easy. Lost two at four months, and then the last one ...' Her voice trailed off and a tear rolled down her cheek. 'He looked perfect to me. I was seven months gone. He should have been all right. Born sleeping, was how your dad put it.'

I was completely gobsmacked. How had I never known about it all? 'When did this happen? How old was I?'

'About four, I think. Your dad told you I'd gone to visit your gran, but I was in hospital. We called him Peter, and I can still see his little face now. After that, we decided never again, I couldn't go through any more. We had you, and we were grateful for that. Broke our hearts to lose him, so I can imagine what Flynn went through. To have your baby in your arms, in your life, for four whole months, and then to have her snatched away. Dear God, life can be cruel sometimes.'

'Oh, Mam.' I didn't know what to say. 'Why did you never tell me?'

'Why would I? It would only have upset you, and for what?'

I was silent for a moment, and she shook her head. 'Don't do that.'

'Do what?'

'I know you, Rose. You've always been the same. You're sitting there now, wondering if I ever wished it was you I'd lost instead of Peter.'

I bit my lip. She was right. I had been thinking exactly that.

Gently, she cupped my face in her hands and turned me to look at her. 'Peter was my beautiful, bonny boy, and I wish to God I'd been allowed to keep him, but never at your expense. Never. Me an' your dad, we knew you'd take it all on yourself, so we said nowt. We were right, an' all. Trouble with you is, you don't know your own worth. Look at all this palaver with

Flynn, for a start. You think you're not good enough for him, but you are! Of course you are. He'd be lucky to have you, any bloke would. Look how you've brought them two bairns up on your own and made a go of your sweet shop. You're a proper catch. Wish you'd see what the rest of us see.'

I gaped at her. Was this really my mother talking? 'But you're always having a go at me, saying how useless I am at everything. And my dad …' I gulped and shook my head.

'Your dad, what?' she demanded. 'What about him?'

'He was so disappointed in me,' I whispered.

She stared at me in shock. 'What the hell are you on about? Your dad was never disappointed in you. What the heck gave you that idea?'

'You did!' I said, stunned at her sudden memory loss. 'On the morning of his funeral, you told me that he'd been so disappointed in me. Do you think I'd forget that?'

She shook her head and stroked my hair, her eyes filled with tears. 'Oh, Rose, you daft ha'porth. I said he was disappointed *for* you, not in you. He hated the way Bazza had abandoned you and Fuchsia, and he didn't trust Jumbo for a minute. He always said he'd let you down, and he was worried sick about you being left with two bairns. He said you were so lovely, so bright, you deserved the best. Bloody hell, how could you think any different? Don't you know how much he loved you? How much we both loved you?'

I could only sob, unable to form a single word.

'I know it must seem sometimes that I'm always having a go at you. I'm just like that. I saw you making mistakes, and I wanted to wake you up. I thought, if I kept on at you, you'd listen, but even when I was saying it, I was kicking meself. You were worth so much more than what you ended up with, Rose. That's what made us sad. Not you. Never you.'

She smiled suddenly. 'But now you've got a real chance of happiness. That bloke of yours, he's lovely. He's not Bazza, or Jumbo. By God, you do pick men with weird names, don't you? Anyway, point is, he's a kind man with a good heart, and what's more he's not skint, and he's got a nice house. Things can be really good for you, from now on.'

I wiped my eyes. 'Did you not listen? I've blown it, Mam. He's dropped me because I acted like a paranoid idiot, and besides, it's all impossible now ...'

'Why? 'Cos of the bairn? But surely a bairn is exactly what he wants?'

I shook my head. 'He said he wasn't ready to move on. He didn't want to replace Emily. That's why he and Lindsey split up. She's moved on, had a son, but he can't. A new baby is the last thing he'd want.'

'You never know till you tell him.'

'I can't. Anyway ...' I looked at her, suddenly hopeful. '... maybe this is all a horrible coincidence? Maybe I'm late for another reason? Maybe I'm not pregnant?'

'Only one way to find out.' She stood up, smoothing down her dress with her hands and fixing me with a determined look. 'Pass me bag. I'll go and get you a test.'

'You can't!'

'Why on earth not? You can't just sit here, biting your nails and worrying for the next nine months, putting it all down to wind.'

'But there's only one chemist in the village, and Mrs Roberts might tell people ... I can't.'

'Okay. Well, where's the nearest chemist outside of this wilderness, then?'

'Farthingdale, I suppose.'

'Right. Well, I'll take a walk to Farthingdale and pick up a test, and then we'll know where we stand, one way or the other.'

'Really?' I was quite astonished that she'd do all that for me. I usually had to beg her just to put an extra slice of bread in the toaster for me, but she was already picking up her bag. There was no turning back. My fate was about to be decided.

****

She was gone for over an hour. I felt mean letting her go on her own, but I really couldn't face walking into a shop and staring at all those pregnancy tests on the shelf. It made it all seem too real, and it couldn't be, could it?

I paced up and down the living room, absent-mindedly picking at my mother's chocolates. She would throttle me when she found out how many I'd pinched, but I needed something, since my nausea had passed.

Flynn's words kept coming back to me, over and over again. "Another baby. I couldn't contemplate it. It seemed cruel, disloyal. As if any child could replace my beautiful Emily".

I remembered the look in his face as he'd stroked the headstone, the pain in his voice. A pregnancy was the worst thing that could have happened. He would never want another baby, let alone one with me. And what about me? How did I feel? Even putting aside the inevitable fact that I would be a single mother, yet again, could I really cope with a baby at my age? I wasn't that far from forty, and I had a business to run. Then there was Fuchsia and Cerise. How would they deal with it? And I'd be tied down again. The thought of all those dirty nappies and sleepless nights was bad enough, but when I looked ahead and saw eighteen years, or more, of schools and tantrums, stroppy teenage years and more financial pressure .... Oh God.

I felt really sick again, and that time, I didn't think it was down to hormones. How could I do it? Go through all that stuff again?

My mother returned home to find me sniffing into my tissue and feeling very sorry for myself indeed. 'What's the matter now?'

'I don't want to be pregnant. I can't face all that again. It's not fair.'

'You reckon?'

'Yes, I do,' I said petulantly. 'I've done all this twice. I don't want another baby.'

'Well, before you start mithering, why don't you take the test and see if you've got anything to whinge about? And thanks for eating all me chocolates.'

'Sorry.' I pushed the tissue up my sleeve and took the bag she held out to me.

After a moment, she sat down beside me on the sofa. 'I don't know if you realise how it works, but you have to actually pee on a stick, not hold it to your stomach and hope it communicates with the foetus.'

'I know. I'm trying to pluck up the courage.'

'Never mind courage. Have you had anything to drink?'

I nodded. 'I've been dying for the loo for ages.'

'Brilliant. The gods are smiling down on you. No waiting round. Off you pop.'

I stood up shakily and headed to the bathroom, hoping and praying that the gods were indeed smiling down on me.

'Well?'

A few minutes later, I was back in the living room, clutching the stick and not even daring to look at it.

'What does it say?'

'I don't know. I can't look,' I admitted. 'Will you do it?'

'Well, hold it out for me, then. I'm buggered if I'm touching it.'

I held out the stick and waited, biting my lip as I tried to read her expression. She squinted at it, then grabbed it from my hand, hygiene issues apparently forgotten.

'Mam?'

She smiled up at me and put her hand in mine. 'Congratulations, pet. You're up the duff.'

CHAPTER TWENTY

The wedding was just a week away, and things were getting a bit frantic. My mother and Alec had had their trip to York and given their interview to *Ti Amo Magazine*. She'd seemed more excited by the afternoon tea they'd had at Betty's than meeting the reporter, but she was quite thrilled that she'd had her photo taken and been told that she was very photogenic. She'd come home floating on cloud nine, and couldn't wait for the issue, featuring her and her long-lost love, to come out.

Alec had assured her that the flowers and cake were all sorted, and he'd met up with Clifford, the landlord of The Kearton Arms, to make final decisions on the menu, which he told my mother was "a surprise". Everything about the wedding would be a surprise to her, since he'd taken over almost every aspect. Mind you, that might have been a blessing in disguise. The only job she had was buying the dresses, and she hadn't even managed that. She couldn't decide on her outfit and was panicking. I was panicking, too, when she finally brought home the dress she'd chosen for me. It made me look like Mama Cass.

I gasped, as soon as I saw the cream chiffon ankle-length gown she was holding up for me. 'I can't wear that.'

'It's your own fault,' she said. 'You refused to wear peach, which only left cream, and this was the only one they had that didn't cling to your bits, and since you insisted you wanted something looser, I snapped it up. Like it, or lump it.'

'Great. Can I lump it, then?'

'No. You're wearing it, and that's that.'

I might have said I wanted something looser, but the dress was like a tent. I could have taken a homeless family in under those skirts. Even my mother looked horrified when I tried it on, and the girls were helpless.

Cerise fell over onto the sofa and howled with laughter.

'Aw, Mam, you look hilarious.'

'You look nine months pregnant,' said Fuchsia.

I caught my mother's eye, and she shook her head slightly, seeming to take pity on me. 'You don't look that bad, pet. Maybe if I get a sash to tie round the middle, it will look a bit better. Here, try the headdress on.'

'Headdress?' I stared at said headband, which was decorated with artificial peach roses and green ivy leaves, and looked to her. 'What did I ever do to you?'

She tutted and shoved it onto my head, standing back and pulling a face at me. 'Dear God, you look a sight. You'll have to get rid of that streak, nothing else for it.'

'I'm not wearing this,' I said, pulling the headband off and throwing it on the coffee table. 'I'm not wearing any of it. Forget it.'

'Don't be a brat,' she said. 'You look proper bonny.'

'Bonny?' I could feel the tears starting. It was all getting too much.

'Are you crying?' Cerise looked aghast. 'Seriously? Over a daft dress?'

'Shut up, Cerise,' said Fuchsia. 'Gran, Mam's right. This is a mess. Where did you get it from?'

'That little wedding shop in Moreton Cross. It was on sale. Eighty quid.'

'You were robbed.' I sniffed.

'Well, that's gratitude,' she said.

'Cerise, why don't you take Gran to Helmston, to that little shop behind the market square?' Fuchsia said. 'They do some lovely dresses there, and they're not bad prices.'

'I can't afford to pay out again,' my mother protested.

'You've got the receipt, haven't you?' Fuchsia said, shutting her up. 'Take that dress back and get a refund. You'll find something much better in Helmston, and Cerise knows what Mam would wear. Think about it, Gran. You're having two VIPs at your wedding, you don't want to make a show of yourself. Go on.'

She was canny, that one. My mother had been delighted when Joe had accepted her invitation to the wedding, and even more excited when he'd asked if he could bring Charlie along as his plus one. She was thrilled that she'd have a celebrity couple at her nuptials.

'Why me?' demanded Cerise, who was turning into a full-blown stroppy teenager. 'Why can't you go?'

'Because I want to talk to Mam about something. It's important, okay?'

I stopped sniffing and looked at her curiously. Fuchsia wanted to talk to me? Well, that was new. My mother and Cerise were obviously shocked by the unexpected turn of events, too, as they didn't argue, but gathered up the dress and receipt and headed out to find something better.

'You think they'll get something decent?' I asked.

'God knows,' Fuchsia admitted, 'but let's face it, they couldn't find anything much worse, could they?'

I gave a bitter laugh and wiped my nose.

'You okay now?' she asked.

'Yes. Sorry. Just felt a bit ... overwhelmed.'

'So I gathered. Not like you, Mam. But then, you've been acting a bit out of sorts for a while now.'

I tucked the tissue into my sleeve and tried to avoid her eye. 'Oh, I'm all right. Just a bit stressed with all this wedding malarkey. I'll be better when your gran's gone and I get my bedroom back.'

She was silent for a moment, then she reached out and took hold of my hand. I was so surprised I nearly fell off the sofa. She didn't look drunk or stoned, so what had happened?

'Mam, can I ask you something?'

I nodded, trying to still the little voice of doom that had started chattering in my head.

'Are you pregnant?'

Bollocks! Where had she got that from? The shock caught

me off guard and I gaped at her. 'How did you know that?'

She sat back and whistled. 'So you are! Christ, I thought I was imagining things.'

I sat back, too, and stared at the gas fire on the wall. God, it was ugly. I really should think about redecorating the place. Maybe when my mother had gone. It occurred to me suddenly that I might have to put the flat on the market. It would be far too small for three children. If I had a boy, he would need his own room—though, come to think of it, even if it was a girl, she'd need her own room, too. She was far too young to share with Cerise and Fuchsia, and be exposed to all their weird ways. And I hardly thought they would welcome *Peppa Pig* wallpaper. Something else to worry about. Where was I going to find somewhere decent to live that wasn't too far from the shop, and that I could afford?

So engrossed in my latest worry, I didn't realise Fuchsia was speaking at first. 'Eh? Sorry?'

'I was asking you when it's due,' she said patiently.

I considered. 'Er, March, sometime,' I said. I looked at her curiously. 'What gave it away?'

'I'd wondered for a few days. You've been quite nauseous, and you look awful in a morning, really rough.'

'Thanks.'

'What clinched it was the look gran gave you when I said you looked nine months pregnant. There was real sympathy in her eyes, and if that's not suspicious, I don't know what is.'

'You're not as daft as you look, are you?' I said.

'Ta very much. So, whose is it?'

Oh hell. How could I tell Fuchsia that I'd shagged her boss and was expecting his baby? She'd be mortified. She may even quit her job in disgust. I probably would have. I mean, how could she face her boss every day, knowing he'd been bumping bits with her own mother? Awkward.

'I'd rather not say,' I said eventually.

She opened her mouth as if to say something, but shut it

again. We sat quietly for a few moments, as though trying to adjust to spending time in each other's company without rowing.

'Mam, can I tell you something?' she said eventually.

'Of course.' I was beginning to think I was dreaming the entire day. Fuchsia was sitting with me, calmly taking the news that I'd gone and got myself pregnant at the ripe old age of thirty-seven, and suddenly she wanted to confide in me, too? It was all getting quite surreal.

'Thing is, it's a bit difficult for me. I've wanted to tell you for ages, but, well, there were problems. Still are, to be honest, but I'd like someone to talk it all over with. Someone on my side, for a change.'

I gulped. 'I'll always be on your side, Fuchsia.'

She looked at me with troubled grey eyes. 'Really?'

'Of course. I love you.' It hurt to hear the doubt in her voice. Had I been such a bad mother? She should have known I was on her side. Obviously, I hadn't done a great job with her. What was I doing, thinking I could raise another one? I must've been mad.

'Mam, I really don't know how to go about telling you this …' She nibbled on her thumb nail, and I waited, not wanting to push her.

I wondered if she was leaving to go to Bristol with Oliver. The thought was so painful, I wanted to grab her and hold her to me and tell her to stay. Oliver Crook! What use was he? He'd never shown the slightest interest in her. She was far too good for him.

'Thing is, I've—I've been seeing someone,' she began, eventually.

I nodded, feeling sick. 'I know. Oliver.'

Her head shot up, and she gave a short laugh. 'Oliver! Not you, too. No way am I interested in Oliver Crook.'

'You're not?' I said, astonished.

'Bloody hell, no. He's an immature tosser. Thinks he's

God's gift to women, too. Got way too big for his boots, that one.'

She sounded about sixty. I grinned. 'Thank God for that. He's a complete twat. So, who *have* you been seeing?' I hadn't noticed any other blokes hanging around, although she had been seeing those mysterious friends of hers lately. I wondered who it was. Still, what did it matter, as long as she was happy?

'You'll be cool with it, whoever it is?' she asked, her eyes full of anxiety.

'Yeah, course. Oh, shit, Fuchsia, he's not married, is he?'

'Would you be disappointed, if he was?'

'Well, yes, of course. Not just for the wife, but for you. They never leave them, you know. Well, except for Jimbo, but I wasn't his wife, was I? They never really break away, and you'll just be left, hanging on, hoping, waiting. And what about his family? Does he have kids? Oh, hell, this is a nightmare.'

She started to laugh. 'It's okay, Mam. He's not married.'

'Oh, thank Christ,' I said.

'He's not a he, either. He's a she. That's what I've been trying to tell you. I'm seeing Pandora.'

'Pandora? Pandora Crook?' Honestly, didn't kids like to fuck with your head? One minute Fuchsia was Camilla Parker-Bowles, the next she was Ellen DeGeneres. 'You and Pandora Crook? You're a couple? You're seeing a girl? Pandora?'

'Is it all right?' She was trembling as she said it.

I thought about all those times I'd seen her hanging round the Crook kids, and all the assumptions I'd made. I thought about her sullen behaviour, the times she'd hidden away in her bedroom, too miserable to make the effort to speak, the lost weight, the sleeping, the depression.

What had Flynn said? Crying in the toilets? No wonder. She'd had all this to go through, and I hadn't even known.

I put my arms around her and pulled her to me. Her body shook against mine, and I kissed the top of her head and told her how much I loved her, and that it didn't matter to me who she was seeing, as long as they made her happy, and of course it was all right.

'I wanted to tell you,' she said, pulling away from me, probably for air, 'but Pandora's scared of how her mother will take it, and she wanted it kept quiet. But I needed to talk it over. It's all right for Pandora. She's had Tally to talk to, and now Oliver knows, and they're cool with it. Cerise is a good kid, but she's too young really, and I felt bad that she took all that grief at school because of me.'

'What grief? What do you mean?'

With a sigh, she told me about her former workmates finding out about her and Pandora, how they'd tormented and bullied her until she couldn't face going into work any longer. It seemed one of her former colleagues was cousins with a girl in Cerise's class, and it wasn't long before the rumour got round that Cerise's sister was a lesbian. They'd been calling her names and mocking her, which Cerise wasn't going to allow. She'd got hold of the ringleader and given her a good pasting. Fuchsia said she'd come home and demanded to know the truth, and when Fuchsia had admitted it, Cerise had given her a hug and said it was absolutely fine, but she wished Fuchsia had had the guts to tell her, because she'd have thumped Carol Andrews a heck of a lot harder if she'd known it wasn't just vicious gossip.

I couldn't believe it, although it all made sense finally. 'So, Cerise knew, too? Who else? Your gran?'

She shook her head. 'No chance. Just Cerise. And—and Dr Pennington-Rhys.'

'Flynn? Flynn knows?' I sat up and drew away from her, my head spinning.

She pulled a face. 'Jesus, Mam, you've just gone ultrasonic. Yeah, he knows. He saw me and Pandora together, you see, and—'

'Together? What do you mean, he saw you together?' I had some truly terrible visions in my head. Where had they been? What, in heaven's name, had Flynn walked in on?

'We were kissing outside the riding school. He was on his way back from a visit.'

'And he asked you about it?'

'No, it was me. I got all embarrassed. He was trying to be nice, tried to get me to confide in you. I lost it. It was all still raw, you see. Pandora had been going out with lads, trying to convince herself that she wasn't gay. That was messing with my head, and why I was so confused and miserable. Then, that day, she told me she couldn't kid herself any longer and wanted to be with me, and I was over the moon, but then she said we had to keep it quiet 'cos of her mother, and she was still embarrassed and I felt really insecure again, and, well, Flynn just copped it. It was all just too much for me.'

'I see.' So, that was what had been going on. But Flynn had never said a word. Not so much as a hint.

'He was really nice to me,' she said, taking hold of my hand. 'Really concerned. He told me I should tell you, that you'd understand.'

'Did he?' I murmured.

She squeezed my hand. 'He's a nice bloke, Mam. He'll make a good dad.'

I swear I felt my heart leap into my mouth. 'How the buggery bollocks did you know?'

'Aw, Mam, bless you. It's so obvious when you're together, when he's around you, when his name's even mentioned. I admit I didn't know you'd actually got that far with him, but good on you. Surprised he didn't take precautions, though, him being a doctor.'

I told her about her grandmother's expired chocolate condoms, and she burst out laughing.

'Oh, Mam, we do get ourselves into some predicaments,

don't we?'

'You could say that. But you have to keep it quiet. I haven't told him yet, and I don't know when I will. He and I are—well, we're not actually speaking at the moment. In fact, he hates me.'

'Does he heck. He doesn't have it in him to hate anybody. You'll work it out, Mam, I'm sure. How can he be without someone like you in his life?' She giggled, and in spite of my misery, I felt a surge of joy at the sound of her laughter. She was holding my hand, and her eyes were warm. She looked like a different person. I felt that, at last, I had my daughter back.

'So, you and Pandora, it's serious?'

She nodded. 'I really love her, and I think she loves me, too. It's just Sophie. She doesn't want to let her down. But the thing is … the thing is, we want to live together. We're going to start looking for somewhere to rent. I know it won't be easy, but we really want to be together, so Sophie's going to have to be told. We're just trying to pick our moment.'

'I think you underestimate Sophie,' I told her. 'She just wants her kids to be happy. That's what we all want. I don't think it will be nearly as bad as you imagine.'

'And I'm sure that things will be fine with Flynn,' she assured me. 'I don't know what's gone on between you, but I'm sure it can be fixed.'

I nodded, and we sat together, my arm around her shoulder, while I enjoyed the feeling of being close to my eldest child for the first time in a long, long time. I wondered if either of us really believed the assurances we'd given each other. Sophie would have a massive shock, and although she did want her kids to be happy, she had an image of what that happiness would involve. I doubted a same-sex partner was what she had in mind for Pandora. It had nearly killed her that Pan had given up university to work in a riding school.

As for Flynn, I didn't think anything could fix that. In fact,

I could only see things getting worse. At some point, I was going to have to tell him he was going to be a father again, and after everything that had happened, I could only see that news inflicting yet more pain on him.

I hated the fact that, yet again, it would be me who was hurting him.

CHAPTER TWENTY-ONE

My mother glowed with excitement as she pulled off my duvet. Ignoring my protests, she threw open the curtains in the living room and spun round, her eyes shining with joy.

'Get up, pet. It's the big day.'

I blinked at her, bewildered. Either I'd had some epic lie-in, or she'd gone bonkers. 'Mam, it's Thursday today. The wedding's not till tomorrow.'

She looked at me as if I were stupid and waved her arm at me dismissively. 'I'm not talking about the wedding. It's today that *Ti Amo Magazine* comes out—the issue with my interview in it.'

Her interview? Apparently, Alec didn't feature at all, then? I wondered if she'd be so excited when it came to actually walking down the aisle and signing her life over to him.

'Do you want a cup of tea?' She beamed.

Hell, it was a red-letter day all right. I sat up straight, groaning as the first wave of nausea hit me. Shit, when would all this be over? I'd never had morning sickness with the other two. That was what you got when you conceived a child with a double-barrelled toff. Working class kids had never given me any trouble. Well, not during pregnancy, at any rate.

'Please,' I murmured, swallowing hard and taking some deep breaths.

'Bacon sarnie?'

'Ugh, don't,' I said, desperately trying to dismiss the image of grease and bacon rind from my mind.

'Aw, still feeling rough? How about a bit of dry toast? That usually helps.'

I shook my head. 'Just the tea please. I daren't risk it.'

'Coming right up.'

I wished she would pick her words more carefully.

She literally waltzed into the kitchen, while I shakily got to my feet and folded up the duvet, ready to stash back under her bed. Frankly, I'd have been tempted to climb back into it and sleep right through the wedding. In fact, I would have liked to sleep right through the next three months, or so, and skip out all this sickness lark, too. Oh, sod it, I'd have happily slept right on and missed the horror show that was labour and childbirth, thinking about it. Let the world roll on without me. That would be nice.

At least I finally had a decent bridesmaid dress, thanks to Cerise. She'd selected a simple V-neck, ivory dress, with an A-line tulle skirt that came to just below the knee, and an ivory sash adorned with a single same-colour rose at the waist.

'You can wear it afterwards, too,' she said, as she watched me parading up and down in it, almost weak with relief. 'It would make a lovely party dress, and only sixty pounds.'

'If she still fits into it,' murmured my mother, but luckily Cerise must have been too busy rummaging in the bag to hear her.

'So, you've finally chosen something?' I asked when Cerise pulled out another outfit.

My mother shrugged. 'Your Cerise picked it. I think it might be a bit plain. What do you reckon?'

I surveyed the oyster silk, knee-length, cap-sleeved dress, and the matching collarless fitted coat. It was elegant and rather classy, and not like my mother, at all. I'd been very worried, imagining walking down the aisle behind Lily Savage, but I approved whole-heartedly. 'How did you manage that?' I asked Cerise, as my mother whisked the outfits away to hang in the bedroom.

'Showed her some really awful, severe dresses first, like something the Amish would wear. By the time we got to this one, she was almost weeping with gratitude.'

I had to admire her. She was one devious kid.

'So, what are you up to today, then?' I asked my mother, as I sipped tea and tried not to think about the washing machine that was tumbling away in my stomach.

'Going to Henderson's this morning, picking up a copy of the magazine, and having a bloody good read. Can't wait.'

'I mean, after that. You must have loads to do.'

She shrugged, suddenly looking deflated. 'No, nothing. Alec and his sister have sorted it all. I just have to turn up.' She reached over and patted my arm, her face brightening like she'd remembered something. 'Meant to tell you last night, Flynn's coming to the wedding.'

I felt the washing machine flick onto spin cycle. 'Why? And how do you know?'

'Well, how do you think? Maurice told me. I invited them both, remember?'

'Well, yes, but I thought Maurice wasn't keen? And isn't Flynn working?'

'Maurice decided he wanted to be there, after all. Feels up to the visit, and said he wouldn't miss my big day for the world. 'Course, he made it a condition that Flynn went with him. Didn't want to be a Billy no-mates, did he? Anyway, Flynn's got a locum standing in, so it's all sorted.'

I took another sip of tea and put the cup down. It was no good. Even that was making me nauseous. I'd probably end up in hospital, on a drip like Kate Middleton, except not half as glamorous. I bet she'd looked fabulous, even with her head in the toilet bowl. Not like me. I'd look like the girl from *The Exorcist*. And there'd be no Prince William to hold my hand, either. There wouldn't be anyone—except maybe my mother. Jesus, how bad could things get?

'Might be a good chance to talk to him,' she said, giving me a meaningful look.

'Talk to him? Oh, yeah, perfect place to tell him he's going to be a father, to a baby conceived during a dreadful mistaken shag, with a gobby woman he can't stand. Are you mad?'

'You'll have to tell him sometime,' she pointed out. 'I don't think you can put that down to marshmallows for very long.'

As if the thought hadn't occurred to me. Of course he

would find out at some point, but not till he had to. I had to get used to it all myself first. I had to be strong enough in my own mind, to cope with his horror at the outcome of our stupid fumblings.

Stupid fumblings? Hardly. The memory of how good it had been occupied my thoughts far more than was good for me, and the knowledge that it would never happen again was too painful to contemplate. So I didn't. It was better to just think of it as a huge mistake, and not dwell on what I'd lost. It wasn't as if he'd ever been mine to lose in the first place.

I wasn't surprised when my mother said I looked shocking and went to get me a ginger biscuit to nibble on. I wasn't sure how much of the sickness was from the baby, and how much was caused by Flynn. Between them, they were going to finish me off.

I dragged myself into the shower, got dressed, and rubbed a bit of blusher on my pale cheeks. Thankfully, after another ginger biscuit, I felt a little bit better.

Fuchsia was very sympathetic, rubbing my back and making me another cup of tea, which I hardly touched, before rushing off to work. Luckily, Cerise was having a lie-in, so I didn't have to put on an act with her. I would have to tell her, too, of course. God knows what her reaction would be. Disgust, no doubt. I'd wait till the first scan was over. I had enough to deal with at the moment.

'Are you up to work today?' Mam asked, as I pulled on my trainers and found a scrunchie for my hair.

'Not much choice, is there? Henderson's will be open now. Are you coming downstairs with me?'

She beamed. 'Going to put me makeup on first. I might be recognised. Do you think people might want an autograph?'

I raised an eyebrow. How many copies of the wretched magazine did she think sold round here? I had a feeling she was heading for a major disappointment. I didn't want to rain on her parade, though, so I smiled and shrugged, and said something about not being sure, and it was a bit early in the day, and perhaps she should prepare for a slow trickle of interest rather than a tsunami? She nodded and seemed happy with that, so I left her to it and headed down to the shop.

Eliza and I must have asked Chrissie about six times that morning if she was sure she'd be okay tomorrow without us. We must have been starting to get on her nerves, because she finally snapped at us that she wasn't completely stupid, and of course she could cope, and we'd roped in Tallulah, hadn't we, and what the hell did we think was going to happen?

'All right, all right,' said Eliza, holding up her hands in alarm. 'We were only asking.'

Chrissie looked ashamed. 'Sorry. Just a bit down at the moment.'

'What is it? Anything we can help with?' I mean, it wasn't like I had any problems of my own. I might as well have gone digging around, looking for other people's to occupy me.

She seemed a bit nervous, but then confessed that Robbie had asked her out. 'It's all right,' she said, trying to appease Eliza. 'I said no.'

'What on earth for?' Eliza asked. 'I thought you really liked him?'

'I do, but he's with Lexi, isn't he?'

Eliza and I looked at each other. 'They've been dating, but honestly, there's no spark there. It's more a friendship thing. She's fond of him, but that's all.'

Chrissie looked stunned. 'Really? Are you sure?'

Eliza laughed. 'Positive. Lexi wouldn't be bothered in the slightest, if you went out with Robbie. You should call him. Go for it.'

Chrissie looked ready to explode, and was halfway up Bay Street, trying to make a call on her mobile before we could say "Bye bye, Lexi".

'Well, that was easy,' Eliza said with a grin.

I nodded. Why weren't my problems that simple to

resolve?

It was about quarter-past ten when the door opened and a woman stepped hesitantly into the shop. I knew her instantly, and had to sit down on the stool behind the counter, as my legs threatened to give way completely. She was wearing a very elegant two-piece grey suit, and her long, dark hair was neat and glossy. How did those women manage it, I wondered? I never looked elegant, no matter how I tried. Some of them just made it look so easy, so effortless.

Eliza paused in filling up a tray with lemon meringue mallows. She smiled brightly at the woman at first, but gradually recognition must have dawned, as she went quite scarlet and looked at me in undisguised horror.

'Can—can I help?' she said, sounding rather croaky.

The woman smiled, looking from me to her and back again. 'I'm looking for Rose,' she said. 'I'm sorry, I don't know her surname. I believe she works here?'

Eliza glanced nervously at me. Well, if I was trying to stay incognito, that look had just given me away. Cheers, mate. Mind you, from the way the woman was looking at me, I had a funny feeling she already knew that I was the one she was looking for.

'I'm Rose,' I said, or rather squeaked. I was painfully aware of my faded jeans, pink T-shirt, and frizzy hair that I'd scraped back into a scrunchie, not to mention the non-too-flattering apron that Eliza insisted we wore in the shop. I felt like Mrs Overall standing next to Claudia Schiffer.

She smiled and held out her hand. I took it, and she shook it gently. I hoped she couldn't feel mine shaking.

'I'm Lindsey. You don't know me but—'

'Oh, I think I do,' I said.

She surveyed me for a moment and nodded. 'I expect you'll think I'm mad,' she said, 'and perhaps I am. It's really nothing to do with me, but, well, I owe him. Could you spare ten minutes, do you think? I really would like to talk to you.'

Eliza looked at me. 'Are you okay?'

I nodded. 'Yeah, yeah, that's fine.'

'Is there somewhere we can talk? Privately?'

I thought about upstairs, but my mother would be reading her magazine, and Cerise would be mooching around. Eliza rummaged in her pocket and handed me some keys.

'Here. Use my place. Gabriel and Lexi are at work, and Amy's at the farm with Joe. You'll have it all to yourselves.'

I gave her a grateful squeeze of the arm and removed my apron.

'Come on, then,' I said to the woman, who suddenly seemed almost as nervous as me. 'Let's have that chat.'

****

We didn't speak as we headed down King's Row towards Tippet's Yard. The cottage was at the end of the passageway, a narrow three-storey building, with steps leading up to the front door. Lindsey struggled on the cobbles as we approached, and for the first time I was glad I was wearing trainers. At least I didn't look like I was about to fall flat on my arse at any moment. Served her right for being so gorgeous and wearing such impossibly high heels.

Trying to breathe calmly, I fumbled with the keys and unlocked the door. Lindsey followed me in and looked around, seemingly rather taken with the cottage's charms.

I was quite glad, for once, that my flat was never empty. I'd have died of shame, taking her in there. My mother had thrown in the towel, declaring that she didn't see why she should flog herself to death, keeping the place tidy, when, quite clearly, her daughter and granddaughters preferred to live like slobs. The result was that the flat had reverted back to its usual disgraceful, cluttered state.

Blessedly, Eliza's place was neat and tidy and well-furnished. Eliza was so proud of her little home. It was her pride and joy, and you'd never find a coat slung over the back of a sofa, or a pair of muddy shoes kicked under the coffee table there. At least Lindsey couldn't find fault with my friend's little haven, even if she'd come to find fault with everything about me.

'Coffee, tea?'

'Coffee would be lovely. Thank you.'

Crap. Did that mean she'd want the proper stuff? I usually just scooped a spoonful of Nescafé into a mug. I walked into the kitchen, and Tessa yawned and looked at me curiously. Not curious enough to climb out of her bed, though. She stared at Lindsey, and seemed to consider whether she merited further investigation.

Lindsey studied the dog a bit nervously. Tessa cocked her head to one side, and I'm sure she looked her up and down. Eventually, seeming to decide there was nothing to be worried about, the dog settled back onto her bed, her head in her paws. Fat lot of good she was. Gabriel always said she was the laziest dog in existence, and he wasn't wrong. Mind you, she was twelve. An old lady in dog years, I supposed. I expected the poor bugger had seen it all and couldn't be arsed any more. I knew how she felt, and I wasn't even forty.

I looked at the kettle and got out two mugs. Stuff it, I didn't see why I should go to all that palaver for this woman. Anyway, I wasn't going to mess up Eliza's kitchen. No chance. I hunted for a teaspoon and brought out the jar of coffee from the cupboard, sneaking a sidelong look at her to see how she'd react. She didn't seem bothered. She was looking round the room, rather admiringly. I could understand why. Gabriel had put in a whole new kitchen when they moved in, with ivory coloured units and wooden worktops. It was very country kitchen, and really pretty, adorned with little vintage signs and bunting. Very girly. Eliza said it was her favourite room.

I poured out two coffees and asked Lindsey if she took milk and sugar. She didn't, which I supposed helped to explain the slender figure. I slopped some milk and sugar into my mug and plonked the two coffees down on the table, pulling up a chair and indicating to her that she should sit down.

She did so and pulled her mug towards her, seeming even more nervous.

'So,' I said, deciding it was time to take control, 'what's all this about?'

'Well,' she said, nursing her coffee as if she needed to keep her hands warm, which I doubted on such a warm August day, 'it's about Flynn. What else would it be about?'

I studied her face. She was quite pretty, but not as sophisticated-looking close up. Her dark hair had the odd grey strand threaded through it, and beneath her makeup, I detected a few freckles. She looked quite tense, and, as it dawned on me that her visit was as nerve-wracking for her as it was for me, my hostility towards her flowed away. She had lost her child, after all. How could I feel angry towards her for anything?

'Look, I know this is absolutely none of my business, but I just had to come. I had to try, at least, to explain .... He's feeling so wretched, and I owe him so much.'

'So you said, but I don't understand why you've come, or what it is you want?' What was there to say? And how much did she know, anyway? Oh, God, did she know I'd spied on them at the railway station? I felt myself go hot at the thought. How humiliating was that?

She took a tentative sip on her coffee, as if she thought I might have poisoned it, or something, then rubbed her forehead as if trying to think what to say. She sat there for what felt like ages before looking at me. She had nice eyes—hazel, I thought, and sort of sad. 'I don't know how much Flynn has told you about me. I gather from your lack of questioning that you realise who I am? That I was married to him?'

I nodded. I was saying nothing. I wasn't going to incriminate myself if I could help it.

'It was a long time ago. We were divorced eight years ago, so, you see, I do understand that this is nothing to do with me, and I promise I'm not here to cause trouble. The thing is, well, Flynn was so happy the last time I saw him. In spite of ... well, in spite of the reason we met up.'

'Emily.' There, I'd gone and done it now. Me and my big fat mouth.

She looked at me and smiled softly. 'So, you know about her? I'm so glad.'

'Are you?'

She nodded eagerly. 'Oh, yes, because it means he's finally talking about her. That's good—a real breakthrough.'

I wasn't so sure about that. I had kind of forced his hand, after all. Reluctantly, I decided that honesty really was the best policy, and, with a great deal of embarrassment, I confessed everything to her.

'So, you see, now he hates me, and it's all over. There really isn't anything else to say,' I finished.

She was gaping at me as if she couldn't believe I'd been so crass as to follow him, to spy on him, and then accused him of all sorts.

'Goodness,' she said finally, 'I see what he means about you.'

'And just what the hell is that supposed to mean?' I said with some indignation.

She grinned, and immediately looked five years younger. 'He said you were a real character. I would never have the nerve to do something like that. Oh, you'd be so good for him!'

Was she taking the mickey? I studied her face carefully, but she seemed genuine. Her eyes were bright with laughter, and she was smiling to herself as she took another sip of coffee. Okay, then, I'd give her the benefit of the doubt. Still didn't explain what she was doing here, or what she wanted though, did it?

'The last time we met, after we'd been to the churchyard

and laid the roses on Emily's grave, we went for lunch in the pub nearby, The Bay Horse. Do you know it? We used to eat there a lot, when we lived in Bramblewick. It's lovely.'

I shook my head. No, I didn't know it, and I didn't give a monkey's about it. What was she here for?

'Well, anyway, while we had lunch, Flynn told me about you. I'd guessed there was something, someone. He seemed different—brighter, happier. It was as if the old Flynn was finally coming back. Anyway, he told me he was seeing a lovely lady called Rose, who was different to anyone he'd ever known before, and that she made him happy—really happy. I can't tell you how pleased I was to hear that. Rose, are you listening?'

I was staring at the houseplant in the middle of the table. I didn't do plants. I was probably the only person in the history of the planet who'd managed to kill off a spider plant, and so I couldn't say for sure what species that one was, and, frankly, I couldn't have cared less. For some reason, though, I seemed unable to drag my eyes away from it, as her words echoed round and round my head. "She made him happy—really happy." I'd made Flynn happy? When was that, then?

'Rose?'

I shook my head. 'Sorry. I just—just, are you sure? I mean, it *was* me he was talking about, right?'

She laughed. 'Of course I'm sure. I knew as soon as I saw the pink streak. He's quite entranced with it, isn't he?'

'Is he?' That was all news to me. I thought he'd hate it. I mean, it wasn't exactly sophisticated, was it? And him a doctor and everything.

'Oh, yes. Anyway, when we parted that afternoon, I went away feeling happier than I had in years. Usually, I get on the train, and I feel nothing but sadness and guilt that I'm leaving him to his misery. This time, I felt quite able to leave him behind, sure that he was finally coming through. It was such a wonderful feeling. I suppose that's why I had to come.'

Finally. Was I going to hear the real reason at last?

'The thing is, I called him the other night. I wanted to ask his advice about a friend. She has a medical problem and is refusing to see a doctor, nothing serious, but ... anyway, that's irrelevant. He sounded so low, so miserable, and I knew at once it was because of you. He admitted that you'd broken up. Wouldn't tell me why, but I could hear the sadness in his voice. So, you see, I had to come, Rose, because if there was any chance at all that I could help to put things right, I'd do it. Anything. I owe him so much.'

'Well, now you know why he ended it,' I mumbled. 'You can hardly blame him, can you? I'm such a clot.'

'Oh, rubbish,' she said. 'That's no reason to finish things. Flynn's a darling, but he can be such an idiot sometimes.'

That cheered me up a bit. She was right. He could be. This wasn't all me, after all.

'So you jumped to conclusions and blundered in,' she continued.

I frowned. All right, no need to rub it in.

'The thing is,' she said, 'anyone else would have told you what they thought of you, sulked for a day or two, and then forgotten all about it. Not Flynn, of course. And I do rather think that I'm to blame.'

'Sorry.' I shook my head and ran my hand through my unruly hair, hoping the pink streak was behaving itself and lying where it was supposed to be, instead of standing up on end like I'd had an electric shock. 'Forgive me if I'm being thick, but how is any of this your fault? And why do you keep saying you owe him?'

She sighed and took another sip of her coffee. 'Because it's thanks to me that Flynn learned how to bury his feelings so deep that he lost sight of what they were. And now it's causing him to lose someone else precious to him, and I simply can't bear it.'

Did she mean me? Really? I was precious to him?

'When Emily died, I took it very badly,' she said, eventually.

'Well, you would. You were her mum,' I said. 'I can't think of anything worse. If I'd lost my daughters like that, well, I can't imagine ...'

'Oh, yes, Flynn said you had two daughters,' she said, smiling. 'So, I suppose you do understand, in a way.'

'Well, not entirely,' I admitted. 'I don't think anyone can really know how bad they'd feel in that situation, but I can kind of guess.'

'It's the worst pain imaginable,' she said softly, tears suddenly glistening in her eyes. 'I thought I was going to die, too. Sometimes, I prayed I would.'

I was silent. What could I say to that, really? My hands went almost of their own accord to my stomach, as I thought about the little life growing inside there, and I found I had tears in my own eyes. How could I have wished it away? However tough things got, I would cope. I would look after the child, no matter what it took. How had I ever thought otherwise?

'Flynn was ... amazing. You know what he's like,' she said with a smile, 'always the noble one. Too bloody kind for his own good.'

I blinked. Had she just said bloody?

'He tried so hard to help me with my grief that he quite ignored his own. You see, I blamed him. It was wrong of me, and so very, very unfair. My only defence is that I was completely devastated, heartbroken. I needed to blame someone, and, of course, he was closest. He was the man of the house and supposed to protect us. You know, when you're in the midst of such pain, feminism quite goes out of the window.'

Well, at least she was honest, I'd give her that much.

'Of course, it was even worse because he was a doctor. I was furious with him because he didn't even try to save her. She was in her cot, just lying there, and I was screaming at him to do something, to resuscitate her. And he just stood there, looking down on her. Then he scooped her up and held her, just held her. He didn't do anything else. Just cuddled her to him, and stared at me with this dreadful look in his eyes.'

I tried to imagine what it must have felt like, finding your baby like that. What had they gone through? How had they coped? Feeling quite ill, I drained the last of my coffee, just for something to do that would stop me crying.

'Of course,' she said, taking out a tissue from her handbag and mopping her eyes with it, 'it took me a while to realise that he'd known from the minute he saw her that there was nothing he *could* do. It was far too late. But I simply wouldn't believe him. It took me a long time to forgive him, and even longer to accept that there was nothing to forgive.

'I was beyond consoling. I cried every day for months. I raged. I was vile to him. I wanted to die. Flynn told me, a long time afterwards, that he'd feared every time he got home from work that he'd find me gone. I mean, gone as in gone to Emily. It was all I talked about. I didn't want him, you see. I just wanted to be with my baby.'

'Oh, God.' I stood up and walked over to the kettle, flicking it on again, in need of something to do. I stared out through the window at the tiny back yard, seeing none of it. In my mind, I watched Flynn trudging home from work, his steps slowing as he walked up the path to his front door, his hands trembling as he reached for the handle. How had he got through it?

'I know.' She sounded as if she were really crying now. I turned back to look at her, and my heart ached for her as she sat there, mopping up her tears and shaking her head as if appalled at her own behaviour. 'I was a total cow.'

'It wasn't your fault,' I said. 'You were grieving. Grief does terrible things. You can't be held responsible for that.'

'That's what Flynn says.' She sniffed and gave a weak smile. 'He's never blamed me for any of it. Not once. But, you see, I was the lucky one.'

I raised my eyebrow in query. 'You think? How?'

'Oh, but I was!' She pushed back her chair and came to stand beside me. 'You see, I was allowed to grieve, Rose, and I did. I mean, I *really* did. I wallowed in it for such a long, long time, and I thought it was never going to end. And it hasn't, not really, but I know how to manage it now. I learnt because I had the luxury of taking my time, going through it with someone there to support me at all times. But Flynn ...'

'Flynn had no one,' I whispered. 'He was so busy helping you through your grief that he didn't get to express his own.'

'Exactly. And you know what's even worse? When I finally started to come out of that long, dark tunnel into the light, I was able to speak about her, to put up photographs of her and remember her with a smile on my face, but Flynn couldn't. He couldn't bear to look at her, or even say her name. After a while, I wanted another baby, another chance. He couldn't bear that, either. I pushed him. I was selfish and cruel. Unthinking. He felt cornered and panicky, and, eventually, I realised that he wasn't coping. Finally, after being so absorbed in myself and my own feelings, I was in a place where I could look beyond that and see how he was actually doing, and it wasn't good. I was shocked and horrified by the state of him. I asked him to go to counselling but he wouldn't. He was acting as if everything was fine, as if our darling baby had never existed. Everything seemed okay on the surface, but he wasn't Flynn anymore. I tried, Rose, I really did, but I couldn't reach him. Eventually, we realised we wanted different things. He couldn't deal with moving on, and I wanted to. Oh, I really needed to. So we agreed to part.'

Noticing her trembling, I put my arm around her.

She gave me a grateful smile. 'It's all right, I'm okay. I eventually met Matt, who's lovely and uncomplicated, and we got married. We had a little boy four years ago. He's called

Christopher. He's adorable. He knows about Emily, and we have photographs of her in the house. Did you notice any photographs of her in Flynn's house?'

I shook my head. 'Not one.'

'You see? That's what I mean. That's why I owe him. I messed him up, and I want him to be well again. When he talked about you, I saw flashes of the old Flynn, the man I fell in love with. It made me feel so happy, I can't tell you. I can't just let you two split up without doing something to make it all right. You do see that?'

'I know, but ...'

'Rose, please. All you have to do is go to see him and tell him your side of the story. I'm sure he'd be willing to listen, and I'll bet he's just waiting and hoping that you want him enough to make the effort.'

She sounded so sure of herself, I felt quite hopeful for a moment. Then I remembered, and shook my head.

'But why? Do you love him?'

'Lindsey, I know you mean well, but there's something you don't know.'

'What? What don't I know?'

I took a deep breath. It wasn't going to be easy, but she needed to know the reason it was never going to work with Flynn. Surely, after everything she'd just told me, she'd see that I was right. There was no way back for us.

When I finished, she was staring at me, and I saw so many conflicting emotions reflected in her eyes, they looked like a kaleidoscope.

'You see?' I said dully.

She sat down and ran her finger around the rim of her coffee cup, deep in thought. 'You know, maybe this is exactly what he needs,' she said finally. 'I know it's a bit earlier than you expected, and it wasn't planned, but that could be for the best. He won't be able to run away from this, he'll have to deal with it. Flynn's not the sort of man to shirk his responsibilities, no matter how he feels.'

'But I don't want him to stand by me because of duty,' I said. 'How could that ever work? And I don't want to force him into dealing with something he can't cope with, either. I don't see a way out of this, Lindsey. I do appreciate you coming here to tell me what happened, and I understand why you want to help, but the truth is, everything you've just told me only confirms that he's not going to want this baby, and I'm going to have to deal with that. I'm sorry, but I really do have to get back to work.'

She stood up and picked up her bag, stuffing the tissues inside it and snapping it shut. 'Of course. I've taken up enough of your time.'

I led her to the front door and opened it, giving her a watery smile, as she turned to say goodbye.

'Please, Rose, just take your time and think about it,' she urged, seemingly unable to admit defeat. 'This could be the best thing that ever happens to him. Please, try to make him see that. Don't give up on him.'

I shrugged, unable to think of anything to say. What did she want from me? I couldn't make promises I couldn't see any way of keeping. It wasn't up to me. I seemed to have had very little say in any of it. It seemed to me the cards had been dealt in our relationship way before I'd ever even heard of Flynn Pennington-Rhys.

'Goodbye,' she said softly. I held out my hand, but she put her arms round me and pulled me into a warm embrace instead. 'Take care. Of all of you.'

Her eyes flickered to my stomach, and she smiled, before she turned away and walked down the path. I closed the door and leaned against it, my heart hammering in my chest, my legs shaky.

It had been good to hear the full story behind the breakup of her marriage, and it had been very kind of her to make the effort to try to repair my relationship with Flynn, but there was nowhere for it to go. Flynn hadn't dealt with losing his first child. I couldn't see any way he would want to welcome another one into his world, although, no doubt, he would offer to pay his way and provide for it. But I didn't want him to "do his duty" by us.

I sank onto the floor and curled up in a ball, letting the tears fall without even attempting to stop them. Thanks to my sobs, Tessa seemed to decide that there was finally something worth getting out of bed for. She padded through the living room and plonked herself down by my side. I buried my face in her neck, and she was very good, not complaining once about the racket I was making, or the fact that my tears were making her fur all damp.

'Oh, Tessa, what am I going to do?' I wailed.

She sighed, as if agreeing it was all impossible, and my sobs grew louder. I didn't want him to do the right thing. I didn't want him to be noble, decent, unselfish. I wanted him to pull me to him, smother me in kisses, and tell me he was thrilled that I was carrying his baby.

I just wanted him to love me.

****

'So, who was she? And what did she want with you?' Eliza demanded, the minute I arrived back at the shop.

Her eyes goggled when I admitted she was Flynn's ex-wife.

'But why was she here? Does she know we followed him to the station? Does she know we saw them kiss? Hey, why was he giving her a kiss? And what was with the roses?'

I stared at her, unable to say a single word.

'Rose? Oh, my God, you look awful. What the hell's going on?'

I had to tell her. I hadn't intended to, as it struck me that just about everybody would know about the baby, apart from its own father, and I didn't really have the right to discuss Emily with anyone, but Eliza was my best friend, and I needed someone to talk to. I'd really had enough. I didn't think I could take much more.

'Why didn't you tell me?' she said, obviously hurt that I hadn't confided in her, especially when I admitted that my mother, Fuchsia and now even Lindsey knew.

'Because you've been going all out to get pregnant,' I said. 'I didn't want to upset you.'

'Why would it upset me?' she said, giving me a hug. 'You are daft, sometimes, Rose. We've only been trying three months. It could take a year, or more, to conceive. I'm hardly going to start panicking, am I? Anyway, you're my best friend. Don't you think I'm more concerned about you? I can't believe you've been going through all this without me.'

'It doesn't matter,' I began.

'Of course it matters,' she said, cutting in. 'Oh, my word, when I think how you took care of me, listened to my never-ending whining, when I was going through all that stuff with Harry and being all confused and lovesick over Gabriel. The least I can do is be there for you now. What are you going to do?'

She had a point. I'd been a rock. And she *had* been pathetically lovesick. 'I don't know,' I admitted. 'Plod on. Give birth. Start the whole flaming childcare rigmarole again.'

'I mean, about Flynn? When are you going to tell him?'

'Oh, I don't know. When I have to. And you have to swear that you won't tell Gabriel. Please. I know you two are like that,' I said, showing her my tightly entwined fingers. 'But I can't expect him not to tell Flynn when they're such good friends and work together. It wouldn't be fair, and I need to be the one to break it to him. Gently.'

'I know. I promise,' she said. 'Mum's the word.'

'Very funny,' I said, and she laughed.

'How lovely, though. A new baby. When ours arrives, it

can be playmates with yours. Won't that be great?'

'Fabulous,' I said.

'I suppose that explains why you've been looking like death warmed up, every morning, too,' she said thoughtfully. 'I just can't believe all this. Poor Flynn. To go through all that and never say a word about it. It breaks your heart, doesn't it?' She was right about that. She shook her head and went to put the kettle on.

Chrissie came through from the kitchen and carefully placed a batch of mint choc chip mallows onto the shelf under the glass counter.

'Ooh, Rose, you're back. Your mother rang about half an hour ago, demanding to speak to you. She wasn't happy when I said you weren't in. She said to go upstairs when you get back. Said it's urgent.'

'Oh, hell's bells.' I groaned. 'What now?'

'Go on up,' said Eliza. 'I'll make the tea when you come back.'

I nodded gratefully and headed upstairs. No doubt, it was another pointless drama to deal with. Had she forgotten to buy the garter she'd assured me she intended to have? Had she discovered that Denise was fully booked, after all, and she'd have to do her own hair for the wedding?

I opened the door and leapt back in surprise, when she appeared at my side, her face positively blue with rage, waving a magazine at me like a demented Oompa-Loompa.

'Thank God you're here,' said Cerise, who was cowering on the sofa and looking a bit nervous. 'See if you can calm her down. She won't listen to me.'

'Calm me down? Calm me down? It'll take more than your mam to calm me down, pet,' said my mother, ramming the magazine into my hand and looking at me with a wild expression in her eyes. She did look a bit unhinged, to be honest.

I had an urge to seek refuge beside Cerise. Safety in

numbers, and all that. 'What's up? Didn't they run the story?'

'Oh, they ran it,' said my mother. 'Pages six and seven. Go on, take a good look. The double-crossing, lying rats. Oh, and so nice to me face, an' all. Pretending to be interested, pretending to be listening! Rubbish! They never heard a word.'

'All right, let me find it,' I muttered, flicking through the pages and dodging past her to sit beside my daughter on the sofa.

'Libel, that's what it is, libel. Or is it slander? I can never remember.'

'Libel, if it's been written down,' said Cerise helpfully.

'Don't encourage her,' I said. 'Ah, here it is.'

I reared away from the pictures of my mother and Alec staring out at me from the pages. The angle was hardly flattering. My mother's head looked enormous, and Alec looked as if he'd borrowed Red Rum's teeth.

'Crikey,' I said, 'I see what you mean. What kind of photographer took those?'

She glared at me. 'Not the photos! Read what it says in the interview.'

I began to read, and chortled when I saw they'd put my mother's age as sixty-four. Bad enough for her, if they'd got it right. She always knocked two years off her real age, so to see they'd added another two must have been unbearable for her. She'd be onto her solicitors at this rate.

As I continued with the article, though, I began to get quite angry. 'Have you seen this?' I glanced up at her. 'They've got Dad's name wrong. Who told them he was called Mike? It sounds nothing like Dave.'

'Oh, do carry on,' she said through gritted teeth.

I did, becoming increasingly wound up as I read that my mother had fallen in love with Alec from the moment she saw him, and it had broken her heart when his parents whisked him away to Cumbria, after deciding he was too young to know his own mind. Apparently, she had never got over him and had married my father, "Mike", on the rebound. It had been a reasonably happy marriage, producing only one child, as there were "fertility issues".

I glanced up at my mother, feeling a rush of sympathy for her. Where had they got this stuff from?

She bit her lip and nodded at me. 'Read it all. Unbelievable.'

I finished the article, my rage rising, as I read that my mother had become a widow when "Mike" died of cancer in his early fifties, and she'd hoped against hope that Alec would one day find her, and get back in touch with her. When she was mugged and featured in the paper, his sister had recognised her, and contacted him to tell him where she was living. By the time Alec got back to Oddborough, she'd moved away, but he contacted the newspaper, refusing to take no for an answer, until they gave him her number. She'd been overwhelmed to see him again, realising that he'd been the love of her life all along, and that she'd never felt like that about anyone else, although "Mike" was a kind man, and had done his best, and they'd rubbed along quite nicely for all those years. Apparently, Alec was the only man who'd ever floated her boat, and she couldn't wait to marry him and finally fulfil her destiny—the destiny she'd been so cruelly denied by their evil parents—to become Mrs Alec Thoroughgood.

'Oh, God,' I said, putting the magazine down.

I felt sick for my father. To be dismissed so casually, as if he hadn't mattered at all, as if he'd just been keeping her warm till bloody Alec got back and took over the reins.

'I know,' she said, tears in her eyes. 'It's not true, Rose. I loved your dad. He was the real love of me life. Alec was just a crush, a stupid childhood crush. I wasn't just using your dad to get over him. You know that, don't you?'

'Of course I do, Mam.' I grabbed the magazine and flicked through it again, finding what I was looking for and holding it out to her. 'See, on this page here? There's a contact number.

Ring them. Speak to the reporter and complain. Tell them you want a retraction, that they had no right to twist your words like that.'

'I should have known they'd get it all wrong,' she said, taking the magazine from my hand. 'They weren't even writing anything down. More interested in the photos. I get the feeling they'd already made up their minds what story they were going to run, whatever I said.'

'They had no right,' I said. 'Ring them now. I'll have to get back to the shop, but Cerise will stay with you. Let me know what they say, all right? Threaten them with legal action, if you have to.'

She nodded, and I made my way back down the stairs, seething with anger. There had to be some way of getting them to admit they were wrong, and to make it quite clear that my dad was much more important in my mother's life than Alec Thoroughgood ever would be. There had to be a code of conduct, surely? Or was I being naive?

I spent the next half hour speaking to the managers of the shops in Whitby and Helmston, who stocked our products, taking their orders for the next deliveries, and tried to push my anger to one side. What an awful day it was turning out to be. I was already shattered.

Cerise popped her head round the door, just as I put the phone down on the last client. 'Can you come upstairs, Mam? Gran needs you.'

I shot back upstairs and found my mother sitting on the chair, looking completely shell-shocked.

'What is it? What did they say?'

'I'll tell you what they said,' she whispered. 'Alec. That's what.'

CHAPTER TWENTY-TWO

At first, I had to rely on Cerise to tell me what was going on, as my mother seemed incapable. Eventually, she started to chip in with bits of information, and I finally pieced together the facts.

It seemed that it wasn't the magazine that had got in touch with Alec, at all. He had contacted them, and offered them the story for their true-life romance slot.

'Five hundred quid, he got for that,' she muttered, 'and the tight bastard never said a word.'

Alec had provided the complete story, and they'd assessed it to see if it was something their readers would enjoy. When they decided it was, they'd contacted Alec, and arranged to meet up with him and my mother.

'But it was only for photos, and to clarify a few extra points with him,' she said. 'No wonder they didn't seem to take any notice of what I was saying. It was Alec they were pumping for information, not me. And I was so busy pouting for the camera like flaming Posh Spice, I didn't even realise. What a mug.'

'You weren't to know,' I said. 'So, Alec told them all that stuff about my dad?'

'Aye. And he must have given them the wrong name for your dad out of spite. He's a very petty man.'

'And the fertility stuff?' I asked gently.

She shook her head. 'He knows nothing about any of that. Obviously, he's made assumptions there.'

'But can't you force them to retract it all?'

'Apparently, Alec signed a statement to say that it was an accurate account of the facts, and then I signed a document that was basically giving them the right to publish. I didn't even read it. Thought it was a release for the photos. Silly cow.'

'Oh, Mam.'

She sat there chewing her nails for a moment. 'I'm going over there.'

'Where? The magazine?'

'Don't be daft,' she said, giving me a withering look. 'I'm going to see Alec. Find out what he thinks he's playing at, telling all them daft lies.'

'But it will take you ages,' I said.

'I'll get a taxi there, and he can flaming pay for it. I want to know what made him do it, and I want to know what the hell he did with that five hundred quid. Tight git. At least half of that's mine, and I think I should get it all, given the trauma he's put me through.'

'Are you sure you're up to it?'

'Oh, I'm up to it, all right. You don't wanna be worrying about that. I'll see you later, pet.'

'Do you want me to come with you?'

'No, it's fine. This is something me and Alec need to thrash out on our own. Don't worry. I'll be home for tea.'

She grabbed her bag and vanished, leaving me and Cerise looking at each other. 'Well!' she said.

'Yeah, you could say that,' I agreed. I felt drained. What time was it, anyway? Not even one o'clock. The day had gone on forever.

I trudged back downstairs, but Eliza took one look at me, turned me round, and sent me back upstairs.

'Go and have a lie down,' she told me. 'Take the afternoon off, we're managing just fine. No arguments.'

I didn't have the strength to argue. I just wanted to curl up on the sofa and sleep and sleep. They could wake me up when it was all over.

****

Fuchsia was furious when she read the article. She'd loved her grandad, and saw it as the massive insult I think Alec had intended it to be.

'She's not going to marry him now, is she?' she demanded.

'I wouldn't have thought so,' I said. 'Not after this. I expect she'll be home soon, and we'll know for definite then.'

Except, she didn't come home. She'd promised to be back for tea, but Fuchsia didn't get home from work till twenty-past six, and she still wasn't back by then.

By seven, I was worried enough to ring Alec. I never thought I'd stoop to that, but needs must.

'She's not here,' he told me. 'She left about two hours ago. I expect she'll be home soon. It is a two hour bus ride, you know.'

Yes, and you have a car, you heartless sod, I thought. 'Is she—is everything all right?'

'Oh, tickety-boo,' he assured me. 'We got it all straightened out. No worries.'

'So, the wedding's still on?'

'Of course, of course. All a silly misunderstanding. See you at the church tomorrow.'

Shit, I thought. How had he managed that?

I put the phone down and told my disbelieving daughters that, apparently, the nuptials were going ahead. They were as thrilled as I was.

'Well, stuff it,' said Fuchsia, 'let's have our tea, then. I'm starving.'

We ate our beef casserole while discussing how much we all disliked Alec Thoroughgood and wondering what the hell my mother saw in him.

'Must be a good shag,' said Fuchsia.

'Like you'd know,' said Cerise slyly.

I nearly choked on a carrot. 'All right, that's enough.'

Cerise laughed. 'You still planning to move in with Pandora, then?'

Fuchsia turned a bit pink. 'Yeah. We've just got to find somewhere decent to rent. And tell Sophie and Archie, of course.'

'Good luck with that,' said her sister, dripping with sympathy.

'You ought to get it over with,' I said. 'No point in putting these things off.'

She fixed me with a meaningful stare. 'No. There isn't, is there?'

I squirmed and busied myself with dolloping mashed potatoes onto my plate. She had a point, I could hardly deny it.

By half-past eight the dishes were washed, the remains of the casserole put in the fridge for my mother, and we were slobbing on the sofa, discussing the fact that, as it was the night before the wedding, she should really be here right now, getting her nails painted and drinking wine, while we fussed over her and tried to pretend we were happy for her.

'Where is she?' Fretting, I rang Alec again. 'Have you heard from her? Only she's not back, and I'm worried.'

'I expect she wanted some fresh air,' he said. 'Or maybe she's met up with friends and gone for a drink. It's her last night as a single lady, after all.'

Like I needed reminding. 'But she'd have rung me, surely? And she's been mugged before. I can't help worrying.' I heard glasses clinking in the background. 'Where are you?' I asked suspiciously.

'Just meeting up with friends. It's my stag night,' he said.

'Cutting it a bit fine, aren't you?'

'Oh, well, I've already had three in the last two weeks. I have a lot of friends.'

How? Who? I couldn't believe he had any, but I simply asked him to tell my mother to ring me, if he heard from her, and then hung up on him. By the time it got to ten-past nine, I'd had enough.

'I'm going to look for her,' I said.

'Where?' said Fuchsia. 'She's not likely to be in the village, and if you head off to Redcar, she could be on the bus coming back in the opposite direction. Ring her.'

'I have rung her, loads of times. Selfish cow isn't answering,' I said, the tears starting to flow. I kept remembering the massive cut on the back of her head and the bruises on her wrists from the mugger. What if it had happened again? What if she'd been taken to hospital and was unconscious, and no one knew who she was? What if she was lying in an alley somewhere? What if she was in a mortuary?

Jesus, Rose, calm down. I knew I had to do something, but what?

'Maurice!' I blurted, hit with a sudden brainwave.

'Who? Oh, you mean that old bloke from Helmston? You think she might have gone there?' asked Cerise. 'Give him a call.'

'I don't know his number,' I said, feeling my blood pressure rising as I spoke. It was all getting too much. I couldn't believe what a shitty day I was having.

'Dr Pennington-Rhys will have it,' Fuchsia said, looking at me. 'Why don't you call him?'

I shook my head. 'I can't.'

Cerise looked puzzled. 'Why not?'

Fuchsia smirked. 'Yeah, why not, Mam?'

I gave her a look of exasperation. 'All right, I will.'

So I did, though my hands were shaking so much I could barely hold the phone. I wasn't sure he'd answer, but he did on the second ring.

'Hello?' His voice was calm and gentle, and I had a sudden image in my mind of resting my head against his chest and begging him to take care of me.

I cleared my throat. 'It's Rose.'

'I know.' Of course he did. My name would have flashed up on the screen. Idiot. 'Are you all right?' He was likely wondering what the hell I was doing, ringing him up at this time of night. Or any time, really.

'I'm ever so sorry to bother you,' I said, 'but I wondered if you could give me Maurice's number? It's just that my mother has had a bit of an upset today, and she went out earlier, and she said she'd be home by teatime, but now it's after nine, and she's not back, and Alec said she's not with him, and she should be home, and I just don't know what else to do.'

'It's all right, calm down,' he said soothingly. 'I'll get you the number. Just a minute.'

He took simply ages. I clutched the phone muttering, 'For God's sake, where's he gone? I asked him to get me the number, not drive to Maurice's bloody house.'

'Rose?'

'Yes?'

'Just to let you know, I've put you on speaker phone while I look for the number. I can hear you, you know.'

'Oh, bugger.'

I was positive I heard him chuckle, but surely not?

'Okay, I have it. Have you got a pen?'

I nodded.

'Rose?'

'Oh, shit, I forgot you can't see me. Yes, yes I have a pen.'

He gave me the number, and I thanked him.

'If she's not there, call me back,' he said. 'I'll help you look. If you want me to, I mean?'

'Thanks. That's really good of you,' I mumbled and hung up.

I rang the number he'd given me, but no one answered. I rang and rang, my mind feverishly running through all the possibilities as to why Maurice wouldn't be at home. Maurice was always home, wasn't he? What if he'd had a fall and was lying in his kitchen, unable to get up? What if he'd been burgled and clobbered over the head? What if my mother had turned up, and they'd drunk themselves unconscious? What if ... oh, for God's sake, Rose, get a grip.

I rang Flynn. He answered immediately.

'Is she there?' he asked.

I shook my head, then realised yet again that he couldn't see me and whimpered, 'There's no answer. What if something's happened to him, too?'

'He's not answering? Right.'

There was silence for a moment, then he said, 'Meet me at the top of Bay Street in five minutes. I'll drive us to Maurice's house. We need to find them. Both of them.'

'Oh, thank you.' I was truly grateful. Sitting there worrying myself sick was doing me no good at all. I needed to take some kind of action.

'Will you ring me if she turns up here?' I asked, pulling on my trainers and jacket and trying not to sound too anxious.

The girls nodded. 'Of course we will, Mam. She'll be fine. You know Gran, she's indestructible.' Cerise smiled.

'And you ring us if you find her,' added Fuchsia.

I hugged them both, suddenly aware of how much they had come on in the last few weeks, and how much I loved them.

As I hurried up Bay Street, I felt all fluttery and nervous when I saw the silver Peugeot sitting opposite The Kearton Arms, facing towards the Whitby road. He'd already turned it round, ready to go. I wondered if he'd spotted me in his rear view mirror. I realised I hadn't put any make-up on, and my hair was still fastened in the scrunchie. Crap. I'd wanted to look all glamorous the next time he saw me, too.

What was I thinking? My mother could be lying dead somewhere, and I was worrying about my frizzy hair. I should be shot.

He leapt out and raced round to the passenger side of the car, opening the door for me in the way that only Flynn could. I gave him a feeble smile and slunk into the seat, clicking my seatbelt and taking a deep breath, as he got in beside me and started the engine.

'Doesn't Maurice have a mobile?' I asked, after wracking my brains to think of an opening line.

He shook his head. 'No. He's not interested. I take it your mother's not answering hers?'

'No.' I swallowed down the panic as I said it, and his eyes softened with sympathy.

He squeezed my hand. 'I'm sure there's a reasonable explanation. She'll be all right, Rose. Try not to worry.'

It took all my strength not to hurl myself against him and howl. Instead, I bit my lip and nodded silently. He let go of my hand and drove off, as I sat there, trying to tell myself that he was just being kind. None of this meant anything. Flynn couldn't help being nice. It was who he was.

I explained about the magazine interview, and what they'd written about my father, and what my mother had discovered about Alec. Flynn seemed very indignant on my father's behalf, but not too surprised about Alec. I guessed he'd sussed out his character from the start, too.

Once the explanations were out of the way, we talked very little during the rest of the journey to Maurice's. I thought he seemed nervous, too, and guessed he was more worried about the fate of the oldies than he'd let on. He glanced at me every now and then, but said nothing until we were almost in Helmston. Then he cleared his throat.

'Fuchsia's doing very well,' he said. 'She's looking much better, too.'

'Yes. She's been a lot happier lately,' I said. 'She told me,' I added.

'Told you? Told you what?'

'About Pandora.'

He looked at me for a moment as if assessing how I was dealing with it. 'Ah.'

'She told me you knew about it,' I added. 'Said you handled it really well.'

'I'm sorry I didn't tell you,' he said. 'It wasn't my secret to confide, and I do know how you must feel, knowing that I kept something like that from you but—'

'It's all right,' I said. 'I get it. Thanks for being so nice to her. It was kind of you.'

He looked surprised, as if he'd been expecting an attack. 'Oh. Oh, well, no thanks necessary. I like Fuchsia. She's a nice girl.'

'I know.'

He seemed even more surprised, and smiled. 'Things are better between you now?'

I nodded. 'They're really good. Better than I ever imagined.'

'That's wonderful.'

I had a feeling he really meant it. He was so lovely. I wished for a moment that he'd pull the car over and pounce on me. It would be really nice to be pounced on by Flynn. Oh, God, my hormones were popping again. Great. And what kind of daughter was I to let my hormones pop, while my poor mother could be in mortal danger?

I daren't look at him again, and we continued the journey in silence, pulling up outside Maurice's house and looking anxiously at the window. There was a light on, so he must have been home. Why hadn't he answered his phone, then? Oh, God, what if he was lying at the bottom of the stairs?

I was out of the car before Flynn had time to do his usual gentlemanly routine of opening the door for me. He followed me up the path and knocked loudly on the front door. We waited a moment, and then Flynn took out a key and opened it up.

The house was deathly silent. There was a lamp on in the living room, but the television was switched off. Flynn went back into the hallway and called Maurice's name. There was no sound from upstairs. We looked at each other and headed into the kitchen. The light was on and the door was open. Moths were fluttering round the bulb, making me duck and squawk and flap my arms like a demented parrot.

Flynn laughed, and I glared at him. 'It's not funny,' I began. 'I hate moths,' but he was nodding towards the garden, his eyes twinkling with amusement.

I followed his gaze, and felt weak with relief when I saw my mother and Maurice sitting in a hammock at the end of the garden, deep in conversation, and each holding a glass of something that looked suspiciously alcoholic.

'Oh, thank God.' I felt quite faint suddenly, and Flynn took hold of my arm, steadying me as I wobbled.

'Are you okay? Quite a relief, isn't it? I have to admit I was much more worried than I let on.'

'I knew it!' I said.

We headed out into the garden, and the two renegade oldies looked up and smiled at us when they saw us, holding up their glasses and calling to us as if they hadn't a care in the world.

'Aw, how lovely to see you both together,' trilled my mother. 'Have some wine. It's delicious. Oh, not you, Rose.'

I glared at her. She'd better not have had so much that she slipped up.

'She can have a glass of wine, can't you?' asked Maurice.

Flynn looked at me, and seemed to be waiting for my answer.

I tried to sound casual. 'No thanks. I'm not bothered,' I said. 'Mam, have you any idea how worried I've been?'

'Worried?' She looked puzzled. 'What about?'

'You said you'd be home by teatime,' I reminded her. 'Why didn't you let me know you were coming here?'

'It was a last minute decision,' she confessed. 'I got off at the bus station at Whitby, and there was a bus to Helmston ready to leave, and I just thought, sod it. Why not come and visit me old mate, Maurice? So I did.'

'Well, thanks very much for letting me know.'

'You could have rung me if you were worried,' she said.

'I did! Loads of times. You didn't answer.'

'I never heard it ring.' She fumbled in her bag then stared at me. 'It's not there. Bugger. I must have left it at Alec's. Sorry, pet.'

'Oh, God.' I crumpled onto the hammock beside her, and she put her arm round me.

'Are you all right?' She looked quite anxious, and I put my head on her shoulder, just so relieved that she was safe and sound. The stupid, selfish old sod.

'Glass of wine, Flynn?' asked Maurice. 'I'm terribly sorry about this. I'd have called you if I'd known you were worrying.'

'Rose did ring here,' explained Flynn, 'but there was no answer, which worried us even more. Of course, if you were out here, you wouldn't have heard it.' He pulled up a garden chair and sank into it, looking at me quite anxiously. 'Are you sure you're okay? You don't look well.'

My mother squeezed me in a rather protective manner. 'Right as rain,' she said. 'Just had a tiring day. Works too hard, doesn't she? And then worrying about her stupid mother, an' all. I don't know how she does it. She's a diamond, this one.'

He nodded. 'I know.'

She beamed at him, and I closed my eyes. Any moment, she'd be telling him what a fabulous mother I was, and how lucky his unborn child was to have such a spectacular incubator.

'I think we should be getting home,' I told her, anxious to avoid such eventualities. The three of them looked at me, and then at each other, as if I was some stern parent, trying to stop their fun.

'You're getting married tomorrow,' I reminded her wearily. 'At least, that's what Alec said?'

She put down her glass. 'Oh, aye. I suppose you're right. Hell, is that the time?'

'I'll take you home.' Flynn stood up, and Maurice sighed and put down his glass.

'I suppose it is rather late,' he agreed. 'It's been a lovely evening, though. I'm so glad you came over, Maisie.'

'Aye, me an' all, Maurice,' she said.

They collected the wine bottle and glasses, and we all headed back indoors. Maurice managed to get most of the moths outside, more for my benefit than his, and shut the door. We walked towards the car, and Flynn helped my mother into the back seat before opening the passenger door for me.

As he climbed into the driver seat, Maurice called to my mother, 'I'll see you tomorrow, Maisie? At the church?'

She looked at him in silence. Flynn and I both turned to look at her. Eventually, she nodded and said, 'Aye, you will. Eleven o'clock sharp.'

'Remember,' he said, 'what we talked about. The offer's there, if you change your mind.'

Flynn raised an eyebrow at me, and my eyes widened. That sounded intriguing.

My mother smiled and waved at him, a lonely figure standing by his garden gate. 'See you tomorrow, pet. Thanks for tonight. It was just what I needed.'

He nodded, and we drove off, leaving him behind, while I wondered what had been said and just what kind of offer Maurice had made to my mother.

****

Mrs MacLean was asleep within five minutes of them setting off. Flynn heard her gentle snores from the back seat and smiled to himself. 'She seems to be okay, anyway,' he said. 'So, the wedding's on, then?'

Rose tutted. 'Looks that way. I wonder what all that was about, her and Maurice?'

'I don't know. Maurice is looking so much better, isn't he? Almost his old self.'

She nodded. 'He certainly doesn't seem so depressed.'

'It's your mother,' he said. 'She's cheered him up no end—really brought him out of himself.'

'My mother?' She sounded surprised. 'Doesn't she annoy

him? She's ever so common, sometimes.'

Flynn grinned. 'Is she? I don't know about that, but she's terribly good fun. She makes him laugh. She's rather good company, I think.'

'Is she?' Rose considered for a moment. 'Maybe a bit, sometimes.' She fell quiet for a moment, perhaps remembering how scared she'd been when she thought something had happened to her. She looked over her shoulder and smiled at her sleeping mother. 'Yeah. She is.'

He turned back to the road, sensing her eyes boring into him.

'You've done a lot for Maurice, yourself,' she pointed out. 'You've really looked after him, helped him to recover.'

'Me? I did nothing.' His smile died, and his hands gripped the steering wheel a little tighter.

'Yes, you did. Not many blokes would go round to an old colleague's house, and cook and clean for him, and take him out for the day.' Her voice trailed off, and he wondered if she was remembering Whitby and what it had led to. He mustn't think about that, whatever he did.

'I should have done it sooner. If I hadn't neglected him the way I did, none of this would have happened. I couldn't cope, you see ...' He glanced in the rear view mirror, but Mrs MacLean was still fast asleep. 'After Emily,' he whispered, 'I couldn't take anyone else's grief. I left him to it. It was unforgivable.'

'You're too hard on yourself,' she murmured. 'You'd been through so much, Flynn, how could you be expected to deal with anymore?'

He went to change gear, and her hand rested on his. He moved his own hand back to the steering wheel, but her hand went with it. He glanced at her. She was looking at him with such sad eyes. He wanted to pull over and grab her to him, hold onto her and never let her go. He was so sorry for the way he'd spoken to her after the whole roses fiasco. He wanted to tell her that, tell her how stupid he'd been, how he'd overreacted. Life without her was so dull, so dreary. He wondered how to go about asking her to forgive him, to give him another chance. He'd been so happy to hear her voice, when she'd called earlier. He knew it was wrong, but he'd actually been glad that her mother had gone missing for a while. It gave him the chance he'd been longing for, to be with her again.

They reached the top of Bay Street, and Flynn switched the engine off. It took them a couple of minutes to wake Mrs MacLean up, and another couple before she was fully with it and able to gather up her bag and get out of the car.

'Eeh, it's a bit nippy, the night,' she said, shivering as Flynn helped Rose onto the path, and they all stood there, looking awkwardly at each other.

'Well, thanks a lot, Flynn,' said Rose eventually. 'I don't know what I'd have done without you.'

'No trouble,' he said. 'Maybe ...'

'Yes?'

He stared at her, trying desperately to communicate how he was feeling. Her own eyes were full of anxiety as they met his. He shook his head. 'Nothing. Goodnight.'

'Goodnight, Flynn.'

'Night, pet. See you at the church tomorrow.'

'Yes, of course. Goodnight, Mrs MacLean.'

He stood there for a moment, watching them begin the descent down Bay Street. He could hear them muttering to each other, and saw Mrs MacLean waving her arms, as if she was trying to make some point.

Once he'd climbed back into his car, he took a deep breath and moved his rear view mirror to look at his reflection. A coward stared back at him. A weak and feeble man, who didn't have the guts to go after the woman he loved. Because he did love her. He knew he loved her. There was no joy in his life without her, and she occupied all his thoughts. Even when he was at work, she was there in the back of his mind. He only had to wander into the office and see Fuchsia sitting there, looking up at him with the same grey eyes as her mother, to be reminded of his stupid behaviour.

How many times had he longed to go to her flat, to knock on the door, to take her in his arms and tell her how much he needed her? How much he loved her? Lying in that lonely bed, night after night, longing to feel her beside him again. He had gone all those years with no one to hold, feeling empty and hollow, but she had filled him up, and now he couldn't bear to be without her.

He stared into his own eyes, anger at his own stupidity and spinelessness suddenly evident in their expression, in the way his reflection glared at him with contempt.

He'd had enough.

He jumped out of his car and began to head towards Bay Street, but stopped short when he saw her marching back up towards him.

She glanced up and stopped, too, but then he was running towards her, and she was smiling uncertainly, and his arms were round her, and he was kissing her.

'I love you.' She couldn't get a word in edgeways as he kissed her forehead, her nose, her eyelids, her lips. 'I love you so much.'

She stared up at him, her dear face cupped in his hands, her eyes wide with astonishment as he told her how much she meant to him, how sorry he was for the way he'd behaved, how much he adored her.

'It's no good without you,' he whispered. 'Nothing's right. I can't stand it. Please, Rose, please forgive me. Please say you'll give me another chance.'

She was shaking her head, and for a heart-stopping moment, he thought she was telling him no, but she was smiling, and tears were rolling down her face, and her lips were on his, and her hands raked through his hair, pulling his head closer to hers. They stood for a long, long time, kissing, murmuring, kissing again.

A gang of teenagers trudged up the hill eating fish and chips. 'Put her down, mate. You're putting me off me haddock,' yelled one.

They jeered and whistled, but Flynn and Rose just laughed and kissed some more.

'I have to go,' she said eventually.

He looked at her, stricken.

'It's the wedding,' she reminded him. 'I need to be at home to help.'

'Of course.' He let her go, telling himself it was a temporary separation. They would be together again. Soon.

'I'll see you tomorrow,' she whispered.

He nodded and kissed her again. Then she turned and began to walk down Bay Street, and he headed to his car.

She'd only been walking a minute or so, when he ran up behind her, grabbed her round the waist and spun her round. She gasped, and he kissed her again.

'I love you,' he told her, fiercely.

'I love you, too. I'll see you tomorrow.'

She was laughing. Flynn laughed, too, and ran back to the car. That time he switched on the engine and drove home. He could wait one more night. They had the rest of their lives together.

CHAPTER TWENTY-THREE

I wasn't sure what time I finally fell asleep. Possibly around four. I woke up at six and rushed straight to the bathroom, where I was violently sick. Lovely. Waiting till I stopped retching, I pulled the chain and rinsed my mouth with water. I stared into the mirror above the sink, at a face that was so pale, I quite scared myself. My eyes resembled currants in a pasty dough face. Well, what did I expect on two hours' sleep and with morning sickness to contend with?

I wondered what Flynn would say if he could see me? Would he still be telling me how much he needed and loved me? I groaned silently and shook my head. How could I have been so stupid? What the hell had I been thinking?

I'd only gone back to him because my mother insisted that I should talk to him, try to at least get things back on a friendly basis, even if nothing could come of it. I hadn't expected him to go all weird on me like that. Why would I? It was so unlike him that, after some sleep, I wasn't sure I hadn't dreamt it. I never imagined, in a million years, that he would behave like that—although he'd been very passionate that night after Whitby. Still, the way he'd kissed me last night, so fiercely, so lovingly, how could anyone have predicted that?

Feeling an ominous tingling again, I rolled my eyes. My hormones were all over the place. That was what had landed me in this mess in the first place. Because it was a mess, and last night, it had got a whole lot messier.

I carried the tumbler into the kitchen and washed it out. They would be up soon, getting all excited about the wedding. My mother would be queening it over us, the centre of attention on her special day. They wouldn't know that, in the space of fifteen minutes, my whole life had tilted, and I had gone from misery to complete ecstasy to desolation.

I shouldn't have encouraged him. I should have pushed him away, made it clear that I thought a lot of him, but that things were going to be strictly platonic between us from then on. There was no way I should have reacted like that. I had practically vacuumed him up. I was a disgrace. And telling him I loved him! Again!

'But he'd told me first,' I muttered to myself, rebelliously.

It doesn't matter, said the little voice of reason. *You know perfectly well that he doesn't have all the information. You do. You should have acted responsibly.*

Oh, bollocks. Why did everything have to be so complicated?

There's nothing complicated about it, said the little voice, calmly. *You're pregnant. Flynn doesn't want any more children. He said so himself. He's not moved on from Emily. You have to let him go.*

Fuck it, said the rebellious voice. *Can't I just make the most of him until he* has *to know? I could get away with this for weeks yet. Think how much fun I could have in that time.*

You heard him last night, said the little voice. *He said he loves you. He means it. He's far too decent for you to mess him around like that. You can't just string him along. He deserves the truth.*

And I deserve some fun, said the rebellious voice. *And, anyway, it's his fault my hormones are popping. Firstly for being so completely gorgeous, and then for getting me pregnant. Surely, the least he owes me is a few good f—*

'Flipping heck, Mam, you look rough.' Cerise padded into the kitchen, yawning and scratching her head. 'Isn't Gran up yet? Shall I wake her?'

'No, leave her for now,' I said, my voice still hoarse from all the retching.

'God, you look awful. You're not ill, are you?'

'You'd look awful if you had to sleep on that sofa every night,' I said.

'True. Sorry, Mam. It must have been rotten for you lately. Well, at least Gran will be moving in with that slimeball tonight, and you'll have your room back.' Her face brightened. 'Hey, and I'll have my room to myself soon, too, when Fuchsia moves in with Pandora. Imagine how much space we'll have.'

I thought about the size of buggies, cots, changing mats, baby baths, sterilising units. We'd have no space at all by the time I'd bought that little lot. I gave her a weak smile and asked her if she wanted a cup of tea.

'I'll make it,' she said. 'Go and sit down before you fall down.'

I practically collapsed onto the sofa and lay there, clutching my pillow and wondering when my stomach would stop spinning.

My mother appeared beside me. "Morning! Lovely day for it, isn't it?' She looked at me and felt my forehead. 'You look like death.'

'Cheers,' I said.

Cerise called from the kitchen. 'Cuppa, Gran?'

'Thanks, pet.' She turned back to me and whispered, 'Do you want a ginger biscuit?'

I didn't really, but anything was worth a shot. I nodded, and she hurried into the kitchen, distracting Cerise with wedding talk while she somehow managed to snaffle a couple of ginger biscuits and smuggle them into the living room.

'Wouldn't say no to some toast,' she called to Cerise, while snuggling up beside me on the sofa and watching in sympathy as I nibbled at the biscuit. 'Bless you. It's not getting any better, is it?'

I shook my head.

'It'll pass soon. At least it's only the mornings. Some people have it all through the day.'

'Thanks,' I said, greatly comforted.

'So, how did it go?' she whispered. 'Last night, I mean? I wanted to ask you when you got in, but I must have fallen asleep.'

'Mam, you wouldn't believe me if I told you,' I said.

'In a good way, or a bad way?'

'Both.'

'Eh?'

'Never mind all that. Is this wedding still really on? Because after the stunt Alec pulled with the magazine, I can't believe he managed to talk you round.'

'Neither can I.' Fuchsia wandered into the room, pulling her hair into a scrunchie and giving my mother a very disapproving look. 'After all that crap about Grandad, how can you bear to even speak to him?'

'It's not that easy.' My mother squirmed, nodding gratefully at Cerise as she handed her a plate of toast.

'Don't see what's hard about it?' said Fuchsia.

My mother took a bite out of her toast and chewed thoughtfully. I watched as a blob of butter dripped slowly down her chin, but looked away hastily, taking a surreptitious bite of my ginger biscuit.

'Alec said he didn't say your dad was called Mike,' she told me eventually. 'He said he distinctly said Dave, and can't imagine where they got Mike from.'

'That's the least of it,' said Fuchsia. 'What about all that stuff about Grandad just being someone you rubbed along with, while you pined away for Alec? Surely, that's not true?'

'Of course not!'

'Well, then?' I didn't want to put pressure on her, but really, how could she possibly forgive him for that?

'He said it was all twisted by the magazine, to make it sound more romantic,' she said.

'And you believe him?'

She twirled a lock of her hair in her fingers, smearing butter all over it, and gave me a helpless look.

'You don't, do you? Oh, Mam, you can't marry him.'

'I never said I didn't,' she protested, but the doubt was in her face plain for all of us to see.

'And what about the five hundred quid?' asked Cerise.

'He said it's paying for a honeymoon. It was meant to be a surprise.'

'So, he's booked a honeymoon?'

'Not yet, but he said he will when the dust settles.'

'What dust? Hardly a romantic metaphor,' I said. 'He could at least have said when the confetti's blown away.'

They all stared at me.

'Since when were you a romantic?' asked Cerise.

My mother smiled at me knowingly. 'Hidden depths, your mam,' she told them. 'Gets that from me.'

'Well, I think he's lying,' said Fuchsia, reaching over and breaking off a piece of toast. 'You can't go through with it, Gran. Simple as that.'

'Really?' said my mother, looking round at us all with wide eyes. 'So, what do I do, then? Stay here, crashing in your mother's bed, while she gets stuck on the sofa till God knows when? That'll really work, won't it? I've got nothing, don't you understand? A few bits of furniture stuck in Flynn's spare bedroom and garage. That's my entire life right there. I've got me pitiful pension, no home, no job, no future. At least with Alec, there's a nice house in Redcar to live in, and a decent income, and the chance of a holiday now and then.'

'And his slimy paws all over you,' said Cerise, pulling a face.

Fuchsia giggled. 'Surely, you don't need sex that badly, Gran?'

'Your gran has a very active libido,' I said, feeling sympathy for her condition for the first time in my life.

'Do I buggery,' snapped my mother. 'I dunno where you get these ideas. I'd rather have a cup of tea and a sticky bun, any day of the week.'

'Eh? But all that talk you gave me the other week? The sexy lingerie? The chocolate condoms?'

Fuchsia and Cerise put their hands over their ears and started singing loudly. My mother looked at them and rolled

331

her eyes, then turned to me.

'I told you, the condoms were left over from me and your dad. And the other stuff—just me trying to convince meself, trying to see if I could summon up some enthusiasm, flick the switch, you know. I thought if I could tell meself enough that I was up for it, I'd believe it in the end.'

'But you're not interested?'

'You must be joking.'

'So, you and Alec have never ...?'

'Oh, aye, once or twice, but to be honest I can't say the earth moved. I'm not even sure the bed moved. He certainly wasn't a patch on your dad.'

'Oh, Mam,' I said. 'Then, why? Please, please don't throw yourself away on him. We'll manage. You know you can stay here for as long as you want.'

She took my hand and squeezed it. 'It's good of you, pet, and I really appreciate it. But you and I know that things are going to have to change, and can you honestly tell me that there's really room for me here on a permanent basis?'

I blinked away tears as I had to admit to myself that, no, I really couldn't. There was no getting away from it. The flat was too small. I didn't know how we were going to cope *without* my mother, never mind with her. And she had no money, nothing of any value to sell. She would never be able to even scrape up a deposit on a decent flat, and I had no money to help her. It was already worrying me, thinking about the amount of stuff I'd have to buy within the next seven months. Because I didn't want to ask Flynn, knowing how he felt, and that meant I'd be trawling the second hand shops, as it was. There'd be nothing spare to help her with a deposit.

She patted my hand. 'Right, then, enough of this. Let's get ourselves glammed up, eh? We've a wedding to get to.'

****

My hair was refusing to behave itself. Even with Fuchsia's super-powered straighteners, it seemed determined to make a show of me and kept springing up all over the place. My pink streak had a distinct kink in it that I couldn't get rid of. My skin looked dull even under the makeup. Concealer hadn't completely disguised the dark shadows under my eyes, and I still felt nauseous, as well as a complete mess.

My mother looked lovely, though. The oyster silk dress and coat suited her strawberry blonde colouring, and I'd never seen her so dignified and elegant. As if resigned to her fate, she was holding her head high, like Catherine Howard on her way to the guillotine.

The flowers had been delivered early that morning—small posies of peach and white roses for me and my mother, and peach rose buttonholes for the girls. Peach didn't suit me. Maybe I should have dyed over my streak for the wedding? I remembered Lindsey's assertion that Flynn loved my pink streak.

Why did everything always come back to Flynn?

Fuchsia and Cerise had made a real effort. Fuchsia had dressed in a bottle green shift dress, and Cerise wore a baby blue skater dress that I thought was a bit short, but I didn't say anything, as I really couldn't be arsed with any dramas. I had enough to worry about. Cerise's hair looked a bit better, with several washes toning down the blonde slightly, and Fuchsia had helped her with her make-up, showing her that, sometimes, less is more. I watched her applying a light dusting of blusher to her sister's face, and thought how lovely it was to see them getting on so well these days. I was proud of Cerise for sticking up for Fuchsia, even though she shouldn't have thumped the girl who mocked her, I supposed, and I was glad she had no problem with her sister's sexuality. They seemed finally to be becoming the loving little unit I'd always dreamed of.

Even my relationship with my mother was so much better

these days. She still had the knack for opening her mouth and making me feel like shit on occasions, but she'd proved to be much kinder and more considerate than I'd ever imagined she could be. I knew she loved me, and that was what really mattered.

We actually felt like a family at last. How sad that it was all about to change. Mam would be moving to Redcar that night. Fuchsia and Pandora would find their own place, eventually, and Cerise would be disgusted to find out that she would soon be sharing her bedroom with a squawking baby.

I couldn't do it to her. The baby would have to stay in my room until—well, probably until Cerise left home, I guessed. I foresaw a long, long time on the sofa. Maybe I should invest in a sofabed. They were quite expensive, but cheaper than moving, even if I managed to sell the flat and find somewhere else affordable. I doubted it, though, especially in the village, and there was no way I wanted to leave.

It had occurred to me that morning, though, that maybe leaving Kearton Bay was exactly what I should do. Obviously, I wouldn't give up my job, and would travel to the village every day to continue there, but maybe I should look farther afield for a home. Maybe Whitby or Farthingdale, or Moreton Cross? That way, Flynn wouldn't run the risk of bumping into the child every day. He could easily avoid Mallow Magic. I didn't think he'd been in the shop, anyway, so that wouldn't be difficult.

Maybe, when the shock died down, he'd be calm enough to agree to occasional access? It would be a shame if our child never knew him. Cerise and Fuchsia never saw their fathers, but both of them were arseholes, anyway. This little one had a gem of a father. I didn't want it to miss out. But then, Flynn had been through enough. I couldn't force him, could I?

A headache had started brewing, and, as we arrived at St Hilda's, I began to feel very sick. I wished to God there was some way I could stop the wedding from happening. It was a travesty. Surely, if God was looking down—and He was supposed to look down on you when you were at church, surely—then He would cause something to put a halt to the fiasco? Maybe a bolt of lightning had struck Alec as he'd entered the building? Highly appropriate, I would have thought, given that he was the spawn of Satan.

The girls kissed their gran and wished her luck, before dashing inside to take their seats.

My mother turned to me and took a deep breath.

'Are you sure, Mam?'

'Of course. Redcar's not far, and his house is fab. He's got a Jacuzzi bath. What more could I ask for?'

Why did churches feel so cold? Even on a sunny August morning, I shivered as we entered the building. I had a very bad feeling about it all, like I was sending my mother to her doom.

My mind raced through all the possibilities that could work and give me the chance to save her from this fate worse than death. If I got a sofabed, she could stay in my room, at least for the time being. I could sleep in the living room, and the baby could sleep in there, too, in its Moses basket. When it got too big and needed a cot, it would have to share with Cerise. How would Cerise react to that, though? Maybe Cerise could have the sofabed, and I'd sleep in the bath? The way it was going that might have ended up being the only option left.

I was so busy trying to work it all out that, before I knew it, we'd reached the end of the aisle, where Alec stood next to another slimy-looking man, who I assumed was his brother-in-law. They had matching cravats, comb-overs and smug grins.

I blinked and glanced round.

Eliza waved to me, and Amy bounced up and down on the pew, obviously excited to see her Auntie Rose looking such a prat. Beside them, Sophie was bursting with excitement to be seated next to Charlie and Joe. She was wearing another huge hat, and Charlie kept ducking every time she moved her head. Pandora was on the other side of Joe, looking very girly in a dress, rather than her usual jodhpurs.

I smiled at her, and she flushed a little and smiled back. I thought how pretty she was, and realised I'd never really taken much notice of her before. I could see what Fuchsia saw in her. I really hoped it would work out for them.

My gaze flickered to the end of the pew, and I caught sight of Flynn. My stomach flipped, and I swallowed, desperately hoping to quell the sudden attack of nausea. He stared back at me with such warmth and love that I found it hard to breathe.

Beside him stood Maurice, looking very dapper in his suit. He gave me a brief smile, but his attention was all on my mother. I didn't think he could believe she was actually going ahead with it, either.

The organist stopped playing, which was when I realised that there had been music. I'd been so absorbed in my own thoughts that I hadn't even noticed. I straightened up, determined to be a good bridesmaid. It was the least I could do for my mother—the very least.

Our vicar, Ernest Cawthorne, smiled at my mother and Alec, then reared back slightly in alarm when Alec flashed his Red Rum gnashers at him. I realised that the camera angle hadn't been to blame, after all, for the dreadful photo in the magazine. Alec really did smile like a Grand National winner, and I didn't mean the jockey.

'Dearly beloved,' the vicar began,

I peered up at the high vaulted roof of the church in desperation. 'Come on, God,' I muttered. 'Do something. You can't really want her to marry bloody Champion the Wonder Horse?'

'It is given that, as man and woman grow together in love and trust ...' droned the vicar.

Love and trust? When the rat had told all those lies about my father *and* snaffled the five hundred quid? Snaffled being quite an appropriate word, given his facial features.

'The gift of marriage brings husband and wife together in the delight and tenderness of sexual union and joyful commitment to the end of their lives ...'

I tried to keep my eyes away from Flynn. Why was it that, on the worst day of my mother's life, all I could think about was how much I'd love to be back in Flynn's bed, being held and kissed and ... Oh shit, pack it in, Rose, for God's sake.

'It enriches society and strengthens community. No one should enter into it lightly, or selfishly, but reverently and responsibly in the sight of almighty God ...'

Was my mother listening to this? She still trembled in front of me. The whole affair was horrendous—like watching an accident unfurl, and knowing it was about to happen, but being completely powerless to stop it.

My own body felt shaky. I really should have had something to eat. A few nibbles on a ginger biscuit simply weren't enough. I could smell my future stepfather's aftershave, and it was quite overpowering. How could she stand him anywhere near her?

'Now we come to the nerve-wracking bit,' said the vicar. 'Always a tense moment,' he added with a smile.

The congregation shifted and laughed.

Alec winked at my mother. His big horsy teeth flashed, as he leered at her. Beads of perspiration dotted his forehead, and I caught the whiff of Brylcreem in his hair.

Taking a deep breath, I tried to steady myself, but I could feel panic rising, and it wasn't the only thing.

The vicar smiled. 'First, I am required to ask anyone present, who knows a reason why these persons may not lawfully marry, to declare it now.'

There was silence, and Alec turned to look around the church. 'Come on, somebody save me,' he joked.

A few people tittered politely. I saw Maurice glaring at him.

Flynn was rising from the pew. Why was he standing up? He seemed to be watching me with real concern.

My mouth filled with saliva. I gave a strangled cry, and the next thing I knew, my stomach heaved, and I threw up all over the floor in full view of a horrified congregation, a dismayed clergyman, and an apoplectic groom.

'Oh, well, that's just disgusting,' said the best man.

Flynn was by my side. 'Are you all right?'

Actually, having finally thrown up, I was feeling a bit better. I nodded, and he handed me his handkerchief. I looked at it and felt tears in my eyes. Trust Flynn to have a hanky.

'Look what she's done to my shoes!' Alec had turned purple, and he pointed to his shiny black brogues, which sported several decorative splashes.

My mother had the bouquet to her nose. She was never good with vomit, to be fair. 'You all right, pet?' she managed before burying her head back in the flowers.

'Of course she's not all right,' Alec snapped. 'She's got a flaming bug, of some sort. She should never have come here. Completely selfish, and now look at the mess she's made.'

'I think we should stop the service and get this cleared up,' suggested the vicar.

'I'll clean it up,' I offered, feeling dreadful.

'Of course you won't,' said Flynn immediately. 'You're obviously not well. You need some fresh air.'

'Honestly, I'm fine,' I said, trying not to look at the pool on the floor and hoping I hadn't vomited on a grave stone, or anything. Church floors often had those set into them, didn't they? I never liked walking on them, though someone had once told me that there were no bodies under there, and that the stones were just memorials. I wasn't too sure, though, and always felt disrespectful stepping on them. How ironic that I may have just thrown up on one. I was sure that if it did have an occupant, they would have much preferred to have my feet on them than the contents of my stomach.

'Never mind all that,' snapped Alec. 'Let's just get on with it. We can clean up after this is over.'

'But it stinks!' said his best man.

Charming.

My mother popped her head out of the flowers long enough to ask, 'Are you all right to carry on, Rose?'

'She can wait outside. I'm not risking any more of that,' said my future stepfather. 'She's standing right behind us. Are you prepared to risk vomit in your hair? Because I'm sure I'm not.'

'You really are all heart,' said Flynn coldly. He took my arm and tried to lead me away, but I wouldn't budge.

'I need to stay,' I whispered to him. 'I have to be here for my mam.'

He must have seen the pleading in my eyes because he seemed to understand.

'I won't have it,' said Alec. 'Stop being a brat and wait outside. You've disrupted our perfect day enough as it is.'

'Leave her alone, Alec,' said my mother. 'She's my daughter, and if she wants to stay, she's staying.'

'Over my dead body,' said Alec.

'Don't tempt me,' said Flynn.

I looked at him admiringly, though I did wish he'd stop doing and saying all those things that turned me on. He was playing havoc with my hormones.

Alec glared at him, but obviously didn't dare say anything else.

'Shall we continue?' asked the vicar uncertainly.

I glanced over at Eliza, who was trying not to laugh, while Sophie fanned herself with the order of service, her face having a distinctly greenish tinge. Evidently, she wasn't good with vomit, either. Charlie looked enthralled. I hoped the service wouldn't end up in his stand-up routine.

'This is a fiasco,' muttered Alec. 'Carry on, Vicar.'

'Oh, really,' said a woman on the front pew on Alec's side. 'This is too much. It's making me retch.'

'Shut up, Martha,' snapped my mother. She turned to me and rolled her eyes. 'That's his sister.'

I gave her a look of sympathy. Fancy marrying into such an appalling family.

I heard giggling and, recognising it, knew that Fuchsia and Cerise were helpless. Suddenly, it all seemed terribly funny, and I started to giggle, too. Flynn looked at me in astonishment, but I couldn't help it. I think maybe hysteria was setting in.

'Will you be quiet!' bellowed Alec.

'Don't speak to her like that,' said Flynn furiously.

'You tell him, pet,' said my mother.

'I beg your pardon?' demanded the so-called love of her life.

'He's quite right. You don't speak to Rose like that. I won't have it.'

'Oh, you won't? So, you're defending her over me?'

'Any day of the week,' she confirmed.

'I'm beginning to think this wedding is a big mistake,' he said.

'Well, give it a few hours, and you'll catch up,' she told him. 'I'm not marrying you. You can shove this wedding up your arse.'

Fuchsia and Cerise whooped, and I felt quite weak with relief, even if it did mean I'd be sleeping in the bath.

'You've gone mad,' said Alec in astonishment. 'It's the fumes from that,' he added, pointing distastefully at the pool of sick on the floor.

'Bugger that,' she told him. 'I'm not marrying anyone who talks to me daughter like shit. Sorry, vicar.'

'Have you any idea how much money I've spent on you?' Alec demanded, wiping sweat from his forehead with his cravat, like a true gentleman. 'Literally hundreds of pounds, that's how much. And you behave like a common fishwife. I can see where your daughter gets it from,' he added, drawing back his lips in disgust and revealing so much of his teeth that I was tempted to try to tell his age from them.

'It wasn't a complete waste of time,' Charlie called. 'At least now we all know what happened to Shergar.'

My mother looked across at Maurice, who'd made his way to the end of the pew and was standing beside Flynn. 'What you said to me last night, did you mean it?' she asked.

'Last night? What's all this, then? Is this Maurice?' demanded Alec.

Maurice ignored him and smiled at my mother. 'Every word, Maisie.'

'Then, I'd like to take you up on your offer, if I may?'

'Offer? What bloody offer?'

I was wondering that myself.

Maurice beamed. 'Of course you may. I'd be delighted.'

'So, this is what's behind it all!' Alec screeched.

His brother-in-law folded his arms. 'Told you she looked common,' he revealed. 'I knew this was a mistake. You've been had, Alec. They've been at it behind your back, all the time.'

'Do you mind?' said Maurice distastefully. 'We don't all have our minds in the gutter.'

'You've been screwing my fiancée?' yelled Alec. 'What's this offer?'

'I'm going to live with Maurice,' said my mother calmly. 'And—'

'I knew it!' Alec swung back his fist and aimed straight for Maurice, who, so busy looking at my mother, didn't even seem to realise.

Flynn had, though, and before anyone could say "shiner", he'd leapt in front of his friend and caught the full force of Alec's punch in his face.

'Oh, Christ, not again,' I said.

My mother whacked Alec over the head with her bouquet, and then kicked him with the full force of her pointy-toed shoes for good measure.

The vicar raised his hands and appealed for calm, but Alec's sister came rushing over and started pulling my mother away from her brother, Fuchsia and Cerise charged at the sister and dragged her off my mother, Charlie had to be physically restrained by Joe from joining in, Maurice exchanged insults with a hopping Alec, and I studied Flynn's face and informed him that, yes, he was probably going to have yet another black eye.

'That's two-all,' he said with a rueful grin. 'Can we call it quits now?'

'I think perhaps you should leave the church,' suggested the vicar, in a rather desperate voice. 'Go to your homes and try to calm down. There will be no wedding here today.'

He wasn't wrong there.

My mother seemed to suddenly be a whole lot stronger and calmer. She turned to the congregation, as Fuchsia held back a struggling Martha, and called, 'Everyone is welcome to head to The Kearton Arms for the reception. There's a buffet laid on, and also a disco, I believe.'

'Yes, that I bloody paid for,' snapped Alec.

'Take it out of my share of your fifty pieces of silver,' she retorted, obviously allowing for inflation. The congregation began to file out of the church, laughing and gossiping about the strangest non-wedding they'd ever been to.

'What a fab wedding,' said Charlie, beaming at me, as Joe rolled his eyes and tried to pull him away. 'Is it always like this round here? Who needs the Edinburgh Festival with entertainment like this?'

Pandora sidled up to Fuchsia and whispered something to her. Fuchsia looked a bit nervous, but nodded and let go of Martha, who glared at her but obviously didn't dare say anything. Cerise said she'd meet us back at the pub, and headed out of the church with Eliza, Amy and Sophie.

'We need to talk,' Alec said to my mother. 'I want to know what's been going on between you and Maurice.'

'I'd quite like to know that, too,' I murmured, and Flynn looked as if he was none the wiser, either.

'Why don't you come to my house?' Flynn suggested. 'Obviously, there are things to be cleared up, and Rose needs a glass of water and a sit down.'

'What about us?' asked Martha, her husband nodding in agreement. 'Where are we supposed to go?'

'The reception?' suggested my mother, scathingly.

'No way. I'm not mixing with that lot, all your common pals,' said Martha.

'Well, sod off home, then,' Alec said, and we all stared at him in shock. 'I want to talk to my fiancée,' he said. 'If you don't like it, just go. I'm going nowhere till I've got some answers.'

'Well, that's charming,' said his brother-in-law.

'He's in shock,' said his sister, sadly. 'Poor Alec. This is all her fault. I'll never forgive her.' She glared at my mother. 'Do you hear me? I'll never forgive you.'

'You're breaking my heart,' said my mother. 'Now, piss off and leave us alone.'

'Are you sure about this?' I asked, as Flynn led us along the road to his house. 'It's not really your problem. I don't see why you should be involved.'

'If it's your problem, it's my problem,' he said, linking his arm through mine.

Oh, Flynn, I thought wearily, *you have no idea*. No idea at all.

CHAPTER TWENTY-FOUR

Flynn let us into the house, and Alec finally shut up moaning as he peered round at the expensive furniture and tasteful decor. As his eyes flickered about, I imagined him mentally totting up the value of everything, and working out how much it had cost. He was a truly repulsive man.

'First thing's first,' said Flynn. 'Rose, would you like a glass of water?'

I nodded. 'Please.'

'Sit down,' he said, 'and I'll bring it to you.'

I sank into the chair and clutched my stomach. It felt a lot easier now, but it was still a bit unsettled. I wondered if I'd feel better if I ate something.

Alec sat on the sofa, right in the middle, as if determined to keep my mother and Maurice apart. Maurice sat on the other armchair, while my mother wandered round the room, having a good nosy.

She gave me a big grin. 'Nice place he's got,' she whispered, giving me a meaningful wink.

I shook my head slightly, and jumped when Flynn appeared at my side, handing me the glass of water.

'Would anyone else like a drink?' he asked.

'Never mind all that,' said Alec impatiently. 'I want to know what's been going on. Have I been cuckolded?'

My mother laughed. 'Cuckolded? What century's that word from?'

'You know what I mean,' he said. 'Have you and that man been at it?'

Maurice looked disgusted. 'Certainly not,' he said.

'I'm not sure I believe you,' Alec said.

'I'm quite sure I don't care,' Maurice replied.

'This is getting us nowhere,' Flynn said. He perched on the side of my chair and put an arm round my shoulders.

I peered up at him. 'You're getting a bruise,' I said.

'I know. I can feel it,' he admitted. 'Are you feeling any better?'

'Much,' I said. 'Though, I could murder a slice of toast.'

'Really? Coming right up.' He jumped up and headed back to the kitchen.

'Aw, isn't he lovely?' said my mother admiringly. 'You've got a good 'un there, pet.' She picked up a frame from the top of the sideboard and stared at it for a moment. 'Is this her?' she asked me. 'Is this the bairn?'

'What?' I looked up, startled, as she held up a photograph of a beautiful baby, all dark, silky hair, and big blue eyes. Flynn had a photograph of Emily in the room? She was laughing merrily at the camera, and, as I looked at her, I felt my heart break all over again.

'Is that Emily?' murmured Maurice. 'Good heavens. First time I've ever seen her.'

I was absolutely certain that the picture hadn't been there the last time I visited. What did that mean? Was he finally coming to terms with her death? Feeling the first stirrings of hope, I tried to quell them. No point in building them up, only to have them destroyed again. I would have to wait and see.

'Who's Emily?' asked Alec.

We all looked at each other, before Maurice said, 'Flynn's daughter.'

'Oh. Well, enough of that,' he said. 'What about this affair, eh? How long's it been going on?'

'For heaven's sake,' said Maurice, 'there's no affair. Never has been.'

'I wondered what was going on. She mentioned your name a couple of times, and I thought to myself, Alec old son, you'd better watch out there. Why is some other bloke sniffing round your lady? Oh, she said it was all innocent, that you were just a friend, but I had my suspicions. And why would you ask her to move in with you, if she was just a friend, eh? Answer me that.'

'Really,' said my mother, 'I can't see that it's any of your business why I'm moving in with Maurice.'

'You're my fiancée!' Alec screeched. 'And if it wasn't for that disgusting daughter of yours, you'd be my wife by now.'

'You're welcome,' I told her, and she beamed at me.

'Thanks, pet.'

'Oh, this is bloody marvellous.' Alec had started sweating again, his cravat dark where he'd been mopping up perspiration. If anything was likely to make me vomit again, that would be it.

Flynn came back with the toast and sat beside me. 'Have I missed much?'

'Alec doesn't believe my mother and Maurice are just friends,' I said, taking a bite of toast and chewing carefully.

'Well, he wouldn't,' said Flynn. 'People like him always assume the worst.'

'What do you mean, people like me?'

'I read the magazine article,' Flynn said, seeming embarrassed when my gaze shot up to him. 'After I got home last night, I wondered what the upset had been about, so I bought a copy this morning. Have to say, it was a disgrace. You completely dismissed Mrs MacLean's marriage to Rose's father, as if it had been irrelevant.'

'That wasn't me, it was the reporter,' insisted Alec. 'And I'm not on trial here. These two are. What was the offer you made my fiancée?' he said, glaring at Maurice.

'Simply that she could come and live with me and share my home—as my friend and companion, nothing else. I still love my wife, even though she's been gone five years now, and Maisie doesn't want, or need, a romantic relationship at this point in her life. Of course, that may change. Either one of us may meet someone else, or perhaps our friendship may deepen, who knows? But right now, we both want a home, a companion, a friend. Maisie makes me laugh. She's been so good for me, and I value her so much and love her dearly. I think we could make a good team, and, happily, she agrees with me.'

'What? And no funny stuff?'

'No, Alec, no funny stuff,' said my mother, but she winked at Maurice. 'Well, not yet, eh, sweetheart?'

He chuckled, and Alec stood up.

'I've heard enough. This is all crap. I know you're pulling my leg, and you've been at it all along. Well, to hell with you. Maisie, I want my ring back.'

'My God,' I said, 'you really are low.'

'Oh, he can have it,' said my mother. 'I was only going to flog it, anyway. Ugly thing.'

'Yes, that's why I thought it would suit you,' said Alec.

My mother glared at him, and I leapt to my feet.

'Just get out,' I said. 'You're a horrible man, and I don't believe for a moment that you didn't tell the reporters all that stuff about my father.'

He curled his lip at me, revealing those disgusting, long, ivory teeth. 'You're quite right, I did. And do you know why? Because that's exactly what your mother told me. Your father was just the mug she latched onto after she lost me. She never loved him, she told me that herself. He could never match up to me.'

'My dad was a lovely man, and worth ten times what you are!' Tears welled up in my eyes, more from anger and frustration. He couldn't hurt me, because I didn't believe a word of it, but I still didn't want to hear those vile words spouting from his mouth.

'Your dad was a feeble idiot.' Alec stood in front of me, hands on his hips, and as he leaned towards me, I reared away from the smell of Eau de Porn Star and Brylcreem. 'Your mother was glad when he popped his clogs, and that's the truth of it.'

'You lying bastard!' My mother was right behind him, and, as he turned to face her, she swung her fist at him and threw a mighty punch. Unfortunately, Alec was too quick for her and ducked, so her hand connected with my face instead, and I found myself falling.

I landed with a thud on the floor. Luckily for me, Flynn had very expensive thick carpet, and I wasn't hurt by the fall. The punch was another matter, though, and I lay for a moment, feeling the familiar throb in my face and shaking my head. Not again.

'I'm out of here. You're all nutters,' Alec said and stormed out of the house.

I vaguely heard Maurice mutter that he could at least have shut the door behind him, but I was more aware of my mother throwing herself at me and screaming, 'Rose! Rose, are you all right?'

'I'm fine, don't worry,' I said, rubbing my cheekbone and wincing. 'I make that three-two.'

Flynn helped me to my feet and kissed me gently. 'You're not going to let me win, are you?' he said, smiling.

'Oh, my God, I'll never forgive meself,' my mother wailed dramatically.

'She's fine, Mrs MacLean. Don't worry,' said Flynn, but she turned on him, her eyes wide with fear.

'I sent her flying. She could lose the bairn!'

Deathly silence took over the room, and as I watched, the shock of what she'd said registered in my mother's face, while amazement filled Maurice's eyes.

My heart drummed frantically in my chest as I slowly turned to look at Flynn.

The colour literally drained from his face. 'The—the what?'

'I'm sorry, Rose,' murmured my mother. 'I didn't mean to let it slip out. I was just that scared.'

'I know, Mam. It's all right,' I said.

'Goodness,' said Maurice. He shook his head, apparently unable to think of anything else to say, and looked anxiously across at Flynn, but Flynn simply stood there, staring at me as if frozen in time.

'Flynn, I was going to tell you,' I said.

'Is it, is it ...?'

'Of course it's yours,' I said, rather hurt.

He shook his head. 'I was going to say, is it true? Oh, my God.' He sank onto the chair and buried his head in his hands.

I looked helplessly at my mother, who looked at Maurice.

'It was my fault,' she said. 'Me and those damn chocolate condoms. They were out of date. I didn't know about expiry dates, you see. I would never have given them to her, if I'd known.'

'Not your fault, Maisie,' said Maurice soothingly. 'Sometimes, these things are just meant to be.'

I went to step toward Flynn, but paused at a babble of voices, and suddenly the living room was full of people who all seemed to be arguing.

'I knew he hadn't shut the door,' said Maurice.

'What's going on now?' my mother asked, as I looked round to see Sophie, Eliza, Fuchsia and Pandora standing there.

'Rose, did you know about this?' demanded Sophie.

'Can you please leave?' asked my mother. 'Now's not the time.'

Sophie didn't seem to hear her. 'Rose, are you listening? Did you know about Pandora and Fuchsia?'

'What about Pandora and Fuchsia?' My mother was suddenly all ears.

Eliza looked from me to Flynn. 'Everything all right?' she mouthed.

I shook my head, and she pulled a sympathetic face, obviously realising why he was looking so shocked.

'Perhaps we should do this another time, Sophie,' she said, pulling on her sister-in-law's arm.

'I just want to know if she knew?' Sophie was in tears now. 'Did everyone know? Am I the last to find out?'

'Find out what?' My mother looked baffled.

'That they're a couple.'

'Who is?'

'Pandora and Fuchsia. Haven't I just said that?'

'Our Fuchsia?' My mother's mouth dropped open. 'Never! You're a lesbian, pet? By, you kept that quiet. I thought you fancied her brother.'

'It was all just a ploy.' Sophie plonked herself down on the sofa and dabbed her eyes. 'How am I going to tell Archie?'

'Archie won't mind, at all,' said Eliza. 'I'm surprised at you, Sophie. I thought you just wanted your kids to be happy?'

'I do, of course I do, but it's all been such a shock. How did you feel, Rose, when you found out?'

'I—I was all right,' I murmured, looking anxiously at Flynn. I wished they'd all just clear off. Of all the times to finally tell Sophie, they'd had to pick now.

'So, you did know!' Sophie was triumphant. 'I knew it. Why did you tell her and not me?' she demanded, raising tearful eyes to her daughter.

'I didn't,' protested Pandora. 'Fuchsia told her. I didn't know she was going to tell her, but once I knew she had, I knew I had to tell you. I'm sorry, Mum. I didn't mean to hurt you, but I can't tell you how hard this has been for me. I've been so scared. I don't want you to hate me.'

'Hate you?' Sophie looked appalled. 'As if I could ever hate you. Is that what you think of me? I was only upset when I realised that everyone knew except me.'

Fuchsia looked at me, her eyes full of tears. I put my arms around her, and Sophie began to cry again. Fuchsia reached out a hand to her, and Sophie looked at it for a moment, before taking hold of it and squeezing it.

'Not many people knew about it,' Fuchsia assured her. 'It was only a few. We only didn't tell you because Pandora was scared of letting you down. She loves you so much. She didn't want to be a disappointment to you.'

'Never.' Sophie shook her head. 'She will never be a

disappointment. I'm sorry she thought she'd let me down. It doesn't matter who you sleep with,' she said to her daughter, wiping tears away with a tissue. 'Don't you know that? I don't care, as long as you're happy and don't push me away. Please don't keep me out of your life. I knew it, you see, I knew there was something you were keeping from me, and that's what was upsetting me so much.'

'I'm sorry, Mum,' whispered Pandora.

I looked round for Flynn, and was shocked to find him gone.

Maurice patted my arm. 'He left a moment ago. Give him time, my dear. He just needs to come to terms with it all.'

I turned to my mother, whose wedding day had devolved into a total fiasco, and to the man who had been just a friend, but was now apparently her new housemate. From them, I looked to my daughter, who had arrived with her girlfriend's family in tow, including the mother who had no idea her daughter was even gay. What a bloody day.

Why was my life always so messy and noisy and crowded? No wonder Flynn couldn't cope. Even without a baby, he would never be able to handle all this, and my life seemed to consist of endless chaotic episodes.

I glanced around his pristine house and tried to imagine him living with all the noise and mess that being with the MacLeans seemed to entail. I couldn't. Flynn Pennington-Rhys was the quiet man. It didn't matter how much time I gave him. He would never come to terms with it. It was all impossible.

CHAPTER TWENTY-FIVE

The Kearton Arms was buzzing. Considering it was Friday and not many people had been invited, there were an awful lot of guests suddenly. I suspected that word had got round that Joe Hollingsworth and Charlie Hope were present. Lots of people popped in, had a drink, scoffed a few sandwiches, begged for autographs and left again, which would have been terribly rude, had it been a proper reception. Since there was no wedding, however, no one seemed to care much and it was basically a free-for-all.

Gabriel and Meggie appeared at lunchtime and stayed for an hour. I saw Eliza head over to Gabriel's side and pull him away from the crowd, where she spoke quietly to him. He glanced over at me, surprise on his face, before he shook his head, and Eliza beckoned me over.

'Gabriel hasn't heard from him,' she said. 'Sorry, Rose. I thought maybe he'd have gone to see him, talk things through with him.'

'Where could he be?' I fretted. 'There's only Gabriel and Maurice he really talks to, and if he's not with either of them, he must be all alone. God knows what he'll do.' I could only think of one other place, and I shivered as a vision of Flynn, throwing himself on Emily's grave, and sobbing with grief, flooded my mind.

'I can't see it being a big drama,' said Gabriel. 'I should think Flynn would love to be a father, once he gets his head round it all.'

'Did you know?' I asked. 'About Emily, I mean?'

He looked at me blankly. 'Who's Emily?'

'Oh, God.'

Eliza squeezed his arm. 'His daughter,' she said gently.

'Flynn has a daughter?' He looked stunned.

My eyes filled with tears, and I turned away. 'I'm sorry, I can't,' I said, and left Eliza to explain to him all about Flynn's sad secret.

My mother and Cerise were sitting with Maurice, at what should have been the top table.

'Any word?' asked Maurice. I shook my head, and he patted the chair beside him, indicating that I should sit down. I did, and he smiled at me. 'I don't believe I said congratulations,' he said.

'Thanks, but I don't feel much like celebrating,' I told him.

'You know, after all the babies your mother lost, and the fact that Matilda and I could never have children, and given what happened to Flynn and Lindsey, I should think you would be extremely grateful to have the chance for a third child. It's a great blessing.'

I felt wretched. 'I know. I am. It's just ...'

'Just what?'

'It's just that, if I hadn't got pregnant, maybe Flynn and I would have had a chance. Not much of a chance, I'll admit, but at least there would have been some chance. Now there's no hope at all.'

'When I first met Flynn,' said Maurice, taking my hand, 'it must have been about eight years ago now—do you know what I saw when I first met him? A broken man, that's what. At first, I thought it was just the divorce. He'd told me bits about his wife, and seemed to be still grieving for his marriage. I was quite worried about him, and I took him under my wing a bit. Introduced him to Matilda, started inviting him round for dinner, that kind of thing.'

He smiled. 'Matilda was very astute. Said there was something else that was hurting him. Something so bad he couldn't speak of it. It was her who finally coaxed it out of him—about Emily, I mean. He never spoke of her to me, and not much to Matilda. We were shocked when we visited his house. Not a single photograph. I mean, it's not right, is it? Anyway, there was a hollowness to him, an emptiness.'

I nodded. 'I know.' What was he trying to do? Make me

feel even more guilty?

'After a couple of years, I retired, and Flynn moved here to go into partnership with Raphael Bailey. We kept in touch regularly and saw a lot of him, but then Matilda got ill ...'

His voice trailed off, and I looked across at my mother and Cerise, who were listening to his story with keen interest. My mother patted his arm and said, 'Go on, Maurice. It's all right.'

'Oh, I know, I know.' He shrugged. 'Flynn seemed fine at first, driving us to hospital appointments whenever he could, shopping for us, taking us on days out, that kind of thing. But as Matilda got worse, his visits grew less frequent. He couldn't face it, and we understood that. Matilda had expected it, and warned me what would happen. She was quite right. After she died, I rarely saw him. It was only very recently that he got back in touch and started visiting again on a regular basis. I was delighted to see him, of course, but do you know what I wondered?'

'What?'

'I wondered why it was that, after all that time, he was still pretty much the same. There had been little progress. He was still hollow. Still stuck in that frozen state.'

'I don't think he is,' said my mother. 'He can be a right laugh, and he waded in like a good 'un when them yobs got hold of our Rose.'

'Ah,' said Maurice, holding up his hand. 'Now, that's the point I'm coming to.'

Well, thank God for that. I thought he'd never reach the end.

'These last few weeks, I've seen a change. At first, it was just sitting with me as I talked about Matilda. He never wanted to discuss her before, but now we look at photographs, and we talk about our visits and our trips out, and we laugh as we remember things she said or did. I thought that was a marvellous breakthrough, but it got better. He started to tell me about Emily.'

'He did?'

'Yes. Never had before. Told Matilda a bit, as I said, but never me. Suddenly, it was as if he wanted to talk about her. He told me about her birth, and about her favourite toys, and about her first tooth, which had just come through when she was taken. And then, finally, he told me about that day. About finding her in her cot, knowing there was nothing he could do. It was too late.'

'Oh, don't,' I said, mopping away tears again. Bloody hormones were turning me into a blubbering mess. 'Lindsey told me. It's just awful.'

'Lindsey told you?' He looked at me, astonished. 'When did you see her?'

'She came to see me,' I admitted. 'She wanted me to give him another chance, put things right. I told her about the baby, and she said I should make him see what a good thing it could be for him. Huh. Fat chance.'

'Well, I never. But she's right, my dear. Flynn is finally grieving. I'm not sure what brought it to the surface, what made him deal with it, but something has. And I have a feeling it has something to do with you.'

'Me?'

'Yes. I wondered if anything could break through that protective shell of his, but that day you turned up at my house, with Maisie here, I saw him looking at you, and I knew that you were his only chance. You must know how he feels about you? Isn't it obvious?'

'But even if he could cope with a baby, I'm far too loud and complicated for him. He has such a quiet, orderly life. Can you imagine him living with someone like me?'

All three of them exchanged glances, then there was a chorus of, 'Yes!'

'You can?' I was quite astonished.

'Best thing for him,' said Maurice. 'You've brought him back to life. Please don't give up on him.'

That was more or less what Lindsey had said. Was I missing something that everyone else could see?

'You can't give up on him, anyway,' said Cerise giving me a knowing look. 'At least one of your kids needs a father it can rely on. I can't think of anyone who'd be better at being a responsible dad than him, can you?'

I shook my head. 'I'm sorry I didn't tell you,' I said. 'I was waiting for the scan.'

'It's okay. At least it explains why you chucked up all over the church. It'll be quite cool not being the baby of the family anymore. I'll be the big sister, at last. But you need to make it up with him, Mam, because I quite fancy living in that big house of his.'

I laughed, but my eyes must have betrayed my doubt, because Maurice leaned over to me and whispered, 'He'll be back, Rose. Just you wait and see.'

By four o'clock, the disco was in full swing, the food had nearly all gone, and my mother had cut the cake and handed out slices to everyone, even people in the bar who had nothing to do with the wedding and didn't have a clue who she was.

'Bugger it,' she said. 'Alec got me ring back, so the least I should get is the cake.'

I watched as everyone danced to *White Wedding* by Billy Idol, smiling as Pandora and Fuchsia rocked the dance floor, looking bright and happy, and very much in love. Charlie and Joe were head banging like Status Quo, and Lexi had dragged Will in for ten minutes, to catch up on the gossip, having heard through the village grapevine that the wedding had been a catastrophe. I saw her pull him onto the dance floor, and couldn't help giggling at his awkward attempt to dance with her. She was laughing so much she was crying, and in the end she just shook her head, pulled him to her, and kissed him on the forehead.

Will looked quite dazed. I watched hopefully. 'Oh go on,' I urged him. 'Grab her, tell her how you feel!'

'Very well.'

I looked up, shocked, to see Flynn standing there looking down on me.

He held out his hand. 'Come with me,' he said.

****

I stood up and took his hand as he led me outside. We walked out of the pub car park and to the top of Bay Street, stopping at the bench by the railings, where he appeared to have left his jacket. I thought that was very trusting of him. Being raised in Feldane, there was no way I'd have left any of my belongings in public view.

'Where have you been?' I said. 'Were you at the churchyard? Did you go to see Emily?'

He touched my cheek, his eyes warm with understanding. 'No. I went to The Hare and Moon, and had a very large brandy and talked things over with Rhiannon.'

'Why?' I demanded. 'And how come Rhiannon knew all about Emily? Because she did, didn't she? That's why she was so sympathetic to you at Easter, and how she knew about the roses. Why confide in her?'

He looked a bit baffled, as if the thought hadn't occurred to him. 'I don't know,' he admitted at last. 'When I moved here, we just got talking one night, and she—well, she has a way of making you tell her things. I can't explain it.'

I couldn't really blame him for it. He was quite right. She did.

'Anyway,' he continued, 'after that, I went home, but you'd all left, so I went into the garden and got you this.' He lifted his jacket, and from beneath it, he pulled out a single flower—a gorgeous pink rose, which he gave to me with trembling hands.

'I know it's not red,' he said, 'and I know they say red roses are for love, but this one's very special. I grew it in my garden.

It's a lovely variety, and it's called *You're Beautiful*. And I'm giving this to you because you are, Rose. You're beautiful. And I love you.'

'But the baby ...'

'It's wonderful.' He smiled, his eyes bright with tears, and pulling me to him, he kissed me softly. 'Don't you understand? It's amazing. I have another chance, and it's all because of you.'

'But you said you weren't ready,' I said. 'You said you could never replace Emily.'

'And I can't,' he said. 'But this baby won't be a replacement. It will be her little brother or sister. And I wasn't ready, but you made me face up to all that.'

'Me? How?'

'That day I took you to the churchyard. Having to tell you about her, it was like something cracked open. I went home after I'd dropped you off, and I finally opened the box of her belongings that I'd kept locked away all those years. It was so painful, I could barely bring myself to touch them, and I panicked and put them away. I thought I couldn't cope, so I decided to go to Maurice's that night, take my mind off it all, distract myself the way I always did.'

'And did you?'

'Yes, but something amazing happened when I got there. I started to tell him about her. Just little bits at first. Oh, Rose, I can't tell you how good it felt to talk about her, to be able to smile when I remembered her. Bit by bit, day by day, I've talked a little more. I took her photograph out of the box and put it in my living room. I started to remember her with love and happiness, instead of tears and pain. Bit by bit, I let go of the grief and the guilt, and I knew it was because I wanted to. For the first time, I wanted to move on. I wanted to be ready to love again. I wanted to love you.'

'So, you don't mind?' I was aware that I was crying again and wondered what the hell had happened to the tough cookie that used to be Rose MacLean.

'Mind? It's the best thing that could ever have happened to me. I'm the luckiest man alive. Look at me! I have a beautiful girlfriend and a new baby on the way. What more could I ask for?'

'Two nightmare stepdaughters, and a gobby mother-in-law, who's shacking up with your old mate?' I said, immediately paling. 'I didn't mean it like that. They're not. She's not—it was a figure of speech.'

He wasn't smiling anymore, and I wondered if I'd scared him off already.

'It's okay,' I said. 'Look, I see now that you're chuffed about the baby, and I'm really happy about that, and of course you can see it as much as you want, but you don't have to saddle yourself with the whole package. I know I'm loud and common and not as clever as you. I know I have a stupid pink streak in my hair, and a wobbly stomach, and my boobs aren't pert and perky ...'

'What the hell are you talking about?' he said, shaking his head in obvious bewilderment.

'You! You're so quiet and organised. You never put a foot wrong, and my life is so chaotic. I mean, first, my mother drags us over to Feldane, and we both get assaulted by yobs, and then your car gets vandalised, *and* you get stuck with my daughter, because I dragged her to the interview and more or less forced you to take her on, and then I was horrible to you when all the time you'd been protecting her, and had been so kind and nice, and I'm just so awful, and your life is so ordered, and your house is so neat and tidy, and mine looks like Beirut, and I'm always showing myself up, and I know I must show you up, too, and you hate embarrassment, and here you are with a black eye, yet again. I'm so sorry I keep doing this to you, I really am—' I ended on a sob, and he looked at me for a long moment before shaking his head.

'So, you think I'm too boring?'

'What? I never said that.'

'Ah, but that was the implication. I'm too dull. Your life is all excitement and impulse and drama, and mine is all safe and predictable and dreary. I see.'

'Flynn, I didn't say that.'

He was walking away from me, heading back to the pub. I stood there, staring after him in dismay. I'd done it again. Why couldn't I keep my big trap shut?

'Flynn!' I yelled.

'Come on!' he called.

I hesitated for a moment, but ran after him. What in God's name was he doing now?

The pub was chaotic. Most people seemed to be on the dance floor. The DJ was playing *The Locomotion*, and it was obviously proving popular with young and old. Even my mother and Maurice were up dancing, and Eliza and Amy were giggling away, pretending to be trains as they chugged around, weaving between the dancers. I didn't think anyone noticed Flynn, as he cut through the crowds and headed for the DJ, but they certainly did when the music stopped and Flynn picked up the microphone.

As all eyes turned to him, I felt myself beginning to tremble and couldn't stop.

Eliza hurried over and put her arm round me. 'What's going on?' she whispered.

'I have no idea,' I confessed.

'Ladies and gentlemen,' said Flynn, his voice booming out through the speaker system. He looked a bit startled at how loud he sounded and swallowed hard before continuing.

'What's he doing?' said Eliza, awestruck.

'I don't know. This is his idea of hell,' I said.

Flynn looked down at the crowd, all gathered round watching him. He seemed terrified for a moment, and I could see the microphone shaking from across the room.

Then his eyes met mine, and he smiled. 'Ladies and

gentlemen, I'm sorry to interrupt your fun, but I have an important announcement to make.'

He did?

My mother and Maurice glanced at me and smiled. Charlie and Joe beamed and wrapped their arms around each other. Fuchsia and Cerise were grinning and giving Flynn the thumbs up. Eliza put her arm round me and squeezed me, her face bright with laughter.

What were they all looking so happy about?

I turned back to Flynn, and he was gazing down at me with such love in his eyes that I suddenly knew and started to cry yet again.

'Rose MacLean, I know I'm a dull, boring chap, with a very mundane existence and a distinctly average personality, but when I'm with you, I start to feel like maybe I could be a bit better, and life suddenly seems to be so much brighter. I know we'll probably argue, and I know I have your two lovely daughters and your utterly delightful mother to win round, but I would like to tell them, and to tell the whole village, and especially to tell you, that I love you with all my heart and soul, and since we have matching black eyes for the second time this year, I feel that we're simply meant to be together. So, darling Rose, will you do me the very great honour of becoming my wife?'

There was total silence, and Eliza squeezed me again as she whispered, 'Well?'

I studied my quiet man as he stood there, doing something that must have been terrifying for him, and suddenly I didn't care about my silly pink streak, or my stretchmarks, or my chaotic life or my noisy family. I didn't care that he was smarter than I was, or had a better job, or was better educated, or that he had a beautiful home that would very quickly become as noisy and chaotic as my little flat. I didn't care because neither did he. All he cared about was that we were together for the rest of our lives, and it was all I cared about, too.

My eyes welled up again. 'Of course I will,' I said.

He likely couldn't hear me properly, as the people around me cheered, and he looked anxious for a moment, till I nodded and smiled, then he jumped down from the stage and was by my side, picking me up and swooping me round in delight.

Eliza sighed. 'Gabriel will be furious he missed this.'

'I'll have to buy a hat,' Charlie decided.

Fuchsia laughed. 'Look at the pair of them with their matching bruises.'

'Match made in heaven,' said Maurice.

'I can't believe my daughter is going to be Mrs Peddleton-Royce,' said my mother.

****

Much later, as we lay in bed, our arms wrapped around each other, and our heartbeats finally settling down back to normal levels, I told him how proud I was of him for having the guts to do something so demonstrative. 'I know it must have been awful for you,' I said. 'You were so brave.'

'Not at all,' he assured me. 'You were so sure that I couldn't face embarrassment. I wanted to show you that I can deal with that. It's only being without you that's unbearable.'

'Oh, that's so sweet,' I said. 'But you're not telling me you weren't scared? I saw you trembling from across the room.'

'I was only a little nervous, that's all,' he said. 'In fact, I shall prove it to you. Every year, on our wedding anniversary, I shall stand up and make a public declaration of my love for you. I'm a changed man, Rose. I can be just as embarrassing as you. You'll see.'

He kissed me, and I felt my passions rising yet again.

His eyes widened. 'My God, you're insatiable.'

'I can't help it. My hormones are popping,' I said. 'And that's hardly my fault, is it?'

'I take full responsibility,' he said, 'and therefore I feel it's my duty to ensure that you are fully satisfied at all times.'

'I'd expect nothing less from you,' I said, and he laughed and pulled me to him, and his lips covered mine, and I was really very glad that my hormones had gone so berserk, after all.

I don't think he will make an announcement every year, you know. But really, when you have the love of a good man, what does it matter?

The End

Acknowledgements

I can't believe that, six months after the publication of *There Must Be An Angel*, here I am again, saying thank you to so many people.

Firstly, I'd like to thank everyone who took the trouble to read *Angel*. I can't tell you how much it means to me that there are people who actually sat down and spent hours of their time absorbed in something I wrote. Thank you to those of you who told me, either in person, or online, how much you enjoyed it. You will never know how much those words meant. They kept me going when my confidence was low and gave me the courage to continue with *A Kiss from a Rose*. I'm especially grateful to those of you who posted reviews on Amazon. The ways of Amazon are a mystery to me, but it does seem that reviews help—a lot! So thank you to those who have already reviewed, and if anyone else would like to do so, or you'd like to review *Rose*, I'd be ever so grateful!

My thanks, as always to my families. That's my real-life family, and my writing family. My mum, to whom this book is dedicated, has done sterling work, telling her friends, neighbours and family all about my writing, and lending her paperback copy of *There Must Be An Angel* to all those who didn't have a Kindle, or couldn't get to grips with the concept of ebooks. Thanks to her, and to my lovely aunt, Diane, *Angel* made it to Tenerife and was passed around family members who live there, and their various neighbours. I'm delighted—and relieved—to say it was enjoyed.

Dan, Lisa, Phil, Jamie, Jemma, Cheryl, Collin, Emma, Sarah, Rick, Becky, Tracey, Graham—thank you for being so supportive, and for continuing to put up with my "Where's Sharon?" act. Love you all, and cuddles and kisses to my grandchildren and nieces.

My writing family, The Write Romantics, are indispensable. I can't imagine how I'd cope without them, and hope I never have to find out. In alphabetical order, huge love and thanks to Jo Bartlett, Jackie Ladbury, Deirdre Palmer, Lynne Pardoe, Helen Phifer, Jessica Redland, Helen J Rolfe, Rachael Thomas and Alys West. I'm so glad we're on this writing journey together. I couldn't wish for nicer companions.

I'd also like to thank Valerie-Anne Baglietto, a wonderful writer, who has encouraged and inspired me. I'm very proud that she read and enjoyed my debut novel, and kindly provided a cover quote. I'm also slightly stunned that I didn't even have to ask her!

Thank you to Julie Belfield for her marvellous editing and proof reading service, and to my lovely beta readers: Jo Bartlett, Julie Heslington, Helen J Rolfe, Alex Weston and Julia Richardson. Thank you for your constructive remarks, attention to detail, considered opinions and kind words. Thank you, too, to the anonymous member of the Romantic Novelists' Association, who read an early draft of *A Kiss from a Rose* as part of the New Writers' Scheme. I was thrilled and delighted with my report!

Hugs to my colleagues at MGP. You've been so lovely, and I'm delighted that so many of you have read and enjoyed *Angel*. I really hope you like *A Kiss from a Rose* as much.

Finally, a big thank you to my other half. Steve, without you, this wouldn't be possible. You support me in every way, you boost my confidence when it's flagging, share my posts, tell people about the books, leave me in peace to work, bring me cups of tea and biscuits, and tell me how proud you are of me. I know it isn't always easy, and there have been sacrifices. I want you to know how much I appreciate it. It's been a long, lonely highway at times, but I wouldn't change a thing. Thank you. xxx

Once Upon a Long Ago

(A Kearton Bay Novel – Book 3)

Lexi Bailey doesn't do love. Having seen the war zone that was her parents' marriage, she has no interest in venturing into a relationship, and thinks romance is for fairy tales. As far as she's concerned, there's no such thing as happy ever after, and she's not looking for a handsome prince.

For Will Boden-Kean, that's probably a good thing. He hardly qualifies as a handsome prince, after all. He may be the son of a baronet, and live in a stately home, but he's not known for his good looks. What he *is* known for, among the residents of Kearton Bay, is his kind heart, his determination to fund Kearton Hall—and his unrequited love for Lexi.

While Lexi gazes at the portrait of the Third Earl of Kearton, and dreams of finding the treasure that is reputed to be hidden somewhere in the house, Will works hard to ensure that his home survives and thrives. When he goes against Lexi's wishes and employs the most unpopular man in the village, she begins to wonder if he's under a spell. Will would never upset her. What could possibly have happened to him?

As plans take shape for a grand ball, Lexi's life is in turmoil. With a secret from Will's past revealed, a witch who is far too beautiful for Lexi's liking, and a new enchantress on the scene, things are changing rapidly at Kearton Hall. Add to that a big, bad wolf of a work colleague, a stepmother in denial, and a father who is most definitely up to no good, and it's no wonder she decides to make a new start somewhere else.

Then she makes a discovery that changes everything—but time is running out for her. Is it too late to find her happy ending? Will Lexi make it to the ball? Will Buttons save the day? And where on earth did that handsome prince come from?

Once Upon a Long Ago will be published by Fabrian Books in 2016.

There Must Be an Angel

(A Kearton Bay Novel – Book 1)

"This lovely book tugged at every heart-string. A treat from start to finish. I loved it!" Valerie-Anne Baglietto.

When Eliza Jarvis discovers her property show presenter husband, Harry, has been expanding his portfolio with tabloid darling Melody Bird, her perfect life crumbles around her ears.

Before you can say Pensioner Barbie she's in a stolen car, heading to the North Yorkshire coastal village of Kearton Bay in search of the father she never knew, with only her three-year-old daughter and a family-sized bag of Maltesers for company.

Ignoring the pleas of her uncle, chat show presenter Joe Hollingsworth, Eliza determines to find the man who abandoned her mother and discover the reason he left them to their fate. All she has to go on is his name – Raphael – but in such a small place there can't be more than one angel, can there?

Gabriel Bailey may have the name of an angel but he's not feeling very blessed. In fact, the way his life's been going he doesn't see how things can get much worse. Then Eliza arrives with her flash car and designer clothes, reminding him of things he'd rather forget, and he realises that if he's to have any kind of peace she's one person he must avoid at all costs.

But with the help of beautiful Wiccan landlady, Rhiannon, and quirky pink-haired café owner, Rose, Eliza is soon on the trail of her missing angel, and her investigations lead her straight into Gabriel's path. As her search takes her deeper into the heart of his family, Eliza begins to realise that she's in danger of hurting those she cares about deeply. Is her quest worth it?

And is the angel she's seeking really the one she's meant to find?

There Must Be An Angel was published by Fabrian Books in March 2015

Printed in Great Britain
by Amazon.co.uk, Ltd.,
Marston Gate.